W9-CLS-843

AFTER HAVANA

AFTER HAVANA

CHARLES FLEMING

ST. MARTIN'S MINOTAUR NEW YORK

www.minotaurbooks.com

Library of Congress Cataloging-in-Publication Data

Fleming, Charles.
     After Havana : a novel / by Charles Fleming.—1st St. Martin's Minotaur ed.
        p. cm.
     ISBN 0-312-30748-9
     1. Cuba—History—1933–1959—Fiction.   2. Racially mixed people—Fiction.   3. Americans—Cuba—Fiction.   4. Jazz musicians—Fiction.   5. Havana (Cuba)—Fiction.   6. Communists—Fiction.   7. Assassins—Fiction.   I. Title.

PS3606.L46A69 2004
813'.6—dc22

                                                                        2003058538

First Edition: January 2004

10   9   8   7   6   5   4   3   2   1

For my mother and my father

AFTER HAVANA

1

The black Cadillac blew out of the driveway at the Tropicana, tires squealing, and shot down Calle 72 toward the water. The car was huge and shiny, a brand-new model with big fins, and it lunged through the night like a shark through the water. The man at the wheel was Del Stevens, an American film actor who had been drinking daiquiris since noon. The woman at his side was a Mexican film actress who was trying to raise a rumba on the radio. They had met at the Hotel Nacional in the early evening, when they were both still well dressed and well mannered.

They had later been joined at the Tropicana by an American banker and his wife and another couple, who said they were from Florida. The Mexican actress didn't believe it. The man was small and dark and obviously Cuban, from his rat-a-tat Spanish to his perfectly polished two-tone shoes. The girl was a blowsy redhead, worn and cheap and about as American as a cheese enchilada.

The little dark man was sitting in the front seat now, pointing through the windshield as the Caddy careened down to the coast. He shouted at Stevens, "Number seven, my freng! Turn on number seven!"

Behind him, in the backseat, the cheap redhead said, "Jimmy! What about El Cruz Azul?"

And her boyfriend said, "Sure, but he have to turn on Calle Siete."

"I'm turning," Stevens growled, and whipped the steering wheel hard and brought the big Cadillac around like a schooner. He accelerated all the way through Miramar and blew a red light going across the river. The radio blared something that sounded hot, but then lost it. The Mexican actress cursed quietly.

A black Security car had been following the Cadillac since it left the Tropicana. Stevens hadn't noticed it, but he saw a black-and-white police cruiser come up behind him just after the blown red light. The officers in the black-and-white cranked up the siren.

Stevens said to the Mexican actress, "Get a load of these jokers. And gimme a cigarette."

She lit one without turning to look at the Cuban police car. "You going to stop?"

"Hell, no."

The small dark man said, "There's a Security car coming, too."

Stevens checked the rearview mirror, and saw the unmarked black sedan. He stomped on the gas, and blew another red light going into Vedado, and clipped the front tire off a bicycle that was just entering the intersection. An elderly shopkeeper went down on the pavement. The Caddy skidded in a bit of water, turning onto the Paseo, but soon was on the Malecón, the broad crescent of coast road that fronted Havana Bay.

The tide was up, and the surf was heavy. Big waves crashed into the seawall ahead of them, sending showers of salt water raining onto the pavement. Stevens could see both cars behind him now. He checked the speedometer: they were doing sixty or better. He screeched past the little park below the Hotel Nacional. For one moment, he thought of his room, and a pitcher of daiquiris, and wished all of this were over. It wasn't fun anymore. It was getting messy. It was going to be expensive, too. They were on an island, racing a brand-new Cadillac across Havana, and the place was lousy with soldiers and cops. Where were they going to run to? He spat his cigarette out the window.

The Mexican actress was hot, though. She pulled close to him and said over the screaming siren, "Faster!"

For one long, clear minute they were alone on the Malecón, open road ahead of them, waves crashing over the seawall. The two Cuban cars and the siren were lost in the splash of the waves on the pavement. The night air, even by the coast, was terribly warm. Stevens was boiling inside, flushed with speed. He tilted his head back slightly and filled his lungs with salty air. Far up ahead, the lighthouse at the Castillo shot its beam out over the ocean, cutting like a machete into the dark.

Coming off the Malecón, Stevens hit the gas hard and turned away from the water and into a broad plaza surrounding a small park with a fountain, a block or so from the Presidential Palace. The actress was still fiddling with the radio but still couldn't find a rumba. Instead came the sound of Radio Rebelde. A gravel-voiced speaker said in Spanish, "No cause will be lost while there is one revolutionary and one gun. No cause—"

Another carload of American tourists was just pulling out from the curb. The driver shot into the plaza in front of the approaching Cadillac.

Stevens jerked the wheel and stepped on the gas, and said, "Turn off that goddamn radio."

But the Caddy lost its grip on the pavement. The big car slid sideways across the plaza, struck a curb, and then jumped onto the lawn that fronted the fountain. Stevens swerved and got the car straight, but it was moving too fast. The big machine slammed into the fountain and with a roar collapsed into itself.

The Mexican actress and the small dark man named Jimmy died on impact. The banker and his wife were crushed to death in the backseat. The redhead from Florida was thrown from the car and struck her head on the pavement with such force that she also died at once. Stevens was thrown from the vehicle, too, spun like a rag doll onto the cobblestone plaza.

The cops in the squad car almost rear-ended the Cadillac as it swerved to miss the carload of fellow tourists. The driver hit the brakes and brought his black-and-white to a halt just as the Caddy crashed into the fountain. The cops were out with their guns drawn, standing in the night as the Cadillac radiator hissed and the front wheels, lifted clear above the edge of the fountain, squeaked to a halt. The cops waited while the black Security car pulled to the curb and stopped. The cops were outranked, and they were scared. They had Americans on their hands. Dead Americans. They held their weapons steady while the Security men got out of their car and stuck their hats on their heads and walked across the plaza to the fountain.

The younger of the two Security men, Cardoso, scanned the accident and the victims as he moved forward. *¡Qué lástima!* So many bodies! And so close to the Presidential Palace. The senior partner, Ponce, stood beside the black Security car. There was blood all over the place. The Cadillac was ruined, but the radio still blared the voice of the rebels, broadcasting from their outpost somewhere in the mountains. "We cannot fail, for we are the heart of the people! There is no turning back! The government of the tyrants must fall. . . ."

Luis Cardoso had grown up near this plaza, not far from the port, down a narrow cobblestone street that had been poor for five generations. He had run through this plaza a hundred times, late for school or kicking a soccer ball or being chased by the baker whose bread he stole. He had splashed in this fountain as a child.

It would need repairing now. And the tourists! One glance at the redheaded girl on the ground was enough. A glance into the car told the rest. Cardoso instinctively took off his hat, then snapped off the radio. The fountain gurgled in the new silence. The people in the car were all dead.

But the driver was sitting up on the pavement, looking dazed, moving his mouth as if he were trying to speak. Something about his face was familiar. An athlete, perhaps. So many of them came down to Havana, baseball players and boxers, to gamble on the roulette wheels and violate Cuban women. Or maybe he was an actor. Havana got many actors, too. Any night at the Hotel Nacional they were crowded into the bar, drinking daiquiris and laughing too loud. One night Cardoso had watched Mickey Mantle introduce John Wayne to Rocky Marciano, who had been brought into the room by Ernest Hemingway. Maybe this American knew those men. Maybe he had just left them at the Tropicana.

It did not matter. Cardoso's partner pulled a revolver from under his suit coat and fired two shots into the American's chest. Cardoso watched as the man slumped backward and lay flat. A pool of blood spread quickly beneath him.

Putting the weapon back inside his coat, Ponce turned to the uniformed policemen. "Get a wagon for the bodies. Fatal automobile accident. Too much rum. Leave Security out of your reports."

The policemen nodded, frightened and obedient. One jumped toward the ruined Cadillac. The other reached for the radio in the black-and-white.

Ponce bent down over the body of the American actor. He reached into the dead man's jacket pocket and pulled out a fat brown billfold. He thumbed through the identification papers, glanced over his shoulder at Cardoso, and withdrew a sheaf of green American dollars. He rose from the body, dusting his hands on his trousers. Cardoso watched Ponce walk casually back to the black Security car.

As he was placing his hat back on his head, Cardoso noticed a young woman watching from a balcony above. *A visitor,* Cardoso thought. Dark like a Cuban, but not Cuban. And not American, either. Black hair, dark eyes, skin the color of chocolate. Very beautiful.

Cardoso watched her return his stare. Then she drew back into the shadow of the balcony and was gone.

Cardoso noted the number on the building, then said to no one in particular, "Bad luck." He raised his hat and stared at the building for a moment. Then he went over to the uniformed cops. "Find out who lives on the second floor at 31 Calle San Lázaro, with the balcony. A foreign woman. Be discreet."

In the car, as they pulled away from the plaza, Cardoso asked, "Who was the gringo?"

"An American movie actor," Ponce said. "On the list of those supplying the rebels with funds and arms."

"Did he have identification?"

"Nothing," Ponce said casually.

"But he was carrying portraits of the American presidents, eh?"

Ponce said, "What presidents?"

"The greenbacks, Ponce. The American money, with the pictures of the presidents on them."

"What a joker you are," Ponce said. "I never know when you are serious."

"Forget it," Cardoso said. "I'm never serious."

María Fuentes was on the beach at Cojímar an hour before sunrise. Already the fishing boats were well away. The stretch of sand was empty but for a few tangled nets and the hull of an overturned boat with the bottom rotted out. The sky was moonless and dark, but clear, and the air smelled only of salt and the sea. It would not rain this morning. The fishermen would have an easy time coming back into port. Her man, Juan Obregón, who was not a fisherman but who had put out with the fishermen in the dark, would be safe. The fishermen would unload their catch on the sand. Juan Obregón would land at a different beach with Carlos Delgado—the man they called El Gato, "the Cat." They would walk to the highway at Cojímar and then take the bus into Havana. Another man would take El Gato to a house in Vedado, where they would get into a car and drive deep into the mountains. Juan Obregón would slip into the narrow streets of Havana and be free.

That was the plan. María Fuentes trusted it no more than she did the tropical weather. Now the wind blew gently and the sea was calm. In an hour the rain could be coming flat across the beach and the sea could be a choppy field of whitecaps, like a graveyard decorated with headstones. The gringos who came to frolic at Varadero adored the sea. They danced beside it in the nighttime, with their gowns and dinner jackets, and swam in it in the daytime, with their colorful bathing suits and wide straw hats and big sunglasses. The sea was their playground, the scenery for the melodrama of their rich, grand American lives. María Fuentes knew better. The sea was a terrible jungle where the men went to hunt for food. Sometimes they did not return.

The sea had taken her own father. He was a fisherman of legendary skill, far more admired than El Viejo, the Cojímar man whom the American Hemingway had written his famous book about. María Fuentes's father had taught El Viejo how to tie a hook, how to mend a net, how to keep a boat steady in rough water. Now El Viejo was famous. He drank *mojitos* all day at the bar of La Terraza with the Yankee clowns who paid money to listen to him prattle nonsense about life and the fish. And her own father slept somewhere beneath the sea.

María Fuentes prayed that Juan Obregón would not join him today. The ports were being watched. Paid informants were everywhere, happy in this rotten economy to make an extra peso when they could—and anxious to stay above suspicion themselves. Batista's men knew that Fidel was raising money and arms in Mexico and that his small band of revolutionaries was training in the mountains. Men presumed to be sympathetic to their cause disappeared routinely from the streets of Havana, and were not seen again. The men smuggling El Gato into the country would be tortured and executed without trial.

María Fuentes herself, coming to Cojímar against Juan's wishes, was in danger. No matter what Juan said. When he left her at midnight, Juan had leaned against the door of her little flat, lighting a cigarette and smiling indulgently: "Don't worry, precious. I am only an old dog, going to escort the cat from the sea. What trouble could there be?"

From the beach, María Fuentes could see the lighthouse at the Castillo standing guard over the port of Havana. The beam swung out from the port and swept across the Atlantic. North to Florida. West to Mexico. In another hour the sun would rise behind her and the day would begin.

Halfway across Havana, Peter Sloan was walking unsteadily through Parque Central. He had left the American women giggling in the bar at the grand Hotel Inglaterra, which stood in the dim light like a wedding cake. He turned his face now toward Old Havana, to the cobblestone lanes of Obispo, O'Reilly, and Obrapia that dropped down to the port. There would be carousing at El Floridita, across the tattered grass of the plaza, and at Bar Monserrate. The Bodeguita del Medio would be clanging with drunks. The Café de Paris, too. Sloan stopped to tie his shoe. He pushed a lock of dark hair off his forehead, then sat on a bench to light a cigarette.

Noise and drunks were spilling onto the sidewalk at El Floridita. Above the swing doors Sloan could see blue-brown cigarette and cigar smoke, swirled by ceiling fans, gathering into clouds above the bar. The sound of a high-pitched horn drifted to him—a Harry James song on the radio, maybe. It sounded like a bullfight. There was laughter, too. The doors swung open. Sloan saw a tall silver-haired man wearing a white linen suit and matching white Panama brim holding court. He was waving a cigar with one hand and holding a finger in the air. Caught in the light, he looked as if he were posing for a statue. Then the door swung shut and he was gone.

Was it Thursday morning? Friday? Sloan wasn't sure. There were windblown bits of newspaper on the ground. One of them would have yesterday's date. But then the date wouldn't matter. It was spring, and it was 1958. Every night was Saturday night in Havana.

It was wild. By all accounts, Havana had been a sweet, sleepy colonial town for a hundred years or more. The Cubans had won their independence from the Spanish in the 1890s. Everything was cool. Folks were making sugar and rolling cigars, and some of them were getting rich. Then this former army sergeant named Batista had taken over the government, and everything went nuts. Batista was friendly with the American gangster community, from the time he'd spent as an exile living in Florida. He brought 'em all down and had 'em set up shop.

Meyer Lansky got in first and made the most of it. He was building the big new Hotel Riviera. He owned a piece of the Hotel Nacional, where his brother, Jake, ran the casino. His Florida pal Santo Traficante set up the casino at the Sans Souci and took a stake in the Capri, where he gave the casino-management job to an old

New York hand named Fat the Butch. Bad guys poured in from Las Vegas, from Cleveland, from New York and Chicago.

Big money followed. The joints were glitzy even by Vegas standards. The mob guys understood entertainment—always had, whether it was in the desert or in New York—and they brought in the best people. They understood what the average gambler looked for in a casino. They built palaces and fitted them with marble floors and crystal chandeliers, easy on the eyes and easy to get to. You could catch a five-hour flight from New York, or a one-hour flight from Miami, take a cab from the airport, get a nice twenty-two-dollar room at the Capri or the Riv, and you were in business. It was exotic and tropical, but it was almost like being at home, too: the stickmen and the ladder men and the dealers were all gringos. The veteran gambler would know most of them from card and craps games in New York or from the tables in Vegas.

And the veteran gamblers came. Lansky was said to be raking off $200,000 a month from the casino operations in Havana. He was giving about half of that to Batista. Meanwhile, the Cuban man in the street wasn't getting much out of the deal. The man in the street wasn't happy about that. There had been increasingly violent riots and demonstrations. These rebels, led by Fidel Castro and his brother Raúl, were getting noisier and noisier. The army was hitting back— rounding up everyone who looked suspicious and doing unpleasant things to them—and the Americans were helping.

So with the government chasing the rebels, the gangsters fighting it out for control of the gambling money, and all the Yanks coming down and getting crocked and throwing their dough around, Havana was hot.

Tonight the city had been full of madness. But now everything was quiet. The streets were empty. Drunks slept on almost every bench in the plaza. Shoeshine boys, barely old enough to wield a brush, slept under the bushes. Prostitutes, those so ugly or unlucky that no house would have them, leaned against the walls in the colonnade, still hopeful so close to dawn. It was a night like any other.

The Tropicana had been filled to the bursting point. They were six deep at the main bar. Taxicabs were stacked up at the curb, crowding in like pigs at a trough, double- and triple-parked as they disgorged men in dinner jackets and women in jewels and gowns.

Inside, from the stage, it had looked to Sloan as if the audience were performing for the band and the dancers, and not the other way around. Onstage was a spectacular tableau—a line of a hundred showgirls in feathered headdresses and shimmering metallic skirts, all twirling and high-kicking to the blaring conga sound. But from the stage, the audience was equally resplendent. Frank Sinatra and Ava Gardner, who were supposed to have split up, were huddled over champagne with Spencer Tracy. Nat "King" Cole was dining with Marlon Brando at a table next to Humphrey Bogart and Lauren Bacall. The American film director John Huston was sitting with some hard guys from New York—Italians, from the looks of them. The dark, handsome Porfirio Rubirosa, said to be the richest man in the Dominican Republic, was whispering with two of Batista's generals. Cantinflas had an entire table of Havana beauties laughing with him over lobster and white wine. Floyd Patterson, the heavyweight champion of the world, sat with a group of American military men. The whole Havana scene was on parade. The only thing missing was Ricky Ricardo, singing "Babalú," with Lucy trailing behind him.

It had ended after midnight. Or rather, the music had ended after midnight. The parade had continued, but without Sloan's assistance.

He had changed clothes in the locker room and slipped outside for a smoke. Large American automobiles were pulling away from the casino, driving down to the coast road back toward the port. Some of the cars would drop tourists at the Hotel Nacional or the Hotel Presidente. Some would go to big private houses in Vedado, to continue the party there. Others would cruise the Malecón, stopping at cathouses like Gloria's or Casa Celia—which were run by Meyer Lansky's guy Chico Fernández. The girls there were as pretty as the ones onstage at the Tropicana, and it was cheaper to sleep with them at Gloria's than to dine with them at the Tropicana.

Sloan smoked a cigarette, watching the cars go. A big black Caddy, so new that you could almost smell the paint, screeched out of the driveway and tore down Calle 72. The guy behind the wheel was an actor. Del Stevens. Sloan knew him from a gangster movie called *Kansas City Kill*. He hadn't seen him inside the casino.

But that reminded him: he had seen Scarfioti, the Spaniard with the Italian name, sit for over an hour with Chico Fernández and two guys who looked like Security. The Security guys had the signature dark suits and heavy shoes, and were out of place in the Tropicana. What business could they have with Fernández? What business could Scarfioti have with Fernández? Sloan couldn't guess, and didn't.

The show was in full swing. The band was playing "A Night in Tunisia." Scarfioti and Fernández, who had not glanced up once, suddenly stood and shook hands as if a deal had been struck.

Sloan would have to get on the horn to Mo about that. It was part of their deal.

The thought of it made him weary. He'd have to get up early, go to the post office, request a *cabina* with a line to Florida, and wait until someone found Mo for him. He'd do it on the way to work maybe. He chucked his cigarette away, skidding it across the plaza past a sleeping shoeshine boy, and got back on his feet.

When things had gotten rough for Sloan, after the bad time in Las Vegas and the very bad time in Los Angeles, Mo arranged the gig at the Tropicana and fronted Sloan the money to get to Havana. Sloan played in the Tropicana band, and kept out of trouble, and kept his eyes open. When he saw something interesting, he reported back to Mo. Scarfioti and Fernández, making any kind of a deal about anything, qualified as interesting.

But that was for later. The sun wasn't up yet in Miami, either. Mo would be sleeping. Sloan still had the rest of tonight to worry over. He wasn't thirsty. He didn't want a woman. If he had, there would have been the two Americans he'd left behind at the Inglaterra. One of them had recognized him from the bandstand, she said, and insisted they all take a taxi together. The girls worked in publishing in New York. They were on vacation. They wanted to see the *real* Havana.

Sloan didn't. He'd seen the real Havana. It was like the fake

Havana, only dirtier. He was polite, though. On the cab ride in to
the center of town, he answered their questions: yes, Hemingway was
a fine fisherman and beloved by the Cuban people; yes, Meyer Lansky
was the power behind the gambling and booze in Havana; yes, the
rebels were gathering strength and sympathy from the underclasses;
and no, he didn't know whether it was true what they said about
Cuban women.

Sloan realized with a start that the American women thought he
was quaint. On the short taxi ride, he had become a bit of local color,
a souvenir of their wild trip to Havana. There was something in the
way the two girls looked at each other just as he was saying,
"Havana's just like Vegas, with bananas and beaches."

One of them winked at the other as if she were taking a snapshot.
Sloan could hear the story retold as Manhattan cocktail-party chatter.
He escorted them into the lobby, pointed at the bar, and said, "This
is the famous Hotel Inglaterra. This is where I get off." And he left
them there.

On his own, he was restless and out of sorts. He wasn't hungry. He
didn't gamble. Old Havana had nothing he wanted. He pushed his
feet off the plaza and began to walk down Obispo. He had a fresh
bottle of good rum in his apartment. He'd go sit on the balcony and
drink the rum and let his head get quiet.

In the distance, down Obispo, he could catch glimpses of the port.
The smell of the sea air grew more distinct. There was a breeze from
the north, a cooling breeze that might be the beginning of a storm
coming across the Florida Straits. As he neared the port, Sloan could
see the lighthouse at the Castillo and the beam of light sweeping out
across the Atlantic. Something was building there now. He could
smell moisture in the air and guessed that rain was coming.

A flat near the water had a radio on, or maybe a record player,
playing that Everly Brothers thing, "All I Have to Do Is Dream." It
made his chest ache to hear it. He moved quickly to the end of the
block.

Sloan didn't like any of the radio music. Because he used to wear
his hair a little long, people said he looked like this kid Elvis Presley,
but Sloan couldn't listen to guys like him. The race record stuff like

"All Shook Up" and "Hound Dog" was all right, but the goopy songs like "Teddy Bear" and "Love Me Tender" were disgusting. And the goopy songs were everywhere. Pat Boone. Johnny Mathis. Ricky Nelson. Andy Williams and Perry Como. It was hard for a real musician to listen to the radio at all.

They weren't playing any of that junk at the Tropicana. Time stood still there. It wasn't 1958. It was more like ten years earlier. The sounds were Basie and Ellington and Dizzy Gillespie and Chico O'Farrill and the Dorsey boys. The bands were jazz bands and they played swing music that made people want to dance and Latin music that made people want to do more than dance. They played mambo and tango and rumba and calypso. Deacon learned the *son* and the bolero. He played music written by Bebo Valdés and Mario Bauzá and Machito—the "afro-cubop" tunes that had been outrageous in 1945 but now were Cuban standards. All that stuff that knocked their socks off at Birdland was gassing the house now in Havana.

Havana time was funny that way. It was time out of time, like one big champagne bubble. Stepping in and out of the Tropicana was stepping into and out of reality. Inside, it was glitz and glitter and wealth. Outside, it was gloom and darkness and poverty and simmering rage. The beggars in the plaza were blind and disfigured. The children in the streets were like bunches of rags and bones. Sloan watched big American motorcars full of tourists slumming with their Hasselblads and Brownies, taking vacation pictures of the local neighborhoods.

It sickened and shamed him. No wonder the rebels were taking target practice in the mountains. The tourists were shooting pictures of the locals, and the locals were shooting bullets at the soldiers. If Sloan were Cuban, wouldn't he be training with the rebels, painting a bull's-eye on Batista's forehead? Maybe. Maybe not. He was only a horn player.

And he was barely that. He was lucky to be playing music at all. He was lucky to be alive.

He had left Las Vegas in 1955 with murder behind him. Worthless Worthington Lee was dead, and the Ivory Coast was over. Haney was dead where Deacon had left him—in a room full of witnesses.

Getting to L.A. without getting noticed was tricky. He'd done it slowly. He stayed a week in Barstow, two weeks in Bakersfield, almost a month in San Diego, and a couple of weeks in Riverside before finally coming in to Los Angeles. Anyone who cared would have been able to figure out where he was headed. He reckoned that the slower he got there, the less likely anyone would be waiting. He sat in L.A. for a full month, living in a ratbag hotel on Central Avenue, playing for drinks and tips in the nightclubs.

Along the way, he'd changed his name. He stopped being Deacon. He started calling himself Sloan. Deacon was a guy with trouble behind him. But nobody was looking for a guy named Sloan.

When no one came for him, and enough time had passed, he went to Hollywood. It wasn't anything he hadn't seen before, but now it all looked different. Everywhere he went—he had drinks at Ciro's and Mocambo and stood on the sidewalk outside the Brown Derby and Romanoff's—was another place that Anita might be. He saw her shadow everywhere. Mo and Haney had both told him she left Vegas with Sherman. But Deacon knew that going directly to Sherman, or going anywhere near Sherman, would be insane. One call, and one cop, was all that separated him from his turn at the hot squat. And he was not ready to sit in the electric chair yet.

But after two weeks of wandering, he got anxious. He was running out of dough. He couldn't get a real gig playing music, because he and his horn were too well known. He wasn't making enough from the little bar bits to pay for a room. Knowing it was the wrong thing to do but not knowing how else to go about it, he grabbed a bus one morning and went to Monolith Studios.

There was a high wall all the way around the place. Lines of tall palm trees decorated the surrounding streets. Everything came and went through the main gate—big sedans carrying actors and directors, big trucks carrying building material, long rigs carrying lights and flats of background scenery. He stood across the street in the shade of a tree and watched the traffic go in and out, trying to figure a way to get past the guards without announcing his presence.

Pedestrians were going in and out, too, mostly working guys with toolboxes or lunch pails.

He stood and smoked another cigarette, and watched, and wondered. He was figuring the best way to try to talk his way inside when a voice behind him said, "What's your interest in Monolith?"

He turned. Behind him was a broad, dark-browed man in a brown suit and matching hat. Behind him were two other men in dark suits standing next to a grumbling low sedan. When the big man didn't get an answer, he said again, "What is your interest in Monolith?"

"Is there a law against standing on a street corner?"

"No. But there's me. What do you want here?"

"I heard a friend of mine is working here. I'd like to contact her."

"What's your name?"

Deacon said, "My name is Sloan."

"And what's your friend's name?"

"Anita."

"Anita what?"

He thought for a moment. He said, "I'm not sure."

The two guys in dark suits snickered at that.

The big man said, "Then you don't know her well enough to visit her here. So, blow."

There was no steam in it. Deacon had been around enough tough guys in his time to know when someone was bluffing and when someone wasn't. This guy wasn't. Pushing people around wasn't a hobby with him. It was his business.

"Have it your way," Deacon said.

The guys in the dark suits looked disappointed.

The big man said, "Don't be back." He and his men got into the sedan and pulled away. They stopped at the corner, though, and waited. When the next bus came along, Deacon swung up and dropped his nickel in the box.

That night Deacon was back. He had taken a bus to Hollywood Boulevard, where he'd had a drink at Musso and Frank. He'd looked in at the Pig 'n Whistle. There wasn't a familiar face in either joint, which was good news and bad both. Then he'd left the boulevard and walked south toward Monolith.

He stopped across from the main gate to watch the traffic, less of it now, come and go. Moonlight fell down through the palms. Sloan stayed in the shadows. But it was less than five minutes before the two dark-suited men from the afternoon were on him again.

Deacon cursed when he saw them, and started to move down the street. The two guys were on him like bums on a baloney sandwich, hammerlocking his head and marching him back to that grumbling low sedan. They tossed him into the backseat and screeched away— through the gates and onto the Monolith lot.

They pulled around the back of a soundstage, yanked Deacon out of the car, and pushed him through the big sliding doors into a dark, cavernous building that looked as though it had been designed for assembling airplanes.

The big guy with the dark brow was waiting for them in a corner, sitting on a metal chair, smoking a cigarette. A radio was playing somewhere in the distance—Prez Prado's "Cherry Pink and Apple Blossom White." The big guy stood up as they approached, and clicked off the radio. He jerked his thumb at the chair.

Deacon sat down. The big guy said, "I had a feeling you'd be back. What's the deal?"

"No deal. I'm looking for my girl. Her name's Anita. She's a friend of Mr. Sherman's."

The two men in suits got quiet. The big guy snorted derisively and chucked his cigarette butt into the corner. Then he hit Deacon hard, so hard and so fast that Deacon and the metal chair went straight over backward. The chair collapsed and Deacon landed flat on his back. He was shaking the stars out of his eyes when the two goons got him by the shoulders and on his feet again just in time for another roundhouse. Deacon went down again, hard, and felt his head light up again. He thought, *Came to Hollywood. Saw stars.* Then he was lifted onto his feet and the big guy gut-punched him and he was on his knees, gasping for air.

That seemed to satisfy them. No one picked him up to hit him again. The big guy stood over him and said, "My name is McClellan. I run things here. No one comes around looking for Mr. Sherman's friends. If I see you again, I'll have you killed. Do you understand me right?"

Deacon nodded.

"Good. Don't come around here again."

Deacon nodded. Then he said, "Where's Anita?"

McClellan's face got blotchy and red. Deacon, kneeling on the floor with his guts aching, flinched. But McClellan didn't move. He nodded to the goons. They grabbed Deacon and got him to his feet again. He was breathing hard and thought he might throw up. *If he hits me again,* Deacon thought, *I'm done. . . .*

Instead, McClellan opened a pack of cigarettes and offered one to Deacon. He took it, stuck it in his mouth, and waited while McClellan shook one out for himself and fired a Zippo. Deacon inhaled and fought back a wave of nausea. He had a sudden thought of a condemned man being given a final cigarette and imagined McClellan standing him up for a firing squad. He'd refuse the blindfold. McClellan would ask him if he had any final words. He'd say—

"I want you off my lot," McClellan said. "And I don't want you coming back this time. What's that gonna take?"

"I just want to know where the girl is, and how she's doing."

"Uh-huh. And what else?"

"Nothing. I want her to know I'm okay."

"And what else?"

"Nothing. I want her to know how to reach me if she wants to."

"And what else?"

"Nothing."

McClellan eyed him, tossed his cigarette away, and said, "Where can she reach you?"

Deacon eyed McClellan back. If he didn't tell McClellan where he was staying, he'd never hear from Anita. If he did, he might be hearing from the cops, or the Feds. Would McClellan put together Sloan and Deacon? Would Sherman know about Haney's death in Las Vegas? Did McClellan seem like the kind of a guy who'd find out about stuff like that? Probably. But Deacon had no other play.

He said, "I'm at the Rosewood."

"Where's that?"

"Downtown. Eighth Street. It's in the book."

"Go home. Wait for a call. I'll see what I can do."

Deacon did as he was told. He was escorted off the lot by the two goons. He got a bus back downtown. He walked to Eighth and sat in the Rosewood lobby, smoking cigarettes, for two days. Twice a day he'd tell the deskman, "I'm going next door for a coffee. Come get me if there's a call." When he came back, the deskman would say, "Nothing, man. All quiet on the Western Union front."

It happened on the third day. Sloan was sitting in the lobby. An enormous car drew up to the curb. The side door swung open. The big guy McClellan got out, buttoned his suit coat, and walked into the lobby. Sloan could see the lump under his arm: he was packing. Sloan got to his feet. McClellan lamped the rest of the lobby, then went to the man at the front desk.

He took a bill out of his pocket, and pushed it across the desk, and said, "Take off for five minutes."

The guy behind the desk said, "Righto," and was gone.

McClellan turned to Deacon and said, "Here's the deal. Shut up, and listen. The girl wants to see you. She's not going to talk to you. She just wants to know that you're okay."

Deacon said, "Do I have a choice?"

"No."

Deacon nodded. McClellan went back outside and rapped on the driver's window. The door of the big car swung open again. And Anita got out.

Deacon's breath caught in his throat. Anita was not a bit more beautiful than he remembered. She could not have been. She was taller, maybe. A little thinner. Coming through the door, almost gliding, she was wearing the black cocktail dress he'd seen her in the night the Ivory Coast opened. That was a nice touch. She was the color of coffee, and there were tears pouring down her cheeks.

McClellan came from behind her and took her elbow. Anita looked at Deacon. Deacon looked back.

He said, "I'm so glad you're all right. Are you all right?"

Anita moved forward and started to speak. McClellan tightened his grip on her elbow. Anita winced, and stopped.

Deacon said, "I've missed you. I was in the hospital. It took me a while to find you."

Anita smiled, and nodded. She opened her mouth again, and McClellan squeezed her elbow again.

McClellan said, "That's enough. Say good night, Gracie."

Deacon said, "Wait a minute. We haven't even—"

He was hit from behind with a heavy sap. The last thing he saw, going down, was the look of shock on Anita's face. The last thing he thought, going out, was to tell her he was going to be fine. But he didn't have the chance. He fell onto the lobby floor like a fighter taking ten, and didn't get up.

Deacon expected to wind up in jail. Instead, he landed in the hospital. Again. Mo showed up. He said, "We've got to stop meeting like this," and Deacon, surprising himself, began to cry. Mo said, "That's all right, now. I'm getting you out of here."

And so he had come to Havana. He hadn't wanted to. But he hadn't wanted *not* to, either. There didn't seem any point to anything, whether staying or going. The cops were on to him, Mo said, and Sherman was going to tell the whole story if Deacon didn't blow. Havana was safe. Mo had some connections there. He said, "You'd be doing me a favor." And Deacon owed Mo a favor. He went.

That was three years ago. In Havana, where he didn't know a soul, he became Peter Sloan full-time. Deacon was dead, permanently this time. Sloan took up the coronet, which was almost a trumpet, so that his horn playing wouldn't give him away. He got a job playing at the Trop. He got a little apartment in Old Havana, a one-room flat upstairs from a restaurant, on a quiet plaza near the port, with a balcony and a view of the street. The scars from the two bullets he had taken at the Ivory Coast healed. His heart hardened. Pretty soon he got so he could hear a song like Rosemary Clooney's "Hey There" and not feel anything at all. Sometimes he thought of Anita, by accident, and stopped as soon as he started.

And once, Mo spoke about her. Sloan was mooning. He had been drinking and he had gotten sentimental. He said to Mo, "Yeah, but she was my girl."

Mo said, "Maybe she was. Maybe she wasn't."

"No," Sloan said. "She was."

Mo cleared his throat and said, "After you left L.A., I had a talk with that guy McClellan. He told me about Anita. He told me some stuff you don't want to know."

"I want to know."

"You probably don't. She was Sherman's girl full-time. Now she's this other guy's girl."

"Who's the other guy?"

"A rich guy. His name is Calloway. He's mixed up in all kinds of stuff, and he's bad news. And it doesn't matter, anyway. Anita, now, she's anybody's girl."

"Except mine." Sloan considered that. "A girl like Anita isn't going to be alone for long. Not if she doesn't want to."

"Not if she's a tramp," Mo said. "You're better off without her."

Now he was home. He would sit on his balcony and drink the rum away, drink the night away, drink the past away. Then he would sleep, and not dream.

It was nearly dawn when Cardoso and his partner returned to their offices on La Rampa. Cardoso, who had driven in from Old Havana, pulled the car down the driveway and into the underground parking garage. Upstairs, two other Security men were interrogating a suspected revolutionary. Cardoso could hear his screams from the garage. The screams got louder as he and Ponce went up the stairs to the ground floor.

Cardoso stopped a junior Security man in the hallway. "What's going on in there?"

"They got a tip this guy knew something about shipments from Key West."

"How long have they been questioning him?"

The junior officer checked his wristwatch. "All night. Since midnight."

Cardoso swore under his breath and followed the screams down the hall.

The suspect was a skinny kid, not more than eighteen, and he was having a bad time of it. Both his eyes had been beaten shut. His face was a bloody mess. His own mother couldn't have identified him. There were burn marks on his chest—they looked as though they'd been made with a car cigarette lighter—and his back had been whipped so badly that the skin was flayed. The boy sat with his head lolling on the chair back, like a boxer exhausted between rounds. The two Security men working him over looked beat, too.

Cardoso came into the room and said, "Men. What's happening?"

"Interrogation," said one of them, a tough, country man named Matos. "We got a tip that this spy has information about El Gato."

"Really?" Cardoso had heard the same rumors. Everyone had heard the same rumors. El Gato was returning to Cuba. How, and when, and what would happen next? That was anyone's guess. So everyone was guessing. "And what have you learned?"

"We're getting close."

The boy was almost motionless. Cardoso drew close to him and took the boy's chin in his hands, and shook him gently.

He said, "Good morning, my friend. How are you doing?"

"Please don't hit me," the young man begged.

"No," Cardoso said. "I won't hit you. What is your name?"

"Fermín."

"Okay, Fermín. You're going to tell me, right now, everything you know about El Gato. These men are tired. They are out of patience. If you don't talk, right now, they are going to beat you until you bleed from your ears and your rectum. Then they will take you to your mother's house and let you die in front of her."

Fermín began to cry, his skinny, bruised body choking up sobs of pain. He said, "But I don't know anything about El Gato. I have *told* them. I don't know anything. I'm a *student*. I only know about agronomy."

The two Security men moved forward. One of them had taken off his big leather belt and was wrapping it around his fist. Cardoso winced a little. The heavy brass buckle must have been what made the gashes in the young man's back.

Fermín heard their feet shuffling and looked up to see Matos and his belt. He began to scream out, "No! Don't hit me again! Tell me what you want to know about El Gato! I will confess! I will confess anything!"

Cardoso said, "Let him go. This is over. Take him out of here and let him go. He doesn't have anything for us."

He left Matos and the other Security officer cursing. He hoped they would not kill the boy. If there was anything to be gained from the interrogation—and obviously there was not any information to be gained—it would be the deterrent to others. But that worked only if Fermín was still alive when he was dumped back onto the streets. If he couldn't talk, couldn't share his terror of the Security men, then it was just another wasted night.

Cardoso kept a cot in the back of his office. It had been a long night. It was going to be a long day ahead, too.

A bare bulb hung from the high ceiling, throwing a bright, ugly light over the office. Cardoso leaned into the mirror and regarded himself. His jawline showed a heavy shadow. His eyes looked tired, too. Only his hair did not need attention. He wore it short, in the military style, which was not the fashion. Most of the men he knew—whether they were cops, crooks, actors, athletes, or casino operators—wore their hair long and kept it slicked back and close to the scalp with brilliantine or butch wax. Cardoso could not. His hair grew in tight, wiry curls.

This raised questions that Cardoso didn't want asked and couldn't have answered. The official census records showed Cuba's population as 70 percent white and 30 percent "colored or mixed." Cardoso suspected that the first number was too high and the second too low, depending on how "mixed" was defined. Between the Spanish conquerors, the Taíno and Camagüey natives they vanquished, and the black Africans they imported as slaves, a lot of bloodlines were mixed. On the street there were men with European features and skin as black as coal, working side by side with men whose blue eyes and straight hair belied their broad African noses and mouths.

A popular song of the day, "El Negrito del Batey," made fun of their plight, these Cuban men of African heritage. Whistling a few bars of the tune became a sly way of suggesting that a man's background was impure, or tainted with black blood.

Cardoso was one of the lucky ones. He was light-skinned and looked European. He had been kidded at school for his curly hair. He had been kidded as a young policeman. Once, in a bar, Cardoso had beaten a man to his knees after the man had started calling him *"el negro."*

With dawn coming, Cardoso undressed in the dark of his office, folding his clothes and draping them over the metal chair behind his desk. The concrete floor felt cold on his feet, the only time that day that he could remember any part of him not feeling hot. He lay back on the cot.

Cardoso had been on the force only a month when he participated in his first interrogation. Escalante, now the captain of the Security forces, had been the lead officer on the case, which involved the kidnapping of the wife of a wealthy sugar baron. Cardoso and another officer had checked out a tip about two brothers who knew the suspected kidnapper. They had tried to bring them in for questioning. One brother had run, and Cardoso's partner—a burly Pinar del Río man named Ramos who was killed on the job a month later—shot him down in the street. The other man came to the police station willingly. He said he knew nothing of the kidnapping. Escalante and Cardoso questioned him for two hours before he began to crack. He had said his name was Meléndrez, that he worked in a café, and that he and his brother Raúl knew nothing of any kidnapping. Cardoso, working the telephone while Escalante continued the interrogation, discovered that the young man's name was Gonzáles, that he worked at a sugar-processing plant, and that he had no brother.

Cardoso returned to the interrogation room and shared the new information with Escalante.

"Excellent work, my friend," his superior said as he left the room. "I am going to get my dinner. Beat the truth out of him and be finished with him when I return."

Left alone, Cardoso confronted Gonzáles with the new facts. Gonzáles denied them. Cardoso thought the young man was brave.

Escalante had already beaten him pretty badly. His left eye was swollen shut, his lip was split, and blood was caked around his nostrils. One of his hands was broken, too, where Escalante had beaten on it with the butt of his pistol.

Cardoso touched the broken hand. Gonzáles winced. Cardoso said, "Tell me the truth. You will die here if you don't tell me the truth. I will cut your hand off and beat you with it if you lie to me again."

The young man paled and said, "But I have told you. I don't know about the kidnapping."

Cardoso cursed and smashed his fist onto the broken hand. The young man fell off his chair and vomited onto the floor. Cardoso forced him to his feet, slapped him until he stopped sobbing, and said, "Tell me now, or I'll kill you."

"Please, no," the young man said. And Cardoso slapped him again. His nose began to pour blood. Cardoso slapped him again, harder this time. The young man fell to the floor. Then he began to tell the truth.

An hour later Escalante returned. Cardoso was slumped against the wall in the corner. The young man had fallen to the floor and could not stand.

Escalante said, "What have you learned?"

"Nothing of value," Cardoso said. "He doesn't know anything about the kidnapping."

"Then why was he lying to us?"

"The man Ramos killed in the street was his boyfriend," Cardoso said. "They are homosexuals. Gonzáles didn't want us to know this. He is afraid he will be fired from his job at the sugar plant."

Escalante began to laugh. He stood over the young man and said, "A homosexual? With a dead boyfriend? *Qué lástima, mi niño.* So sad! Go and eat now, Cardoso. I will finish here."

Cardoso turned and left without looking back. He was halfway down the hall when he heard the pop of Escalante's revolver.

Lying in the cool of his office now, Cardoso was sickened by the memory. It turned out, he remembered, that the wife of the sugar baron had been murdered in her own bed, by her own husband. Fifteen or twenty men were interrogated before the sugar baron, overcome with shame, had written a confession and shot himself. Gonzáles and his boyfriend were two of about six suspects who had not survived.

Cardoso lay flat on his cot, hoping sleep would take him soon.

Matos had taken Fermín downstairs, surprised that the young man could still walk, and pushed him into the back of an unmarked Security car. He drove through the breaking dawn out of Vedado, down Calle 17 to Calle L, and across Calle L into Havana Centro. Fermín had been picked out of a bar on Zanja and had said he lived in a building on Neptuno. Matos stopped the car near the corner of Neptuno and Galliano, in a canyon of apartment blocks that sat in the shadow of the Capitolio. The street was empty and quiet but for the rumble of the big Security car.

Matos got out slowly and listened, and went around to the back door and pulled Fermín to the curb. He dropped like a sack of rags, whimpering as he fell. Matos resisted the impulse to kick his teeth in. Instead, he left him crying in the gutter.

When the Security car was gone, the street came back to life. Two cats slipped out of the shadows and resumed picking at a pile of garbage. A pair of agile young men appeared at the corner and with sidelong glances at the apartment doors moved down the sidewalk to where Fermín lay. They picked him up, draping his arms over their shoulders, and moved off.

Still crying, Fermín said, "I told them nothing, *compañeros*. Delgado is safe." Then he passed out. The two men dragged him to the end of the block and were gone.

Nick Calloway had arrived at the Floridita bar shortly after midnight. He'd taken the girl to the apartment, and seen her upstairs while his driver waited, and then gone on into Old Havana. The driver was purring somewhere, engine running, while Calloway drank and threw money around. He'd come in and seen no one he knew except the bartender, Faustino, who'd greeted him like an old friend. An hour later Calloway had gathered a small audience at a table near the door. Two of the men with him were journalists, one

Yank and one Brit, who'd been drinking hard all evening and now were of no use to him. Two others were American military men from Guantánamo. They were drunk, too, but not so drunk that they were telling anybody what they did at Guantánamo. The last was a Spaniard, Calloway thought, a rich-looking gent with a shiny bald head who did not drink much or say much but seemed to know more than either of the journalists about what was going on in Havana.

After ordering a second tray of drinks all around, Calloway said to him, "How soon will the rebels take Havana?"

The hairless Spaniard laughed and said, "Señor, the rebels will never take Havana. They can have the mountains. They can take Santiago or Santa Clara. But they will never take Havana. The United States will not let them."

The military men said, "That's right," to that. The British journalist said, "Rubbish."

Calloway said to the Spaniard, "But I hear they are quite close already and have revolutionary squads all around the city."

The Spaniard smiled. "They are children, and students, without arms or training. Batista's generals will kill them all. With help from Coca-Cola, of course."

Calloway said, "Let's have some more drinks. Faustino! ¡Más mojitos!"

For several more hours Calloway drank and the phone did not ring. No one said, "Call for Señor Calloway!" How long should he wait? He said to the Spaniard, who amused him more and more, "We must have an evening of jai alai, and another of cockfighting. You are a man who can make a wager."

"Don't bet on it," the Spaniard said. "I have lost a million pesos!"

Still the phone did not ring. The man at Cojímar would have set sail by now. Delgado would arrive. Or he would not. Calloway should be at home, with the girl. But still he waited.

Calloway thought wistfully of a time, years ago, in the California desert. He and his crew had just set another series of speed records. They had retreated afterward to the hotel at Furnace Creek. Night had come, and with it reporters from some of the papers. Calloway and his crew sat on the terrace, laughing and making speeches to one another and drinking champagne. A photographer from one of the San Francisco papers was blasting flashbulbs at the men as they toasted their success. It was, even Calloway understood, a great story: the tall, athletic millionaire playboy, camped in the Death Valley sand like a bedouin, with his mechanics and engineers, far from his Beverly Hills estates and Wall Street fortune, celebrates the smashing of his own land-speed record.

Amid the flashes, a billowy, gossamer figure appeared on the patio. She was about nineteen, and blond, and lithe. She came next to him and, settling gently as a leaf, sat on his lap.

Calloway said, "What's all this?"

The girl said, "You broke the record. You win a prize."

Calloway said, "What's the prize?"

The girl said, "I'm the prize."

It had depressed him terribly, and it was the only thing he really remembered about breaking the speed records. He had stayed with the girl that night, and several nights after. But he had stopped racing shortly after. Now he was in Havana, with a different girl. Who was the prize this time, he wondered—the girl, or him? He was the one with the money.

One thing he liked about the Cubans: they did not like him because he was rich. They liked his money. The men in the hills wanted him to spend his money. But no one liked *him* for that. One night in the beginning, in Mexico City, Fidel had said to him, "Keep your money, amigo! You are a good man, but you have no heart for revolution. Let us start a baseball team instead! We many never beat the tide of the imperialist United States. But perhaps we will defeat the Yankees of New York, on the baseball diamond!" Only later did Fidel begin to accept Calloway's financial support. They had never talked baseball again.

Now the boat from Mérida would arrive. Delgado would come in. Calloway said to the Spaniard, "You are a shrewd man. You will win back your million pesos. Call me at this number, and we will bet together on the horse races. Or, if you like, on the rebels."

The Spaniard smiled. He said, "At what odds, señor? And on which side?"

*   *   *

Even so close to dawn, she was not able to sleep. Was it the tropics? People said the tropics did things that stirred the blood. Hers was stirred anyway. After the dry desert heat of Las Vegas and the palm-shaded poolside of Los Angeles, this damp Caribbean warmth was welcome—enveloping, embracing, a balm after the hot blast she had endured for the past several years. Still Anita had not slept right. The big apartment near the sea had a balcony open to the night air. The crash of the waves over the Malecón unsettled her. So did the smiles of the men in the street, and the cries of the street vendors, and the poverty she saw on the street corners.

An hour earlier she had come in from an evening at a nightclub with Calloway. She had been standing on the balcony, smoking a last cigarette, taking the cool night breeze into her, wondering if an aspirin would chase away her headache. There had been a terrible accident, right in the plaza below her. A big American car, moving fast, full of tourists, had lost control and slammed into the fountain. A police car and another big black car had arrived seconds later. A man in a dark suit had shot the driver of the big American car.

Anita had never seen a man shot before. It was horrible. The man had been sitting up on the plaza, bleeding from the accident. A woman had been thrown from the wreck and was lying, bloody, on the pavement. There were other bodies in the car, not moving. The car radio was blaring a man's voice, saying something—Anita remembered enough Spanish from her childhood and from living in Shipton Wells to get the sense of it—about "the cause" and "the struggle."

The man in the dark suit walked right up to the driver and shot him in the chest while the other policemen stood and watched. Then the man in the dark suit had calmly gone back to his car. Another man, also dressed in a dark suit, had at that very moment looked up at her—and had seen her looking down. There was no one else on the street. For a second the two of them stared at each other—a man in the street, a girl on the balcony, and the bodies of the dead people by the fountain.

Just like that night in Las Vegas, at the Ivory Coast, when Deacon and Worthless were shot.

Anita shivered and crawled out of bed. She went to the sitting room. One lamp shone there. She took a cigarette from a box on the coffee table and went to the bar to mix a drink.

It was the second shock of the night. Hours earlier, with Calloway in the nightclub, the big one with the enormous floor show, she felt for a fleeting instant that Deacon was there, in the room.

Of course, he was not. She knew he was in New York. Or she had been told he was in New York. But there was something in the moment, something in the music, something in the room, that made her feel he was close at hand.

Anita draped herself over an armchair in the sitting room and felt that again. It was warming to her, enveloping like the Havana night. She could feel him close to her. He was close to her. He would always be. She had loved him. She had loved *only* him. No matter what had happened with Sherman, no matter what happened after Sherman, no matter what happened now, with Calloway, Anita knew Deacon would always be the only man she would ever love.

Anita put out the cigarette and took a sip of her drink. It was bourbon and water. Not ladylike, Sherman had told her. A low-class drink. It was Deacon's drink. She hadn't told Sherman that. She hadn't told Sherman much.

On the street below, an ambulance had finished carrying away the bodies of the accident victims. Anita could hear the voices of the driver and his helpers. There was a scrape of metal as a truck with a hook on it began to drag the crushed American car off the ruined fountain.

Deacon might be dead, she knew. Sherman had promised her, after that morning in Los Angeles, that he would not be hurt. But she knew what Sherman was. And his men, especially the man McClellan, frightened her. McClellan had told her, on the drive back to Hollywood on the last morning she had seen Deacon, that he would have the trumpet player killed if he ever came near her again. She knew that part was true.

Now there was no more Sherman in her life. For two years she had been his pillow and his punching bag. He had an awful lot of money, and he had bought her a little bungalow in Brentwood. He treated her better than he treated his own wife. He gave her jewelry and clothes and a car. But he was also a pig, and he treated her like a whore. A high-class whore. For every repellent thing he wanted in bed, there were extravagant gifts. Sherman got her a charge card at Robinson's. In two years she had made two purchases. She had bought Sherman two Christmas presents.

When her twenty-first birthday came, there was nothing Sherman could buy her that she desired. He said, "You must want *something*. A woman always wants *something*."

She said, "I don't want anything. I only want to learn things. Maybe to paint, or play piano."

Sherman, aghast, said, "Do you think you have talent? Please, for God's sake, don't tell me you think you have talent."

"No," Anita said. "But I'm bored."

"So I'll get you music lessons."

"No. I want a library card."

She began to read. At first she took home one book at a time. She read novels, love stories mostly. The first book checked out on her card was *Little Women*, a strong recommendation from the librarian. Reading it was like chewing wallpaper paste. Anita did not finish it. Then the librarian had recommended *Wuthering Heights*. That was more like it. Then, on her own, Anita discovered *The Great Gatsby* and *Tender Is the Night*. They broke her heart. Then she discovered Willa Cather, *My Ántonia* and *The Professor's House*, and the books of Sinclair Lewis—especially *Arrowsmith*. And she understood then that she was not alone—that other men and women had lived and felt all the things she was living and feeling.

The books became more real to her than the life she was living. Sherman and his visits were just interruptions. He came and went. She read, and she was happy.

One day, coming out of the Brentwood library with a stack of books in her arms, Anita slipped and twisted her ankle. Several volumes went sailing as she fell. A man stepped smartly from a foreign coupe parked at the curb. He was tall and tanned and broad-shouldered, and had hair the color of silver.

He said, "Leave the books," and took Anita by the arm and steered her to a bench by the library door. He knelt in front of her and took her calf in his hands. They were large and cool. He explored her ankle gently and said, "You haven't sprained it. Lucky thing, in those heels. I'll get your books."

Anita said, "Thank you."

The tall man went down the library walk picking up books, then set them on the hood of his coupe and walked back to her.

"I apologize for not introducing myself," he said. "I'm Nick Calloway."

She knew the name. A big name. A big name with money. *Another* big name with money. She said, "My name is Anita."

"I'm very pleased to meet you," Calloway said. "Even under such unfortunate circumstances. Or not so unfortunate, maybe. Your ankle is not injured. And now we are going to be friends."

Anita said, "Yes."

The rest happened quickly. She thanked Calloway, took her books, and drove home. He found her, by telephone, the following day—she didn't know how, but men like that can do things like that. He asked her to lunch. Perhaps because he was a big name, she felt safe in going. She would never have gone to lunch with any of the other men—Sherman's friends, mostly, from the studio—who made passes at her. But this man was different. He was strong and gentle and unafraid. So she was unafraid. They had a discreet lunch in Beverly Hills, and several days later they had another.

When Christmas came, she did not buy a present for Sherman. Instead, she arranged for the house and the car to be returned to him. She kept some of the clothes and some of the jewelry. And her library card. And she moved in to the Calloway mansion in Holmby Hills.

Now the dawn was coming. Anita could see the light changing over the bay. Calloway was off in the casinos or drinking at a club, doing his business. She didn't know what his business was. She didn't want to know. He was kind to her. He was a gentleman. He treated her like a lady. He even loved her, she thought. That was enough, to know that.

She went to the window and pushed the shutters closed against the rising light. *Sleep,* she thought. *And keep Deacon safe.*

Dawn was breaking as Sloan turned into the plaza off Obispo. He shuffled up the stone stairs of his ancient building and stabbed in the dark until he got the key in the lock. On the floor, revealed as the door swung open, was a little yellow envelope with the initials IT&T stamped on the left corner. A telegram? Sloan had never received one in Havana. He took it with him to the bathroom, where he got a glass out of the medicine cabinet. He cracked the seal on the bottle of Ron Rico, poured out three fingers, and sat on the balcony.

The telegram was from Mo. It read, TROUBLE. EXPECT ME. MO.

Sloan always expected trouble. Now he could expect trouble and Mo. He folded the telegram and stuck it in his pocket. Saluting the dawn, he gave his attention to the rum.

It appeared at first that the light on the horizon was the rising sun. But after watching it for thirty minutes over the bow of the wretched, pitching little boat, Carlos Delgado realized that it was the light of Havana. He had never landed in his homeland by boat. He did not know what his island looked like over the sea. He was learning—that, and a thousand things he never expected to learn. He never wanted to know how to shoot a man, how to field-strip a British Enfield rifle, how to build a grenade launcher from a piece of sewer pipe, how to make camouflage face paint from mud and tobacco, or how to sleep soundly, on the ground, in the pouring rain, with nothing but a Panama hat for a poncho. But he knew how to do all those things now, and did them cheerfully. Delgado kept his eye on the horizon, lit another cheroot, and said to Juan Obregón, "About another hour, my friend, and the sun will be up. What do you think?"

Obregón rose and peered at the horizon. He said, "The swell has slowed us down. We will land before dawn, I think."

It was a nasty little boat, a fishing boat called *El Encanto* that Armando, the sullen captain, had purchased in Mexico. It leaked and stank of gasoline and did not look as if it could take another two hours in the choppy sea that tossed them now. In the battered wheelhouse Armando stood now, scanning the coastline. Delgado did not like his gruffness—because it was not real gruffness. It was fear, disguised as tough-guy stuff. *Fear of what?* Delgado wondered. *Not the fear of the sea that plagues me,* he thought, *for he is a fisherman. Not the fear of political trouble,* he thought, for Obregón had told Armando nothing about Delgado except that he was to sail in from the Yucatán. *So, fear of what?*

On the horizon Delgado could see lights now, dead ahead, on a shoreline that was slowly emerging from the darkness. *It must be a village,* he thought. But then the lights were gone. Armando sailed forward. Delgado went to him. He said, "I don't know this part of my country. What is the village where we are to land?"

"La Plata," Armando said.

"Is it near Cojímar?"

"An hour, by car."

"Is that it, ahead there?"

"Yes."

"Excellent," Delgado said, and went back to stand beside Obregón. Did he know? He looked very calm. He did not know. But Delgado did. Armando was a traitor, and this was a setup.

Delgado had grown up in Varadero, where the Yankees came with their dollars and their disgusting appetites. He knew the coastal towns the way he knew the lines of a lover's body. He had never sailed into the port here, but he knew there was no village named La Plata. And he knew from the shadows of the mountains that were slowly taking shape before them that they were quite close to Cojímar. The man Armando was lying. That explained his fear.

Delgado put another match to his cigar and said to Obregón, "It is good to be home, my friend. Thank you for everything you have done."

Ten minutes later the outline of the shore had become quite distinct. Delgado thought he could hear waves crashing. He could see a white line of sand, or breaking waves, perhaps a mile ahead of them. There were no lights on the shore now, but there would not be. The men who were waiting there would have binoculars. They would have seen the boat approaching.

Delgado went to the wheelhouse. He said to Armando, "Obregón is sick. Do you have a towel, or a rag?"

Armando jerked his head at the floor of the wheelhouse. "At my feet," he said.

Delgado knelt down and found a tattered bath towel. He wrapped it several times around the muzzle of his pistol, a nickel-plated .38 that Fidel had given him a year before. Delgado stood and said to Armando, "*Viva Cuba libre,* my friend," and shot him once in the back of the head. Armando fell forward onto the wheel and then collapsed.

Obregón had not heard the shot. He was leaning over the side, sick from the pitching, stinking boat, peering out at the horizon. Delgado set the nickel-plated revolver on the floor of the wheelhouse and went to the opposite side of the boat. He strapped on a knapsack into which he had packed, wrapped in plastic, a gun, a compass, some water, and a little food, and slipped over the edge, leaving everything else except the thousands of American dollars he had taped to his body. Too bad about the pistol. It would not survive a jump into the sea, and there was no time to wrap it. Too bad about the cargo, the boxes of guns and ammunition. Too bad, too, about Obregón. Perhaps the Security men—or whoever was waiting where Armando was planning to land—would let him go.

The water was freezing. There might be sharks. Delgado was not much of a swimmer. But there was nothing to do but swim. With luck, the men on the beach would keep watching the boat until Delgado had gotten clear of it. With luck, he would not be carried from the sea into the swamps—which is exactly what had happened, eighteen months before, when Fidel and Raúl and their band had sailed *Granma* into Cuban waters. *¡Esto pinta mal!* What a terrible show they were making of this revolution.

Delgado tried to relax and let the tide carry him. Come, Security.

Come, sharks. Come, all. He wished he were in the Sierra now, with Fidel. For strength, he repeated his comrade's slogan: "No cause will be lost while there is one revolutionary, and one gun. . . ." He kept swimming.

2

It was late morning before Cardoso emerged from the dark cool of his back office into the front of the Security station house. Sometime in the early-morning hours the storm had come. Now the sky was slate gray and low, and the streets ran brown. Rain pounded on the windows. Cardoso shook the shoulder of a boy napping in the station-house lobby. He handed him a five-peso note and said, "Get me *café con leche* and some *pan con mantequilla*. And some fruit."

The smell of fear hung in the air like smoke. Cardoso raised an eyebrow at a smug young officer named Bustillo, who was said to be a nephew or a cousin or something of Fulgencio Batista. His role within Security was unclear and he never did any police work, but his fellow officers believed he made regular reports to the Presidential Palace, and feared him. Cardoso went over to a sergeant named Colón who was lazily working a typewriter at a corner desk.

"What's going on?"

Colón said, "Bad news. The thing in Cojímar went badly. Captain Escalante is very angry."

"Was it Delgado?"

"Maybe," Colón said. "He wasn't on the boat when they boarded it. He had gone overboard. After killing the captain."

Cardoso whistled through his teeth.

Colón said, "On the other hand, we seized several crates of guns and ammunition."

"Coming in from where?"

"Mexico. But the guns are all American."

The boy returned with the steaming coffee. Cardoso excused himself and went into the back room. Good day to stay low. He had to file some paperwork on the incident involving the Americans who died in the crash at the fountain near Old Havana. He had a meeting at midafternoon with a gentleman, a European, who might have something useful to tell him. He had a dinner that night with a young woman, an actress, who might be useful in other ways. In the meantime, he would have to dodge Escalante. The captain was a powder keg under the best of circumstances—an angry man with a great capacity for violence—and these circumstances were not the best.

For months the Security forces had been frustrated by the rebels and their operatives. A year before, four assassins had murdered Escalante's predecessor—shot him dead, at four o'clock in the morning, as he and his wife and another couple stood laughing in the lobby of the Cabaret Montmartre. Since last fall Havana had suffered a series of sabotage attacks on municipal buildings and utilities. Gas and electric plants had been hit repeatedly, resulting in power outages, work stoppages, and blackouts. One night more than a hundred bombs had exploded around the city simultaneously, paralyzing most of Havana for the twenty-four hours it took the Security forces and the army to restore order. Bombs exploded in government offices, water-pumping plants, rum distilleries, banks, and police stations—all at once. It was an unnerving show of force, and of political resolve and military coordination, for the rebels.

Then in March a group of rebels had staged an assault on the Presidential Palace. The predawn raid had failed but had still left dozens of soldiers dead and wounded.

Cardoso himself had slept at the station house that night, as he had last night. He was roused into consciousness by the raised voices of his fellow officers. A military convoy had been overtaken just outside Havana, a radio car was reporting. Moments later, as Cardoso was stepping into his trousers, there was an enormous blast, coming from the area near the university. Cardoso grabbed a sidearm and went into the street.

A pitched gun battle, lasting over an hour, took place on and around the university steps. Five rebels were holed up in one of the administration buildings. They had rifles and grenades and some kind of crude rocket launcher, and by the time Cardoso got there they had already destroyed two Jeeps and a truck and killed five soldiers. Ten or more of their comrades had raided the convoy and made off with a great deal of ordnance and matériel.

But the real battle was at the palace. Thirty armed men had crashed three trucks through the barricades there and stormed the front steps. The soldiers guarding the palace were caught napping. None survived. Ten rebels died in the plaza trying to blast their way up the front steps. Twenty other rebels made it into the building. They gunned their way from the lobby to the second floor before Batista could be awakened and dressed and hustled from his bedroom. Another twelve or fifteen soldiers died while the president was escorted down a seldom-used service staircase and out the back of the palace. A pair of roadsters sped off. Batista was safe. It was another two hours before the rebel commanders realized that their quarry had slipped away. By then more than half of their own men had died fighting their way to the upper floors.

The escape and the victory had done nothing to strengthen Batista's regime. The students and the workers were increasingly with the rebels. Security forces had put at least ten underground newspapers out of business in the past year alone. There were always two new ones, seemingly within a matter of hours. Radio Rebelde, the voice of the revolution, still broadcast from the Sierra Maestra, where Fidel Castro and his men lived and trained and grew mythical.

Now the spring was not going well. The blasts continued—at a Coca-Cola bottling plant, at a cigar factory, at a sugar refinery, all in less than a week. Security forces raided an apartment near the university and seized small arms and grenades and a printing press, and found evidence that American sympathizers were supplying the rebels with weapons and financial support. The arrest and interrogation of union leaders and others known to be involved with the rebels yielded nothing except further evidence that the Cuban people, in sharply rising numbers, had lost faith in the Batista government.

So Escalante and his counterparts around Havana had stepped up their vigilance. There were more arrests. The interrogations at station houses continued. The torture chamber at El Principe prison— where the more promising interrogation candidates were sent after "briefings" at the station houses—became a full-time operation. The rebels and the students called it Paraiso because it was set high on a hill and because so few of their comrades returned from it. And because so few of them cracked.

That part concerned Cardoso more than the rebel bombs. People who could not be tortured into signing confessions or revealing the names of their accomplices made Cardoso very uneasy.

Like last night, with the boy Fermín. Matos would have killed him, kept interrogating and torturing him until he died, and then thrown him in the rubbish heap.

There was a time when that sort of thing hadn't bothered Cardoso much. He was a career police officer. He had come to Havana as a policeman, a simple, studious young man from a village in the mountains of Santa Clara. He was well pleased to get a job with the Havana police. He had been very well pleased to be promoted into the Security service. He worked diligently, kept long hours, and had no pretensions about his work. He was doing the job he was paid to do. He had orders. He was a policeman.

The past year had wounded something in him. He had shown, over a decade of police work, great endurance and a real aptitude for the identification, pursuit, and apprehension of criminals. He was dogged. He never quit. Usually the men he arrested went to trial, and then they were always convicted. Sometimes he could not bring them in, though. He had killed a dozen men in the ten years he'd worked in Havana. He regretted only that he hadn't gotten convictions. He regretted nothing about killing them. They were guilty men.

But this was different. At Paraiso Cardoso had seen a police interrogator rip away pieces of a young man's nose with pliers while other officers looked on without expression. Cardoso had seen another officer drive nails into a man's skull using a framing hammer. He had seen a group of men strap a student to a metal chair, naked, and then force electric wires into his penis. The men laughed when the current went on and the student began to scream. Late one night Cardoso had seen four officers strip a young woman naked and begin to apply a similar technique to her. Later, aroused by the interrogation, the officers raped the young woman. Then they slit her throat.

That wasn't police work, and it was ineffective, besides. Either the Security men were arresting the wrong suspects, or the suspects were too tough to crack under questioning. Cardoso was losing his stomach for it. And it was far from over. The news today about Delgado was very bad—for the Security forces and for anyone in custody. It would be an ugly night of interrogation for anyone being held at El Principe. Paraiso was going to be busy. Cardoso pushed aside his breakfast, lit a cigarette, and called the boy to get him some typing paper and another *café con leche*.

María Fuentes had dozed on the sand for an hour or so before dawn, and for an hour or so after. The beach was quiet. The fishermen and their boats had gone out in the darkness. They would not be back before late morning. The coming of the sun, which rose somewhere under the horizon behind Varadero, was sudden. It was dark, and then it was not. María was asleep, and then she was not. For a few minutes she gazed at the sky, dazzled by the palms waving overhead, buffeted by the warm breeze that came off the water. Then she tightened her shawl around her and slept again.

Now the sun had gone. Clouds gathered. The warm breeze had

turned into stiff, cold bluster. María woke up as the rain began to
fall—first a splatter on the sand, then a deluge. The water churned
before her. There wasn't a sail on the horizon. María dashed to a low
clump of date palms growing out of the sand, but the wind was
pushing the rain almost horizontal across the beach. She was soaking
wet in a matter of minutes. Then a whistle: a man was crouched
underneath an overturned fishing boat beached for repairs and was
waving to her. María scrambled across the sand.

The man was old and leathery. He pulled her underneath the hull
of his weathered boat and said, "Inside, daughter. Here is a towel."
While she was drying her face and hair, the old man produced a mug
of coffee from a pot sitting on a bed of graying charcoal. The rain
pounded on the wooden boat hanging over them. He said, "Drink
something hot before you catch a cold, daughter."

"Thank you."

"It is nothing. A cup of coffee and a towel, to be joined by a beautiful woman? It is nothing." The old man patted María's shoulder.
"But tell me, for the love of God, what are you doing on the beach
during such an ugly storm?"

María told him. But not quite. She told him her brother had put
out with some men, that he had lost his job at the General Motors
automobile plant in Havana, that he thought he might try his hand at
fishing, and that she was waiting for him to return safely from the sea.

Much of that was true. Her man, Juan Obregón, had worked at
the GM plant in Havana, building American cars for the Cuban market, until some months before—when he and ten of his comrades
who had been meeting secretly with workers from the Pontiac plant
at a café on Cárcel were arrested and then discharged from their factory jobs. And Juan had, in fact, put out with some men the night
before—not to go fishing but to rendezvous with the boat from Mexico that carried Carlos Delgado and his guns and ammunition for the
rebels. And she was waiting for him to return safely from the sea.

She said, "But now I am worried, because of this storm. Will the
men be safe?"

"Men in boats going to the sea are never safe," the old man said.

"But your man is lucky to have a woman waiting for him on the beach."

"My brother," María corrected him.

"Your man," the fisherman said, and laughed at her. "I am old and half blind from the sea, but I am not a fool. I knew your father well, *mi niña,* and your father had no sons."

María hung her head. The old man patted her shoulder again. He said, "And I know all the fishermen here. Your man put out today with two boys named Pepe and Enrique. Pepe told me, 'We are going as three and returning as two.' He did not think anything of it, and neither do I. Did you bring cigarettes?"

María had. She and the old man sat under the hull of his boat and watched the rain pound the beach. Nothing moved there. María guessed it was ten o'clock, or later. Still nothing appeared on the horizon. María, drowsy from the drumming of the rain on the boat, made a pillow of the old man's towel and curled down into the sand. She slept again.

Carlos Delgado had been in the water an hour or more when the rain began. He shouted out—to no one, to the sea, to God—"A rainstorm! What next?" He was getting tired. The tide had carried him out, away from shore, and then had drawn him back toward the beach. But he had fought the tide going out, and now his legs were like cement and his shoulders ached. He bobbed, the bubble of his knapsack holding him to the surface, then swam a few strokes, then bobbed some more, as the rain puckered the sea around him.

When the light had come all the way up, Delgado was able to see the coastline clearly. He did not recognize it. The boat he had abandoned was long gone and nowhere in sight behind him. That was excellent. The Security forces would be looking for him there, if they were looking for him at all. And the fact that the captain had lied about the landing suggested they would be looking for him somewhere.

But this stretch of coastline ahead of him was unfamiliar. It was mangrove swamp, with dark weeds growing down steep banks to the water. Delgado focused his eyes and tried to find a strip of white, where a beach would be. As the light dimmed and darkened with the storm, he thought he saw one. Could be the foam of waves crashing over rocks. Could be a nice sandy beach. He aimed for it, kicking his leaden legs and swimming forward.

It took forever to get there, but it was beach after all. A last gentle wave swished over Delgado's head and pushed him into the sand. The water close to shore was so much warmer that it felt like a hot bath. Delgado was tempted to lie in it awhile.

But the beach was exposed and unsafe. He shook some of the water from his clothes, headed across the sand into a grove of low-growing palms, and squatted there.

A path led out the back of the grove. Good news. Someone, from somewhere, walked to this place. That meant there would be people not far away—peasants, of course, who could almost certainly be depended upon to offer a stranger fresh water and perhaps a bite to eat.

Delgado moved into the grove in squishy boots. He unstrapped his knapsack and drank deeply from the bottle of water. He unpacked the pistol from its plastic cover, then unpacked his Panama hat. Everything looked undamaged. He stuck the Panama on his head and the pistol in his waistband, and moved into the woods.

The rain had stopped before he came to a farmhouse. There was a clearing. Patches of red dirt showed evidence of farming. A brace of oxen was tied in a pen. Smoke rose from a wooden shack. Delgado fell to his haunches and watched.

The dirt fields were growing yucca, Delgado saw. At the edges of the fields, shaded by palms, were small coffee plants, enough for one or two families. The thatched-roof wooden home, the typical Cuban house known as a *bohío,* was quiet.

But then the door swung open and a young woman emerged swinging a bucket. She clucked once and a collection of chickens appeared from under the house. The girl began to toss chicken feed across the yard. Delgado decided to move.

The young woman was not startled. She saw. She threw the rest of her feed. She turned and waited. Delgado advanced upon her, hands visible, smiling. He knew he was dashing when he smiled. He wore his black hair and his mustache long. His face was very dark from training and living out of doors. When he smiled, the white of his teeth shone like the sun. He smiled now, coming across the yard, and took the Panama hat off his head and bowed. The girl did not smile back, but neither did she run.

"Good morning," he called to her. "I am sorry to bother you and interrupt your work on this lovely, sunny day. But I have lost my way. My boat capsized in the storm, and I was forced to swim to shore. Can you tell me where I am?"

The girl, clear-eyed and unafraid, said, "You are on the farm of my father, Raúl Moncada Fernández."

"And where is your father now?"

"In the fields with his men."

"And you are left alone?"

"Yes."

"Then you can make some breakfast for me, and we can dine together!"

He smiled again, as broadly as possible. The girl smiled back. She said, "Of course. I am happy for the company. Come and sit."

As she walked away from him, Carlos Delgado thought, *It is because I do not want her. If I wanted her, she would feel afraid. She is safe because she knows I want nothing from her.*

"Tell me your name, young woman, that I may tell the people of Havana I have met an angel."

"I am Gabriela. Do you want a *café con leche?*"

"An angel!" Delgado said. "Yes."

Because his building faced west, Peter Sloan was not awakened by the rising sun. Dawn had come just as he was drifting into sleep, a third snifter of brandy sniftered down, legs stretched out, on the balcony of his apartment near the port. Old Havana was quiet at dawn. Here, on Plaza Vieja, the business of the night ended late and the day started slowly. Sloan might have slept until noon, head lolling on his chest, the cobblestone plaza with its plane trees and burbling fountain quiet beneath him.

But the rain came before he had slept his fill, pattering at first on the roof, then splashing onto his face, and then turning into a downpour. The sky was almost black with it. The plaza was full of water. Sloan shook himself awake, slipped inside his apartment, and slipped out of his wrinkled jacket and trousers and into a dressing gown. He stuck his head out the apartment door and whistled.

Minutes passed before Pedrito, the young boy from the second floor, knocked at this door. Sloan and Pedrito had an understanding. Pedrito ran little errands for Sloan. Sloan got things for Pedrito that his mother wouldn't allow or couldn't afford.

Today Sloan pointed at his wrinkled suit. He said, in halting Spanish, "Clean this. Two hours, no more. Here is money for you, and chocolate. And bring me a café."

The boy was off like a shot, clutching the peso notes and the chocolate bar, leaving the suit behind. Sloan had to whistle him back. Chagrined, the boy left again, clutching the peso notes, the chocolate bar, and the suit. He said, "Two hours. No more," as he left.

Usually the boy stopped to ask questions. He was fascinated by the scars Sloan carried on his chest, perhaps because when he first asked about them, on another day like this one when Sloan had asked him to have his suit cleaned, Sloan told him they were the scars of a bull. He told Pedrito that he had been a bullfighter in Spain and that a brave and powerful bull had gored him in the chest, twice, before falling victim to his cape and sword.

Pedrito was only seven years old. He believed Sloan's story—for about half an hour. By the time he returned with the suit, he had decided Sloan was lying. And he said so. Sloan laughed and admitted he had made up the entire story. He had never been to Spain, he said. He had never even seen a bull. The injury, in fact, was a war wound. He had been stabbed in the chest by Japanese jungle fighters, on the island of Molopongo, during the Battle of China.

Pedrito gaped, wide-eyed. Sloan said, "Many men were killed. I myself was shot twice."

"With a *rifle?*"

"With a *rifle*," Sloan said. "And a *pistola*. And a *cañon*."

Today he was back in ten minutes with Sloan's *café con leche*. Sloan thanked him and gave him another coin, and reminded him, *"Dos horas. No más."* The little boy nodded and left him alone.

Sloan drank his *café* and had a smoke. Through the balcony doors he heard the rain slow and stop. The life of Old Havana began again. A street vendor cruised by, selling fresh fruit. Sloan could hear a local woman, perhaps Pedrito's mother, haranguing the vendor. Something to do with bananas. Sloan hummed "Yes! We Have No Bananas!" to himself. Was that a Cuban tune? He thought not. Bananas came from all those other places where Americans made themselves so welcome—the Dominican Republic, Guatemala, El Salvador, Nickelcigarua, Bananamala.

In Cuba, it was sugarcane and cigars. That's where the money was. That's where the American money was. The so-called Dance of the Millions, the sugar boom that blew Cuba into big money between the two World Wars, had blown the big Yankee moneymakers into Cuba. They'd taken over the sugarcane businesses. They owned the country's railways. They controlled the country's iron ore. They'd made a market in the United States for Cuban products—pineapples, bananas, molasses and syrup and rum, and cigars—and they owned all the shipping companies, and many of the packing companies and refining companies, that got those products off Cuban soil and onto American tables. By the early 1950s, Cuba was the number-one exporter of sugar in the world. Everybody wanted a little piece of the action.

That's why, Sloan guessed, even the Americans were getting worried about these rebels in the mountains. The rebels were monkeying around with *American* money. They were burning sugarcane fields and tobacco farms. The blackouts and the interruptions to water service, and telephone service, and gas service—these were just mosquito bites on the backside of Batista, the cat who the Americans were helping occupy the presidency. But the burning of the fields was a real assault on American interests.

Every time he overheard a conversation these days, it seemed, the topic was revolution. "What do you hear?" everyone asked. "What is happening in the mountains?" When Sloan saw men like Scarfioti huddled up with men like Chico Fernandez, he knew they were talking about the same thing: How much longer do we have? How much money can we smuggle out of the country? How much more money can we make before we get *thrown* out of the country? How much trouble are we in if we don't get out in time?

Sloan could hardly have cared less. He didn't have any money. He didn't have any way of making money. He wasn't going to be in any trouble no matter who was running the big show. He was just a horn player, and he played the same way no matter who was footing the bill. Guys like Scarfioti didn't interest him. The rebels didn't interest him, either. Were they the good guys, or the bad guys? Or rather, were they the better guys, or the worse guys?

Sloan didn't care. Not any more than he cared about the stuff that scared folks back home. Everyone was obsessed with the Russians. Everyone was building bomb shelters. There were Commies here and Commies there. The Americans had fought the Nazis in Germany and the Fascists in Italy and had beaten the imperialists in Japan and fought a draw with the Communist Chinese in Korea. Now everybody was ready to fight the Russkies.

Not Sloan. He wasn't ready to fight anybody, anywhere. He liked to say he was a lover, not a fighter. But he wasn't really much of a lover. Not lately. He had inherited the locals' disdain for tourists, but he had never acquired the tourists' taste for the locals. He'd meet these American girls slumming around Havana and find them childish and vulgar and dull. But then he'd see the Cuban girls in the streets and find himself predatory and creepy. Most of the men he knew from the States behaved as if all the women of Havana were harlots, available and for sale. Sloan didn't feel that way, but he knew that some of the women thought he did. That soured him. He'd catted around his first six months in Cuba. He'd done the drunken crawl to Casa Celia or Gloria's—one or both or which one, he couldn't later remember. He'd picked up or been picked up by a couple of broads from the street. He'd had an uncomfortable dinner with a rich kid, a spoiled Havana society girl who'd spotted him onstage at the Trop and made a sort of hobby out of him. That was pretty demoralizing. He understood what the girls in the street felt. He took the rich girl back to his apartment, anyway, and made love to her furiously for several hours before sending her home. He still felt shame when he thought about it.

So he didn't think about it, and he didn't get much action anymore. His principal interests were his horn, his bottle, and his bed—in that order. He wasn't that wild about getting up in the morning or spending the day getting ready for work, even though with the way he drank, it sometimes took most of a day to get his head clear enough to get to work. He wasn't that wild about any of the people he knew, even though he was friendly with some of the greatest musicians alive. He wasn't that wild about Havana, even though it was balmy and sweet and very welcome after the dry heave of Vegas.

But he was wild about the music. A couple of drinks and a couple of minutes onstage, and Sloan was transformed. Everything clicked. Thirty minutes into the show, six nights a week, Sloan was a happy man. He stayed happy through two sets and half a dozen drinks. He'd have a couple before, and a couple during the break, and sometimes would even sneak a shorty onstage with him if he was suffering from hangover.

He took the happy feeling with him when he left, too. The night air was swell, the stars were often out, and the sea smelled wonderful. Sloan would pack up his horn and have a couple more drinks before setting off. He'd go down to this little club or that. Sometimes he'd sit in and blow some more. Sometimes he'd just listen. Always he would drink—not enough to get really stinko, but enough to stay above, or away from, or apart from, the things that troubled him. On nights like that he didn't think about his past or Anita or the things that might have been. He thought about the song he was playing or the song he was hearing or the drink he was drinking, and it was all just *fine*.

Sometimes a whole week or more would go by, and it would *all* be just fine. Then he'd have a bad night. Anita would appear to him in a dream. Somebody else would be there, too, sometimes—Worthless or Mo or Sumner or Haney. Someone from that bad, bad time. Then Sloan would go on a bender, and two or three days later that would be over, too. Time passed. Three years had gone by in this way.

By noon the boy Pedrito had come back with the suit. Sloan had bathed and shaved and put on a clean shirt and a necktie. His shoes needed a shine. He'd get that on the plaza. He gave Pedrito another coin and went downstairs.

The streets were busy and the air was hot and damp. The cobblestones were dry. But the air was heavy, and smelled of food—cooking oil, onions and garlic, cumin and *sofrito*. Sloan slipped on a pair of sunglasses against the bright light and bought a sweet roll from the bakery at the end of his street. He went up Obispo, headed for the plaza at Parque Central, looking for Havana Brown.

Havana Brown was a black cat, an American, who'd been in Cuba a long time. The story went that he'd come down chasing one woman and ended up catching another and had stayed to get married to yet a third. He had been a legendary Chicago piano player, back in the days before Basie and Ellington changed the way the keyboard sounded. What with the Cuban women, though, and the rum and the passing of time, Havana Brown hadn't touched the ivory in years. He made his money shining shoes and getting his picture taken by tourists in the park in front of the Hotel Inglaterra.

Sloan found him resting on a bench in the shade, a newspaper folded on his lap, eyes shut, napping in the middle of the day. Sloan was deciding to let him sleep when Havana Brown eased his peepers open and said, "Come sit down and get a shine on yo' shoes."

Sloan put the last of the sweet roll in his mouth and did as he was told, reaching for a cigarette as he sat. Havana Brown rolled up the cuffs on Sloan's suit pants and said, "Tell me what's new in the life of *you*."

"Nothing shaking but the leaves on the trees, man."

"I don't believe it, son." Havana Brown opened a can of blacking, swabbed a rag through it, and smeared some on Sloan's shoe. "You look like a man who's been busy."

"Not me," Sloan said.

"You know them cats that got killed this morning?"

"No," Sloan said. "I didn't know anybody got killed at all."

"Some Hollywood actor. Del Stevens. With a carload of Yankees." Havana Brown closed the lid on his blacking and began to wipe the excess polish off Sloan's shoes. "Got liquored up and ran their car into the front of the president's house. An actor and his girlfriend, and some banker from Miami and his wife . . . Whole mess of dead folk."

Sloan remembered the Cadillac squealing away from the Tropicana. He said, "What kind of car was it?"

"Big-ass Caddy."

Sloan whistled through his teeth. That was the car. "All of them killed in the wreck?"

"Maybe not," Havana Brown said. He lowered his voice and added, "Maybe just injured. Somebody say the Security men on the scene shot the driver dead—after the wreck."

"What for?"

"I don't know, and I ain't gonna guess," Havana Brown said. "My momma didn't raise no stupid chirren. 'Cept one, maybe. And I ain't stupid like I used to be. I hear what I hear, and after that I mind my own business."

With that, Havana Brown snapped his rag taut and began to give a rhythmic, popping buff to the tops of Sloan's shoes. The shine came up like a sunrise, and the snapping patter of the rag was like the sound of the Tropicana rhythm section. When he'd finished, Havana Brown had little beads of sweat dotting his forehead.

Sloan said, "You ever want to play some piano, you'll let me know, right?"

"If that ever happens, you be the *first* to know. But don't hold your breath. You'll turn blue and die."

Sloan got up and drew a ten-peso note out of his pocket and left Havana Brown laughing.

He wondered, as he did every time he got a shoeshine from the man, whether Havana Brown knew why the folks called him Havana Brown. He lived in Havana. He was brown, more or less. But "Havana Brown" was a breed of rabbit. There wasn't anything rabbity about Havana Brown. He was a strong old man, with strong old fingers and strong old hands. He had played the piano. Now he polished shoes. There wasn't anything meek or mild or defeated about him.

Still, Deacon thought, *Please don't let me end up here. Please don't put me in a place where I can't play music, where I wind up having to shine shoes just to keep myself fed. Please don't let me die old in a banana backwater like this, doing donkeywork for guys with their futures still ahead of them.*

He could not possibly have said who or what he was talking to. But the wish not to wind up like Havana Brown held his attention halfway across Old Havana.

He left the shoeshine bench and went across Parque Central, walking without hurry toward Vedado. The streets were busy after the rainstorm. Newsboys hawked morning papers on the sidewalk. A fruit vendor with a cigar stuck in his craw was calling out, "Melon. May-*lone*." A florist caught Sloan by the lapel and said, *"Para usted, amigo,"* and stuck a stubby carnation in his buttonhole.

Why is it, Sloan thought, that a Cuban, or a Mexican, can call a man "amigo" and have it sound so nice? Back home, if a guy called you "friend" or "my friend" or "pal," that was usually the last thing he said before taking a swipe at you. People would not say, "How are you today, my friend?" Instead, guys said stuff like "I tell you what, *pal*," or, "Listen up, *friend*," and then they'd poke you in the nose. Round here, when folks said "amigo," it seemed to actually mean they were feeling friendly.

Sloan went down Calle Neptune. By the time he got to the steps of the university, the sun had come all the way out. Puddles of rainwater were turning to steam. The air hung heavy again with the damp. A flatbed pickup carrying a load of black-faced stevedores squealed to a stop at the curb, and the stevedores tumbled to the sidewalk, flicking cigarette butts into the gutter and calling out to one another.

"*¡Cafécito!*" one shouted.

"*Y limonada,*" replied his companion.

"*¡Y cerveza!*" called another.

A dozen of them or more scrambled into the open doors of a café-bar. Sloan could not have said, as he watched them go, how many were black, how many white, and how many mixed.

That was one of the funny things about Havana. It wasn't like the States, with the whole race question and the civil rights thing. (Sure, he'd said to a guy one night at the Trop, because *no one* has any civil rights in Cuba, other than the ones they can buy.) Color was not the great divider it was back home. The racism wasn't legalized, either. There weren't any WHITES ONLY or COLORED ONLY signs hanging over lunch counters or water fountains or hotel lobbies. Race didn't separate people so automatically, or so permanently. The darker people were more gathered up at the low end of things, and the lighter people were gathered up at the top. Sloan had performed a couple of times at the Havana Yacht Club, for example, and at the Havana Golf and Country Club, and that was almost entirely filled with white folks. But everywhere else, in the middle of everybody else, it was all mixed up. You'd stop at a lunch counter to grab a bite, and it was a checkerboard of black guys and white guys and everything in between. You'd stop in a café-bar for a beer or a coffee and, depending on the neighborhood and the time of day and who was working on what and who was taking a break, it could be all white guys one day, all black guys the next day, and all mixed the day after that. Sloan's apartment building in Old Havana was about fifty-fifty, he reckoned—though the owner was white and the janitor was not. Any time there was a crowd on the street, it was a mixed crowd.

But you could have a black shopkeeper right next door to a white shopkeeper and no one noticed. You could drop in on any working-man's dive any midnight and find drunks, black and white, drinking cheek by jowl. The brawls that broke out weren't about color. Most places Sloan went, it was a mixed bag of mixed-blood folks. After the crappy way things had ended in Las Vegas, that was comforting.

But that ended when Sloan got to work. The crowd at the Trop was a crowd of Americans. They weren't paying big money to see a bunch of darkies pound the skins onstage. With the exception of a big-name celebrity singer—when Ella Fitzgerald headlined, or Basie or Ellington was in town, or when Celia Cruz played—the Trop was for white folks only. There were Cuban musicians in the band, of course, and Cuban dancers all over the stage. But even through the fluff and feathered boas, beneath the towering headdresses and behind all the sequins and makeup, you could see they were all white girls. No place for Negroes onstage at the Trop. And very little in the audience. Like the Havana Yacht Club, the Trop was for people with big money, and the color of the big money in Cuba, like the color of big money everywhere, was green on white, not green on black.

For a minute there, in Vegas, with the opening of the Ivory Coast, that might have changed. It might be changing now, even. Sloan never asked Mo about what had happened in the desert after he'd left. Worthless Worthington Lee was dead. Anita belonged to another man. Beyond that, the harmony of black and white in America was none of Sloan's business.

Sloan grabbed a paper off a news vendor on La Rampa. The sun was beating down now. He thought for a moment he might buy an ice cream and sit with it in the park. But the sun was too strong. He thought instead that a *café con leche* at the bar of the Hotel Nacional might be better. But the crowd there depressed him—all Yankee tourists showing off for one another. He went instead down the hill from La Rampa toward the sea, toward the Hotel Presidente. He'd grab his *café* there and read his paper, away from the noise of the Americans.

Calloway came in late and went to bed alone. He did not speak to the girl. He did not touch the girl. He had not touched her, in fact, in weeks. She didn't want him to, and he knew it.

In the beginning she had seemed more willing. Eager, even. Or maybe just grateful. Calloway himself was so ardent that he might have mistaken one for the other. He was intensely attracted to her. Everything about her enflamed him—her coffee-colored skin, her smell, her eyes, her body. Even her murky past excited him. He didn't know where she came from, exactly. But he knew she'd been involved with some rough customers in Vegas, and had worked as a waitress in a roadhouse, before Albert Sherman brought her to Hollywood. Her people were, obviously, of mixed blood. She never spoke of any of it. Calloway didn't pry.

For a year he had waited for her to warm to him. He was a patient man and a tender lover. He was willing to wait for what he wanted, and willing to work for it. He knew that he had satisfied her, physically, in bed. But he had failed to win her. Anita would not love him. He knew this, and it hurt him, and it made him long for her in a way he had never longed for anything. He ached, sometimes, watching her walk across a room.

Had bringing her to Havana been a mistake? Maybe not. She seemed to be enjoying herself. She shopped a little and went on excursions around the island. At night they went out—to the San Souci or the Hotel Nacional or the Tropicana. They danced, ate very well, and after dinner threw money at the roulette wheel.

Last night he had taken her to the Tropicana for the huge floor show. They had arrived in the middle of one of the big production numbers. The stage was overflowing with statuesque women dressed in bright gowns and florid headdresses, parading their long legs and shaking their high, feathered backsides. Even there, even then, Anita turned heads. Not just the tourists, either. The *waiters* stopped and stared.

Calloway had felt a rush of pride. And then a sense of loss. *See what I got, fellas?* he thought. *I don't got it.*

For the next half an hour Calloway did not speak to her. They sat. They drank champagne. They ordered a meal. She watched the stage with a rather childlike wonder. His sense of tenderness slowly returned.

Calloway wasn't a monster. He'd had money and power long enough to understand the limits of money and power. There were some things you simply could not make other people do. No. That wasn't it. There wasn't much of anything you couldn't make other people *do*. But there were things you could not make other people *feel,* or think, or believe.

He had her companionship. He had the pleasure of doing things for her. He had, for a while, enjoyed the pleasure of doing things *to* her. That part was over now.

He had awakened the concierge, coming in, though it was after three o'clock. He told the slippered, sleepy-eyed man, "I need to be up at ten o'clock. Have the girl come with plenty of coffee,

American-style, and breakfast for the lady. Got me?" The concierge had nodded. Calloway had gone to sleep certain that he would have to wake himself at ten and call down for coffee then.

He was wrong. At 9:45 he snapped awake. At 10:00 there was a rap at the front door, then the sound of a key in the lock, followed by the rattle of dishes and cups, and another, quieter rap at the bedroom door. Calloway got out of bed, put a dressing gown over his pajamas, and said, "Thank you," through the door.

Anita was asleep on the other side of the vast bed, curled like a kitten into her pillow. Calloway reached for the heavy blinds. The streets below were slick with rain. The sky above was cloudy, but the sun was beginning to break through. He let the blinds fall back and enclose the room in darkness. She might need to sleep. He did not. And he had a meeting this morning that meant a great deal to him.

Thirty minutes later, after a shower and shave, a cigarette and a mug of the *Americano* coffee that was stronger and thicker than anything anyone had ever been served in the States, Calloway was dressed. He left a note for Anita and left the apartment.

The carpet in the lobby smelled musty. Calloway got a noseful of it coming down the elevator. That was one of the drawbacks of staying in apartments instead of hotels. You didn't get the photographers and the reporters and the hangers-on. But you didn't get the snap-your-fingers service, either. Calloway owned several hotels in San Francisco. He was too well known to use them with any degree of ease. He was too well known to use the ones here in Havana, too. He'd speak to the concierge and simply have himself billed for the new carpet.

The heat and energy in the street were astonishing after the cool quiet of his building. Stepping out onto Paseo Martí, Calloway asked the doorman to fetch him a cab, and watched the passing scene while he waited. Every imaginable conveyance was on the street, splashing the puddles and collapsing the air with their sounds of gunning engines and honking horns. There were big American Fords and Chryslers, many of them built here in Havana, competing for space with growling, thundering motorcycles. Enormous trucks fought their way over the potholes, carrying bananas, drums of cooking oil, pineapples, and stalks of sugarcane. At the corner a policeman in a white pith helmet and matching white gloves waved his hands and wagged his finger in a vain attempt to bring order to the chaos of traffic. Calloway's taxi skidded to the curb. He slid into the backseat and said to the driver, "Hotel Nacional."

The meeting itself was scheduled to take place in a flat on Calle 15. Calloway didn't dare take a taxi there, though. He had been warned, enough to believe the warnings, to take precautions. Havana was full of spies. The rebels had put the populace into a heightened state of alarm, and the Batista regime had put them into a heightened state of terror. Calloway wasn't particularly scared of anyone. But he took the hint. He planned to get out at the Hotel Nacional, looking to his driver and anyone else like any other Yankee *turista*, and proceed on foot from there to the house on Calle 15. He'd have his doorman, the taxi driver, and the doorman at the Nacional to vouch for him, should trouble arise.

Indeed, there were two goons in black suits, sitting in a black Security car, by the Hotel Nacional's broad front doors. Calloway spotted the car, coming down the hotel drive, framed by the tall, waving royal palms. As the taxi drove past, he got an eyeful of the goons—dour, heavy-faced, obdurate. The face of the Batista regime. He slid a wad of bills into the driver's hand and said, *"Gracias, amigo,"* and left the taxi.

The Security guys meant a change of plan. He'd intended to walk straight back up the Nacional drive and out into Vedado. That would look odd, though, to someone looking for something odd. Calloway went up the three wide steps in the Nacional lobby, tipping the doorman as he went by. Inside, he took a left, heading toward the big lobby bar, but then took another left and went down the steps to the garden level. There was a barber shop there, and a beauty parlor and a travel desk and a clothes shop where a man could get suited for tennis or golf or sailing. Calloway went past them, out a doorway leading to the garden, and down another palm-lined walkway. He thought he remembered a side entrance to the street. He was right. He got back into the streets of Vedado without being seen by the Security guys. The record would show the wealthy American Nick

Calloway stopping at the Hotel Nacional, arriving by taxi, overtipping the doorman, and heading for the bar. At eleven o'clock on a weekday morning. Like any other gringo on holiday.

Anita heard him come in and heard him fall asleep, heard him wake up and heard him rise. She knew he would call down for his coffee, pour himself a cup, and then shower and shave while the coffee cooled. He'd have his first cigarette with his first sip of coffee, sitting in his dressing gown and pajamas, and look over whatever the morning mail and morning newspapers had to say. Then he'd pour a second cup of coffee and get dressed. This was his routine.

And she would pretend to sleep through it all. That was her routine.

It had been a year since she had taken up with him. This was the first time they had been out of the country together, or stayed anywhere together that was not one of his houses. His routine did not change. Late nights. Early mornings. Coffee and a cigarette and the papers, first thing. Then out to meet someone. And he never bothered her.

She lay in bed for a long while after he left, dreamy, disappointed, disenchanted. The automobile accident on the plaza, and the shooting, had disturbed her. She had slept fitfully. She had intended to tell Calloway about what she had seen, when he came in. But when he came in, she lay still, silent, pretending to sleep. Would he want to know? Would he need to know? Was it his business? Perhaps. Everything was his business—the movies, oil, airplanes, hotels, real estate. He had so much money that it touched everything and went everywhere. Even to Cuba. Not for the first time she thought, *What am I doing here?*

Not for the first time. She had thought it a hundred times. She had thought it when, as a teenager, she let herself be mauled by the pharmacist she lived with as a runaway. She had thought it while she fought off the attentions of her vile "uncle" in Shipton Wells. She had thought it again, over and over, as Albert Sherman heaved himself onto and off of her, sucking air like an animal, never having the heart attack she wished for him.

She thought it again, now, with Calloway—but not the same way. With Calloway, it wasn't a cry for help or of self-pity. With Calloway, it was just a simple wondering. *Why me? Why not someone else? Why, of all the girls in the world, would he want me?* Being in bed with him was not awful, as it was with the ones who came before. It wasn't nice, exactly, but it wasn't horrible, either. Calloway was a gentleman. He was gentle. He did not force himself on her. He did not hurt her. He did not make her want to hurt herself.

But still, she thought, how sad. She slid deeper into the bed.

If Anita had never begun to read books, perhaps she would never have learned that love was supposed to be more. She might have gone on thinking that love was duty, that love was work, a kind of business deal in which the man gave his protection and his pocketbook, and the woman gave her sex.

But she had begun to read books. So she knew that some women, sometimes, felt something different and had something different. That's how she knew what she had had with Deacon was real.

That was the only time she had not thought, *Why me?* or *What am I doing here?* She always knew, with Deacon, that she was exactly where she was made to be, doing exactly what she was made to do. And it was the only time and place, in her entire life, that she'd felt that way. She *knew*, with Deacon. He was the one for her, and the only one. And she believed she was the one, and the only one, for him.

When she heard the woman sing, "I was made to love you," she knew what the woman was singing about. She was made to love him. Only him. Except everything had gone all wrong.

It would not go right again, she thought. She had been given her chance, and her chance had been taken away. It wouldn't come again. She was made for one man. That man had come and gone.

Her head ached when she finally slipped out of bed. The light outside was glassy and bright. She pulled the curtains slightly, letting a sliver of it into the room, and went into the front half of the apartment.

Calloway had left a note. It said, *Good morning, darling—or good afternoon! I will be away until 5:00. We are dining with the American ambassador at 8:00. You'll find Guillermo downstairs with the car. Go and buy yourself something extravagant.*

Anita crumpled the note in her fist as she went to the telephone. When a voice answered at the other end, she said, "Coffee, please. And juice. And aspirin." Then she hung up.

An hour later she had bathed and had her coffee and a cigarette, and made up and dressed in a bright blue sheath and matching hat. Guillermo was waiting for her with the enormous black car idling at the curb. Anita went out the doorway and slid on a pair of sunglasses. The door to the car swung open. Alicia, who was either Guillermo's wife or Guillermo's sister or Guillermo's assistant or something, was already seated inside the cavernous automobile. She waved and said, "Goose morneen!" and shook a wristful of big paste-jewelry rocks at Anita. "Go inside!" she said. Anita got into the car, stepping gingerly and with a sick stomach over the rivulet of water running in the gutter, pushing the carcass of a dead rat downhill toward the sea.

Guillermo and Alicia waited. Anita knew they wanted to go shopping, where it would be expected that she buy something for them as well as something for herself. Instead, though, she said, "Take me to Varadero."

Guillermo said, "To the beach? In the rain?"

"It is not raining," Anita told him.

"Yes, but it is rain again," Guillermo said.

"To the beach," Anita said. "We will have lunch on the beach in Varadero. And then shopping."

Guillermo brightened. He said, "Yes, señora. Varadero and shopping."

Señora, Anita thought. *I am already a señora. How entirely sad.*

It took Guillermo fifteen minutes of maneuvering the big car through traffic before they were on the Malecón and headed east and pushing out of the city. Then they were clear. The highway was empty but for military trucks carrying soldiers and farm vehicles carrying sugarcane. Few tourists went to Varadero from Havana.

Most people who wanted to go to Varadero stayed in Varadero. The government and the police did not advise driving back and forth. The rebels had attacked military convoys on the highway, and the government wanted the road clear. They wanted everyone to stay indoors and silent so that the only people moving about would be easy to identify as rebels, Anita figured.

What a shame. It was a beautiful day. The hills rose away from the sea in waves of green, lush and full of life. The sun shone on the blue water, and the sand glittered where it met the waves. The air felt like perfume. What a shame. How could anyone fight anyone on such a day and in such a place?

It must be the money. That's what Anita thought, anyway. Men fought whenever there was something to fight over. She hadn't understood that before she came down to Havana. She had thought of Cuba as just another one of those banana-colored countries where they had sandy beaches and snappy music. The first week in Havana, though, she had seen what the excitement was all about. The casinos in the big hotels were astonishing, even after what she'd seen with Deacon in Las Vegas. The casinos here were not bigger, but they were more lavish and more colorful. Calloway had taken her to the Sans Souci and the Capri and the Tropicana. The Tropicana! It was magical. You sat at a beautiful table, with linen and crystal, in a grove of palm trees, actually *outside,* under the stars, the night air perfumed with the smell of jasmine and gardenia, the music from the orchestra swirling like water by the shore. It was like nothing Anita had ever seen.

But the men were like the men she'd seen all her life. They were like the hard men she'd seen in Las Vegas. At every other table, it seemed to her, mixed in with the tourists and their wives and the glamour girls and the Cuban smoothies, there were those tough guys with the flinty eyes and the flat, expressionless faces. Calloway had pointed out Jake Lansky to her in one of the casinos and told her he was the brother of the most famous gangster in America. She thought he was horrible looking. Another night, or maybe later that same night, Calloway introduced her to George Raft, who ran one of the casinos and who looked as if he'd spent his whole life practicing to be a gangster. The practice had paid off. He looked mean and cold and bloodless. Calloway was surprised that she wasn't impressed.

"Horrible," she said, and shuddered while he laughed indulgently.

They came now upon a fishing village, half an hour from Havana, where on the beach men were dragging boats from the water to the sand. Guillermo said, "This is Cojímar. You know Hemingway? *The Old Man on the Sea?*"

Anita nodded her head. She did know Hemingway, and his book about the old fisherman. She had not read it. But he was famous in Havana. People spoke of him as if he were one of their own, a Cuban who happened to have come from America or something.

Guillermo said, "The old man lives here in Cojímar."

Anita said, "I see." He was a real old man? How dull. Anita preferred to think writers made up everything. It depressed her to think of a writer like Hemingway writing about a real fisherman. Why? Why not let the fisherman be? Could his story be as interesting as a make-believe story? No one's story was that interesting. Life was not that interesting. It took books to make life interesting, books or movies. Otherwise, life was just what happened to people. Which was usually sad.

Farther on, Guillermo had to slow the car almost to a stop to let a herd of cattle clear the road. A farm girl with a stick drove the animals off the highway and into the brush. Anita wondered what *her* life was. Maybe another book for Hemingway. *The Young Girl and the Cow*. That would be at least as exciting as an old man and a fish. Anita giggled to herself.

Alicia, on the seat next to her, peered out the window and said, "Look the man."

Anita turned to follow Alicia's gaze. There was a man, a very handsome man in a Panama hat, with a black mustache and intense black eyes, standing under a tree by the side of the road. He saw the two women staring, removed his hat, and smiled, showing a row of brilliant white teeth.

Alicia gasped and said, *"Coñó. Qué hombre tan guapo."* Anita kept her eyes on the man. He placed his hat back on his head and, after the big black car had passed, dashed up the embankment onto the highway and down the other side. Anita turned and watched him disappear into the brush.

Guillermo, his eyes on the rearview mirror, said to Anita, "A rebel soldier."

"How do you know?"

"He is a rebel. A revolutionary."

"How can you be sure?"

"He is not a *campesino* or a *guajiro*. He has an expensive hat. He is a city man. Why is a city man here in the country? He is a rebel. A communist."

There was no point in arguing. Anita said, "Let's get to Varadero. I'm hungry now."

She turned her head again as Guillermo sped on. The man had gone.

There were soldiers on the road to Varadero. They stopped the big American car and rudely commanded Guillermo to get out and show them his documents. Anita could hear several words she knew being thrown about by Guillermo and the soldiers. *Americano* was one. *Señor Calloway* was another, and *gringo* and *yanqui.* One of the soldiers, an ugly, brutal-looking man with a heavy gut, leaned into the driver's window and ogled Anita as if she were for sale. He said to a comrade, "*Está puta . . . riquísima, mi socio.*" Anita knew what *puta* meant. She held her tongue. The soldiers laughed and waved the car through.

Guillermo, back on the road, said, "The rebels make trouble on the Varadero road. Trouble for tourists."

"The soldiers make all the trouble," Anita said. "There are no rebels here. Only disgusting soldiers who want to push everyone around."

Guillermo heard her rage. He said, "Yes, señora," and kept his eyes on the road.

Anita could almost smell the money as Guillermo got the big black car into the village itself, across a narrow bridge where soldiers stood guard and onto a long, narrow spit of land that stretched along the sea. The streets were beautifully paved, without a pothole in sight. There were paved sidewalks, too, without missing cobblestones. The shops were freshly painted. The trees had been trimmed. Everything was shiny and new. Even the sun seemed brighter. There were no poor people here. Where had they gone? Perhaps they had all become rebels, Anita thought. She said to Guillermo, "Let's have lunch."

"Where, señora?"

"I don't know. Let's drive and look."

Guillermo took the car down to the beach road. There were Americans, or white people anyway, everywhere. They strolled on the road, wearing shorts and golf shirts, some wearing nothing more than bathing attire. Everyone had sunglasses. Some of the men carried bottles of beer or glasses with ice. On the sand were brightly colored umbrellas, under which gathered squads of young people in shades of white and red and tan. Off the beach a ski boat skidded by, pulling a beautiful young man who waved at someone wading into the surf.

An open car drew up next to them at the corner, and two young men leered over. One of them, clearly an American, said to Anita, "Hey, *chica*." Anita rolled up the window, and said to Alicia, "Don't speak to them." Guillermo rolled on.

There were hotels and restaurants everywhere, and they all had the same clubby look to them. There were couples everywhere, too, and such young people. Perhaps they were no younger than Anita, but they looked like children in their bathing suits and sunburns and sandals. At each building Guillermo would slow down and glance in the rearview mirror at Anita, then cruise on. Her look hardened with every block.

The beach went on for several miles, the strip of sand widening and narrowing, the blue and green of the coral-reefed water lapping gently at the shore. Anita said, "Here, Guillermo," at a bend in the road where a stately building sat with a discreet sign over it reading VILLA CAPRI. Anita said, "We'll stop here."

It was a hotel-restaurant. There was no one on the front steps, and no one on the porch that appeared to wrap around three sides of the building. Anita picked up her pocketbook, smoothed the wrinkles from her sheath, and, Guillermo and Alicia trailing behind, walked up the stairs toward the entrance. At the top of the stairs she stopped, and turned, and said, "I'll be one hour, no more. You may want to get some lunch yourselves?"

Guillermo nodded and said, "One hour, señora. No more." He and Alicia remained standing beside the car.

Anita went across the wooden porch and through a screened swing door. Inside it was dark and cool, and she had to remove her sunglasses to see the lobby clearly. There was a registration desk at one end of the room and what appeared to be a captain's station, unmanned, at the other. Behind that, Anita could see a dining room and a few couples bent over their plates. Farther on, behind the dining room, was a veranda where other couples and groups were lunching. Anita went forward, feeling as she passed the registration desk a pair of faces turn and stare. She did not look over at them. She'd gotten enough of that in Los Angeles—that look that said "If you don't belong here, we'll make you feel like you don't belong here." The secret, Anita had found, was to behave as if *they* did not belong here, wherever "here" was, and to always act as if you owned the place yourself. Often as not, with Calloway, that turned out to be the case anyway.

A dark and aged Cuban gentleman, his skin the color of maple syrup, came from behind a screen and took his position at the captain's station. He nodded solemnly at Anita and raised an eyebrow. He said, "Yes?" in heavily accented English.

Anita said, "Good afternoon. I'd like lunch."

"Ah," the Cuban said sadly. "We are not serving lunch."

Anita eyed the dining room and the diners and the veranda and the diners there. She said, "What do you mean?"

"We are closed."

Anita watched the couples lunching, long enough to let the captain see what she was watching. He glanced over his shoulder, then turned back to Anita.

"Hotel guests only," he said.

Anita nodded and clutched her pocketbook. She said, "Can you suggest another restaurant nearby?"

The Cuban looked pained. He said, "I am afraid there is nothing here, for you. The restaurants are for Americans only."

"But I am American."

"Perhaps," said the Cuban, "but . . ." He held his hands out, palms up, as if in surrender.

Anita said, "I see." She opened her pocketbook, removed her passport, and then fingered out a fifty-dollar bill. She folded the bill in half and held it up for the man to see, in one hand, while holding open her passport with the other.

She said, "This is my money. This is my passport. I am an American citizen. I am traveling in Havana with Mr. Nick Calloway. We are dining tonight with the American ambassador to Cuba. And I am going to eat lunch *here*. You could stop me, but I promise I will make you regret it."

The captain stared at her, then at the floor. He had not taken the fifty-dollar bill or the passport from her. He turned and looked over his shoulder at the dining room. No one was paying him the slightest attention.

Anita said, "I'd like the small table by the window."

The captain led her there, defeated. Anita sat and removed her hat as the man unfolded a menu and placed it on the table before her. She removed a compact from her purse and checked her makeup. And then felt a welling of big tears in her eyes, and thought again, *Why me? What am I doing here?*

By lunchtime Cardoso had finished writing up his report on the automobile accident. It was delicate work. It had to be, for it was a pack of lies, and copies of it would be read by his superiors and probably by someone at the American embassy. A little investigation had determined the identities of the other victims. They were of no importance. But three of them were American, which meant complications. They were funny like that. The Americans always treated death as if it were some kind of personal affront. They demanded an explanation. Cardoso's explanation: These people are dead. They are no longer living. They are at peace. That should be enough.

The tension at the station house was palpable. Cardoso had sent

the boy out twice for more *café con leche,* and each time, pulling his
head up from his report and the spread of documents identifying the
dead Americans, Cardoso had smelled the smoke of bad feeling. Now,
his report completed, he was looking forward to getting out. He had
a midafternoon meeting with a European, of which nationality he did
not know, who seemed keen on the subject of the revolution. He
seemed to know a great deal more than the average tourist should
need to know. He wanted to talk. They would meet for a coffee or a
cocktail at the Hotel Presidente, and Cardoso would listen and perhaps learn something. Cardoso had no expectations. He was like a
fisherman, checking his traps. He might catch something, or not.

First, though, he must file his report with Escalante. He took up
the clean copies of his report, shuffled the notes and documents into
a pile and placed them on his desk, and straightened his tie and put
on his suit coat. Escalante cared about such matters.

Cardoso found him at his desk, ear cupped to the phone, a fat
Upmann presidente wedged between his teeth. Escalante motioned
Cardoso toward a chair across from his desk.

He was a broad athletic man going rapidly to seed. This was the
work of the revolution. Escalante had been a tremendous sportsman
in his youth. He had performed patriotic feats of strength and skill
for his country at the Olympics in 1932 and 1936. After that, he had
continued to box, to play golf and *béisbol* and tennis. He had sparred
with Hemingway and earned the writer's respect in the ring.

But the revolution had taken him away from all that. These pur-
suits made undignified use of his office. He had begun to eat and
drink more. He was getting soft outside, even as he calcified inside.
Cardoso, who had known Escalante for ten years, was appalled by the
man he had become. Escalante the sportsman, Escalante the laughing
left fielder, the long-ball hitter, Escalante of the terrifying overhead
smash, was no more. Instead, there was Escalante the assassin and
Escalante the torturer.

He said into the phone, "It is of no importance. Eliminate him.
Confiscate his property. Report back to me."

Then he hung up the phone and said without preamble, "The rebel
Delgado has landed somewhere near Guanabo. He abandoned the

ship we were watching, murdered its captain, and swam ashore. He is alone. He is armed. He is yours to find. *¡Oye tú, Redondo, ven acá!*"

A rabbity sergeant came through the door, panting. He said, "*¿Sí, señor?*"

"Give Lieutenant Cardoso the reports on Carlos Delgado. Quickly!" Escalante waited for Redondo to vanish, then said to Cardoso, "You may take a car and two men and whatever weapons you need. This is of supreme importance. I do not want Delgado in the mountains, or in Havana. I want him removed."

Cardoso nodded. He said, "I understand. But I do not want a car, or two men. I will go alone. I will get a car that is not a Security car. I will requisition the weapons I need. It isn't much. I will need some money, though."

Escalante scowled. "You are soft, Cardoso. You make men speak with money. A policeman doesn't need money to make men speak."

"Not if he is willing to kill them," Cardoso said. "But I will be speaking to *guajiros*. Most of them will know nothing. It is easier to find out what they know if I spend a few pesos. Especially if I am in a hurry. Otherwise, how many would it be worth killing? And how long will it take to kill the ones who know and will not talk?"

"Don't bore me with the details," Escalante said. "You have your orders. Leave at once. You should start at Cojímar. There is a man there who was found on Delgado's boat. A Havana man named Obregón. I am told he knows nothing and says nothing. You can change that."

Cardoso began to explain that he had a meeting with a promising source, a European who had information—probably for sale—about the rebels. Then he stopped. Escalante was not a man who took explanations well. He understood action, and results, and did not want to know how the results were achieved. He would not know how Cardoso spent his afternoon. Or what time he arrived in Cojímar.

It was not Sergeant Redondo but Ponce who returned with the document folder on Delgado. Ponce slithered in, smirking, and slid the papers across Escalante's desk.

He said, "Big job, this. Especially for a policeman who goes easy on revolutionaries."

Escalante said, "Go shoot someone, Ponce. We're busy now."

Ponce laughed, a shrill, dry laugh, and said, "I have shot everyone already, *Capitán*. If you allow me to go into the mountains . . ."

Escalante said, "Go. Into the streets. Do your job. Allow Lieutenant Cardoso to do his."

"With pleasure," Ponce said. "He will go fishing at Cojímar and bring back an empty net."

"Out," Escalante said.

Escalante waited until the door had swung shut behind Ponce's narrow back. He removed the presidente from his mouth and said, "By the way, here is the information you requested on the American girl who witnessed the car accident this morning." Escalante slid a manila envelope across his desk. "What is your interest in her?"

"Only romantic," Cardoso said, and forced a smile.

"Ah," Escalante said, and stuck the presidente between his teeth. He drew the manila folder back and placed it in a desk drawer. "I will hold it as a reward, then, for the capture of El Gato."

The old man had left her, and María Fuentes was alone again when she awoke. The beach had become busy. Boats were coming in from the water. The sun was struggling out from behind the clouds. Men were stretching nets to dry in the sun, hoisting barrels of fish to their shoulders, and marching their catch across the sand to trucks that had drawn off the highway.

María brushed sand from her dress and went down to the water. Nowhere in the rush of men and nets did she see Juan Obregón. Or the old man who had sheltered her under his boat. Or anyone else familiar. Several of the men ogled her as she passed. One said, "Ay, little sister. Come to the sea with me." María shot him a vicious look and kept moving.

Her man was not there. She scanned the sea before her. No boats were running to shore. The horizon was clear. María Fuentes returned her attention to the boats on the beach.

Two men with a small sailing boat sat mending nets and staring at her. María Fuentes caught their gaze. There was something guilty in it. She went to them at once. She said, "You are Pepe and Enrique. Where is the man you took to sea?"

The two men stared at her. They were both young, and hard, and burned a bark brown from the sun. One of them, the younger, said, "We took no men to the sea but ourselves."

"You are lying," María Fuentes said. "You do not need to lie. He was my husband. His name was Juan Obregón. I do not need for you to tell me why you took him to sea, or what you saw there. I only want to know where he has gone."

The young men stared. They said nothing.

"Please," María Fuentes said. "I only want to know where he has gone."

The young men stared.

"Please," María Fuentes begged. "I will pay you again what you were paid to take him with you."

"No," the younger man said, staring at the sand. "It is not necessary. We do not know what became of him."

The young man looked around at the other fishermen and at the trucks and men inspecting the barrels of fish by the road.

He said, "We took him out to meet a fishing boat that came from Mexico. It was a big boat, white with blue markings. He got on board. The boat went away. That is all."

María Fuentes said, "Did you see the other men on the boat?"

The younger man winced. He said, "No. It was dark."

"Were they Cubans?"

"Perhaps," the younger man said quietly. "Or no."

María Fuentes said, "What time was it? How long was it before you met the boat?"

"An hour from Cojímar," the younger man said. "To the east."

María Fuentes said, "Thank you."

"For nothing," the younger man said.

"For speaking," María Fuentes said.

The old man was gone. There was no one in Havana for her to speak with, either, nor in Cojímar. If Juan Obregón was gone, she had no one. And now, with Juan Obregón gone, there was no one to ask, no one to tell, nothing to do, perhaps, but wait.

* * *

The Calle 15 location was a subdued, unremarkable two-story house with a wide porch across the front and a balcony porch on the second floor. There was a patchy garden growing roses and gardenias, and a pair of carob trees straddling a stone walkway. Calloway went up the walk as casually as any door-to-door peddler, feeling like the Fuller brush man—here with the answer to all your household cleaning needs, and all your local political problems. He rapped twice at the heavy front door. Within seconds it creaked open and a young woman's voice said, "Come in, Señor Calloway."

The front room was dark, after the bright sun outside, and felt stale and unused. There were two wing chairs facing a fireplace. Off to the left was a door leading to a dining room. The air smelled of cooking oil and garlic. The young woman, who was dark and round, said, "This way." Calloway followed her down a murky hallway to a staircase, and up the staircase to the second floor.

There was activity everywhere. Two women cranked a mimeograph machine in one room. In another room two young men wearing black berets and smoking cigarettes stuffed papers into envelopes. In yet another, two men and a woman were bent over a wide kitchen table that was covered with dry-cell batteries, coils of electrical wire, and what appeared to be sticks of dynamite. A bomb factory. The three worked on, casually glancing up at Calloway as he passed. One of the men winked.

In the front room, lit by windows open onto the balcony Calloway had observed from below, two men sat at a long wooden table, smoking cigars and studying a map of Cuba, laid flat on the table, onto which one of the men had been drawing circles and arrows in red ink. The two men rose immediately upon Calloway's arrival.

"Señor Calloway," said one, a stocky, powerful-looking man with a line mustache and bright eyes. "Welcome. Thank you for coming to see us. I am Dalcio. This is Javier."

The second man rose and extended his hand. He was whip-thin and tall, with a long, sad face and deep-set eyes. He said, quietly, "Señor."

Dalcio said, "And you have met Nilsa already."

The short, round schoolgirl smiled politely and sat at the head of the table. Calloway nodded at her and shook Dalcio's hand.

"I'm pleased to meet you all," Calloway said. "How goes the battle?"

"Today, it is not so good," Dalcio said, and sat in front of his map. "Please, sit down, señor."

Calloway did. Dalcio sucked on his cigar and said, "Today, we have some bad news."

"About Carlos Delgado?" Calloway asked.

The tall, thin Javier narrowed his eyes at this. Dalcio glanced at him and smiled.

He said, "Yes. About our friend El Gato. He is missing. How did you know?"

Calloway said, "I didn't know. I guessed. I was expecting some word of his arrival last night. I never got it."

Now Dalcio narrowed his eyes. He said, "Why were you expecting some word?"

"Because I paid for the goddamn boat!" Calloway said, and laughed. "Cost me a fortune. I had to buy the whole thing off a crook in Mérida, and promise to let him have it back after he made the crossing. My part of the deal was that I would be contacted here in Havana when Delgado arrived safely."

"And no one contacted you."

"No," Calloway said. "What happened?"

"We don't know. Ah, here is *café*." One of the young men came into the room carrying a tray with coffee and milk on it. Dalcio said, "Thank you, *mi amigo*. Put it here. Nilsa? *¿Café con leche?*"

"*Sí, por favor,*" Nilsa said. "And Mister Calloway? You like coffee?"

"Not now," Calloway said. "Had mine, already. What happened with Delgado?"

Javier spoke now. His voice was low and steady, an actor's voice. He said, "There has been no word from him. The boat was seized by Security forces, offshore near Cojímar. The captain had been murdered. Delgado was not on board. That is what our sources say."

"And you believe them?" Calloway asked.

Dalcio said, "Yes and no. Our source is a policeman who is close to Security. He is usually dependable."

"If Carlos is killed, or a prisoner, we can know about that," Nilsa said in bad, schoolgirl English. "The police say so."

"This is what we believe," Dalcio said. "The capture of Delgado would be a great triumph for the Security forces. They would make an announcement if they caught him or killed him. They have said nothing. We believe Carlos escaped the boat. There was only a sailor on board when the Security forces took it. And the murdered captain, of course."

Calloway watched the three of them sip their coffee. None was over twenty-five. The girl should have been in high school, and Javier in a local theater production. Dalcio would be . . . a car salesman or a volleyball instructor on the beach at Varadero, seducing American divorcées. Instead, they were making bombs and revolution at a safe house in Vedado.

Dalcio smiled and said, "We are not worried. Carlos is El Gato, no? He is the cat. He has not used all of his nine lives yet. Perhaps he has not even wasted one on this journey to his homeland. We will wait. Here is what we can show you about our activities in the Sierra Maestra."

Dalcio turned the wide map around on the big oak table to orient it to Calloway's seat. He pointed at a bright red ring near the southernmost corner of the island of Cuba. A town near the ring was called Bayamo. To the southeast of that was a town Calloway knew, Santiago.

"This is our headquarters now," Dalcio said, pointing to the ring. "This is the camp in the mountains where we have made our base of operations. Everything is done from there."

"By telephone?"

"By telephone. By messenger. By Radio Rebelde, sometimes. The telephone is not always safe. It is not always working, if we have planted bombs," Dalcio said, and grinned.

Calloway laughed at him and said, "You *like* making bombs."

Dalcio said, "Amigo, I *love* making bombs."

Javier nodded gravely and said, "He makes very good bombs."

Dalcio returned to the map. "This is the territory we now control," he said. "These are the towns and cities we can control when we decide." Dalcio swept his hand west from Bayamo, across more than half the country. "We can expect to take control of everything else, except perhaps Havana, within a month."

"And Havana?"

"By the end of the summer," Dalcio said.

"Without fail," Javier said.

"Shall we eat lunch?" Nilsa asked.

Calloway watched as a meal emerged. There was a loaf of crusty white bread, bottles of cold beer, and bowls of some kind of vegetable soup, followed by large flat serving dishes of rice, black beans, fried chicken, and a sort of yellow fried potato. As many diners as plates converged on the big oak table—four more in addition to the ones Calloway had already met. Each new face greeted him with a hesitant smile. No one introduced these soldiers. When they had all seated themselves, Calloway said, "I am sorry I cannot stay. I have another appointment. May I speak with you, Dalcio, for a moment?"

Dalcio rose and then said, "If you speak to me, you speak to us all. What is it?"

All eyes rose from the table and rested on Calloway. He felt momentarily ill at ease and insignificant—an unusual feeling, for him.

He said, "I want to know what happens with Carlos Delgado. I have spent a lot of money on him. If he is alive, in fact, he is *wearing* a lot of my money. It is very important to me that he arrive and that the money go to fund this revolution."

"Why?"

The voice came from the table. Calloway turned. Was it Javier? All the rebels looked at him with calm, expectant faces.

Calloway said, "Why? Why what?"

It was Javier. He said, "Señor Calloway, you are a capitalist. You are an imperialist. You have made your fortune off the backs of the workers, in aviation, in oil, and in ownership of property. Why have you become a revolutionary for Cuba, when you are a capitalist at home?"

"Because the revolution in Cuba is just, and it is right," Calloway said. "Besides, it is unavoidable. Batista will fall. The revolution will succeed. There is no other way."

Outside, back on the street, leaving the cool of the house and the shade of the wide porch and the carob trees, Calloway wondered why Javier had asked that and whether his answer had been satisfactory.

He turned west, away from the safe house, heading away from the Hotel Nacional, opposite from the way he had arrived. Would anyone be watching him? Anyone other than Javier? Perhaps. No sense in making it easy for them. Calloway went a few blocks down Humboldt, then turned down the broad, palm-lined Paseo, which led down the hill from Vedado to the sea. He could walk to the Hotel Presidente, as any tourist might, and take a much-needed cocktail at the bar there. How odd for him to be nervous. If the rebels had been intending to kill him, now that they'd gotten his boat, carrying their passenger and his money, they had been given their opportunity and had not taken it. Calloway stuck his hands in his pockets and went down the hill, almost whistling.

Watching him go, from the second story, Nilsa said to Dalcio, "We should have warned him about tonight."

"And told him what?" Dalcio asked. "That we are destroying a gasworks?"

"Just to stay away from the river, perhaps."

"Unless he is visiting the Cementerio de Colón or touring the gasworks at midnight, he will be unharmed. Gringos don't go to places like that. He will be rolling like a drunk at the Tropicana."

"We still should have warned him," Nilsa said. "He is our future."

Dalcio colored and turned from her. "He is the past," he said. "He is a remnant of the colonialist, imperialist past. He is a resource. We are the future, of a free Cuba for free Cubans. There is no room for a man like that in our future."

Peter Sloan bought a Spanish-language daily from a kid in front of the Presidente and then crossed the lobby and took a seat in the bar. He fired up a cigarette, the last in the pack, while he waited for the waiter to come to him. The room was quiet. There were two American tourists drinking tropical booze at a table by the window. There were two Cuban businessmen sitting near them, over *café con leche* and some kind of pastry. At the far end of the bar was a dark-haired woman wearing sunglasses and a scarf, her nose in a paperback book. She glanced up briefly as Sloan sat, then put her head down again— *Not a pro, then,* Sloan thought. The bartender was polishing wineglasses and hanging them on a rack above his head. He nodded at Sloan as he sat—he'd seen Sloan at his bar before, though the nod signified nothing.

Sloan went through the paper slowly. His Spanish was weak—he could order a cocktail or a meal and exchange greetings, but that was about it—but he could make out most of the main news from the headlines and the pictures. Today's reports were about baseball in the States—the Yankees and the Brooklyn Dodgers, who had recently become the Los Angeles Dodgers. There was a story about Tim Tam, the horse that had won the Kentucky Derby and the Preakness. And then there were stories about the rebels in Cuba.

The front page was given over almost entirely to a plane crash. Sixteen foreigners and five Cuban nationals had died when a Cubana de Aviación airplane crashed into a hillside near Punta de Cigarros, near Varadero. The government blamed the revolutionaries. The revolutionaries denied it. Their leader, this character Fidel Castro, issued some sort of statement. Sloan struggled through. It appeared to suggest that the U.S. government had shot down the plane. No, that wasn't it. It said that at any moment the Yanquis might attack innocent Cubans, in support of Batista's illegal regime, in reaction to something like the unfortunate death of the Americans on board the Cubana airplane.

So, dead Americans. More dead Americans, after the car crash that Havana Brown told him about. Mo wouldn't like it. Sloan didn't like it. He didn't like *anyone* dead, though—not dead Cubans, not dead rebels, not even dead soldiers. He'd seen enough dead guys in Las Vegas. He'd seen Worthless shot down before his eyes, just as he had watched the cops kill his friend Sloan, the bartender whose identity he had been obliged to take when he left the desert.

The front page had a picture of fiery wreckage. *Campesinos* stood by watching the plane burn, the men shirtless and wearing straw hats, the women in raggy cotton dresses. Two children held their mother's hand and gazed at the flames. What a thing to see! They'd never forget it.

A waiter interrupted Sloan's musings and took his order for a *media-noche* sandwich and a beer. The white-jacketed young man, a smooth operator with slicked-back black hair and a Boston Blackie mustache, ran the ticket to the kitchen and came back fast with the suds. Sloan said, "And again," and handed the kid a folded five-peso note.

A silver-haired man came into the room just as Sloan was sluicing down the first long swallow of beer. He was familiar to Sloan, but just barely. A man he'd met. A man he'd seen sitting in the front row at the Trop. A man he'd known in Vegas? That was always his fear. He turned his head away and thought. One of Mo's pals? One of the crowd from Chicago? The man moved with a physical ease that some politicians had, and some athletes and some rich guys. It was the kind of ease that came from being the most important person in the room, the kind of self-confidence that said, "Whoever *you* are, *I'm* here now. And I rate."

When he glanced up again, the silver-haired man was moving toward him. He smiled at Sloan casually, sort of professionally, and went on by, and Sloan registered: he was some kind of tycoon, a rich American whose picture Sloan had seen in the papers. Oil? Hollywood? Sloan thought maybe the latter: the man's suit was too well cut for an oilman. Sloan watched him lamp the woman at the bar, and the two Cubans, and the tourists with their tropical cocktails. One of the Cubans, Sloan noticed, put his eyes on the silver-haired man and left them there for quite a while. This Cuban was a good-looking guy who wore his hair cut very close to his skull. He looked like a boxer. He was wearing a black suit, white shirt, and narrow tie and the heavy shoes the Security officers always seemed to wear—for what? For kicking in faces? Why did they all have the same big shoes?—but not the thuggy face that always went with them. Sloan then recognized his companion. He was that guy Scarfioti, whom Sloan had seen huddled

with Chico Fernandez at the Trop. He was wearing his linen suit
underneath his signature shiny, hairless head. And now he was hanging out with a Security guy? This Scarfioti got around.

The Security man and Scarfioti stopped and stared at this man
with the silver hair.

The silver-haired man didn't notice. He wasn't meeting anyone.
He stood at the bar and drew a cigarette case out of his breast pocket
and settled in for a smoke. Just another Yank looking for a five-
minute break. Sloan went back to his paper and waited for his sandwich to arrive.

Cardoso knew the American's face from the papers. He was a big
wheel in the movie business and the aviation business, Cardoso
thought, whose paperwork he'd looked over a week or so earlier. Cardoso made a point of reading the details on any rich or famous Americans and Europeans who registered in at Rancho Boyeros, Havana's
international airport. This guy—Carroway? Callahan? No. Callo-
way—had flown in from Miami with the intention of staying ten
days, on a pleasure trip, with a companion to whom he was not married. They were staying in an apartment in Vedado, Cardoso remembered—unusual for a gringo, not to stay at the Nacional or the
Presidente. Unusual, anymore, for them to stay in Havana at all.
Increasingly, the tourists came in at Boyeros and went directly to
Varadero and stayed there. It was bad for the casino business and
rough on the nightclubs, but Cardoso understood. Yankees on vacation were not interested in rubbing shoulders with revolutionaries
throwing bombs. They did not come to Cuba for blackouts—except
the kind you get from drinking too much. Cardoso could not blame
them. He had never taken a proper vacation in his life, but he understood. He could not imagine how much business this airplane crash
at Punta de Cigarros would cost the country. If it turned out the
rebels were to blame, *coñó!* What a reprisal the Americans would
demand. The voices from Washington were already screaming at
Batista to put down the insurrection. The flow of arms into Batista's

military bases had been unceasing. But even that was changing. The American ambassador Gardner was in, then out, and he had been replaced by a coolheaded stockbroker named Smith. In March the White House had officially ended all shipments of arms to Batista. Unofficially, of course, guns and money kept arriving. But there would be no more tanks or trucks or bazookas. Now the government had to get its arms the same way the rebels did—smuggling them in, one boatload at a time.

Cardoso said to his companion, the bald-headed gentleman wearing a linen suit, "Have something else to drink. It will be hot today, now that the rain has gone. How about a rum and Coca-Cola? I think I will have one."

"Rum and Coca-Cola—just like *las Hermanas Andrews,*" his companion said with delight. "I know the song."

Cardoso snapped his fingers and the waiter, his pencil-thin mustache quivering slightly, came at once. *"Dos ron con Coca-Cola,"* Cardoso said. The waiter scurried away.

"It's a bad business, the rum business, isn't it?" his companion asked. He was a Spaniard. He'd survived his own country's civil war. He'd fought there—well, he'd taken his money and run, which was its own kind of fight—and had run into trouble again in '41 in France. Now he was an American, with business interests in Havana. His name was Scarfioti. Cardoso knew more about him than he would be comfortable knowing Cardoso knew. That was Cardoso's job.

"It has been better," Cardoso said. "The rebels have burned the sugarcane fields. They have attacked the distilleries and processing plants. The price of sugar has remained stable, but that cannot last."

"Nothing lasts," Scarfioti said. "But here is a friend of mine. Señor Calloway!"

The silver-haired man had been about to sit when Scarfioti called to him. Cardoso congratulated himself on having gotten the name right. Calloway. And, of course, he and Scarfioti would know each other. They were both citizens of the world, members of the great international society of powerful men with money. A society that would never admit such a small man as Cardoso.

Scarfioti rose. Calloway came toward them, smiling. He extended his hand and said, "We meet again, my friend. How is the gambling business?"

"Excellent!" Scarfioti said as he rose to take Calloway's hand. "I have not made a single wager all day. I am ahead! This is my friend Cardoso. He is a policeman. I am sure he knows everything there is to know about you."

"How efficient," Calloway said, and shook Cardoso's hand. "My name is Calloway. But you know that."

"He knows everything," Scarfioti said. "Especially the things you do not want him to know."

"How sad for him, then," Calloway said. "That leaves nothing new to learn, does it?"

"My friend exaggerates, señor," Cardoso said. "I know very little."

"It is a lie," Scarfioti said. "He knows all about the horse races and the cockfights. They are all fixed, as you say. He knows all about casinos. They are all legit. He knows everything!"

"Maybe you know this," Calloway said, and leaned in close to the policeman. "I asked our friend here, just last night, to give me odds on the rebels. I asked him how long it will be before the rebels take Havana. He told me they will never take Havana. What do you think?"

"I think I want to know why you want to know," Cardoso said with a smile.

"It is a sporting question only," Scarfioti said quickly.

He looked, to Cardoso, suddenly ill at ease. Calloway, on the other hand, did not.

Cardoso said, "It is not a matter of sport. Many people have lost their lives already."

"And now, last night, this plane crash," Scarfioti said, and clucked his tongue.

"Yes," Cardoso said, "and many more deaths last night, in Havana and in other cities, that did not receive stories in the newspapers. This is so, every night."

"How long, then, before the rebels are in Havana?" Calloway asked again. "How would you advise a betting man to make his wager?"

"I would advise him not to bet at all, señor," Cardoso said. "Especially a foreigner. The rebels may never come to Havana. They may be defeated in the mountains. They may be victorious in the mountains. But no good can come for the foreigners from their victories. Every success for the rebels is a tragedy for the foreigners."

"Really?" Calloway ground out his cigarette. "The rebels will not cooperate with foreign businesses, if they succeed?"

"Never," Cardoso said. "That is almost the only sure thing. That and rum. Here are our *cócteles*. Bring another, for Señor Calloway."

The little waiter said, "At once, *Jefe*," and dashed away.

"*¡Jefe!*" Calloway said. "What a grand title. I want to be a *jefe* myself."

"To your health," Cardoso said, and gulped at his rum and Coca-Cola. "And to Cuba."

Sloan watched the three men talk, over his *medianoche* and beer. It was all just a game of checkers to him. These guys weren't his problem today. His problem today was Sloan—how to get Sloan enough sleep, how to get Sloan up in time, how to get Sloan bathed and fed and watered and slapped into shape for the evening ahead. Now, two hours after rising, he had done half his day's work. He had two beers down his gullet, which calmed his nerves and settled his stomach, and he'd eaten a fine *medianoche* sandwich, and he'd had a little stretch of the pins, walking over from Old Havana. Now he'd walk to the Trop, have a coffee with the cats backstage, and clean his instrument in preparation for the night's show.

Sheesh, what glamour! A musician's life! *It's not for everybody,* Sloan thought. *It'll do for me, though.* He flagged the pencil-thin mustache as it whizzed by with another tray of rum and Coca-Colas, and said, "How 'bout a check?" When the boy whizzed by again, he dropped a slip of paper on the table. Sloan peeled off a few faded Cuban bills and left them there.

Outside the air smelled of salt and sea. A little afternoon breeze had come up. The worst of the heat had passed, and the storm was gone altogether. They would have a big crowd tonight at the Trop.

Sloan set off down to the Malecón. He could walk along the coast, hook back up to Calle 11, cross the Almendares River into Miramar, grab a taxi from there, and still make his call time.

Going past the side windows of the grand Hotel Presidente, he could see the silver-haired man's head gleaming in the dark of the bar. Nothing else rose from the gloom. Sloan lit a cigarette and went across the street to the coast.

3

The *guajira* was gone when Delgado awoke. She had left him with nothing—not a good-bye, not a trace that she'd even been there. Judging from the sun, he had been asleep only a short time. It was early afternoon. Delgado smelled the air and listened. Smoke from a wood fire came from somewhere nearby—a cooking fire, probably, at the farmhouse the girl kept for her father. She would be preparing the evening meal. Delgado rose and shaped his hat back onto his head. He had slept, because he had been safe, and he was awake and ready to move now.

I have very little advice for the young revolutionary, he said to himself as he began to march toward the hillside. *If you intend to overthrow a repressive government, with or without the support of the people who are repressed, two things are mandatory: Shoes, and sleep. You must have good boots, and you must sleep every time the opportunity arises. That,* Delgado thought, *is all I have to offer. The military maneuvers, the underground communications network, the campaigns of sabotage and suasion, are nothing without good boots and plenty of sleep.* Now, with both, and a midday meal, Delgado felt he could revolutionize the entire world. For today, though, he would attempt to begin his march into the Sierra Maestra.

There would be no hope now of finding the men who were to have met him at Cojímar. They would be dead or arrested or in hiding. The boat would have either drifted to shore or been found by the Security patrol boats. The captain's murder would be known. The good man on the boat, Juan Obregón, would be in custody if he had not been shot or had not escaped. He did not look like a runner, though. He looked like a lot of Cuban workingmen—eager and willing, but weak. They had been beaten down too long, too severely, by a political class so strong. The idea of true victory was only a fantasy. And that won't sustain a revolution.

After an hour's walk Delgado came to a highway. The coast was not far. This would be the road to Matanzas, perhaps, and Varadero. It was the only road from Cojímar to the mountains. It wound along the seashore, from the little fishing village out to Guanabacoa, to the big port town of Matanzas, to the Yankee playground at Varadero, and from there up into the mountains at Colón and Santa Clara. That was where he needed to be, Santa Clara and beyond, in the regions where Batista's men could no longer go. How far? Two hundred miles or more to Santa Clara. A long march, for a single man, alone, without food or water. Still, it was better than the alternatives.

There was no trail beside the road. Delgado took the pavement and walked with the sun burning the back of his neck.

Presently there came the sound of an automobile. Delgado stepped off the shoulder of the road into an overhang of greenery, and waited.

It was an American luxury car, a big black sedan—a Chrysler or a Cadillac, Delgado thought. It was moving fast. As it approached, Delgado could see that the driver was taking care to miss the potholes in the pavement. It was not a government car. It was not a country man's car, either. Yankees, then? Probably. Delgado stepped slightly forward and watched.

There were two women in the backseat, one clearly Cuban, one perhaps not. She was wearing a brilliant blue dress and sunglasses.

Delgado instinctively raised his hat and smiled broadly. *¡Ay qué bonita!* The car sped on.

A mile farther on, the roadside trail reappeared. Delgado dropped from the road into the woods. If he pressed on, perhaps he could walk as far as Santa Cruz del Norte. There would be villagers there, on the outskirts. He could beg or buy a meal. Then, having slept an hour this morning, he could walk all night if necessary—or until the rain returned. For today, he thought, he would be fine. The sun had passed the meridian, anyway, and was now shining on his back as he walked. *It is always best to have the sun behind you,* Delgado thought. *And your future straight ahead.*

The old man had found her sitting alone on a bench in the plaza, where she had been sitting for hours, her nerves almost entirely unraveled. She had smoked half a pack of cigarettes and had drunk a *café con leche,* but otherwise had sat silently since she left the beach in the morning. She did not know what else to do. The old man saw her and was glad he had come. He had no good news for her, but sometimes bad news was better than none at all.

"*Escúchame, mi niña,*" he said, and sat beside her on the bench. His feet were bare and broad and leathery from a life without shoes. "I have some news for you. Your man is with the police. His boat was taken by the Security men. They did not find what they were looking for. But they are holding him just the same."

María Fuentes nodded and said, "Holding him." The old man seemed honest and true, a strong, old fisherman like her father. But could this, too, be a trick of some kind? Of course it could. It could be anything. So she said, "I do not know what you mean."

The old man understood. He said, "*Ay,* daughter. Of course you do not know what I mean. I hardly know it myself. I will tell you only that there is a police station on Calle Colón, there behind us. Perhaps you will go and learn something there."

"You are very kind," María said.

"Good luck and bless you," the old man said as he rose and moved across the plaza on his worn, wasted feet.

When he had gone, María Fuentes rose and left the plaza in the opposite direction. She had no other way but the police station. She knew that Juan Obregón would tell her to go home, if he could tell her anything, that she risked being jailed herself by going to the police for information, that she should return to Havana and wait. But she could not wait. Waiting was for the old. Waiting was for the weak. And for the wise, Juan Obregón would tell her. She was not old or weak, or wise.

The station was a whitewashed blockade near the center of town. A group of miscreants clung to its front steps as if to a sinking ship—a cripple, a blind newspaper vendor, a man selling fruit juices from a cart that had lost its wheels, two drunks, and several mountain women who were probably waiting for their men. The women sat dozing on the broad steps, sitting with shawls draped around their shoulders. They looked as if they had been waiting forever.

María Fuentes went up the steps and through the heavy wooden doors. Inside, it reeked of urine and cigar smoke. Behind desks sat several officers in mismatched uniforms, some unshaven, all smoking. Two men in dark suits were playing cards at a table in the corner. They eyed María Fuentes with professional interest. The uniformed policemen hardly noticed her. Why did the absence of decent uniforms bother her? It made them look barbaric. Perhaps it made it possible for them to act with more barbarism, too. Without real uniforms, they were not real policemen, and so they were not accountable to the same set of rules. As if there were rules anymore.

María Fuentes went to the man nearest the door and said, "Excuse me. I am looking for information. On my husband. His name is Juan Obregón."

The man looked up sharply. Then his features clouded over. He was a heavyset man of early middle age. His khaki shirt was stained and filthy. He needed a shave. He needed a lot of things. He looked María over with filmy eyes and said, "Come here."

María Fuentes sat at a chair next to his desk, which was inches deep with papers and forms and old newspapers. The burly policeman lowered himself into a chair facing her. Two other policemen came and stood behind her. She could feel their presence. One of them reeked of rum. One was smoking a rank cigar. The heavyset policeman winked at one of them and said to María Fuentes, "Tell me that again."

"Juan Obregón," she said. "I would like information regarding Juan Obregón."

"We know nothing of Juan Obregón," the policeman said. "Who are you, and why are you asking about him?"

María Fuentes told them as little as possible. Her man—she claimed him as her husband, because she felt she might have some rights as a wife that she would not have as a girlfriend—had lost his job at the car plant in Havana. He had gone to sea with some fishermen. He had not returned. She had asked at the harbor and on the beach. No one had seen him. She was worried.

"We know nothing of this," the policeman said. "Who was he fishing with?"

María Fuentes told them a little more. Two men, she said. Cojímar men. Perhaps brothers. She did not know their names. Perhaps they had been reported missing?

"We know nothing of this," the policeman said again. "You are wasting valuable police time. Perhaps your man is with another woman."

María Fuentes winced. How pathetic. And how cruel. *These men,* she thought, *control the fate of my man. And my fate, too.* She said, "Oh, I hope not. I am afraid for him. I am afraid to be alone. I would do anything just to find out what has happened to him."

It worked. One of the men behind her placed a heavy hand on her shoulder. She could smell the cigar smoke on his fingers. He said, "Now, now, woman. Don't be worried. I will help you."

María Fuentes turned. He was acne-scarred and fat, with a soggy cigar stuck between his teeth. He smiled when she looked up at him. It was a horrible smile. María Fuentes thought, *No. I can't. Not even for Juan Obregón. But, of course, this animal doesn't know I can't.*

She said, "Would you help me? Could you?"

The heavyset policeman grunted and laughed. He said, "He will help you. Indeed, he will help you. Perhaps when he is finished, I will help you myself."

Several other policemen in the room laughed out loud at this. María Fuentes was chilled but resolved. The acne-scarred policeman had a gun and a holster slung from his belt. *If I get his pants off . . .* María Fuentes felt nauseated and weak at the mere thought of it. *Yes, and then? His pants are off, I have the gun, and then?*

She said, "Show me Juan Obregón first."

The acne-faced man said, "But we know nothing of this Obregón. We pulled no fishermen from the sea today. But you will come with me into the cells. Perhaps there is a man there who uses another name. Perhaps he is your man."

"Yes. Thank you." María Fuentes rose. She hadn't even thought of that. Juan would never use his own name. She said, "Show me."

The men in the black suits watched as she passed. One rose and went across the room, behind her, and conferred with the heavyset man. The other policemen watched and exchanged winks. Like laughing dogs. The policeman with the cigar led her to a heavy metal door that swung into a hallway. He took María's arm and drew her forward.

The hallway faced a row of cells. The stench was appalling. There was little light. Men—scarecrows and skeletons—crouched in the darkness. María Fuentes's stomach lurched. She thought, *Please, God, don't let him be here.*

The policeman squeezed her arm with his big hand and said, "This way," and steered her down the hallway. The cells yielded nothing but horror. None of the men crouching in the darkness looked familiar to her. They passed six such cages, six men or more in each of them. At the end of the hallway was a room, the same size as the cells, but with walls and a door in place of bars and a gate. The policeman, holding tight to her arm still, swung the door open and pushed María Fuentes inside. When the door closed, there was almost no light at all. The room held only a metal table and two chairs. There was silence but for the policeman's raspy breath. María Fuentes backed away until she was against a wall, then moved along the wall into the corner. The breathing did not advance on her. She heard a metallic clicking and then the clump of something heavy being laid on the table. *His gun belt,* she thought. Then she heard his zipper. In the near-darkness now, she saw him advance toward her. María Fuentes formed a plan. *Wait until he is quite close. Drop to the floor. Scamper past him. Grab the gun. Pray it is loaded. Threaten to shoot.*

Yes, and then?

When the policeman was almost on top of her, María fell to the floor and dashed past him on her knees. She ran her shoulder into one of the table legs, and a sharp pain shot up her neck and into her head. She rose unsteadily and felt for the tabletop, but she was off balance and teetered away instead. The policeman said, "*¿Qué bolá, María Magdalena?* Don't you want it?" María leaned forward and felt again for the gun belt.

Then the door swung open and the room filled with light. The policeman stood clutching his crotch with one hand and his trouser tops with the other, breathing hard. María crouched in the corner. In the doorway, silhouetted by the light from outside, stood a man in a black suit and black hat. He said, "Get out. Take your gun," and then turned to María Fuentes. "Sit in the chair," he said sharply.

When the policeman didn't move, the man in the suit said again, "Get out now. And turn the light on."

The policeman grunted past her, tucking himself and his shirt-tails into his trousers, scooping up his gun belt and hurrying out the door. He threw the light switch as he went. The room lit up. María Fuentes stood and placed her hands on the back of the metal chair. Her shoulder ached and her head spun slightly. The man in the black suit said, "Sit." He removed his hat, placed it on the table, and sat opposite her.

He was a nice-looking man, clean-shaved, with tired eyes and a low, flat voice and hair cut very close to his scalp.

"Tell me your name," he said. "And your address and your relation to Juan Obregón. And do not tell me anything that is not true. I will know if you lie to me. Do you understand me?"

"Yes," María Fuentes said.

"Good," he said. "My name is Cardoso. I apologize for the police-man. For *all* of these policemen. They are . . . not properly trained. Tell me about Obregón."

María Fuentes told Cardoso almost everything. She told him

everything but the truth. Cardoso took a small notebook out of his jacket pocket and made tiny markings with a pencil. He listened to her with interest but without comment or expression, making notes, nodding. He had warm brown eyes that seemed sympathetic. But then he was a professional policeman, María Fuentes reminded herself. *This is what he does all day—this, and worse—extracting information from people who do not want to talk.* María Fuentes told him about the morning and the old man on the beach.

"And did he know the two young men with the boat?"

"Yes," María Fuentes told him, then caught herself. She could not use their names, could she? She said, "They were called Raúl and Pedrino. They are from here, from Cojímar."

Cardoso wrote this in his notebook and said nothing, but his expression changed. He had heard her hesitate. *That is the first lie,* he thought. *She has given them new names.*

"Go on," he said.

"That is all I know," María Fuentes told him.

"No," Cardoso said. "That is not all you know."

The Security man smiled at her, and waited.

"But, I have told you everything," María Fuentes said.

"Not at all," Cardoso replied. "Not at all."

He smiled at her again and tapped the table lightly with the end of his pencil.

A man screamed horribly from somewhere down the hall, perhaps from one of the cells. It was eerie and heartbreaking, both. Cardoso winced, then smiled softly. María Fuentes stared at him, then looked off in the direction of the scream.

Cardoso said, "Ah. There he is now. *¡Qué lástima!* They will hurt him."

"Hurt who?"

"Why, Juan Obregón, of course. Perhaps you would like to tell me more about him now?"

The scream came again. María Fuentes felt a rush of blood to her brain and was faint.

Cardoso said, "It is better if you tell me what you know—much better. These things do not end well. But it will end more quickly if you are helpful."

It sounded almost like an apology. It sounded like the truth, too. María Fuentes looked into his warm brown eyes. He was not lying to her. It did not occur to her to wonder how he would know the sound of her man screaming—when she, herself, in fact, did not.

She said, "If you will make them stop, I will tell you what I know."

"Good," Cardoso said. "Wait a moment."

The heavy metal door swung shut behind him. María Fuentes waited and began to weep. When the Security man returned, he sat again and touched her hand across the table.

"You are a good woman," he said. "You love your man. You will help him now."

He took the little notebook from his pocket, and the little pencil. He said, "Tell me this, first: who arranged for Juan Obregón to meet Carlos Delgado?"

Late afternoon was Sloan's second-favorite time of day at the Tropicana. He couldn't have said, exactly, what time his favorite time was. It came about midnight, if it came at all. The room was full. The dinner service was over. The patrons had all had plenty of rum and Coca-Cola and gin and tonic and champagne. Sloan himself had already had four or five drinks, too, in the dressing rooms or from a flask he kept in his horn case and transferred before showtime into his jacket pocket. He felt calm and rich inside. The orchestra was calm, too. And at some point in the second set, everything clicked. Sloan felt strong and alive, and the music simply poured from him. All he had to do was lift his horn to his lips. The orchestra swung. They might be doing "Babalú" or "Punta Fresca," a mambo or a merengue or a samba or a swing. It didn't matter. For about ten or fifteen minutes, everything was right.

Now the cleaning crews had come through already. The carpet shone. The tables were set. The china and stemware were out and glistening, and there were fresh-cut flowers on all the tables. The chandeliers in the big room were lit. There was soft music playing in the big room.

In the casino there were men, mostly, bent over craps tables and roulette wheels or sitting for blackjack. The poker table in the very back was full—it was always full, no matter what time of day or night. A few of the men had cocktails. A few had cigars. None had the head of steam that came in the middle of the night, though. No one was insane yet.

Sloan went across the vast Tropicana lobby, past the casino and into the big room. He nodded hello to a couple of black-skinned bus-boys whose names he did not know and to a light-skinned waiter whose name might be Pablo or Pedro or Pedrín or something like that. Sloan played it safe and said, "Hiya, Peewee," and got a wink back. Ahead of him, going toward the stage, were three dancers from the line. They were not yet transformed. They were just average good-looking girls—pale, tall, dark-haired Cuban girls with nothing special to recommend them. One glanced over her shoulder and saw Sloan coming behind, and turned back and whispered to her friends. The other two turned and giggled. One waved. Sloan winked and said, "Lovely ladies, good evening."

He didn't know whether they spoke English. But he knew that in two hours, after undergoing the magic of costume and makeup, when they hit the stage, they would be the most beautiful women in Havana—graceful, swaying birds of paradise, with perfect skin and high, pert breasts and broad Cuban smiles and legs that ran from the floor right up to their tail feathers.

Corman, the entertainment director, was on the floor already, seated at a front table with a pack of cigarettes and a pot of coffee. Sloan waved from across the room. Corman put a hand up and crooked a finger, motioning Sloan to the table.

Trouble? Over what? Sloan was pretty sure he hadn't done anything wrong, lately.

Corman was a short, shiny guy, almost hairless, with a brittle, irritated look on his face—always. He said, "Siddown, Sloan. Have a coffee?"

"No thanks."

"Sit anyway. We had cops here this morning. Looking for witnesses."

"I haven't seen anything, boss."

Corman frowned. "Everyone says that. I haven't even told you what they were looking for."

"Was it Security guys?"

"That's right."

Sloan smiled. He said, "In that case, I *definitely* haven't seen anything. My entire life, I haven't seen anything."

"Very funny. Here's the squeeze. A bunch of Yankees left here last night after the second show. They got drunk and got into a car and drove toward Vedado, in a big new Cadillac, and got theirselves killed."

"So?"

"So, the cops want to know what they were doing before they wrecked the car."

"Drinking, sounds like."

"Yeah, *and?* That's what they want to know."

"Search me, boss. I'm just the cornet player."

Corman scowled. He said, "Yeah, *and?* That's what you always say."

"It's all I got to say," Sloan said, and rose.

"The guy driving the car was an actor, name of Del Stevens. There was a lawyer with him, and his wife, from Miami, and some other folks. All croaked."

"Some accident."

"Go away, Sloan."

"Already gone, boss."

Backstage, the dressing rooms were beginning to overflow with feathered beauties. The metamorphosis had begun. Halfway through the transformation, they looked like something Noah rejected from the Ark—half feathered, half flowered, half human and half angel. Two of them stood in the hallway, wearing nothing but high heels, fishnet stockings, and pearls. Sloan averted his eyes and shot down toward the men's dressing rooms.

About half the orchestra was already there. A craps game was going in the shower room. A crooked craps game, Sloan would guess. In his limited experience hanging around with musicians, the guy with the dice, or the guy *with* the guy with the dice, won an awful lot more often than he lost. Sloan knew from hanging around stickmen and boxmen in Las Vegas that a pro could load a set of dice so that only a pro could tell the difference. A game like this, no matter who brought the dice, wound up getting played with rockers.

Sloan waved to a couple of men standing with their hats shoved back on their heads and exasperated looks on their faces. Good way to get hurt? Tell 'em they were getting shivvied in a crooked craps game. Sloan didn't know them *that* well.

He stopped in front of his locker and sat down next to a swell sax player, a Mexican named Santiago who had come in to replace Corrales, a Cuban who, they said, had gone to join the rebels in the Sierra Maestra. Sloan said, "*¿Santiago, qué bolá?*"

"What theese *qué bolá?* Everybody talk *qué bolá.*"

"What's happening, man. It means 'what's going on?'"

"Theese Cubans don' espeak Espanish right."

"They don't speak English right, either. You doing okay?"

"Me? Chure. I fine."

"That's good, then. Say, I sure like what you were doing last night on 'Tunisia.' That thing right before the break—dot dat dibble dibble DAH DAH. You know?"

Santiago smiled. "I know. Chure, *I* know. And *you* know. And Baby Root know, and he say no more monkey bizzyness."

"Baby" Ruth was the bandleader, an American whose real name was David Ruth. He was not related to the ballplayer George Herman "Babe" Ruth but had got stuck with the nickname because musicians gave *everybody* nicknames and because David Ruth had the face of a child. He was fat and mean-spirited and almost entirely unmusical. It was remarkable that he had a career as a bandleader. It was remarkable that he was even *alive,* given the way he treated his musicians.

"Ruth doesn't know anything," Sloan said. "He wouldn't know real music if it bit him."

"Maybe I goin' to bit him myself," Santiago said.

"You wouldn't like the taste," Sloan said. "Forget it."

Because he came in wearing a suit, because the suit he wore to play in was the same suit he wore to do everything else in, Sloan was always done before everyone else. The other guys had to shower and shave and get suited up, and they had to gossip and complain and shoot craps and smoke cigarettes and tell lies and swap phone numbers and borrow ten bucks and pay ten bucks back and show one another dirty pictures. Sloan didn't have to do any of that stuff, except smoke cigarettes. He slipped out the side door now, as he had done the night before.

The late-afternoon sun was throwing long shadows and golden brown light over the landscape. The palms in front of the Trop waved and swayed gently. Sloan thought they looked like those Hawaiian broads, those hula dancing girls. He'd like to see that one day. He'd like to see a lot of things. He thought of the car full of Americans that had spun past last night, the ones that Havana Brown and now Corman had told him about. They wouldn't be seeing any hula girls. He thought of Anita. Maybe she'd go to Hawaii. Maybe she was in Hawaii right now. Maybe the sun he saw setting in the west was the sun she would see rising in the east, wherever she was, in just a couple of hours. The idea warmed him, somehow. It *was* the same sun, wasn't it? The sun that set for him now would rise and warm Anita, somewhere, today. He saw her riding in an open car in Hollywood, or walking on the beach at Santa Monica, or strolling on the boardwalk at Avalon. Or dancing in a grass skirt in Hawaii. Sloan saw Anita's perfect brown body dancing before him.

And it all went sour, just like that. It wasn't good to think about it too much. Probably no good to think about it at all. Sloan flicked his cigarette butt into the street, took a big slow slug from the flask of whiskey, and went back inside. Showtime, soon.

Anita was sitting in front of the low wooden vanity, finishing her makeup, when she heard Calloway come in the front door of the apartment. She was wearing only a slip and suddenly felt cold. She'd left open the two big windows that looked out over the plaza and toward the sea. A balmy soft breeze had been blowing all afternoon, with no memory of the morning's rain on it. Now, with Calloway back in the flat, there was a chill in the air.

In the mirror she saw him come into the room and approach her. He was carrying a bouquet of some kind of tropical flower and wearing a big smile. Her heart softened a little. She thought Calloway was fifty or older. Sometimes he looked about eleven.

"Good evening, darling," he called to her, and placed the flowers next to her on the vanity. His lips were cool against her cheek, and he smelled pleasantly of cologne—with the faintest suggestion of something else. Anita wrinkled her nose.

"A good day?"

"An excellent day," he said. "Profitable in every way. Now tell me about you."

Anita finished her eyeliner and watched him in the mirror as he sat and crossed one leg over the other and regarded her with affection. Or pride of ownership. Anita was not sure what he felt. She wasn't sure it mattered, either.

She said, "I had Guillermo drive me to Varadero today. For lunch, and shopping."

"You had a fine day for a drive."

"Yes," Anita said. "Not so fine for the lunch. We stopped at a place on the beach. They refused to serve me."

She watched him start and color. He uncrossed his legs and put his hands on his knees and leaned forward, lines creasing his forehead. Anita thought, *Isn't it interesting that he doesn't need to ask me why they refused to serve me?* Calloway said, "Go on."

Anita smiled at him in the mirror. She said, "Don't worry. I didn't make a scene. Well, just a little one. The maître d' told me the restaurant was closed for lunch—but there were thirty people eating lunch, right then. Then he told me it was only open to guests of the hotel. I asked him to recommend another restaurant. He told me they were only open to *Americans*."

Calloway's face had darkened considerably now, and his knuckles were white as his hands pressed down on his knees.

"So . . ." Anita said, "I took out my passport and a fifty-dollar bill, and I said to him, 'This is my passport. This is my money. If you refuse to seat me, I promise I will make you sorry for it. I'll sit right there by the window.'"

Anita smiled pertly at him in the mirror. Calloway's face was relaxing slowly.

He said, "And?"

"And . . . I had lunch. Coquilles St. Jacques."

"And?"

"A little chewy."

"No," Calloway said, "I mean, and what happened?"

"Nothing. I ate, and watched the beach. And watched the people on the beach. The maître d' never came near me again."

"And the other restaurant guests?"

"No one paid any attention at all."

"I see," Calloway said. "Well, congratulations. You have done in one afternoon what will take a hundred years to do in Alabama and Mississippi. What was the name of the place?"

Anita thought, *Tell him, or not? What will he do with the information? What will he do to that maître d' with the information?*

"Villa Capri," she said. "It's right at the end of the beach. Guillermo can tell you where."

"I'll have him take me there," Calloway said. "In blackface. And I'll order hog maws, chitlins, poke salad, and watermelon pie."

Anita said, "Very funny, big man. Now, will you let a girl get dressed?"

Calloway rose and went to her and put his hands on her shoulders. They were large and soft and cool—always cool. He was like a snake, or a lizard—always cool. He leaned down and kissed her again on the cheek.

He said, "I'm afraid we've got to go to that Tropicana again tonight. One of the perils of tourism—everyone wants to show you the Tropicana. Including the American ambassador. I hadn't the heart to tell him we'd already been."

"I'll wear coconut shells and peacock feathers."

"Perfect, darling. Shall I mix you a drink?"

"Make one for yourself. I'll wait."

Calloway switched on the radio and set about building a scotch and soda. He'd missed lunch, between one thing and another, and the cocktails he'd had with Scarfioti and that odd policeman had made his blood feel thin. A scotch and soda now was probably a bad idea. He mixed the drink anyway, lit a cigarette, and dropped into an armchair. The breeze came in from the sea. The music was soft and tropical, rhythmic with horns that swelled and swayed like palm trees. Calloway stubbed the cigarette out and put down the cocktail. *Five minutes*, he told himself. *I will rest for five minutes. Then I will shave and put on a clean shirt. Then I will take Anita to meet the ambassador.*

It was a fool's errand. He had nothing to say to the ambassador. He'd met the man before, several times, across boardroom tables and at political functions. He was a know-nothing, blowhard Washington phony, a guy who'd never gotten far in business and now was not going to get far in the diplomatic corps.

Calloway resented the invitation, which came almost in the form of a summons. But it wouldn't do to irritate the man or arouse suspicion. He wouldn't be on the job much longer, anyway. All Calloway needed, really, was for him to remain asleep at his post for a few more months.

Calloway didn't reckon it would take more than six. The Cuban kettle was about to boil. The insurgents in the hills were gaining momentum. The government resolve was weakening. Public sentiment was shifting. The whole thing was going to blow before the end of the year. The rebels would take Havana, and Batista and his cronies would flee or face execution. Or the rebellion would be beaten down and the leaders would be killed, and Batista would rule for another couple of years.

Calloway was betting on the rebels. But everything would hinge on what happened after they took over. Either the rebels would embrace American money and American interests, or they would not. And the Americans would send an invading force to protect American interests, or they would not.

If they didn't, Calloway was in very good shape. He had siphoned enough money to the rebels, and expressed enough real sympathy for their cause, to earn himself the front position. He reckoned he would angle for the hotels, the airline, and the sugar refineries. He would settle for the hotels and the airlines.

The five-minute rest became fifty. Calloway napped with his chin on his chest. He snapped awake just as Anita was coming into the room. She was dressed in black, with black stiletto heels, a string of black pearls, and black gloves that came to just below the elbow. She was stunning.

Calloway said, "You look wonderful. You always look wonderful. Shame on that man from the Villa Capri. I'm going to get dressed. Can I make you a drink first?"

"Please do," Anita purred, and went slowly across the room toward him. "And turn up that music a little, will you? It's sweet."

Mo awoke with a start just as the plane was hitting the Havana runway. He'd slept all the way from Florida. He was tired. He'd almost missed getting to the airport on time. He'd spent the morning with the people from Miami, and they had insisted on going out to Hialeah for the first three races. He'd known it was going to run him short on time. He'd insisted on taking his own car and driver—even though he knew it made the tough guys from Miami nervous—because he knew it was going to get soggy with drink and horses, and he knew he would miss his flight if he wasn't careful. He'd been right. There was a great deal of drinking at the field clubhouse, and the first race had gone off without anyone having even placed a bet. Mo thought Lichtman was going to have a heart attack. He hated missing a race. Mo had left them right after the third. Lichtman had bet right on that one and on the second. His heart was probably going to hold. Meyer Lansky wouldn't be looking for a new man in Miami anytime soon after all.

Havana was a different story. Meyer had already shifted a lot of his interests out of Cuba. He saw the future—it wasn't hard to see, and it wasn't pretty—and he'd made his play. Mo was sure Meyer was doing the right thing, but he wasn't sure Meyer was doing it at the right time. It might be too early to get out. One thing Mo had learned in Europe after the Big Show: there is always a lot of money to be made during a crisis. For every action there is an equal and opposite reaction, the boys in the lab coats said. When a government falls or a war comes to an end or a war begins, whenever there is cataclysmic change, all the normal rules change, too. And in the blink between the old rules and the new, there is great opportunity.

Mo was in Havana to see the opportunity.

Coming out from Rancho Boyeros airport, it didn't look like there was any opportunity for anything. The road was crowded with bicycles, oxen, peasants, and donkey carts, all carrying vast bundles of green crap. Mo asked his driver, a New York Italian that Meyer had supplied, "What the hell is that stuff everyone's carrying?"

"Sugarcane," the driver said. "They make rum out of it. And sugar. And syrup, you know, for pancakes and all."

The driver piloted the car through the parade of poverty, watching for potholes, flashing his lights and mashing on the horn, pushing the people aside as he moved slowly toward Havana. A bicyclist went down right in front of them as the driver hit the horn. The driver cursed and stopped. Mo said, "Take it easy. We got time."

It was an hour before they made the Tropicana. Mo was beat. He needed a shower and a pot of coffee and a fresh suit of clothes. He'd insist on having all that before he even spoke to anyone. He'd make Meyer's guy handle the guys at the Trop. Meyer's people in Havana had insisted he cancel his reservations at the Hotel Nacional. They had a bungalow at the Tropicana, not open to guests, that Meyer kept for his own entertainment. They insisted he stay there. Mo didn't like it. He was already too beholden to Meyer. And Meyer had a way of expecting things in return. He hadn't told Mo what he wanted in return. Indeed, Mo had nothing Meyer *could* want in return. Mo had sold all his interests in the desert—the Starburst, the Thunderbird, the Ivory Coast, were no longer his—and liquidated all his assets. He controlled nothing. He had no weight. He had no connection anymore to the guys in Chicago. He was just a businessman now.

Still, he was greeted like visiting royalty. The Tropicana manager escorted him to Meyer's bungalow. Bungalow! It was bigger than a house and lavishly decorated, and came with a staff. An elderly Cuban with a vast mustache stood like a cigar-store Indian. The manager said his name was Carillo. When the manager had returned to the lobby to see about Mo's bags, Mo said to Carillo, "Do you speak English?"

"Yes, sir. I do."

"Excellent. Would you please draw me a hot bath, pour me a gin and tonic, and have my dinner jacket laid out for the evening?"

"At once, sir. Perhaps you'll take your drink in the library?"

"Library! Like Meyer can read!" Mo laughed. "Show me to the library!"

Two hours later Mo felt like a civilized human being again. He'd had the gin and tonic in the library and another in the bath, and then had a shave, and had ended with a nice cool shower. Carillo had asked if he wanted someone sent in for a rubdown. Mo had said, "Later. Now, the monkey suit."

At just before ten o'clock, monkey-suited and with a fresh gardenia in his lapel, Mo told Carillo, "See that I get a good table and a waiter that speaks English, will you?"

"Would you like to order now?"

Mo said, "Sure. Have 'em bring me a steak, plain, medium, and a potato, plain, with salt. And a bottle of champagne. A big bottle. With several glasses."

The manager was waiting outside his door when Mo emerged from the bungalow. He said, "I hope you want to see the show?"

"Naturally," Mo said. "Wouldn't miss it."

"Perhaps you would like to meet some of the girls after the show?"

"Perhaps."

"You can tell me, if you do."

The manager escorted Mo down to the lobby, which was filling up with gentlemen and ladies. The bar was already full. The main room was filling up, too. More than half the tables were already occupied.

And why not? It was glamorous. Even for a guy accustomed to Vegas, this was pretty hot stuff. The ballroom was huge, and the ceiling opened directly to the night sky. There were palm trees growing all around—great big swaying coconut palm trees, in huge pots, rising right up to the roof—as well as ferns and banks of flowers. The air reeked of gardenias and jasmine. Waiters came and went as swift as swallows. The clink of glasses and silverware tinkled beneath the swelling sound of an orchestra, hidden from view.

Mo said, "Can you put me near the horns?"

The manager said, "Near the horns? What horns?"

"The horns in the orchestra. I want to be near the horn players."

"Of course, señor. But, why?"

"I like horns."

"Yes, sir" The manager snapped his fingers at a waiter crossing before him. He said, *"El numero trece, y apúrate,"* and then said to Mo, "He will arrange this now. This way, please."

The waiter scurried forward and turned a table for four into a table for one faster, almost, than one could say those words. The table was next to the stage, which rose on several tiers from the floor. Mo could feel the orchestra, behind the scrim, warming the room with music. The manager snapped his fingers some more as Mo sat down, and a bottle of champagne and an ice bucket arrived, along with a big cut-glass ashtray with a box of matches and a fat Havana stogie resting on it.

Mo smiled, reached into his pocket, drew out a twenty-dollar bill, and palmed it into the manager's hand. He was home. It might be Havana, and they might have palm trees and gardenias growing right there in the room, but now it was just a nightclub, playing that nightclub music for a crowd of well-heeled nightclub smoothies, and Mo felt right at home. *No matter where you go,* he thought, *it's the same deal. Rich folks look the same no matter where you go, and the music and the champagne are always just as they should be.* Mo said, "Here's how," to himself, and put a glass of the bubbly to his lips.

Delgado had walked steadily eastward for several hours before the heat of the day began to wane. He had stayed near the highway, retreating into the brush every time he heard an automobile approaching. Delgado reckoned that once he got east of the turnoff for Varadero, he could start hitchhiking. Today, there was too great a risk that one of the cars coming down the highway could be a government car of some kind. The nicely dressed people inside could be Security agents, or worse. After the turnoff for Varadero, the only vehicles on the highway would be the broken-down trucks of the working people or the brand-new cars belonging to Batista's men. It would be easy enough to know which ones to flag down and which to hide from.

By sundown, Delgado's road had come back parallel to the ocean. To the north, due north across the water, was Key West. The water stretched away from him in sheets of bright blue and green, the color changing with the coral beds beneath the surface. Farther out, where the blue became richer and darker, was where the big fish ran. There were marlin and swordfish there, the long, sleek, powerful billfish that so captivated the Yankee sportsmen. He knew it could not be otherwise, but the fact of it depressed him: Come to Cuba, home of beautiful things! The fish! The women! Hunt them down and kill them!

After dark he came to a small village on the coast. The distance from Havana made it right for Santa Cruz del Norte, but it was very small and there were no signs on the highway. Delgado walked a quarter mile of spur road down to the beach, and from there into a small plaza. There were few people about. It was time for the evening meal. He could smell dinner cooking from a dozen wood fires, and smoke rose here and there from the thatched huts scattered among the pines and palms that sheltered the shore.

Delgado was not a country man. He didn't really know country ways. But he forced a smile onto his face, took his hat in his hand, felt to make sure his pistol was still tucked securely into his pants, and stood in front of a low hut and said, "Hello?"

Two young men, one wiping his hands on his pants, emerged. Both had long, stringy mustaches and wore the boiled white shirts and pants of field-workers, and one appeared to be missing his left eye. He appeared to inspect Delgado with only faint interest. He said, finally, "Yes?"

"Good evening," Delgado said. "I am walking the road to Santa Clara. I do not know this village. But I am hungry and I need a bed for the night. I have a little money."

"It is good," the man with the eye patch said. "You will need a little money, for there is neither restaurant nor hotel here. This is Bahía Negro. Santa Clara is many days' walk."

"That is fine," Delgado said. "I have many days for walking. But I need food and rest tonight. Can I eat and sleep in Bahía Negro?"

"You'd better see Señora Galvan. She keeps a room. Orlando will show you."

His companion looked surprised, but nodded. "Come," he said. "It is not far."

"Thank you for your guidance," Delgado told the man with the eye patch. "I will pay Orlando for your services."

"No matter. Go with him to Señora Galvan. She will feed you."

The house of Señora Galvan was another thatched *bohío,* indistinguishable from its neighbors. Orlando walked there silently, padding on bare feet, with Delgado clumping behind in his heavy boots. Orlando did not speak. He simply stopped in front of a thatched box of a hut and nodded.

Delgado reached into his pocket to take out a small bill. Orlando waved this away. He nodded again at the hut and left Delgado there.

Señora Galvan was ancient and tiny and bent. She pulled Delgado through the door with a hard, wiry hand and showed him to a back room with a dirt floor and a low pallet in the corner. She drew a sheet and pillow from a storage chest and pushed them into Delgado's arms. She said, "Are you hungry also?"

"Very."

"Good. I am an excellent cook," the old woman said. "You will eat well. Come."

Delgado sat at a wooden table in the front room, spooning black beans over rice, eating chunks of chicken simmered in tomato and garlic, while Señora Galvan watched protectively over him. She said, "The chicken is fresh. The garlic is not from this village. Tomatoes are not hard to grow. A child can grow a tomato. I get dried beans and rice from my nephew in Havana. He will come here tomorrow. He has a job with the government. He is a fool."

"Where are your sons and daughters?"

"All gone. I had three boys and one girl. The girl married and went to Camagüey Province. She works in a shop. Her husband is a military man. I do not see her now."

"And your sons?"

"All gone."

"I am sorry. A mother should not be alone."

"A mother is always alone. Eat more rice and beans."

After the meal Señora Galvan said, "Come sit with me." She showed Delgado to a pair of rocking chairs, rough-hewn and ancient, by her front door. She said, "We will sit here. I will tell you something. My sons are not gone. But they are not here."

"Where are they?"

"In the mountains."

"Ah," Delgado said. "They are fighting."

"Yes."

"With Fidel."

"Yes."

"And you miss them, and you worry about them."

"Yes."

Delgado's heart swelled. He said, "I am returning to the mountains myself. I also am going to fight with Fidel. Perhaps I can carry a message to your sons. They will want news of their mother in Bahía Negro. Are they called Galvan?"

"I do not know what they call themselves now, but I will give you mangoes to take to them," the old woman said. "It is difficult to get mangoes in the mountains. But you can grow tomatoes there. A child can grow a tomato."

"I have heard this," Delgado said. "But now I must sleep."

The old woman nodded from her chair. She said, "Listen to me. Sometimes in the night I wake up and make myself a cup of coffee. Be careful that you do not shoot me with your pistol, eh? Put it under your pillow."

Delgado smiled and said, "After such a grand meal, I will sleep without waking. Good night."

Sleep did not come at once, though. His legs ached. Delgado was not accustomed to the walking. This was good training, then. He would be ready for the mountains again, before he got there.

He had been fit and young when he and Fidel began. Delgado had been one of the 134 rebels who staged the attack on the Moncada police barracks in Santiago de Cuba in 1953. Three of the men died in the fighting. Sixty more were caught and executed on the spot. The rest were captured. Fidel and Delgado were among them. The trial was swift and the judgment severe. Each received a fifteen-year sentence, to be served at the rough military prison at the Isle of Pines. Both he and Fidel were middle-class young men—Delgado a doctor's son, Fidel the child of a sugar plantation owner. There was outrage at the length of their sentences. Perhaps the people did not understand the true seriousness of the crime. The papers treated the Moncada assault as youthful high spirits. It wasn't. He and Fidel and the others wanted arms from the barracks in order to mount a full-scale revolution.

The public outcry was heard, though. He and Fidel served less than three years. They were released and exiled. They went together to Mexico. Two years later, having raised funds and support from their base in Mexico City, Fidel sailed back to Cuba on a leaky wooden boat named *Granma*. He and eighty comrades landed in December. Only thirteen survived the battle that followed. They escaped into the mountains. Delgado had gotten word, almost two weeks later, that Fidel and his brother Raúl had survived the landing. Fidel wrote to him: *Stay. Find money. Then come home.* Delgado had spent the next six months traveling Central and South America. Twice he had been to New York. The money was not difficult to find. Arms and men, though, were difficult. Delgado sent what he had across the water, to the mountains. From there, Fidel had rebuilt the revolutionary force, which now numbered in the thousands.

And now he was going back to join them. How many days' walk? Many days. Delgado tried not to think about his aching legs. He would be strong, soon. He would hold a rifle again, and fight. He took the pistol out of his waistband and put it under his pillow.

Dinner with the ambassador was glacial. Anita had corralled her energy and charm, and when she and Calloway arrived at the Tropicana she was ready to shine. She would smile and flirt and make Nick pleased that he had brought her. No one ever said to her, "This is your job." But she knew. She was a little bit like the heads that hunters hang on their walls as trophies to show their prowess. Her job was to hang brightly on the wall as Calloway's trophy.

She needn't have bothered. They were met at the front door of the Tropicana, amid the swaying palm trees and the swinging searchlights, by a Tropicana factotum in a dinner jacket. He escorted them, over a series of mumbled explanations, to a banquet room at the rear of the grand casino, making apologies for their host and promising he would soon be with them. "Matters of state," he said repeatedly, as if that meant anything to anyone.

Calloway laughed and said, "Never mind all that, young man. Bring us some champagne and we'll be just fine."

The ambassador was another half an hour in arriving. Calloway had already ordered a second bottle of wine and asked Anita for the third time whether she didn't want some caviar or pâté or something. The factotum returned and said, with great and unnecessary ceremony, "Señor Calloway, may I present the American ambassador to the Republic of Cuba, Señor William Dickens."

The ambassador was a sour man with halitosis and a rotten hairpiece, wearing a wrinkled linen suit. He was not really the ambassador at all. Calloway had explained to Anita, on the ride over from Vedado, that the new ambassador was a man named Semper. He had recently replaced Arthur Gardner. Semper was a stockbroker, a midlevel Wall Street man Calloway had known fairly well years ago, when he lived in New York. This was Semper's assistant.

Calloway rose from the table, though, as if he were meeting the king of Spain. Dickens came to them, eyes shining, hopeful and out of breath. He extended his hand at Calloway, who said, "Ambassador! How nice to see you! Please come join us."

"Well, well," Dickens said, blowing bad breath across the table. "Very nice. Howja do."

"This is my friend Anita, Ambassador."

Anita rose and bowed slightly, as she had been taught to do. Dickens greeted her without interest—"Howja do," he said absently. His eyes had not left Calloway since he had come into the room.

"Sit," Calloway said. "We're drinking champagne. They say it's French, and I imagine we have to believe them. What's your drink, Bill?"

"I prefer 'William,' actually," Dickens said. "I can never think of 'Bill' without thinking of ducks. Don't you see? And I only drink rum. When in Rome, you know . . ."

"Excellent policy," Calloway said. "Now, where's the ambassador?"

The dinner was unimaginably dull. Anita ate sparingly, the bitterly won lunch still sitting heavily on her, and tried to appear interested in the conversation. But it was not interesting. Even Calloway wasn't interested. She could see it. He ordered an immense seafood platter, a grand assemblage of lobster, prawn, fish, and shellfish, then nibbled at it without appetite.

The assistant to the ambassador, the foul-smelling man with the toupee, prattled on about investment opportunities, sugar and grain futures, government contracts, and the political complexion of the Cuban senate. Calloway listened and nodded, periodically saying things like "Is that right?" or "You don't say."

When Dickens left to take a telephone call—"It may be the ambassador," he said breathlessly—Calloway turned slowly to Anita and said, "I believe the little Dickens is the most tedious man I have ever met. And he has foul breath. I'm sorry I dragged you along for this."

"It's nothing," Anita said. "You're the one who has to listen to him."

"Good God, you don't think I'm actually listening to him?" Calloway answered. "Perhaps he'll be assassinated by the rebels."

"Nick, don't."

"You're right. Too much to hope for. I'm going to call for the waiter and see if we can get this over with now."

Calloway went to the door and stuck his head out. Music swelled and then softened as the door opened and closed. The orchestra was swinging. It was time for the first show. A waiter was at the table with the bill almost before Calloway had taken his seat. Dickens returned, hard behind him. Calloway tapped his watch, put his finger in the air, and said to Dickens, "Showtime! I promised Anita we wouldn't miss a minute of it."

Dickens said, "Oh," and looked terribly disappointed.

"But I've taken care of the bill, and I want to thank you for spending so much time with us this evening. I can see you're a busy man, with a hectic schedule."

"You have no idea," Dickens said. "There are some days—"

"Thank the ambassador for us, too, will you? He knows how to reach me, if need be. Thank you again."

They were free of him and strolling across the vast lobby. Calloway whispered something to the factotum, who had reappeared as the bill was changing hands, and the little man escorted them into the main ballroom.

The fountains were lit. The palm trees, hot with colored lights, shone like towers of fire. The stage was a riot of dancers in flowers and feathers. The orchestra hit a high note, and the colors all went to pink. It was like the jungle blooming.

Calloway said, "Follow that little fellow there," and pointed. The sea of tables and men and women shiny in black and white parted before them. The little man drew them on to the front of the room, just off center, until Anita felt she was almost part of the show. The dancers high-kicked and spun before them, and the thrum of the orchestra seemed to become one with her own heartbeat.

Calloway said, "Is this all right?"

"It's perfect," Anita said.

"We'll have more champagne, then."

The music rose and fell like the tide, carrying Anita along as it swelled and softened. The wine was wonderful. Her head was light and airy and clear. The trees and the fountains twinkled with lights, and the dancers were like wild exotic birds winging before her.

Then the music stopped, but for the rumble of the kettledrums. A man in a tuxedo stepped up to the microphone as the dancers flocked to the front of the stage. The emcee said, in heavily accented English, "Ladies and gentlemen, welcome to the world-famous Tropicana— where all your dreams come true! Welcome to the heartbeat of Havana! Home of the most beautiful girls in all the world! Where the rhythm of the drum beats out the jive of the jungle! Ladies and gentlemen, enjoy!"

A silver-haired man in a dinner jacket had risen from a table adjacent to theirs and was approaching the stage as the emcee unspooled his spiel. Calloway watched the man move toward the orchestra pit, a hand in the air as if in greeting.

Then he saw Anita. She had turned, half rising from her own seat, and was staring as if at a ghost. Her face had gone pale. Her body appeared almost to quiver. Her eyes were fixed on the back of the silver-haired man moving away from her. Then she suddenly turned and caught Calloway staring.

She said, "Please excuse me. I'm sorry. I must go to the ladies' room."

She was out of her seat and gone. She didn't look back. Calloway sat down and kept his eyes on the silver-haired man, who now was shaking hands enthusiastically with one of the horn players, a dark-haired, handsome young man who, leaning down from the stage, didn't look as Cuban as the rest of the musicians.

How vexing. Calloway was confused—an unusual, and uncomfortable, sensation. Anita had seen something upsetting. It was the silver-haired man in the tuxedo. He must be someone she knew. Someone from Las Vegas? Probably. To Calloway's practiced eye, the man looked just a little bit slick. A little cheap. Nice enough looking, Calloway saw. Expensive clothes. Well groomed. But slightly cheap somehow. He was coming back from the orchestra pit, sheepishly edging past the other customers. No spring chicken, though. He was easily Calloway's age. And sort of . . . *worn*. Tired. He had been smiling as he left the orchestra. Now he was without expression as he turned away and sat.

How vexing. Calloway turned and looked to see if he could catch the captain's eye. He could certainly get the captain or one of the waiters to tell him the man's name. But there was no waiter or captain in sight. Calloway poured himself another glass of champagne and wished Anita would come back. If he saw her face and it was calm, he would become calm, too. If not . . . he would know that he had a problem to solve.

Then he caught a waiter's eye, and got the man to the table. Calloway nodded toward the stage and said to the waiter, "That man there, with the silver hair. I want to know his name and I want to know where he is staying in Havana. Understand?"

The waiter looked, saw who Calloway meant, and nodded.

Calloway stuck a fifty-dollar bill in his hand. He said, "It's very important. And it's a secret. Understand?"

"Yes, señor. I will go at once."

Out of the corner of her eye, Anita had seen the silver-haired man in the tuxedo rise and begin to move to the stage. She noticed, but didn't. It was just the movement that caught her attention, which she then returned to the stage. The dancers were in a line. There must have been a hundred of them. The emcee was going on about the heartbeat of Havana, "whair oll jew dreen construe," but she wasn't listening. Then the dancers were bowing and retreating. The man with the silver hair came into her line of sight again as he moved closer to the stage, and suddenly Anita saw him clearly.

It was Deacon's friend Mo, from the Starburst. The owner of the Starburst and that other hotel-casino. She had met him the night of the catastrophe at the Ivory Coast. He was the man behind Worthless Worthington Lee, the man who bankrolled the Ivory Coast. His name was Mo. Here, now, in front of her, in Havana.

And then she saw what Mo was looking at. He was reaching up to the stage, into the orchestra, and was shaking hands with one of the musicians. And the musician was Deacon. He was holding a horn in one hand and shaking Mo's hand with the other, smiling like a big kid. His hair was shorter. He looked thin. He looked *wonderful*.

And her head went *zoom* and all the blood rushed from it, or to it, and she was dizzy and hot and on her feet and staring at Calloway and she said, "Please excuse me," and ran from the table.

In the ladies' room, trying to compose herself, she thought, *What am I to do?* Whatever it was, she knew, she'd have to be fast about it. Calloway was no fool. He would have seen the look on her face. He would want to know what it meant. Wouldn't he? He was also a gentleman. Any other man she'd ever been with, except Deacon, would have beaten her over a thing like this. But Calloway? He certainly wouldn't beat her. How would a gentleman handle this?

An older American woman, clouds of powder and scent clinging to her wrinkled pale face, said to Anita, "All you all right, my dear? You don't look well."

Anita said, "I'm fine. Thank you. I've just had a little shock. But I'm fine now."

"Are you sure? Shall I call someone?"

"No. I'm fine. Thank you."

Anita smiled and rose and went to the door. She took a deep breath. She left the ladies' room.

The orchestra was swelling and the dancers were on the stage again and the room itself was dark. Anita did not look at the musicians. She kept her eyes forward, sweeping across the room, until she found Calloway. He was watching the stage with the slightest of smiles on his face. He turned and looked in her direction, half rising from his seat as he saw her approaching. When she got quite close, he stood and took her chair and pulled it out for her.

He said, "You've missed nothing. Are you all right?"

"I'm fine, thank you," she said as she sat.

"Are you sure? Should we leave?"

"No, Nick. I'm fine." She watched his eyes. She saw concern, and affection. She said, "I just got dizzy, all of a sudden. It might have been something I ate."

"An allergic reaction, perhaps," Calloway said. "To that little Dickens."

Anita smiled. Then her eyes filled with tears. She turned away. She knew, just like that, that Calloway knew. The line about Dickens was the clue. He was making a joke, giving her an alibi, helping her cover up the truth. Could he know the truth? No. But he knew something.

So that was what a gentleman would do.

Anita said, "Give me a cigarette, will you? I feel like a cigarette."

Calloway had never, in two years, seen Anita smoke. Whatever this was, it was pretty big. He did as he was asked, but kept his eyes on Anita. She did not once, not then and not for the next thirty minutes, look again at the silver-haired man. She kept her eyes on the stage. She looked dreamy and faraway and lost. Lost to him, anyway. She finished the cigarette, her hand shaking slightly as she stubbed it out. Not five minutes later, she turned and said, "May I have another cigarette?" The waiter came and poured them champagne. Anita took her glass and began to stare at the stage again.

The music ended. The dancers melted into the scenery. The houselights came up. Anita looked exhausted, pale and worn. But her eyes shone. She looked drugged or feverish, or both. Calloway kept his eyes open for the waiter. No sign. A man he hadn't seen before arrived with the check and waited while Calloway peeled bills off the bankroll in his pocket.

Then he saw the waiter, standing with his back to the wall. The waiter raised his eyebrows at Calloway. The silver-haired man was just leaving, passing in front of the waiter. Calloway said to Anita, "Will you wait for me here, one minute?"

"Of course," she said.

Calloway went to the waiter. He took another fifty from his pocket. The waiter whispered, "His name is Mo Weiner. He is an American. He is from Las Vegas. Maybe he is a gangster. He is a friend with Meyer Lansky. He is staying here at the Tropicana, in the apartment of Meyer Lansky."

"Is Lansky here, too?"

"No, señor. He never comes now. He is in Miami."

"Thank you. Not a word of this to anyone. Understand?"

He showed the waiter the second fifty-dollar bill. The waiter nodded. Calloway put the bill in his hands.

He said, "I want you to follow him. Stay close to him. I will be back here in exactly one hour, and I will meet you in the lobby, and you will show me where he is. Understand?"

"Yes, señor."

"You can do that?"

"Yes, señor. But maybe I lose my job."

"I'll take care of you. Just don't lose *him*. One hour, you understand?"

"I understand."

Calloway went back to the table and drew Anita up to him. They joined the stream of Americans and Europeans drifting away from the stage. Anita seemed drowsy and limp. Calloway said, "Poor

Guillermo. He has had a long day. Varadero at dawn and Vedado at midnight."

"Is it midnight?"

"Long after midnight, darling. Look. Guillermo's there."

The night air was cool and sweet after the crowded ballroom. There was a breeze coming up from the sea. Anita felt swoony and light. She let Calloway steer her into the back of the Cadillac and slid across the seat to make room for him.

Deacon was alive. He was here in Havana. She would find a way to see him. How? Somehow. He was playing in the orchestra. So, he was *here*. Not passing through, but staying here. Mo Weiner looked like a tourist, wearing his tuxedo and applauding the Tropicana dancers after each number. But Deacon was *here*.

Calloway said, "Did you enjoy the Tropicana as much the second time?"

"Oh, more," she said. "Thank you."

I will meet the little waiter, Calloway was thinking. *He will take me to this gangster. I will confront him.* With what? You couldn't get to a man like Weiner with money. Gangsters were notoriously greedy, but they couldn't be bought like that. And you probably couldn't scare a gangster, either. They were scary guys themselves, and they didn't threaten easily. Most men could be moved by greed or fear. Some men could be moved *only* by greed or fear. But what about the man who can't be moved by either? What was left? Only his humanity, if he had any. Calloway laughed at the thought. *I'll appeal to his humanity. I will ask him, as a gentleman, to release her. And, because he is a gentleman—and he* must *be a gentleman, if Anita loves him—he will understand.*

The streets were empty. The drive back to the apartment was quick and quiet. Anita stared out the window, which she rolled down a bit as they passed along the sea by the Malecón. Waves crashed over the seawall, where couples clung to each other in the shadows. Calloway watched them, and watched Anita, and sighed. This, then, was not to be. He had always known her heart was elsewhere. Now perhaps he knew where.

At the apartment Calloway thanked Guillermo and, though there was no need, pressed a twenty-dollar bill into his hand as he said good night. He said, "Keep the car running."

Upstairs Calloway said, "Can I mix you a nightcap? I'm having a brandy."

"No, thank you," Anita said. "I'm still feeling a little dizzy. I'm sorry, but I think I'll just go straight in to bed."

She went to him and kissed him lightly on the cheek. The impulse to take her in his arms was almost overpowering. Almost. Calloway wasn't a brute. She had said, as clearly as if she had written him a note, *I am going to bed* alone. *I don't want you near me.*

Moving away from him, she said, "Thank you again, for tonight."

Calloway opened the big shutters that let in the night and the sea. The streets below were silent. There was a slight rumble of waves on the seawall. He settled into the sofa with his brandy, letting his head loll back on the cushions, and considered his options— one or two fewer than he'd had at the beginning of the evening. When he was certain Anita would not be coming back into the living room, he put down the brandy and wrote her a note. *Gone out for that nightcap. Love, N.*

On the way to the door, he had a short, unhappy thought. He paused and went to a bureau drawer, from which he withdrew a small silver pistol. He stuck it into his inside jacket pocket.

Guillermo was waiting at the curb, dozing behind the wheel, with the Cadillac engine purring like a big cat. Calloway opened the back door, slid into the seat, and said, "Let's go back to that Tropicana."

Guillermo rubbed his eyes with the back of his hands. He said, "Is close."

"I know it's closed," Calloway said. "Let's go there anyway."

Anita heard the main door swing shut. She had gotten undressed already and lay naked under the sheets with the lights out. But then the door swung shut and the wall behind her head shook. She waited a full minute, listening intently—someone coming in? someone going out?—and heard only silence. She slipped out of bed and into a nightgown, and went into the front room.

Empty. She saw the note. Her heart began to race. This was her moment.

Moving quickly, Anita threw on the black dress she had just hung in the closet and the black shoes she'd just put away, not bothering with a slip or stockings, and drew a shawl around her shoulders. She spent a quick minute on her face—lipstick, a brush through her hair, no more—then grabbed her pocketbook and was gone.

The apartment lobby was dark and creepy. The night watchman was asleep. She went fast across the lobby tiles without waking him. Then she was outside.

Anita went down the block to the plaza. There were no taxis there. She continued on to the Malecón. A black Security car cruised past. Out of it a face leered at her. Anita was careful to stand in the light. She knew that prostitutes worked this end of the boulevard by the sea. They stood in the shadows of the buildings and waited for cars to draw slowly to the curb, then strode forward to offer them- selves for sale. Anita went back to the apartment.

The night watchman was dozing on his stool in the lobby. Anita said to him, "Excuse me. I need a taxi."

The watchman got to his feet and said, "Taxi! Lady. Yes. A moment." He dashed out of the building and into the street.

Minutes passed. The street was silent. A creaking yellow taxi came along and slid to the curb. The night watchman got out. Anita gave him five pesos and got in and pulled the door closed behind her. She said, "Tropicana, please." The driver, an ancient man with a florid nose and thick black glasses, said, "O-kay. Five dollars."

It was an outrageous amount. Anita gave it to him and said, "Go fast."

Sloan had cleaned and put away his horn and talked a bit with some of the other musicians. Many of them were making plans—a craps game, a card game, a cathouse. Sloan said things like "Sounds like fun" or "Seven come eleven," but he never joined them. He locked his horn away and went back into the ballroom and out through the main lobby doors and into the lobby bar. The bartenders were mop- ping up there. A few Americans were still drinking at the bar. It was technically closed to locals, and it was off-limits to employees. The management didn't want the tourists trying to buy the dancers right there in the lobby bar.

But the tourists wouldn't know that Sloan was one of the musicians. He was just another Yank drowning his sorrows. He slid onto a bar stool and said, "Give me some of that scotch on the rocks, will you?"

The bartender scowled—the late hour, probably—but poured the drink and set it in front of him. Then he saw who was talking and said, "Oh, it's you, Sloan. How's it hanging?"

"Loose and to the left. How you doing?"

"Okay. Tired. Long day. I pulled a double."

"Ouch. Hope you collected some coin."

"Mucho dinero."

"Then you won't need this."

Sloan slid a five-dollar bill onto the bar and drank off the end of the scotch. The bartender poured Sloan another deep drink and set it in front of him.

This Mo business was no good. Sloan was beholden. Mo had saved his life. He'd nursed him back to health in Vegas and then financed his flight from the cops. Then, when Sloan had tracked Anita down in Hollywood and the Vegas thing became a problem again, Mo had helped get him out of Hollywood. He'd found him a gig at the Tropicana and bankrolled his run out of town. And then not taken a dime back when Sloan tried to send him some money for the airplane ticket.

So Sloan had been a good soldier. He'd sent Mo lots of little bits of information. Mo indicated he'd made good use of them. Sloan tipped him to the sale of the Havana Hilton. He tipped him on the burning of the sugarcane fields and the assault on the Presidential Palace, long before any of that stuff was making the American papers. Mo had been only mildly interested in the news that Chico Fernández was rubbing elbows with Scarfioti in the main Tropicana ballroom.

Mo, leaning into the orchestra tonight, said, "That's not what I'm here for, but it's useful to know."

"What are you here for?"

"Ah!" Mo said and laughed. "That's the $64,000 question. I'll have to tell you all about it. Maybe we can have lunch this week?"

"You say when, Mo."

"I can contact you here?"

"Sure. I play six nights a week."

"Grand. You sound good, by the way. You don't mind playing the cornet?"

"Well, it's not a trumpet," Sloan said. "But it's a horn."

Mo slipped back into the audience. The music came up again. The girls swarmed forward. When the show was over, Mo slipped away without Sloan's having seen him go.

Sloan was only slightly curious about the lunch. Mo's business interests had never interested him. Even the opening of the Ivory Coast, which had been Mo's obsession when Sloan worked for him in Las Vegas, had only been the window dressing to his meeting Anita. All he remembered about that time, really, was what he remembered of her. The thought of Worthless Worthington Lee, and of Thomas Haney, ached like a wound that had not properly healed. But that was never what he thought of first when he thought of that time.

Tonight, sitting over his scotch at the Tropicana bar, he tried to think that stuff away. Sometimes he'd imagine meeting someone new, someone who would bring his heart back to life and chase Anita out of there. But he knew it wasn't going to happen.

So instead he said, "Why, yes, thank you, I will have another cocktail," and the bartender smiled and glugged scotch into his glass.

It was unusual. Mo didn't know how unusual. He hadn't spent much time in Havana. He didn't know how they did things down here—how business was conducted, how deals got done, how money was made. When word came that an American financier named Calloway wanted to see him, now, at one in the morning, Mo said, "Sure. I'll meet him in the lobby bar." Why not?

Then he called the concierge, who woke the manager, who told him what he knew about Calloway. Big money. Oil. Airplanes. Movies. Real estate. No Havana investments. Mo thought that was interesting. Real estate? Could word have gotten around that he was interested in the Hilton? Only through Deacon—or *Sloan,* he reminded himself. He wasn't Deacon anymore.

Mo had been sitting in his room with a cocktail, the radio turned down low, restless despite the long day, puzzling over his next move. Or rather that is what he had *meant* to be doing. He was, instead, thinking about Deacon, when he was still called Deacon, and Worthless Worthington Lee and the Ivory Coast and the fiasco it became.

He was thinking about Worthless's ugly death, and then Haney's very satisfactory death, and then Deacon's escape, and the girl, and the rest of it.

He himself had come away clean. He finessed the sale of the Thunderbird to a consortium of local boys, led by Marquez and Truxton. The sale of the Starburst, after that, was easy work. The Ivory Coast took a little longer, but it finally went, too.

Now he was solo. He was out from under the guys in Chicago. He wasn't really tied to Lansky. This Calloway could be the local link he needed. Mo splashed some cold water on his face and headed down to the lobby bar from his bungalow.

The manager was waiting for him outside the door. He said, "Good evening, señor. I will take you to the American Calloway."

Mo wouldn't have picked him out otherwise. He looked nothing like an American financier—whatever that was. *American financier* said fat and bald and vulgar and hungry. This guy looked like a movie actor *playing* an American financier. He looked like Cary Grant as Foster Atkinson III, steel magnate. He was tall and lean, silver-haired and tanned, and very well groomed. Coming across the lobby bar, Mo could see the self-confidence on the man. He stood tall but easy, a cigarette in one hand and a rocks glass in the other, very attentive but very relaxed. Very *poised,* Mo thought. Poised for what?

The manager caught Calloway's eye. The American set down his drink and dropped his cigarette into an ashtray, and brushed his hands lightly against each other as he stepped forward. His smile was professional, wide but businesslike. He extended his hand. Mo reached for it and said, "Mr. Calloway. Good to meet you."

At that moment Mo noticed Deacon—no, *Sloan*—sitting by himself at the bar. He shook Calloway's hand and gave Sloan the slightest nod of the head.

Calloway said, "Mr. Weiner. Thank you for making time to see me on such short notice. Is there someplace private we can talk?"

"Anything you have to say to me can be said in the open," Mo said. "What are you drinking?"

"Scotch," Calloway said.

"We'll have some of that, then."

The manager said, "Scotch, señores," and scampered away.

Calloway said, "That boy's a regular jackrabbit."

The voice was softly Midwestern, or maybe had once come from Texas. Calloway had a bit of the cowboy to him, despite the Hollywood sheen. He had that openness that goes with the West, Mo thought. Wide smile, open face, easy gait. Athletic. He himself was the opposite. He was small and compact and reserved, with tight eyes and a tight smile. He didn't give away much.

He gave Calloway nothing. He waited instead for Calloway to come to him.

Calloway lit another cigarette, offering the custom-cut, leather-and-gold case to Mo, who declined. Calloway said, "Do you enjoy the local cigars?"

"Very much," Mo said. "A fine smoke."

"I buy them for my friends in Washington," Calloway said easily. "But lately they've been saying that I'm supporting an evil regime and a corrupt economy. I disagree. I tell them, 'I'm burning the fields, one cigar at a time.'"

Out of the corner of his eye, Mo saw Sloan rise from the bar and move toward the door. Mo raised a hand in salute. Calloway turned in time to see Sloan wave and slide from the room.

Mo said, "What's on your mind?"

Calloway said, "I'll be blunt. I'm here in Havana with an old friend of yours. Her name is Anita."

Mo's eyebrows shot up. He glanced at the bar, where Sloan had been sitting. Calloway saw his look go there but didn't chase it. He waited. Mo said nothing.

Calloway said, "She came down here with me. She's living with me in California. You know who I am talking about?"

Mo said, "I do."

"We were at the Tropicana tonight, in the main ballroom. Same time as you. She saw you there. And I saw her reaction."

Mo said, "Did you?"

"She doesn't know I'm here."

Mo said, "I see."

Calloway waited. Nothing came back at him. Mo's face was absolutely clear. You could read nothing on it. *Good poker player,* Calloway thought. *Tough in business. Likable, probably. But not a nice enemy.*

Calloway said, "She hasn't told me too much about what happened to her up in Las Vegas. She hasn't told me that much about what happened to her in Hollywood, either, with Sherman. She was glad to leave him, though."

"I imagine she was," Mo said casually.

"Then you know him," Calloway said.

"Well, not to sleep with him," Mo said. "But he didn't seem like a lot of laughs."

"You get the picture," Calloway said. "She's been with me since then. I'd like to keep it that way."

"I can see that," Mo said.

"And I'd do a lot to keep it that way."

Mo raised his eyebrows again. A threat? An offer? What *was* on this guy's mind? He said, "She's a beautiful girl."

The manager returned to them, at last, with a tray carrying a bottle of scotch whiskey, an ice bucket, two glasses, and a syphon bottle. The two Americans looked only at each other. Mo said, "On the rocks, please."

Calloway said, "Soda with mine."

"Right away," the manager said, and began to pour the drinks. Neither man spoke until he had left.

Calloway said, "Your business is no business of mine. Unless you make it my business."

Mo said, "I don't plan on making my business anybody's business, Mr. Calloway."

"Then I can assume you're not interested in contacting Anita?"

"You can assume anything you like."

Calloway winced. He shifted in his seat and took a long drink of his scotch.

"Perhaps I'm not being clear enough," he said.

"I think you're being pretty clear," Mo said. "Why don't you tell me what you want?"

Calloway relaxed. He'd said his piece. He'd put his cards down. And Mo would play. That was always the first hurdle—getting the other guy in the game. Once he was in the game, things could happen.

Calloway said, "I want you to stay away from Anita. What do *you* want?"

Mo said, "I'm here as an investor, Calloway. I see Batista's hold on things coming apart. The rebels in the hills are going to be in the cities soon. Change is coming. I like change. I like being around when change happens. I'm going to squeeze in here for a while and try to make a little money for myself."

Calloway nodded. There wasn't going to be any fighting. There would just be some good, old-fashioned horse-trading.

He said, "I can probably help you there. I've done a lot of favors for people who do business here. Including Mr. Lansky. If you're hooked up with him on this."

"No," Mo said. "I'm here on my own. Meyer's finished with Havana. That's why I'm here, really. I couldn't be moving in if he wasn't moving out."

Calloway sipped his scotch. He said, "Do you want to own something, or run something?"

"Run something. Casinos. That's my line."

"And hotels."

"Before," Mo said. "Not now. Or not here, anyway. The future's too short for it."

"Then why casinos?"

"A crisis, or right before a crisis, is a good time to be in the gaming business," Mo said. "And this is going to be a crisis."

"Which way are you betting it'll end?"

Mo smiled. "I'm not betting at all, Mr. Calloway. I'm *taking* bets. How about you?"

"I'm not sure," Calloway said. "Batista's a bum. But he's our bum, isn't he?"

"Is he?"

Again, Mo's face gave up nothing. Calloway, who didn't impress easily, was impressed.

Mo said, "What's available?"

Calloway thought, then said, "The Sunset's in flux. You can move in there, more or less immediately, if someone applies the right leverage."

"What about the Presidente?"

"I can deliver the Presidente, too. Not the Nacional, though. Not the Tropicana, of course."

"No. What about the Miramar and Las Golondrinas?"

"Perhaps," Calloway said. "You're spreading awfully thin if you go all four of those."

"I'd take the Miramar *or* Las Golondrinas. Not both."

"The Miramar, then," Calloway said. "I can arrange that."

Mo said, "Good." There remained the question of Calloway's end. Depending on what he wanted, Mo thought he'd best not appear too pleased. Or too eager. So, again he waited.

The bar had gone quiet. The room was now almost empty. A bartender stood sloppily at his station, slowly wiping invisible stains from the bartop. Two men who were probably Security sat in the corner, heads back, puffing in silence on a pair of fat Havanas. Calloway looked up and around, but found no waiter. Mo reached and poured him a fresh drink, then dropped a couple of ice cubes into his glass and gave it a blast of soda from the syphon. And waited.

Calloway tipped the glass at him and took a long draft. He kept his eyes on Mo's. In time, he said, "I'm going to want a promise from you in return."

"What is it?"

"I want you to stay away from Anita. And I want you to make her stay away from you."

Mo said, "You have my word."

Calloway nodded without smiling. He said, "Good. I'll make the arrangements. I will set up a meeting for you with the Sunset people for tomorrow. No, I mean today, of course. I will try to get the Presidente as well. The Miramar will take two days. I am lunching with the owner over the weekend. It's a polo lunch. Do you ride?"

"I don't even watch," Mo said. "The closest I'll get to a horse is bribing a jockey."

"That won't be necessary here," Calloway said. "The horse races are already fixed."

Calloway got to his feet. He pulled a twenty-dollar bill from his pocket.

Mo said, "Please. You are my guest."

Calloway put the bill away. He said, "Thank you, for being a gentleman about this."

Mo said, "Forget it," and shook Calloway's hand. He stood and waited while Calloway left, watching him to the door. Calloway went out without glancing back. *Proud. Strong. Good man to have on your side. But that, unfortunately, will never happen,* Mo thought. *Not when he figures out he's asked the wrong guy to stay away from his girl.*

The driver pretended to be lost. He fooled around on a back street and wound up in Miramar, near the sea. Was he trying scare her? Too late. She was already scared—too scared to be frightened by some creepy old Havana hack. At some point he pulled to the side of the road and said to her, "Is vairy vairy far. Maybe, fi' dollars more."

Anita said, "No," and grabbed the door handle.

The driver said, "O-kay. Two dollars more."

Anita said, "At the Tropicana. Go."

The driver smiled—broken teeth, yellow, with bits of food between them—and drove on.

When they arrived, she slid across the seat and got out without a word. The driver said, "Señorita! Two dollars more!" Anita walked off without looking back.

The doorman seemed to hesitate before he grabbed the big front door handle and pulled it open. Did she look like a tramp? Of course she looked like a tramp. What else was she? Leaving one man in the middle of the night and going to another? *Tramp is a nice word for it,* she thought.

The lobby was empty. Anita went quickly, clicking her heels across the broad marble floor, to the big ballroom. There was no one there. The orchestra pit was ghostly, a graveyard of music stands, their arms outstretched in supplication or despair. She left them there and went back across the lobby to the bar.

Calloway was standing at the bar, huddled over a drink with another man. With Mo. She went very cold inside, then very hot. How could this happen? Calloway could know Mo, because men like Calloway always knew men like Mo. But here, tonight?

Anita left the bar without being seen. Her face was on fire. She went past the doorman, then stopped and said, "Where do the musicians stay?"

The doorman, who was very old and very black and had eyes the color of root beer, said, "What musicians?"

"The ones in the orchestra. Do they live here?"

"No, miss. They live in Havana."

"Do you know Deacon?"

"No, miss."

"The horn player? American?"

"No, miss."

The snaggletoothed cabdriver was still parked in front of the casino. He saw her, smiled horribly, and pushed open the back passenger door. Anita thought, *I would sooner crawl.*

"Go aroun' the back," the doorman said quietly. "Some of the boys might be there."

"Which way?"

"That way," he said, and cocked his thumb over his shoulder.

Anita went that direction fast. There was a concrete walkway going off through the bushes. It was dark. Anita felt afraid and small and alone. But she said to herself, *Nothing worse is going to happen to me than has happened to me already.* She thought of the wretched long nights in Brentwood, dying of loneliness but praying Sherman would stay away from her. She thought of her "uncle," heaving himself onto her, at the coffee shop in Shipton Wells. Dead, now. She thought of Worthless, and the Ivory Coast. Dead, too. So many people dead behind her. And Deacon, gone—but not gone now.

Whatever was ahead of her was not worse. Anita kept going.

The concrete walkway circled around the back of the building. There was a parking lot there and a loading dock. Several men in white jackets and hats stood smoking cigarettes. Beyond them, spilling out of a doorway, stood several others in dark suits. One of them was carrying a guitar case. Behind him, she could see, men were playing cards in an overlit room.

One of the men in a white jacket saw Anita coming and said something to the others. They turned. One whistled, which got the attention of the dark-suited men in the doorway. They turned, too. Anita went toward the dark-suited men. Someone in that card game would know where Deacon was.

When she got to the doorway, a slick, light-skinned Cuban stepped to her and said, "Hey, baby. What's shakin'?" The man behind him, a darker-skinned Cuban, said, "*¿Qué bolá, chica?* You wanna kees me?"

Anita looked past them into the card room. The men parted. Inside, a man with a cigarette dangling from his lips and a spread of cards in his hands glanced up and said, "Who you lookin' for, sweetie?"

"Deacon," Anita said. "He's an American. A horn player."

The man said, "We don't got no Deacon. Maybe you'd like somebody—"

"Please," Anita said. "He's tall and dark and he comes from Las Vegas. Is he here, or not?"

The men stared at her. She turned and left them, and went back across the parking lot and circled around toward the front of the building. Catcalls followed her. *Fine.* He wasn't there. Maybe he would be there tomorrow night. She'd come back. She'd wait again. Let them call out if they wanted. She'd come back and she'd wait and she'd come back again. She would come back and stand like some brokenhearted widow, watching the sea, day after day, for her man—

And there he was. Anita got to the corner of the building. There he was. He had a cigarette in one hand and a suit coat draped over the other. His dark hair hung over his forehead. He was raising his hand to someone—someone she could not see.

She ran to him, sobbing as she ran. She called to him but made no sound. A cab slid up to him in the driveway. Deacon threw his cigarette onto the ground. Anita tried to call again but couldn't.

Then he was in the taxi, and she was there. She put her hand on the door and slid across the seat and into his arms. His lips were on hers and she was crying and breathless and he was breathless, too. He reached past her, pulled the taxi door closed, and said to the driver, *"Hacia el Malecón."*

The driver yanked away from the curb and headed for the coast.

Deacon held Anita and kissed her, and held her some more. Her hand was tight in his. Her body pressed into his. He could feel the heat coming off her in waves, and the smell of her filled him. Her cheeks were wet. His chest was tight. It was just as it had been before, but stronger. She was a *woman* now—all woman. And he was terribly aroused, which embarrassed him. It did not embarrass her. She felt him go hard where she held him, and she was electrified. She pushed closer to him and put her hand on him, and felt him shudder.

He said, "Wait. Whoa. Stop it now."

"Don't make me stop."

"No," he said. "Wait. Talk to me for a second. Why are you here? *How* are you here?"

Anita slid slightly away from him. She pushed her hair off her face. She smiled, girlish and giddy, and said, "Does it matter now?"

"No," Deacon said. "But tell me."

"I came here with a man named Calloway. We . . . live together. He took me to the Tropicana, and I saw Mo. And then I saw Mo go up to the stage, and I saw you together with him."

"Who's Calloway?"

"He's just a man. He's nothing."

"You live with him?"

Anita nodded. "But he's nothing, really. I can't believe I'm here with you."

Deacon said, "I know. Come."

He held her tight to him. The driver had made his way down from the Tropicana, across Miramar and into Vedado. He dropped down the Paseo, deserted now, to the Malecón. There was a little moon. The sea shone. The lights of the shoreline drive stretched up and away to the Castillo, like a crown.

Deacon said, "I have an apartment in Old Havana. Can we go there?"

"Yes," Anita said, and squeezed close to him. "Please, yes."

Deacon threw a shutter open when they were inside, but left the lights off. The light from the moon was enough.

He said, "Can I pour you a drink?"

"No."

He made one for himself and said, "Sit, here. I'll be just a minute," and went to the bathroom. He threw some cold water on his face and patted himself dry. He couldn't look in the mirror. His heart raced. He took a long draft of the brandy, which tasted sharp and sweet after the Tropicana's scotch.

Anita was in bed when he came back into the room. Her black dress was draped over the chair he'd left her in. Her heels had toppled over on the floor. She lay on her back, with the sheet pulled over her breasts, the moonlight spilling onto her through the window. His breath caught in his throat. He had never seen anything so beautiful.

He pushed off his shoes, threw off his shirt and tie, stepped out of his trousers, and was in bed with her. She was on fire, and she was wet and he was close to her and inside her. It was like nothing he had ever felt. Deacon rose and fell with her, as if they were the sea, as if they were swimmers on the sea, beneath the sea, diving at the bottom of the sea, like one swimmer sailing over the sea. Deacon felt drugged and wild and complete.

She did not know how long it lasted. It felt like forever. When it was over, they lay close, his head on her breast, both of them silent and sedated. The breeze smelled of the sea.

Listening to her breathe, feeling the heat of her skin next to his, Deacon knew: *This is where I am meant to be. This is what I was born to do.* He felt safe and strong and right. He felt *home*.

He put his face next to hers and said, "I love you. I will never let you leave me now."

Anita curled into him and said, "Yes."

They made love again. When it was over and Deacon lay crushed and spent beside her, Anita began to cry. Deacon wiped her tears away and asked her what was wrong.

"Nothing," she said. "I'm just happy."

Deacon rose at last and went to his suit coat and got out a cigarette and lit it. Standing naked in the dim light, he inhaled deeply and blew smoke at the ceiling, and said, "So, what do we do now?"

Anita said, "I don't know. But we stay together."

"Yes," he said. "That part I know. What about the rest of it?"

"I don't know," she said. "But if we stay together, the rest of it won't matter."

At precisely the stroke of midnight the enormous municipal gasworks building in eastern Vedado erupted in a ball of gas-fed fire. Vibrations from the blast could be felt as far away as the old *fortaleza* to the east and Mariel to the west. The flames were visible on the Malecón, miles away, and down the coastline at Miramar. Windows were shattered in factories along the banks of the Río Almendares. Gas lines to homes in the section just west of the Cementerio de Colón ignited in ribbons of fire. Three homes were burned to the ground as their occupants stood dazed and illuminated in the street.

Sitting in the darkened living room of a modest house on Calle 15, seven young revolutionaries quietly saluted one another. One of them said, "Congratulations, my friends. We are one step closer to freedom from tyranny."

Cardoso got back to Havana after midnight. Had it been an hour or two earlier, he would have tried to make a date with his actress. But not at midnight. They hadn't slept together yet. Coming in past the Castillo, the lights of the city bright before him, he thought of all the places he might stop for a drink before bed. But all of them were places he went to work—the Floridita, La Bodeguita, the Monser-rate, were all places he drank because of what he would see and hear. He took no comfort from them. He'd do better to go home.

The interrogations always drained him. He didn't take to them the way Escalante did, or Matos. The beatings horrified him. What went on at El Paraiso horrified him. Even the questioning wore him down. He'd got the Fuentes girl to tell him about her man, about how he'd gone in a boat to meet Carlos Delgado, who was coming back to Cuba with guns and money. She had told him how her man, Obregón, had been working with some radicals operating out of a house in Vedado. She didn't know the address or the names of the radicals. But she knew some of them drank in a café on Zanja—the same café, perhaps, where Matos had picked up the poor kid they'd tortured at the La Rampa station house.

When he was finished, he took her down to the cell where her man was being held. He wasn't hurt too badly. His eyes were black-ened and his nose was broken, but he was standing, and he didn't limp when he walked. Cardoso had him released—Escalante would scream, if he found out about that—and told the least stupid looking of the Cojímar cops to have him followed back to Havana.

After María Fuentes and her man were gone, Cardoso spent two hours combing the Cojímar cafés and bars. If the citizens knew any-thing, they weren't talking. Most of them were fishermen. They were hard and poor and not afraid. Cardoso had nothing to offer them and nothing to scare them with. He bought a few drinks, had a few drinks, and got nothing.

But when he was leaving, two young men, boys not even in their teens, came and stood by his car. One of them, a bashful-looking kid with long eyelashes, said, "Are you looking for El Gato?"

Cardoso said, "I am."

"He was here," the boy said. "Will you give me money?"

"I will give you money if you tell me where he is *now*."

The bashful boy said, "I do not know where he is now. But I know where he went. He went with my cousin to Bahía Negro."

Cardoso said, "Ah. That is good information. Here are five pesos."

The boy's eyes grew huge.

Cardoso said, "I will give you five more if you tell me where he went after Bahía Negro."

"But I don't know."

"Tell me your cousin's name, then, and I will give you two pesos."

"My cousin is Orlando Cruz."

Cardoso gave the boy his two pesos, then gave two pesos to his companion. Public relations, he thought. He got into the unmarked police car and began the drive to Bahía Negro.

But there was nothing for him there. He found Orlando Cruz—a brutal-looking young man with a terrible future ahead of him—and, after applying considerable pressure, managed to get him to admit that Delgado had been in the village. There was no more he could take from him, though, without violence.

He told Cruz, "Lie down now."

The man's face drained white.

Cardoso said, "I mean it. Lie down now. On your face."

Cruz slowly got to his knees, his eyes on Cardoso's. Then he lay down. Cardoso saw his lips moving—praying. Cardoso thought, *Good. You'd* better *be scared.*

He said, "I will ask you one question. If you answer me, and you tell me the truth, I won't shoot you in the back of the head. Otherwise, you will die like a dog in the dirt."

Across the village, an old woman named Galvan woke and rose from her bed. From the side of her hut she could see activity: there was a car, and a man. One of the Cruz boys was being questioned.

She went quickly to her back room and shook the visitor awake by the shoulder.

"You must leave now," she told him.

"Yes," the man said. He was on his feet, pistol in one hand, boots in the other.

"There are government men in the village," the woman said. "Go to the mountains. Look for my sons. Be strong for your country."

"Thank you—for your sons and your home. You are a hero to the revolution. Good-bye."

And he was gone, off into the night on silent feet. Señora Galvan went back and lay on her pallet. The Cruz boy was not her concern.

Cardoso knew the young man was afraid. He could feel him quivering as he put his foot on the back of his neck. But the young man wasn't a fool, and he wasn't a revolutionary. Cardoso said, "This is the question. The rebel Delgado is in your village right now. Where is he?"

The young man choked back a sob and said, "The house of Señora Galvan."

Cardoso removed his foot. He said, "Stand up and show me."

The boy led him across the village to a thatched hut. But, of course, Delgado had gone. The old woman inside said she had been asleep. She didn't look it. But it was hard to know, with old people. They either looked as if they never slept or as if they slept all the time. This one looked as if she had not been to bed since Batista was a boy.

She said, "I have nothing for you. Go away."

Cardoso walked through her hut. There were two soup bowls next to a pot of stewed chicken. Both had been used. He lifted one to his nose and sniffed. They had been used recently.

Cardoso said, "Señora is a fine cook. Rice and beans with chicken, and plenty of garlic. You use a lot of cumin."

"I have been cooking for many years, señor."

"I am sorry I missed my dinner tonight. Perhaps I could dine with you, another day."

"I do not cook for strangers."

The old woman had a face like a block of mahogany. Cardoso would learn nothing from her. But he understood. Delgado had been, and gone. Cardoso walked through the hut. There was a low window in back. Perhaps Delgado had gone that way. The surrounding woods were thick and deep. There was a half-moon—not enough to track with. Perhaps, if he had dogs or knew the village better . . .

He would not find Delgado tonight.

When the old woman woke him, Delgado leapt through the window and ran fast through the village, then slipped into the trees and hid in the brush. He got his boots on and pushed deeper into the woods.

It was slow going, but the rain had left the ground wet and the brush was silent as he walked.

How long had he been sleeping? It was a good sleep. But he had been dreaming, too. He'd had a nightmare. The same nightmare. Always the same nightmare.

He dreamed of his own death. Or rather, he dreamed that he had died. That part of the dream was always the same. He had died— sometimes in battle, sometimes of sickness, sometimes at the hand of a traitor. Now he lay, dead, but conscious. And someone was doing dreadful things to his dead, helpless body. He was dismembered. He was disfigured. They cut at him with knives, ripped the fingers from his hands, gouged out his eyes. And he could not leave them. He could only watch, paralyzed and horrified, as they tore at him.

It was the only thing that frightened him. But it frightened him a great deal.

He shook the terror off him now. This was not the time to be afraid. He had told all who knew him that he must be cremated upon death, no matter where or how he died, and that at all costs his body must not be allowed to be taken by his enemies. He had done what he could. Now was not the time to be afraid. Delgado used the moon to light his way. There was no sound behind him. The government men, whoever they were, whatever they knew, would not take him tonight.

Near dawn, standing by the window, smoking a cigarette, Sloan said, "It gets so quiet here at night. It's strange, for such a big city."

"Don't they all get quiet at night?"

"No," Sloan said. "Some cities never get quiet at all. New York goes all night. The Cubans are real human beings, though. They eat and drink and laugh and sleep like real human beings. Americans . . . I don't know about most Americans. I thought we were normal, until I came here."

"Come back to bed with me."

Sloan held her a long time. They talked quietly. He told her about leaving Los Angeles, coming to Cuba, working at the Tropicana. He told her about Mo coming to town.

"I saw him with Calloway tonight."

"You saw Mo with Calloway?"

"At the Tropicana."

"They know each other?"

"They were talking, at the Tropicana, when I came looking for you."

Sloan's head puzzled over that, spun, came up with nothing. He said, "Why would he know Mo?"

"He knows everyone. He's very rich, and powerful."

Sloan smiled to himself. *Great. Another rich and powerful guy that doesn't like me.* He said, "Does Mo know you're with me?"

"No. He couldn't. I didn't know I would find you tonight. And he didn't see me, when I came looking for you."

"So Calloway doesn't know, either."

"No. Stop talking so much."

"Yes."

Sloan fell asleep just at dawn. The sun came up from somewhere far behind them. The light rose from dark gray to light gray, slowly. The sound seemed to rise slowly, too. On the street, people began to move. Anita held Sloan close, felt him breathe, felt his heart beat.

This was her place. She was sure now. She didn't know how she would leave Calloway. But this was the place for her. *If we stay together this time,* she thought, *the rest of it won't matter.*

4

The two Havana cops were like cops anywhere. They stood in Calloway's apartment, slow and slovenly, staring at it as if it were a museum exhibit. One of them pushed his hat back on his head and whistled while the other examined the foreign brands of liquor on the cocktail trolley.

Calloway brought them Anita's passport. They stared at her picture. The one with his hat pushed back whistled louder. The other one said, *"Ay, coñó. ¡Qué bonita!"* and then added, "What time she go away?"

"After midnight," Calloway said. "I left the apartment around midnight. I came back around two o'clock. She was gone."

The scent of her hung in the air. Calloway hadn't touched anything. Anita's bedclothes had been turned back. Her closet was full of dresses. Her suitcases were stacked there, too. Her jewelry had not been touched. Her passport and other papers were tucked into a

dresser drawer underneath a pile of neatly folded handkerchiefs and
scarves. Calloway had returned from his meeting with the mobster
from Miami. The apartment was empty. He was concerned, but he
waited until dawn before he began to feel real panic. He had horrible
visions—Anita overpowered by thieves or kidnappers, Anita afraid,
Anita being harmed.

The policemen almost laughed at him. The one who hadn't whistled tapped Anita's passport photo as if it were all the evidence he
needed.

"Maybe she have another man," he said.

"She go with another man," the other policeman said.

"Nothing can be done," said the first.

"Thank you, gentlemen," Calloway said, and showed them the
door.

There was little enough to go on. Calloway spoke with
Guillermo and Alicia, Guillermo's woman. They knew nothing.
Guillermo looked aghast, saying over and over, "But señor! Is
impossible!"

The night watchman was more helpful. He had seen Anita go out,
he was certain, sometime very late. After midnight. Long after midnight, maybe. She had been wearing a black dress and a shawl. She
had gone into the street and walked down to the plaza, but then she
had returned and asked him to find her a taxi. He had done so. A
friend of his had driven her away.

Calloway said, "Who is the friend?" and handed the night watchman ten dollars.

The watchman's eyes brightened. He took the bill and said, "He
name Raúl."

"Bring him to me," Calloway said, and handed him another ten.
"Now."

The night watchman went off like a shot. It was hours before he
returned. The taxi driver, a nasty piece of work with a gin-blossom
nose and huge yellow teeth, said he remembered Anita.

"Pretty lady," he said. *"La llevé a Tropicana."*

Ah. She went to the Tropicana. Further inquiry yielded this: The driver had waited for Anita to come out of the nightclub. He had wanted the fare back to the center of town. He had waited in the driveway. At one point she had come out again, alone. He called to her. She ignored him and went back into the building. Then she came out again and got into another taxi, with another man. They drove away.

The taxi driver had not gotten a good look at the man. It was dark. He was dark, the hack thought. He was smoking a cigarette by the curb, then got into a taxi. Then the lady came out from behind the building and jumped into the cab with him. They drove off. The driver did not know where they went. He didn't know the driver of the other cab. He didn't remember the color of the other cab.

Calloway told the driver, and then had Guillermo say it for him, slowly and in Spanish, "If you see her again and you contact me, I will give you a hundred dollars. If you bring her to me, I will give you five hundred dollars."

The taxi driver almost swooned. *¡Coñó! Five hundred dollars!* He said, "I will find your woman!" and ran off into the night.

The day following Anita's disappearance, Calloway arranged a sit-down for Mo and the people from the Sunset. Calloway did not mention Anita to Mo, who was all business. Within an hour, over coffee in the Tropicana dining room, the Sunset people were ready to allow Mo to take over the casino and restaurant. They would continue to operate the hotel. The rest was his.

The following day, Calloway escorted some men from the Hotel Presidente to another meeting at the Tropicana, which ended in a similar fashion. Mo would have the inside track to take over the casino operations, if he could provide Lansky's blessing and if he could front the hotel owners a month's worth of his proposed rake. The key man, a very pale Cuban named Navarro, made these demands in a quiet, breathy voice.

Mo frowned and said, "You guys are being pretty tough on me. You don't trust Americans?"

"No, no," Navarro said. "We do not trust *Jews*. But Mr. Lansky will tell us if we can trust *you*."

"Great," Mo said. "I'll get recommendations from Goebbels and Himmler, too."

"I do not know these men," Navarro said.

"Too bad," Mo told him. "You'd like 'em."

After the meeting, when the Presidente people had gone, Calloway said, "This is going well. I think the men from the Miramar will come on board now, too. They are all sheep, these businessmen. One moves, they all move."

"Excellent," Mo said. "I owe you. You got any idea how you'd like the favor returned?"

"Yes," Calloway said. "There is something I could use your help with: Anita has disappeared."

Calloway watched Mo's face. It gave away nothing. His eyes were still and held Calloway's gaze.

Calloway said, "She went out the night you and I met, at almost exactly the time you and I were meeting. She didn't come back."

"You've been to the police?"

"Yes. They are fools."

"That's . . . four days? Since she's been gone?"

"Three days."

"I'm sorry," Mo said. "That's rough. I don't know what I can do to help. Do you think she's left the country?"

"No. Her passport is still in the apartment. I think she's been kidnapped."

"I'm sorry." Mo thought for a minute. He had not seen Deacon— or rather, Sloan—in several days. But then, he hadn't been looking for him. He said, "There hasn't been any note, though, or a phone call, from the kidnappers?"

Calloway shook his head.

Mo said, "What about these Security guys?"

"What about them?"

"Aren't they sort of high-grade cops?"

"I met one recently. At the Presidente. He didn't seem the Sherlock Holmes type to me."

"Worth a try?"

"Maybe." Calloway got up and stood tall. He didn't look like a guy in trouble, Mo thought. He carried himself like a guy who'd just sunk a hole in one. You couldn't buy that kind of confidence, and you couldn't fake it. Mo was impressed. Most guys would be slumped over a shot glass.

"If there's anything I can do to help, you'll tell me," Mo said.

"Thank you," Calloway said. "And I'll let you know about the Miramar. I'm seeing the owners tomorrow at the polo grounds. You can expect a call, from me or from one of them, by Sunday."

Calloway left Mo in the Tropicana lobby and went away down-hearted. He hadn't expected Mo to know anything. He hadn't known what he'd do if Mo had told him anything, either. If Anita had gone to him, Calloway thought, he'd have felt Mo's temperature rise when he spoke of her. But what would he have done then? How do you get a girl off a gangster?

They had a day—a long, perfect day.

It wasn't that first day. That day was only nearly perfect. After the long, draining night, Sloan and Anita slept late into the morning. It was noon before either of them stirred, and almost three o'clock before Sloan got out of bed. Anita still slept, Sloan had a smoke, sitting with one shutter open, looking out over Plaza Vieja. Then he washed and dressed and went down to the street for coffee and juice. Anita was just waking up when he got back to her. They drank their coffee while she slowly emerged into the day.

It passed too quickly. They went back to bed for a while. Sloan went back down to the street for cigarettes. He had a girl from a restaurant on the corner prepare two plates of lunch and send them up. He and Anita ate in bed, lounging like a lord and his lady, lazing away the late afternoon.

In the evening he went to work. She told him she would stay in. She wanted to sleep, and rest, and think. She was worried about what was supposed to happen next. So was he. That night, though, he had only to go to work, try to find someone who could cover for him the next night, and then try to get home as early as possible.

All that went well. His friend Santiago, the sax man from Mexico, had a cousin who played cornet. Santiago said, "He's okay. He can play anything."

Sloan said, "Have him play *quiet,* will you? That's the key. Tell him it's not an audition. I'll lay some bread on him if he doesn't mess up."

Sloan was half worried that Baby Ruth would notice and object, and tell Corman. Baby was funny that way. He was a good guy but unpredictable. Sloan might be able to go to him and tell him that his girl had just arrived from the States and that he wanted to take her out on the town, and Baby might say, "Knock yourself out." Or he might not. He might say, "If you want to keep this job, you'll be here." And either way, if Baby took it to Corman, Sloan would be out of a job. Corman wasn't reasonable, ever. Sloan had seen him can people for much less.

He understood he might be next. He decided he didn't much care. Havana was swell. The Trop was swell. But this was different.

He came back in after midnight. Anita was sitting up in bed, reading a Spanish-language newspaper. She threw down the paper and he threw himself into her arms. In the dim light as he undressed, she saw for the first time the scars that Haney had left on him the night the Ivory Coast opened. She touched them and cried, and he told her about Mo and the hospital and the cathouse and how he recovered. He didn't know whether Anita knew he was the guy who killed Haney weeks later. She didn't ask. He didn't say.

They didn't leave the bed again until noon.

The sky was blue and cloudless when Sloan pulled the shutters open. Plaza Vieja was brimming with life. Music played from somewhere. Sloan went into the street for coffee and juice and pastries. He and Anita ate and drank their breakfast, sitting on chairs in front of the open window, gazing down at the plaza. Sloan pointed out his favorite bench and his favorite café. He told her of a hundred nights when he'd sat right there on that bench, staring at the sky, thinking about her, wondering whether those same stars were shining down on her somewhere. He said, "To tell you the truth, one night I thought: *She's in Hollywood. The only stars looking down on her are probably Montgomery Clift and Rock Hudson.*"

Anita said, "Yuck. That's creepy."

After breakfast Sloan took Anita down into the street. She was jumpy about it at first. Sloan said, "If he knew where you were, he'd have broken down the door already. Wouldn't he?"

"Yes."

"Then he doesn't know where you are. There'd be no reason in the world for him to look here."

Sloan walked her up Obispo to Parque Central. He showed her the Hotel Inglaterra, where they had a drink in the lobby bar. He took her past the big cigar factories, the Partagas and the Upmann, where the rich aroma of warm, dry tobacco filtered out into the street. They walked down Lamparilla, Anita transfixed by the little dress shops, until they were at the water. Sloan bought her a cold drink at Los Marinos while they waited for a boat to take them across the water to the old fortress.

On the water, the sun dazzling in her eyes, the wind in her hair, Anita said, "Do you bring all your girls here?"

Sloan said, "I've never brought anyone here at all."

"I'd bring a girl here, if I had a girl."

They walked to the old fort, and Sloan bought her a long, lazy lunch at La Divina Pastora, the tourist joint built into the side of the ancient fortress. Sloan was shocked at the prices and disappointed by the food, but Anita was enchanted. Before them the sun sparkled on the water, the little boats went by, and Havana rose across the bay.

Anita said, "It's so beautiful," and got misty-eyed. "*You're* so beautiful. All of this is so beautiful. I can't bear to think about all the time we weren't together."

"That's over. We're together now."

"Can we stay together? I mean, *can* we?"

"Sure," Sloan said. "Why not?"

Anita didn't answer.

After lunch they were drowsy. Or they called it that. Sloan guided Anita back to the apartment, where she fell upon him. It was dark when he opened the shutters again. Before she was entirely awake,

Sloan said, "Stay here in bed. I'm going to run out for something. I'll be back in half an hour. I'm going to get your dress cleaned." He scooped up Anita's black dress and her shoes, and took them out of the apartment.

On Lamparilla there was a dress shop where Anita had idled in front of the window. Sloan had a nodding acquaintance with the family that owned it. He went there now. The family was named Corales, and the shop was still open. Using his best Spanish, which he knew was woefully inadequate and probably very amusing to everyone but him, Sloan said, "I need another dress, just like this, but not black. And, how do you say it? Stockings? And the other clothes, the clothes for, you know, *under*. Do you understand me?"

"Of course, señor," the Corales woman said. *"Perfectamente."*

Sloan had a *café con leche* at a shop across the street and read the headlines in the evening paper while the Corales woman did whatever she was doing. Sloan calculated in his head. *At this rate,* he thought, *after the lunch and the dress and the drinks I'm going to buy on the terrace, and the dinner I'm going to buy at El Molino, I can afford to keep Anita with me for . . . a week? Maybe she won't need a new dress every day.* Sloan finished up his coffee and went back to the dress shop. The Corales woman had finished the dress and had wrapped it in paper with the old dress and the shoes and the underclothes. Sloan paid and thanked her and went back down Lamparilla to his apartment.

Anita was sitting at the window, dressed in only her slip. Sloan thought he'd faint—she was that beautiful. He put the package down and went to her.

An hour later they were sipping rum and Coca-Cola at La Terraza, the rooftop bar at the Hotel Inglaterra. Havana glittered below them. Sloan glanced about. No familiar faces. But, of course, he realized, he didn't know Calloway's face. Any reasonably attractive Yank over the age of thirty could be the man who was looking for them. If, indeed, he was looking. Would Sloan look for Anita if she'd disappeared? Only until his dying day.

The dinner at El Molino was perfect. Sloan ordered a chicken *cazuela* for them both. It came baked in a clay pot, smothered in spices and aromatic vegetables. They drank a bottle of Spanish wine. The band played sweet, sad songs.

It was after midnight when he took Anita's elbow and steered her back into the street. Cutting across Parque Central, Sloan saw Havana Brown with his shoeshine box, and before he could wonder whether it was a good idea, he had said hello to him.

"Sloan! How you fixed?" Havana Brown called out.

"I'm grand, Mr. Brown. Grand. This is my friend Anita."

"How you, Anita?" Havana Brown struggled to his feet and extended a horny, dark hand, then withdrew it and bowed instead. "What's a beautiful girl like you doing with a bum like Sloan?"

Anita said, "Just lucky, I guess."

Havana Brown laughed and laughed. They left him laughing still, sitting down again on his shoeshine box. Sloan led Anita down to Plaza Vieja. The apartment was silent. The bed was cozy and cool.

He said, "Tomorrow night, you know, I'll have to go back to work. I don't get a day off, officially, until Sunday."

Anita snuggled close to him in bed and said, "I don't care. I will wait for you here. I'm never leaving you again."

The morning after his long night in Cojímar, Cardoso put to use the information he'd squeezed out of the girl María Fuentes. The tail on Juan Obregón had yielded nothing, so far—or the cops following him were too thick to learn anything—but Obregón was probably smarter than they were. He wouldn't lead them anywhere right away.

There was more value in the café on Zanja where the girl had said her boyfriend's radical colleagues gathered.

Cardoso took three uniformed officers with him and made a sweep of the joint about an hour after lunch. The room was crowded. He sent two officers around to the back door while he and the third officer went through the street door. The room went quiet and Cardoso said, "You are all under arrest. Remain seated. I want to see your identification papers."

As Cardoso expected, several young men dashed for the back door. A young woman went the other way, for the front door. All of them were apprehended and held at gunpoint while Cardoso inspected their documents. Two other young men were suspicious enough that Cardoso had them detained, too. He and the plainclothes officers returned to the Security offices on La Rampa with six detainees.

The afternoon that followed was long but profitable. One of the two young men Cardoso thought suspicious turned out to be a well-known thief who was wanted on all sorts of charges. The young man with him was clean. Cardoso knew he would see him again, for he had the criminal way about him. But for now Cardoso sent him away.

With the young men who'd tried to run, Cardoso struck gold. They were members of a rebel cell that had been operating out of a house on Calle 15. The least-likely-looking of them, a powerfully built young man named Dalcio Segundo, had crumbled almost immediately and given up the address of the house. From the others, Cardoso could extract nothing. A middle-aged man named Roberto could be made to say nothing, not even his last name, despite several extreme beatings. The other man, who had a long, sad face that made Cardoso think of Cervantes and who was named Javier Morán, was similarly unforthcoming. And the girl was hopeless. She was a short, round butterball of a thing, cute and plain and bright-eyed. She looked like a homemaker, like a girl who would be most comfortable frying *plátanos* and baking *flan*. Her name was Nilsa Fernández. Cardoso did not have the stomach to beat her, but there were other ways to coax information out of suspects. The four had been separated for several hours when Cardoso had the girl brought to him.

He immediately told her that her three friends had all died during their interrogations, but not before the one named Dalcio had told them the address of the house on Calle 15. Cardoso said his detectives were preparing to storm the house now. They would not need to go in shooting, Cardoso said, if the girl would tell them what to expect there.

The girl had nothing to say. She looked soft as pudding, but inside she was as hard as rock. Cardoso said, "Your friends from the café on Calle Zanja have died like animals. Do not force me to deliver the same fate to you. You are young. You have your life before you. You have the chance to live—to marry and have children and grow old in your kitchen. And all we need to know is this: Where is Carlos Delgado, and where is he going?"

The girl said nothing. Even later, when Escalante himself arrived and took over the interrogation, she said nothing. The captain came into the room, puffing on a freshly lit cigar, and stood behind Nilsa while Cardoso spoke to her. Then Escalante grabbed the girl from behind, placed his large hand across her small face, and held the fiery red tip of his cigar against the side of the girl's neck. She flinched and whimpered, but when Escalante removed his hand from her mouth, she had nothing to say.

Cardoso left them, half sickened. He was fairly certain the girl would die. He knew she would not talk. He took half a dozen plain-clothes officers and went to the house on Calle 15.

It was, of course, abandoned. Cardoso had known it would be—it would have been fifteen minutes after the arrest of the four radicals. It was possible to round up suspects. But it was not possible to stop Cubans from talking. Information and gossip traveled above the speed of sound.

But the raid was successful in other respects. Cardoso's men seized bombs and bomb-manufacturing equipment and a footlocker containing three rifles and several boxes of shells. They seized a printing press and boxes of leaflets. They found a cache of small arms and ammunition, and a radio transmitter—a crippling loss, Cardoso knew, for the rebel cause. All the identifying characteristics of the house, though, had been removed. There were no identification papers, no passports, no address books, no codebooks, no printed information of any kind besides the leaflets that exhorted workers to revolt. And there was no money. From the debris in the kitchen and the number of dirty plates and glasses, Cardoso guessed that as many as fifteen people had been living or meeting in the house—but there was no guessing who they were, now that they'd gone. Perhaps Escalante would produce more from his interrogation than Cardoso had. Probably not, though. He'd only produce more corpses.

By the end of the night, Escalante had come to Cardoso and said, "You made one mistake with the rebels you arrested today. The girl is not associated with them."

Cardoso nodded. He said, "How do you know?"

"Take a look at her, if you have the stomach for it," Escalante said. "She is innocent. But she may not live to tell anyone that ever again."

"What about the others?"

Escalante smiled a hideous smile. He said, "They won't talk anymore now, either. One of them confessed to involvement in last night's gasworks explosion. None of them would take responsibility for the girl, though."

Cardoso thought. Could he have been mistaken? He said, "The girl ran from the café along with the men when we came through the door."

"Perhaps so," Escalante said. "But I am telling you, she is no revolutionary. I did everything but rape her myself."

"I admire your restraint," Cardoso said.

"You saw her face," Escalante said. "And that body! Like making love to a pumpkin! It was not restraint, I assure you. And she is not one of the rebels."

"If you are certain, Captain," Cardoso said.

"I am certain, and I am correct," Escalante said. "Have her released. And have someone explain that we will pick her up and finish the job if we hear any gossip about what happened to her today."

"Right away," Cardoso said.

The girl was in terrible shape. Cardoso did not have a weak stomach, but this was difficult even for him. He could not bring himself to touch her, though it was clear to him that she would not be able to rise or walk without assistance. He had two patrolmen get her out of the cell and into the back of a police car.

Once she was seated, Cardoso knelt next to her. Without looking into her eyes, without looking at her bloodied, slashed, and swollen face, Cardoso said, "We will not ask you any more questions. We will take you home, or to a doctor. Where do you live?"

The girl would not speak.

Cardoso said, "Please, only tell me an address. We will take you there, wherever there is someone who can care for you. Just an address, or the name of a street."

The girl would not speak.

Cardoso wondered whether she had been so severely damaged that she could not understand him. He put his hand on her knee—and she flinched. He said, "This is not a trick. Believe me. You need medical attention. There is no doctor here. Where do you want us to take you?"

The girl turned slightly toward Cardoso now. Her lips parted. Cardoso leaned close to her, to listen. The girl said, in a low, cracked voice, "Take me straight to the devil, you animal, so I can see you burn in hell."

Cardoso snapped back and stood up. He said to the patrolman, "Take her to the café on Zanja. Leave her on the street there. Don't hurt her."

Going back through the station house, head down, face burning, Cardoso almost bumped into Ponce. The smirking lieutenant said, "Good evening, killer of rebels. Congratulations on the Vedado raid."

Cardoso nodded.

"Quite a triumph," Ponce said. "Quite a seizure, too. Guns and ammunition. But no money?"

Cardoso said, "No. No money."

"Really?" Ponce said. "Or have you collected it already?"

Cardoso left him.

Cardoso had been raised in the Catholic Church. He had been christened, had taken his catechism, and been confirmed. There could be no confusion on this point. If there was a hell, he would surely burn eternally there. The hoarse, whispery sound of the girl's voice would not leave him that night. An animal, she had called him. But it was worse than that. He was not an animal. He was a man.

That night, after Calloway had told him about Anita's disappearance, Mo dressed and had dinner alone in his room. After dinner he went directly to the main ballroom. The captain knew him by now and didn't ask if he had a reservation. He did accept the ten-dollar bill

Mo palmed him, though, and led him to a table near the front. Not eager to appear too obvious, Mo ordered a bottle of champagne and gazed at the diners around him, at the band, and at the bandleader and singer before he allowed his eyes to drift over to the section of the orchestra directly in front of him.

Deacon wasn't there. Or rather, Sloan wasn't there. Mo wondered whether he had made a mistake. He looked down at the other end of the orchestra. No, he hadn't made a mistake. The horns were all assembled at this end. He counted the saxophones and the trumpets and the trombones. There was a guy sitting, holding what could be a cornet. But he wasn't Sloan. When the band took its next break, right after a swinging version of Count Basie's "April in Paris," Mo slid up to the orchestra and caught the cornet player's eye. He pulled a five-dollar bill from his pocket and waved it at him.

The cornet player came down to Mo and said, "*¿Qué bolá, hombre?*"

"No Spanish," Mo said. "Where's Sloan?"

The cornet player looked blank. He said, "*¿Cómo?*"

"Yeah, yeah, sure," Mo said. "But where's Sloan?"

The cornet player shrugged. Mo thought, *Okay, so he understands enough to shrug.* Mo pulled a bigger bill out of his pocket and held it in front of the guy. He said, "Let's try this one more time, okay, Paco? My name is Mo. Got it? *Mo.* I want to talk to Sloan. You tell Sloan, 'Call Mo, now.' Savvy?"

The cornet player took the twenty-dollar bill and said, "You bet. I tell him."

Mo laughed. He said, "Good gag. You played me like a trout. Tell Sloan to call me right away, here at the Trop."

"*¿Cómo?*"

"Very funny. Don't push it."

The show didn't interest him after that. Mo left the table and told the captain, "Have that champagne sent to my room, will you? With a fresh bucket of ice."

Once he was alone, Mo lit a fat Upmann and poured himself a glass of champagne, and sat with the radio on. He could listen to the music from the ballroom, right here in his room, without having to see the faces of the tourists. Better, like that. He listened for an hour or more, wondering when and if the phone would ring, dozing in an armchair, until the champagne was gone and the Upmann had started to go bitter. The phone didn't ring.

María Fuentes prepared a plate of food for Juan Obregón, placed it before him, and watched him, again, push it away and refuse to eat. This had happened several times that week. Since Juan refused to speak to her about what had happened on the boat and in the jail cells, María could only guess how he had been damaged. He would not answer her questions. She asked if he needed a doctor, if he was afraid the Security men would come back for him, if he was afraid the rebels were angry with him, if he was afraid that Delgado was dead.

"Don't ask me about El Gato," he hissed at her. "He is safe. He is already in Santa Clara, God willing." He refused to say anything more.

By week's end, he wasn't talking to her at all. The arrests of the rebels from the Calle 15 house had shaken him. María watched his face go white as he read the newspaper accounts. They were sitting in a café near Plaza Vieja. It was Saturday afternoon. Juan said, "Well, it's over now," and withdrew into himself.

The following Monday, María went directly from her job to Juan's apartment. He answered the door, looking even more ashen and drawn than he had on Saturday. He obviously had not eaten. *Just as well,* María thought: she had bought two sacks of food at the market. She would cook for him.

But Juan would not open the door to her. He held his shoulder against the door and said, "I do not want you here. Go away."

"But why?"

"I do not want you here."

"What have I done? What has happened?"

"What have you done!" Juan said. "You have killed them! You cooperated with the police."

"I was trying to save you," María said. "I *did* save you. You are free."

"And they are all dead. I am finished. Go away."

María knew that Juan was a proud and stubborn man. He now

looked like a desperate man, too. An insane man. She knew from experience that there was no talking him out of something once he'd made up his mind. There was only waiting until he changed his mind.

She said, "I will be cooking chicken at my home. Come and eat when you are hungry."

But he did not come. Tuesday and Wednesday passed. María returned to his building. When Juan did not answer her knock, she went to the lobby and found the manager of the building. He himself had not seen Juan in almost a week. He agreed to open Juan's door.

But he insisted that María wait in the hallway. It was the gentlemanly thing to do, he thought. Juan could be locked in an embrace with another woman.

There was no other woman. The manager felt stillness in the apartment. He wandered from the front room into the bedroom. The bed had been slept in but not made—for several days running, he thought. There was an unhealthy smell in the room. Juan Obregón had not washed for several days running, either, the manager thought. He went to the bathroom.

Juan Obregón was in the bathtub, lying on his back in a pool of his own blood. His throat had been cut. His mouth gaped. His eyes stared. He had been dead for two or three days. The manager went back out to the hallway and said to María Fuentes, "He is not here. We must contact the police. Go home. I will have someone inform you when the police arrive."

María went. No one contacted her. She waited, and was frightened. But she was a strong woman. She could be frightened for only a short period of time. She went back to the apartment. The manager told her that Juan Obregón had been found dead in his apartment. He told her the police said that a heart attack had killed him.

María knew that it was not true. She couldn't have said why. All those days without food, without sleep, could surely cause a man's heart to fail. But the apartment manager was lying to her. Juan Obregón had not died of a heart attack.

He had been murdered by the police. That was a fact. One way or another, directly or indirectly, María knew, Juan Obregón had been killed by the Security men. By the police. By the government. He had been a proud, intelligent, passionate man. But the work at the automobile factory had been deadening. Attempts to improve conditions for the workers had proved futile. The company had fired the workers who rallied for better conditions. Juan had embraced the revolutionary movement because he had been given no choice. And he had been pushed to the brink of death and insanity by the Security men who were investigating his links to the revolution. The Security men might just as well have gone to his apartment and shot him in his sleep. They had killed him. María was alone.

Because she had tried to save Juan by telling the police about the café on Zanja, she, in fact, had killed Juan Obregón. The police had only helped her. The murder was really hers.

She sat for a long time at a café in Plaza Vieja, thinking about Juan, thinking about herself, thinking about the waste her life had become. She had been a good child. She had grown into a woman, tall and shapely. Men found her beautiful. She had fallen in love with Juan. They had made plans for a future together. Now there was no future.

Or, there was no more of that future. The Security men had not killed María Fuentes. There was no future for her in Havana. Perhaps her future was somewhere else.

She would go to Santa Clara. She would follow the rebels into the mountains.

María Fuentes paid for her coffee and went to her apartment to pack a bag.

It was slow going to Santa Clara. The roads east of Colón were littered with the wreckage of the revolutionary struggle. Past the city of Matanzas there were two burnt-out tanks, once the pride of the Cuban military, abandoned by the side of the road. They were American-made and almost new. Carlos Delgado's heart swelled with pride. *Our people are impoverished, oppressed, beaten down and broken, and the government cannot kill us with tanks.*

Delgado said to the truck driver carrying him down the road, "What happened to these tanks?"

"The rebels blew them up."

"But how?"

"Who knows?" the driver said. "They have their ways, I imagine."

Indeed, Delgado thought. *They have, indeed.* The truck driver let him down outside of Colón.

It took him several days to travel from the village where the old woman had helped him escape from the Security men into the mountains. Delgado walked most of that first night, then slept most of the next day in a hollow under a bridge. The next night he walked again. He saw nothing to suggest that the Security men were on to him. So the next day, he took the road again and tried to flag a ride. One truck driver took him all the way to Colón. Delgado walked into the city and ate lunch at a workingman's café, standing on the street at a counter eating a sandwich of roast pork. He desperately wanted sleep after that. He walked past a city park, where men without work were dozing on the benches and sprawled on the grass. It wouldn't do, though. That was a very easy way to meet the police. He walked until he was on the outskirts of Colón and then began waiting for another ride.

It was dusk before he got one. A man with a flatbed truck was going to Remedios, near Santa Clara, to bring back a load of coffee beans. Delgado offered him money for the ride. The man refused. Delgado said, "Then perhaps you will let me help you with the driving."

The man laughed. He had a lined face the color of dried tobacco. He said, "No one can drive this wreck but me. And even I can't drive it half the time. It is temperamental."

"Then I will buy a meal for us at the next town."

"No, señor," the man said. "There is no town until morning. There are some oranges in a sack behind the seat. Have an orange. Then you will go to sleep. I can see from your face you are tired. Even the cat needs to sleep sometimes."

The hair stood up on the back of Delgado's neck. He said, "The cat?"

"Yes, even El Gato, señor." The man turned to Delgado with a smile. "I remember you from the old days. Welcome home to Cuba. Now sleep. We will be in Santa Clara before dawn."

*   *   *

His friend Scarfioti reminded Calloway that he had an acquaintance on the Security force. His name was Cardoso. They had met over drinks at Hotel Presidente, one afternoon before Anita disappeared. Calloway had not forgotten. But he had no faith in the Batista police forces—a point that he made cautiously to Scarfioti.

"It is not a question of corruption, my friend," Scarfioti said. "There is great poverty here, in a country of great wealth. There *must* be corruption. But what does it matter? You do not seek justice. You seek action. Money can buy anything in Havana."

"You're right," Calloway said. "Where do I find this Cardoso?"

"We will go to La Rampa together, tomorrow."

Calloway insisted on going alone. He said he would meet Scarfioti for a *café con leche* the following day, and then left him on the street. He found Cardoso in the cold, cement-floored Security offices. A frightened-looking junior officer in a stained uniform pointed at a bench and said, as if he were issuing a command to a dog, "Sit." Calloway stood with his hands folded behind him. Cardoso emerged presently from a dark hallway and beckoned Calloway to follow him to his office—another dark, cold room with cement floors.

Cardoso bade him sit, and offered him a cigar. Calloway took the chair but declined the smoke. Cardoso lit a cigarette.

He was better-looking than Calloway remembered—blunt and square-jawed but not crude. His eyes were soft, and his features were somewhat delicate. Calloway wondered idly whether the policeman was all the way white. A lot of Cubans weren't, he'd been told.

Cardoso blew smoke at the ceiling and said, "How is your friend, the Spaniard?"

"Scarfioti? He's not a friend," Calloway said. "He is only a man I see in the casinos and the hotels. I know nothing about him."

"That is probably a good thing," Cardoso said. "I think he is a man looking for trouble."

"I have trouble now," Calloway said. "That is what I am here to speak with you about."

Cardoso said, "Tell me."

There wasn't much to tell. Calloway described Anita, gave Cardoso the address of his apartment, and told him the few pertinent details of the night of her disappearance. She was there when he left. She was not there when he returned. The building's night watchman had seen her go out. A taxi driver had taken her to the Tropicana, where Calloway himself was in a late meeting. The taxi driver said he had seen her leave the Tropicana with a dark-haired man sometime after that. These were the only known facts.

"She took nothing from the apartment?" Cardoso asked.

"Nothing."

"Would she have had much money?"

"Very little, I would think," Calloway said.

"And no passport."

"No. I have it here."

"May I?"

Calloway slid the passport across the desk. Cardoso took it up gently and opened it. Calloway did not see his expression change.

But his feelings did. He had recognized the address at once as that of the building where he had seen the dark woman on the balcony the night that the American film star was shot and killed. Now he had her picture. And her name and age.

Because it was the correct thing to say, he said, "She is very beautiful."

"Yes, she is."

"Who else does she know in Havana?"

"To the best of my knowledge, she knows no one," Calloway said. He thought it best to keep her acquaintance with Mo Weiner to himself for now.

"Well, we will see, señor," Cardoso said. "I will have photographs taken of this passport, and I will circulate the photograph to the police and Security forces. Do you have someone watching your apartment when you are not there?"

"There is the night watchman," Calloway said. "And I have a driver, who has a wife, and they are usually there if they are not with me. Why?"

"She will return to the apartment, I think."

"For her passport?"

"For something. If she is not kidnapped, or murdered, she will return to the apartment," Cardoso said quietly. "I am sorry to be so . . . indelicate. Would you like me to assign someone to watch the building for you?"

Calloway said, "I will assign someone myself—my driver. He is known around the building already and will not arouse suspicion."

"Very well, señor," Cardoso said.

Calloway rose and said, "Thank you for seeing me on this matter. I had hoped we would meet again, but under more pleasant circumstances."

"Perhaps the next time," Cardoso said. "We can include your friend from Spain. How goes his wagering?"

Calloway said, "He did not tell me, so he must be winning a great deal of money."

"Not betting on the revolutionaries, I hope."

Calloway smiled and said, "Why? Have they made advances?"

"Just the opposite, señor," Cardoso said. "Just this week we arrested and destroyed a group of rebels operating here in Havana— just here in Vedado. They were making bombs there, in a nice house in the middle of a nice quiet street."

"Good for you," Calloway said. "And the rebels are all in jail?"

"Some of them are in jail," Cardoso said. "Some of them did not survive the arrest and interrogation."

It was not more than Calloway could bear—the sensation of Nilsa's face and Anita's face melding together in his mind—but not for long. He turned and stepped to the door, saying over his shoulder, "What a pity—for everyone involved."

"Yes," Cardoso said. "You may come back anytime, for the passport of your friend. Or I can send it to your apartment."

"Will you send it?" Calloway asked. He would not willingly spend another minute in this cold, concrete place.

"It will be done," Cardoso said. He extended his hand. "I will contact you as soon as I have any information. It will remain confidential, of course, until then."

Calloway left the Security offices and walked up La Rampa to the park at the top of the hill. Children were strolling with their mothers. Lovers sat together on benches beneath the trees. Calloway took an empty bench. The park reminded him of the Tuileries, without the Eiffel Tower.

The cold of the police station would not leave him. The sun felt weak. The thought of Anita, in danger, in pain, would not leave him. He had not imagined how much it would hurt to have her taken from him. But he'd had no reason to imagine that, until today.

Alemán had been sent to fetch Nilsa from the safe house. He thought the idea a terrible one. She was in very poor condition, and her eyes were swollen almost shut. She would not be able to see across the street, much less be able to recognize anyone across a street.

But he was not giving the orders today. The orders came from Vicente Chibás, who had been elected cell leader after the arrests of Javier, Dalcio, Nilsa, and the others. Vicente said, "An American is meeting with the Security forces. If it is the same American, Nilsa will know. *Only* Nilsa will know."

Alemán had brought her. She had a shawl around her shoulders, another covering her head, and was shivering despite the warmth of the day. Alemán held her arm and guided her to La Rampa, into a café that faced the Security offices.

When the tall, silver-haired American left the building, Nilsa said, "Yes. He is the man."

"Shall we follow him?"

"There is no need," Nilsa said. "That is the man who came to the house on Calle 15. His name is Calloway. Take me back now."

Leaving the café, Alemán removed his cap with his right hand and dusted it off against his right leg—the prearranged signal. Down the block a man named Diego stood up and folded the newspaper he had been studying, and began walking up the hill toward the small park. He was half a block behind the tall American. He tucked the newspaper under his left arm and stopped at the corner to light a cigarette. It was another prearranged signal: he had the American and would not lose him.

By evening, Diego had followed the American halfway across
Vedado. Calloway went to the Hotel Presidente and had a drink in
the lobby bar with someone who might have been the hotel manager—someone who worked there, anyway. Then the American
went to the Hotel Nacional and had another meeting in the big bar
there, with two men who certainly were Nacional employees.
Diego recognized one of them from the newspapers, where there
were often pictures of the man posing with movie stars and the
other celebrities who stayed at the Nacional. The American left
that meeting and was picked up in front of the hotel by a long
black car driven by a dark-skinned Cuban. Diego flagged down a
taxi and followed them. The black car drove to an apartment building on Calle San Lázaro. The American left the car and driver at the
curb.

Diego did not know what to do. He did not want to lose the
American. But he did not want to simply sit and watch and wait,
either. He hit upon a plan. There was a flower shop at the corner.
Diego went there and bought a spray of roses. He came back down
the sidewalk hesitantly, as if he were checking the addresses on the
buildings, and entered the American's building, and waited a
moment in the lobby before coming back out. He studied the number over the door, looked up and down the street, and then pretended
to notice the car and driver parked in front. He went around to the
driver's open window. He said, "Help me, amigo. I have flowers for
Señor Calloway, the American. Is this not his building?"

"¿Cómo? ¿Qué dices?" the driver said. He had been sleeping, and it
took him a moment to focus on the man with the flowers. "Señor Calloway—yes. He lives here."

"What apartment? I have to deliver the flowers."

"Second floor, my friend. He has the second floor to himself."

"Muchas gracias, señor."

He took the flowers inside. He told the elevator operator to take
him to the third floor.

He had the apartment number. Now he was hoping for a trash bin
and a stairwell. He found the stairwell and went back down the back
of the building, still holding the fragrant bouquet. The stairs

dumped into an alley. Diego set the flowers on the ground there. Perhaps a woman would find them and think they were left by a secret admirer. Perhaps they would rot in the gutter, like everything else in this wretched country. Diego went down the alley to the end of the block and back around the corner.

The long black car sat. Diego went into a corner café, and asked for a *café con leche*. He sat, too, and watched and waited and smoked cigarettes. It was two hours before the tall American came out the front of the building and got into the backseat of the big black car. Diego was too slow getting outside, though. The black car was off and gone before he could find a taxi. Well, no matter. He had the apartment address. That was more than they'd sent him to do. He went up the street to the corner and waited with the other working people for the next bus.

In the car Guillermo said to Calloway, "Señor?"

"To the Miramar."

Guillermo drove there in silence.

Day was breaking and the sun was almost up. Carlos Delgado sat on the hood of the hulking beast of a truck, which the driver had pulled to the side of the road sometime during the night. Delgado had awakened and felt chilly. He had climbed down from the truck in the dark and pulled himself onto the hood, warm from the heat of the engine, and fallen asleep. The truck sat at the top of a sharp rise. Behind them was a carpet of green. Before them the sky was going from blue to pink as the sun's first rays crept from under the clouds.

Delgado slid down from the hood. The driver was crumpled into his seat, his knees drawn up to his chest, his cheek mashed against the window. He had said almost nothing to Delgado during the long drive, preferring instead the growl and grumble of the big engine, and the grind of the gearbox. Delgado had his thoughts to himself.

This wasn't useful. A certain amount of self-reflection was a fine thing. A necessary thing, even. A man should endure one prison sentence, in his early years, in order to better know himself. But only one, and a short one at that. After, it is better to stay in action. Too much reflection made for poor revolutionaries. Too much reflection made for a heightened awareness that the odds were not in one's favor, that justice would seldom be done, that death before dishonor was often the only sustainable ambition.

He had dreamed his nightmare again last night. He had been assassinated by a traitor, shot in the back of the head on the beach at Varadero by a member of his own cell. Now his dead body lay in the sand while his enemies laughed and stabbed it with long knives.

There was a stream a hundred feet or so from the road. Delgado went there for his morning ablutions, urinating against the side of a tree, then washing his neck and face in the chilly mountain water. He was mopping himself with a handkerchief when he heard the thrum of the truck motor. He moved quickly back to the road.

The driver was beside the truck, pissing against a rear tire. He said, "Good morning, my old friend. I thought I had lost you."

"I was washing. There is a stream down the hill."

"I will wait to wash until we arrive in Santa Clara," the driver said. "There is a fine restaurant there. We will eat and have *café*."

Delgado swung up into the cab. The driver ground the truck into gear and pulled onto the road. In twenty minutes they began to see workers walking with lunch pails, women pedaling bicycles into town, knots of schoolchildren marching to their classrooms.

Santa Clara was Carlos Delgado's favorite city, after Havana. In fact, though he told no one this, he preferred it to Havana. He could not say so, because the architecture of the city was so entirely colonial. The Spanish had built and designed the city's center in the European style. The grand Parque Vidal, the Palacio Provincial, the Teatro de la Caridad, in their now-faded grandeur, reminded Delgado of a past that never existed—or not for men like Carlos Delgado, anyway. He would not have lived in the Palacio, and he would never have been welcome at the Teatro. He would have been a bootblack in Parque Vidal, perhaps, or at the very most a violin player in the orchestra at the Teatro. The city's faded history was like all history, written by the victors, full of lies and fiction. Still, it warmed something in him to see Santa Clara once more.

The truck driver said, "We will stop and eat near the center."

"Not me," Delgado said. "I will leave you there. You have done me a great favor. I will not return the favor by spoiling your breakfast."

The driver laughed and said, "If you didn't want to spoil my breakfast, you should not have snored all the way into the mountains."

Delgado patted the man on the shoulder. He said, "You are a good man. Thank you. Be careful as you drive back to Havana, eh? I understand the rebels have been on the roads. I will send the word around that they are to look out for you."

Delgado dropped down at the corner of the broad Parque Vidal. It was busy already. Children and their nannies played on the grass. The old men were already in place, their cigars and newspapers in hand, ready to waste another fine morning smoking and gossiping.

Passing a bench of old men, Delgado read the headlines: REBEL GROUP SMASHED IN HAVANA one read. A VICTORY IN VEDADO read another. Delgado found a newspaper vendor at the corner of the park and bought a copy. The story was there, along with details on the arrests of Nilsa Fernández, Javier Morán, Dalcio Segundo, and several others who were not identified.

This was a bad blow. The house in Vedado had been headquarters in Havana for a long time. Much of the planning for the attacks on the public utilities had been done there. Delgado did not know what new actions were being scheduled. He could not know how much would be lost now. Nilsa had run the Havana office almost single-handedly. She knew more about rebel activity than anyone outside of the men training in the mountains with Fidel and Che. Her death was a terrible loss. As were the deaths of Javier and Dalcio and the others.

Santa Clara was ugly to him suddenly. This was colonialism. The blood of men and women like those in the Vedado house had built the Palacio Provincial and the grand Teatro and the graceful central park. Many thousands more had died filling the bank accounts of the men who ruled them. Enough of architecture. Delgado was glad to be returning to the business of blowing up buildings and tearing down civilization. He and Fidel and Che and the others would build it again, for the people, without spilling the people's blood to do it.

He had been told of a café near the square that was home to the Santa Clara cell. It was called Los Remedios. Delgado strode the streets around the central park until he saw the sign, a battered, hand-painted depiction of a baseball player swinging a bat.

Delgado was hardly through the door. The truck driver he had left half an hour before shouted to him, "Hey, amigo! What took you so long?"

Three men sitting with him turned to the door and began to laugh. Delgado, chagrined, said, "Why didn't you tell me you were going to Los Remedios?"

"What kind of revolutionary would tell such things?" the truck driver said. "Why didn't you tell me yourself?"

Delgado sat with the men. The truck driver introduced himself and told Delgado the names of the men. He called for *café con leche* and a plate of food. Delgado accepted a cigarette from one of the men. Soon they were chattering at him, peppering him with questions—about the boat from Veracruz, about the landing at Cojímar, about the assault on the house in Vedado.

"Tell me one thing," Delgado said quietly. "Who talked? How did the police learn about the Vedado house?"

"No one knows," one of the men said. "But we believe it might have been the man captured at Cojímar."

"What man?"

"The man in the boat with you," the truck driver said. "He was captured by Security when they boarded the boat. The captain of the boat was killed, but this man was captured and interrogated."

Ah. Delgado was surprised. He did not know Juan Obregón before the boat ride, but he did not look like a man who would talk. On the other hand, the men on the Security payroll could make anyone talk.

Delgado felt the shadow fall on him once more. He saw himself, dismembered on the beach.

He said, "Enough of bad news, my friends. Tell me of your success in the mountains."

Sloan was sailing. He was sent. He had Sam Cooke in his head: "Darling, you . . . send me. I know you . . . send me." He had intended to walk from Plaza Vieja down to the Malecón and grab a bus. But he walked to the Malecón and just kept walking. The waves were crashing against the seawall, the spray going rainbows where the sun shot through it. There were old men with fishing lines and young men with young women. Cars rumbled past. Beyond, the water went blue and green and brown over the beds of seaweed and coral. Sloan walked all the way into Vedado before he saw a bus for Miramar and grabbed it.

There was nothing much doing at the club. It was too early. He had called Mo and asked if he could drop by. He was going to cruise the locker room and see about getting that kid Santiago to get his cousin to keep covering his shift.

But there was no Santiago in the locker room, and no cousin. Sloan asked a marimba player named Guzmán whether he'd seen either of them. Guzmán said, "I don't see nobody, man." Sloan left him and went for Mo.

He had lunch all laid out. Nice touch. He was coming out of his bathroom wearing a silk dressing gown and smoothing his hair back with a silver-handled brush when Sloan was shown into the big apartment. Mo smiled and welcomed him, saying, "I thought we might have a bite. I don't know what it is, but these guys seem to know how to sling a meal together."

They did. There was chilled lobster and cold poached salmon in a hollandaise sauce, and asparagus tips, and vichyssoise. Mo pulled the cork from a bottle of white wine and poured just as a white-jacketed waiter came through the door and started ladling out bowls of soup.

Mo said, "Say when. And how."

"How."

"Sit down, and tell me about this thing with Anita."

Sloan was surprised. Mo said, "Relax. I had a visit from Calloway. You know who that is, right?"

Sloan nodded. He and Mo sat at a linen-covered table decorated with silverware. The waiter set the soup bowls before them and began serving the lobster.

Mo said, "He came here to see me, couple of nights ago. First he came to see me because he had this idea that I was in Havana to snatch Anita away from him. That's because he saw her looking at me in the Tropicana. In fact, obviously, it was *you* she was looking at, but he didn't know that. We started talking business, and it turned out there was some business for us to do together. So we set up some things."

"Casino things."

"Casino things," Mo said.

"I guess he's a pretty big noise in the States," Sloan said. "Big money."

"Big, big money," Mo said. "Most of it legit. Down here he's connected, but mostly legit, too. He knows rich people. And down here that means he knows the people who run things, because they *are* the rich people. So we make some arrangements. Then he comes back to see me—and not on business. Anita has disappeared, and he thinks I might know something about it. Do I?"

Sloan said, "No, you don't. She's with me now. The thing with Calloway is over."

"Calloway doesn't know that. He thinks she might have been snatched."

"Snatched?"

"Kidnapped."

Sloan said, "Oh. That's bad. That means cops."

"Maybe not. Rich folks don't like cops anymore than poor folks do. Cops are a middle-class thing. He might not go to them at all."

"He won't if I get to him first."

Mo raised his eyebrows at that. He said, "Relax. Eat some lobster." The waiter had arranged the shellfish and salmon and asparagus on the plates, which he now set in front of them. Mo put a fork in the air like a conductor waiting for his orchestra to settle.

He said, "This looks fine, doesn't it?"

"Yeah. Do you know where Calloway stays?"

"He's got a place in Vedado. An apartment he keeps there."

"Do you know where it is?"

"No. I can find out. But I think it's a rummy idea, you going there."

"You're probably right. But it's a better idea than him going to the cops and getting them involved."

Sloan had lost most of his appetite before they finished with the soup. The lobster didn't make much of an impression. Over coffee Mo said, "You owe me ten bucks. I bribed a guy in the band ten bucks to find out where you lived."

"Did he tell you?"

"No. He took the money and I didn't see him again."

"Good. I don't advertise where I live."

Mo laughed. "You're a man of mystery. Don't make too big a mess of this thing with Anita."

"I don't plan to."

"I'm serious," Mo said. "Calloway's a big boy. He could swing a lot of mallet down on you if he decided to make that his business."

"I understand," Sloan said. "But what am I gonna do? I can't let her go, unless she wants to go, and she doesn't seem to want to go. I could run off with her, but where? Calloway's got resources. He's got friends in Cuba. He's probably got those kinds of friends everywhere."

"Maybe you're safer here than anywhere else, then," Mo said. "You'll let me know if there's anything I can do to help."

"You're the man, Mo. Thanks. Again."

Sloan cruised the locker room again on the way out, and this time he found Santiago's cousin sitting in front of an open trumpet case, polishing his horn. Sloan put a hand on his shoulder and said, "You are Santiago's cousin. My name is Sloan."

The man looked up. He was only a kid, hardly old enough to drink. He said, "You . . . Sloan?"

"That's right. You are the cousin of Santiago."

"Santiago . . . my *primo*."

"Cousin," Sloan said. "I got it. The band, it's okay? The Tropicana music?"

The kid smiled. He said, "Tropicana . . . s'wonderful!"

Sloan reached into his pocket. He dug out a wad of bills. There was one twenty in there. He peeled it off and gave it to the kid.

He said, "You play again tonight and tomorrow night, okay?"

"Okay!"

"Good kid," Sloan said.

Outside, Sloan felt suddenly drained. This was all wrong. This was a bad idea. The girl was not his girl. She belonged to someone else, someone rich and powerful who was going to crush Sloan like a bug. Sloan didn't have the money to keep Anita properly. He didn't have the money to protect her properly. He was a guy with a great future—behind him. All that promise, all that career, he'd shot all that the night the Ivory Coast blew up. He'd shot some of it into his arm. He'd shot what was left of it the night he killed Haney. He had no place left to go if he was run out of Havana. He didn't have anything to offer Anita. She had been his once, and he had lost her, and having her back again was . . . Was what? It was the nicest thing that had ever happened to him. He thought of her, as he had left her, cradled in his bed—warm, the color of toast, sleeping like a child. So, it was all wrong. And so what? It was all wrong. It would have to stay all wrong, then, until it was all right. Sloan flagged a taxi out of the queue and said, *"Plaza Vieja, por favor."*

Anita was alone when she awoke. Light filtered through the heavy wooden shutters. Peeking through them, she could see activity in Plaza Vieja. It must be midday. There was a note in the front room: *I have gone to meet a friend, and then to work. I will be back after midnight. I love you.*

Anita went back to bed and curled up in the sheets, burying herself in the smell of him, the smell of them together. She was loved and warm. But she knew she was not safe. She and Deacon would be left alone for a while, but this would not last forever. Calloway would be looking for her. Calloway wouldn't stop looking. Sooner or later he would find her, and Deacon. What would that mean? She imagined he was capable of jealousy. She was certain he was capable of violence, though he had never behaved violently toward her. She also knew that he had people working for him—not just Guillermo and Alicia but other, darker people—and that they were probably capable of anything. If they hurt someone, it would be Deacon.

For him, then, not for herself, she made a decision. She must go to Calloway. If she waited for him to come to her, or for his people to come to her, someone would be hurt. If she went on her own, at the very least, she knew that Deacon would not be hurt.

Anita got out of bed and washed and dressed quickly. She put on again the simple black dress she had left the apartment in that first night, and took with her only her purse. At the bottom of the note Deacon had left for her, she wrote, *Me too. I love you. A.*

There was a queue of taxis just off Plaza Vieja. She took one. The afternoon traffic was heavy. It was slow going. Workers were digging a hole in the pavement along the Malecón. The taxi crept along the seawall. Anita saw the man that Deacon called Havana Brown with his shoeshine kit, sitting alone facing the water. Lovers walked hand in hand. Anita closed her eyes and breathed in the damp, salty air. It was forever before the taxi got clear of the construction and made its way into Calle San Lázaro.

The big black car was not parked at the curb in front of the building. Anita saw neither Guillermo nor Alicia as she went in, nor even the building manager. The lobby was empty. The elevator operator took her to the second floor wordlessly.

The apartment was empty, too. Calloway was not there. Anita felt faint, and guilty. She had composed a sort of speech in her mind, full of apology and defiance. Now, with no one to give it to, she poured herself a whiskey and sat with the glass in an armchair facing the window, shivering.

Vicente Chibás arranged for himself and two others to watch the apartment on San Lázaro. There was no plan. It was just a stakeout.

He posted one man in front of the florist. He was a country bumpkin, new to Havana, named Alvarez. Chibás and Jaime Cabral posted themselves at a café on the corner. They drank *café con leche* and smoked cigarettes and pretended to read the morning newspapers.

For hours, nothing moved. There was no sign of Calloway. Nilsa and Alemán had made the identification. Chibás had done the necessary backgrounding. Calloway lived on Calle San Lázaro, in high style, occupying the entire second floor of an apartment that looked out over the plaza and the Malecón. He was staying there with a dark-skinned American woman, maybe a Negress, who was reportedly a great beauty. Calloway's business in Havana was unclear, but he had met several times with an American gangster named Mo Weiner. Weiner was connected to Meyer Lansky.

Vicente Chibás hated them all with a special rage. They were everything he loathed about the lawless, soulless power of American imperialism—the money, the gangsterism, the high living off the backs of the poor Cubans, the sexual adventuring with dark-skinned women. . . . Everything about it enraged him. He sat in the café, smoking furiously, reading headlines.

In the late afternoon there was a high whistle from the street. Alvarez was standing on the corner, his gaze facing the San Lázaro apartment. A taxi had pulled to the curb there. A dark-skinned young woman in a black dress got out of the taxi and went on stiletto heels up the steps of the apartment building.

Chibás was on his feet. He said to Jaime, "That's his woman. We're going in."

"On what orders, *compañero?*"

"On *my* orders. You can come with me, or stay."

Jaime trailed after him. He made a signal to Alvarez—we're going, you're staying—as they went up the stairs and into the building.

They stopped in the lobby. Jaime could feel the heat radiating off Chibás. He said, "Let us wait, and make sure."

"We can't wait. Calloway will come in soon, if we wait."

"So what, then?"

"We take the girl. It is a good plan. We take the girl, for a kidnapping."

"Kidnapping? We are not kidnappers."

"Listen. This is a good plan. We will take the girl. We will hold her. We will use her to get information from Calloway, about how he exposed the safe house on Calle 15. We will also use her to get Calloway's *money*. He is very rich."

"It is a bad plan. These are criminal things."

"Calloway is a criminal. He is a gangster imperialist, come to Cuba to rape the people. We are acting in self-defense only."

There was no winning. Chibás had decided. He was not discussing now. He was explaining. Jaime said, "Promise me we will not hurt the girl."

Chibás appeared to think it over. He pulled the weapon from his waistband and checked for ammunition. He had a full wheel. He said, "That is also a good plan. We will not hurt the girl. *Vámonos.*"

Calloway had been in the Floridita for too long. He had drunk too much. He had learned nothing. He had been waiting and watching for . . . what? Something, or someone. He had thought he would know what it was when he saw it. Now he felt old and foolish, a juggler among the clowns. He told Faustino the bartender to mix him another pitcher of drinks. And then another.

Scarfioti had come and gone. He was keen to go cockfighting. Calloway didn't like it, and said so. "A man with a cock of his own shouldn't trifle with another man's chickens."

Scarfioti didn't laugh. Maybe he didn't understand Yankee English. Now he was gone. Calloway directed Faustino to drive his tray of daiquiris into the back corner.

Ava Gardner was there. Without Sinatra. Without Hemingway. Calloway didn't know when or how she'd arrived, or with whom, but she'd collected a group of men around her in seconds. *Like flies on . . . honey,* he said to himself, trying not to be sour. She was very beautiful. And a rummy. One of his film companies had briefly entered into a contract with her to make a series of pictures about heroism during World War I. The producers had reckoned that because of her close relationship with Hemingway and because of Hemingway's book *A*

Farewell to Arms, the deal would be a cinch—get Gardner, get the rights to the World War I book, maybe even get Hemingway to write something new. It had blown up in their faces. Gardner's people had demanded money up front—Calloway believed they may even have called it "earnest money," which was pretty amusing—and Gardner had drunk it all away.

She was still terribly beautiful. Tragically beautiful. Not beautiful like Anita. Maybe beautiful like Anita would be if the next ten years were very hard on her. If she survived the next ten years. The very idea of Anita at forty hurt Calloway in the chest. He pointed to the back table and said to Faustino, "Put her there, pal."

Soon he had attracted his own small crowd. He was a wealthy American with a pitcher of fresh drinks. His face was known. His reputation was known. He had drunk with some of these men, and been drunk with some of these men, before. He couldn't, in his current state, remember any of their names. But their faces swam before him and collected little details.

"What about your racehorse?" he said to one, a lawyer from Miami, who he suddenly remembered was running ponies at the track.

"Out to stud," the man said. "Or the glue factory. He finished out of the money three weeks running."

"That reminds me of a joke," Calloway said. "I won't tell it. And what about your sugar mills?" He recognized another man, who'd developed a plan to buy up sugar plantations and refineries as the revolutionaries were burning them down.

"A brilliant plan," the man said. "Batista's men are all crooks. I have spent more buying off clerks and officials than I have spent buying land. So I own half of Matanzas. But I cannot go there because the rebels control all the highways."

"You're taking it well. Have a cocktail."

"Cheers! To the revolution!"

"To the crooks!"

"To Cuba!"

The men clinked glasses and toasted. Someone from Ava Gardner's table shouted *"¡Olé!"* It rang hollow and stupid. Calloway thought of

Hemingway and the men he wrote about—dry, angry, humorless men with broken spirits. Hemingway himself had not seemed such a man, when Calloway knew him. But it was impossible to know what a man's face was hiding. He looked over at Ava Gardner. She was shimmering, glistening, laughing—and miserable inside, perhaps. His own face was hiding anxiety and an aching loneliness.

He had drunk too much. He had learned nothing. The thing he had been waiting for was not here. The man who would come to him with bad news was not coming here. Not tonight, anyway. He said, "My friends, I leave you. Faustino! Beverages for everyone."

He handed the bartender a wad of bills, going out—some Cuban, some American. He had no idea how much. He had no interest in it. He would go home. The apartment would be empty and would smell of Anita—her perfume, her soap, her scent. He would lie awake and alone.

Guillermo was at the curb with the long black car. He leapt from the driver's seat and got the door open just in time for Calloway to pour himself in.

Anita heard footsteps outside the apartment door. She straightened up at the little writing table near the window and braced herself. She had more or less decided what to tell Calloway. She would tell him now, depending on how much drinking he had done. If he'd been out with the men at El Floridita . . .

But the man who came through the door was not Nick Calloway. He was a Cuban with yellow eyes and bad skin. Behind him was another Cuban, round with dark eyes and torn trousers. Anita thought, *My God, something terrible has happened.*

The men were all the way into the room before either of them spoke. The one with yellow eyes said, "Where is he?" Anita realized only then that he was holding a gun at his waist and pointing it at her.

She said, "He is not here. No one is here."

"*Bueno,*" the man said to his companion. "Take her."

They were quick. The round man shot across the room and took

Anita by the neck. He put his hand on her mouth and began to tie some kind of scarf around her neck. He smelled of garlic and cooking oil. He pushed the scarf over her mouth. Anita's eyes never left the weapon in the other man's hand. When the round man had her secure, the yellow-eyed man stuck the weapon in his waistband. He said, "*Y las manos también,*" and the round man began lashing Anita's hands behind her with some kind of scratchy rope.

"*Vámonos,*" the yellow-eyed man said. The round one began pushing Anita to the door.

Then the lock rattled again. Anita gasped behind the scarf. Calloway would come through the door. The yellow-eyed man would shoot him.

It was another Cuban. He came through the door, crouching, holding a gun. Then the yellow-eyed man fired once. The man went down in the doorway. Anita's ears rang in the silence. The round man loosened his grip on her arm and said, "*Ay, Dios. ¡Es Alvarez!*"

The yellow-eyed man pulled the body through the doorway, the heels dragging through the deep carpet. He said, "*Vámonos,*" again. The round man pushed Anita forward, staring at his fallen comrade. He said, "*Ay, Dios,*" again. His companion hissed at him, "*Cállate.*"

The two men hustled her down a back stairwell that Anita had not even known about. It stank of onions and urine. Or perhaps that was the two men. Or perhaps it was the smell of her own fear. Anita's breath came short and sharp, and her head was light.

The air outside was heavy and wet, and it was very dark behind Calle San Lázaro. The men pushed her along an alley. When she tripped and began to fall, though, the round man caught her and pulled her up gently. Maybe . . .

At the corner there was a car waiting. The yellow-eyed man with the pistol yanked the trunk open. The round man steered her toward it. He said, "I sorry, lady." The yellow-eyed man pushed him out of the way and pulled a canvas bag over Anita's head. She was lifted roughly from her feet and shoved into the trunk of the car. The engine started. The trunk slammed shut. Anita felt herself gagging on the scarf, which had gotten twisted behind her neck. The car lurched forward. Anita banged the back of her head against something cold and steely. The car lurched to the left and accelerated with screeching tires. Then everything went black.

Guillermo had a difficult time getting Calloway up and out of the car in front of the Calle San Lázaro apartment. Calloway was drunk, and he was heavy and cumbersome as only a drunk can be. Twice Guillermo had him on his feet. Twice Calloway sat back down in the big black car and attempted to return to his nap. Guillermo was thinking about whether he should go inside and wake Alicia. That would mean leaving Calloway alone on the street. He could lock the car, perhaps, and then—

A sharp report came from inside the building. It sounded like a gunshot. Guillermo changed his mind about leaving Calloway in the car. There was enough trouble already. Between the police and the Security and the rebels, nothing was safe in Havana anymore. Especially not a rich American, drunk, passed out on the street, in the middle of the night. Guillermo threw all his weight into it and got Calloway on his feet and moving up the apartment building steps.

The night watchman had disappeared—off getting drunk himself, Guillermo imagined. He was a useless old bum. He imagined the *viejo* was the uncle or grandfather of the building manager, an old nuisance being kept out of trouble and off the street with a job running the elevator. A job he wasn't even able to do properly. Guillermo mashed the button, wedged the door open, and got Calloway inside.

Calloway said, *"No más mosquitos, amigos."*

Guillermo said, *"No, señor. No más."*

Some scent caught Guillermo's nose. He was pulling Calloway off the elevator. The American's big shiny shoes seemed to be twisted into each other. Calloway was a stumbling drunk, and he was stumbling now down the hall. Guillermo saw that the apartment door was ajar. His heart leapt. That was the scent. The young *mulata* had returned. Guillermo pushed open the apartment door with his foot.

A man lay bleeding on the floor on his back, just inside the apartment. Calloway stumbled past him, headed for his bedroom. Guillermo shut the door behind him and let Calloway go on. He knelt and gingerly felt the man's neck. The body was very warm. But there was no pulse. The smell of perfume in the room was quite strong now. There was also another smell, a sharp, metallic smell. Guillermo thought that might be from the gun that killed the man on the floor.

There was a crash from the other room. Guillermo shot to his feet. His heart leapt again as he ran into the bedroom.

Calloway had fallen onto the bed. He lay on his back, his jacket halfway off. He had knocked a lamp off the bedside table. Guillermo loosened Calloway's tie and removed it, then unbuttoned the top of Calloway's shirt. He untied his big shiny shoes and slipped them off. He went to the bar, poured a tall glass of fresh water, and put it on the bedside table where the lamp had been. Calloway was snoring.

Guillermo stood over the body in the front room. It had bled onto the carpet. There would be some difficulty in cleaning that. And some difficulty in covering up the killing. Guillermo sat on his haunches. It was a poor man who lay dead on the floor. It was a workingman, wearing cheap clothes and shoes. He was just a young man, too. *¡Qué lástima!*

There was nothing to be done. Guillermo went out of the apartment and shut the door behind him. He would go downstairs. He would wake Alicia. He would wake the building supervisor. He would call the police. There was nothing else to be done. He would protect the American. He would tell the truth. Perhaps the *mulata* killed the poor young man on the floor? That was not Guillermo's business. His job was protecting the American. Protecting his *mulata* was not part of that anymore.

Cardoso got the call just as he was dropping off to sleep. He had stayed late at the station. He had filed paperwork. He had read a file from another officer who had done some follow-up work on the arrests and interrogations of the suspects from Calle 15. In the late evening he had sent a boy out to get his dinner, which he had eaten at his desk.

He had been very lucky, really, with the way things had gone in Cojímar. He had been sent there to catch Carlos Delgado. The revolutionary had slipped away from him. Cardoso had come back with nothing. Delgado had been in Cojímar, had run to Bahía Negro, and had left—maybe by only minutes—before Cardoso had tracked him there. Then he was gone and the trail was cold.

But the interrogation of María Fuentes and Juan Obregón had kicked up the information that turned into the raid on the house on Calle 15. Everyone appeared to have forgotten, for the time being, that Delgado had escaped.

Cardoso knew the reprieve was only temporary. Escalante missed very little and forgot nothing. He would hold on to Cardoso's failed pursuit of Delgado, and he would use it to his own advantage one day.

For now, though, Cardoso was being treated with a kind of respect. The campaign against the rebels had been going so badly for so long that this recent victory was seen as a great victory. Cardoso knew better. It was only a moment. The rebels would have contingency plans against exactly this sort of defeat, and they would have gone into action as soon as their people were in custody.

About midnight, Cardoso was interrupted by the smug officer named Bustillo. He looked like he had been drinking: his eyes were red, and his face was slack and lopsided. He was rather handsome, like his uncle the president, in a brooding, heavy-browed way. *He must be very stupid,* Cardoso thought. Otherwise, his uncle would have secured him a better, or easier, or at least more lucrative job. How much could he earn, as a Security cop, even if he padded his income like the other officers, shaking down pimps and prostitutes?

Bustillo leaned on Cardoso's door and said, "Cardoso, big hero! Escalante wants you. There's been a murder."

Escalante was in his office, his fat face wreathed in cigar smoke, his big feet up on his desk. He grinned at Cardoso. Bustillo turned on his heel and was gone, smiling lopsided at some private joke. Escalante said, "Sit, sit," and pointed to a chair with his cigar. Cardoso lowered himself into the chair and folded his hands in his lap.

Escalante said, "The woman that interested you so much—the

American Negro woman who is kept by the American Calloway—is now a suspect in a murder case."

Cardoso said, "Tell me what has happened."

"She has been missing. Tonight she returned to the apartment of the American. She was not alone. Shots were fired. A man has died, shot once in the belly."

Cardoso said, "Who is the man? Is it her rich American?"

"No," Escalante said. "His name is Alvarez. He is one of the rebels associated with the group on Calle 15."

That dropped like a stone into water. A dead rebel from the Calle 15 group, in Calloway's apartment, shot by Calloway's girl . . . This made no sense. Those two worlds did not overlap.

"Could it be a personal matter? A lover's quarrel?"

"That was my first thought as well," Escalante said. "Until Officer Colón described the body of the dead man to me."

Cardoso said, "And?"

"The man was quite ugly," Escalante said. "And badly dressed. A poor man, and an ugly man. The American woman is very beautiful. He was not a boyfriend for her. No more than you are."

Escalante's smile was awful. He continued, "Although, *una mulata y un mulato* . . . Together perhaps you could make one true *negrito*." He began to whistle the song "El Negrito del Batey."

Cardoso forced himself to be calm. He said, as gently as possible, "If you want to question my ancestry, Captain, I suggest you stand up and do it like a man. Otherwise, let us talk about the American woman."

Escalante heard the challenge and let it fall. He said, "What else do you need to know?"

"Where are you holding her?"

"We are not holding her at all," Escalante said. "She has disappeared."

Cardoso said, "What, then?"

Escalante pulled his feet from the desk and dropped them to the floor. He said, "*¡Bobo!* Bring us brandy!" Within seconds there was the sound of scampering feet and clinking glasses from the outer office.

Escalante said, "You are a fine policeman. You will find out where she has gone. You will go to Calle San Lázaro now and learn what you can. You will remember that this is a rich American, with powerful friends, and you will speak cautiously with him."

Cardoso did not see any reason to tell Escalante that he had already met with Calloway, right in this building, on the subject of the girl's disappearance. He would go to Calle San Lázaro, to the second floor, to the balcony where he had first seen the girl, and he would ask the questions and listen for the answers.

Escalante's boy came in with a tray and put it on the police captain's desk. Escalante shooed him away and began mixing himself a drink.

Cardoso said, "Nothing for me, thank you. I must go to San Lázaro now, if I am going. It is late, and I am tired already."

"Take Bustillo with you," Escalante said.

"Why? If I needed a partner, I would need a real policeman."

Escalante laughed. "You take your work too seriously, my friend," he said. "Perhaps it is because you take yourself too seriously."

"I'm sure you are right," Cardoso said. "If I were not so tired, we could have an interesting conversation on the subject. Good night."

Bustillo was at the curb, smoking a cigarette and staring at a window across the street. Cardoso said to him, "If you are not too busy, Captain Escalante says you are to accompany me to Old Havana. I need a partner for this murder in Calle San Lázaro."

"Okay," Bustillo said. "But wait. The woman will be nude, in one minute."

Cardoso followed his gaze upward. A heavyset woman with long black hair was undressing in a third-floor window. Cardoso said, "I'll give you one minute, then. I'll come with a car," and left Bustillo to stare.

They were quiet on the drive over. Cardoso let his thoughts wander. This was one kind of police work, puzzling over the possibilities. He could imagine the girl involved with the rebels. He could not imagine how. He could not imagine Calloway knowing about it. Or being involved himself. *Americans make poor spies,* Cardoso thought. *They are too open, too honest, too simpleminded. And too arrogant. Are the women perhaps better at it than the men? Women tend to be less arrogant, of course. Unless they are very beautiful. And the American girl is very beautiful.* Cardoso let these ideas drift around in his head, watching them as if they were clouds forming and breaking apart in the sky.

The street was crowded with citizens. Two uniformed policemen were trying to keep them away from the building. Cardoso parked the car and pushed through, Bustillo trailing him, and got into the lobby. He told one of the policemen, "Do not let anyone inside for a little while. Not anyone."

The night watchman took them to the second floor. He said he had been sleeping and had not taken anyone upstairs in hours. Cardoso could smell the booze on his breath. He said, "What hole were you 'sleeping' in? What is the name of the bar?"

The man said, "In Calle Galliano, near the Malecón."

Then they were on the second floor. There was a small foyer. One door into the apartment stood open. Cardoso, going in, saw the soak of blood in the carpet. He saw, too, the furrows in the carpet going across the threshold—two of them, made, he imagined, by the toes or the heels of someone's shoes, someone who was dead or near dead when he was dragged inside the apartment.

Inside, just inside, the body of the dead man lay on a darker stain of carpet. Cardoso noted the position of the body, the position of the hands, the shape the man made. He did not appear to have been moved since he was brought into the flat. He wasn't going anywhere on his own, either. He'd been dead several hours, Cardoso reckoned. The blood pooling around him was blackening and looked sticky in the hot night air.

Cardoso said to Bustillo, "Stay here. Take notes. Act like a policeman."

Bustillo laughed. He said, "You are enough policeman for both of us, amigo. I will go downstairs and have a drink."

Calloway was sitting on the sofa. Cardoso could smell the alcohol on him before he had come halfway across the room. The American looked more dazed than drunk. Cardoso pulled a chair near the sofa, and sat.

He said, "Señor Calloway. I am sorry to meet you again, in such circumstances. Tell me what you know about this."

Calloway said, "I only know what you can see with your own eyes. There is a dead man in my house. I don't know him. No one saw him come in. Someone has killed him. No one saw that person come in, either. And Anita was here, but now she's not."

"Ah," Cardoso said. "How is it known that the girl was here?"

"She had begun packing a bag. She had collected some of her things."

"Which things?"

"Her personal things. Photographs. Some clothing."

"These things are missing?"

"No. They are in a suitcase on the bed. She was packing, apparently, when . . ."

"When what, señor?"

"When whatever happened must have happened," Calloway said. His eyes were rather desperate, Cardoso thought. But they didn't appear to be hiding anything.

Cardoso said, "And what do you imagine happened?"

Calloway said, "I have no idea. Someone shot someone. Someone is dead. Anita is missing. Again. Or still."

"I am sorry for you," Cardoso said. "We have some information on the dead man. You will remember that I told you earlier about the arrests of some rebels who were operating out of a house in Vedado? This man was connected to that group of rebels."

Calloway said, "The group on Calle 15? That group of rebels?"

Cardoso said, "Yes, exactly."

Cardoso realized, to his dismay, that he had never told Calloway that the arrests had taken place on Calle 15—only that they had taken place in Vedado, on a street in Vedado. It confused and irritated him to realize that Calloway knew something he should not know. It was late. Cardoso was tired. Ordinarily, such a piece of information would have excited him. Now . . . it wearied him.

He said, "Can you tell me what connection your friend would have to these rebels?"

"None," Calloway said. "She knew no one in Havana. This is something different, I'm afraid."

"And what is it, Señor Calloway?"

"I don't know."

Cardoso left him. He looked in the other rooms. He inspected the suitcase the girl had been packing. It was as Calloway said. She, or someone, had assembled some personal effects but had not finished the job of packing them into the bag. It was sitting open on the bed, half filled. Neatly folded shirts and dresses and a pile of underclothes were on the bed next to it.

Cardoso came back into the front room. He said, "I will leave you now, Mr. Calloway. I am sorry for the trouble you are having. Tell me one last thing, only. Do you keep a weapon here in the apartment?"

"No," Calloway said.

"And your friend? Did she keep a weapon?"

"No."

"You're quite certain?"

"Entirely certain," Calloway said. "Anita wouldn't know what to do with a pistol."

"And you?"

"I'd know what to do with one," Calloway said. "If I had one."

"Of course, señor."

Cardoso went downstairs to look for Bustillo. He was not in sight. The neighborhood was full of drinking establishments. Bustillo could be in any of them. Cardoso decided not to find out. He got into the Security car and drove away.

Cardoso didn't like what he'd seen. He didn't like what he'd heard. The whole thing was rotten. Calloway was lying about something. He knew more about the Calle 15 arrests than he should. He was telling less about the murder in his apartment than he should. And the girl was in the middle of it. The most logical explanation, he suddenly saw, was this: Calloway was involved with the rebels. The enemies of the rebels had taken his woman. Who were the enemies of the rebels? The police, and Security. So, the girl was probably being held at El Principe, a guest in Paraiso.

But of course she was not being held at El Principe. She was gone. And it made no sense at all to Cardoso. Though it was against policy and would likely result in a tongue-lashing in the morning, Cardoso decided to drive the borrowed Security car to his home and sleep. He was too tired to do anything else. The streets of Vedado were empty and dark. Cardoso crossed town, went past the Cementerio de Colón and over the river, and was home.

Tomorrow, he thought as he dropped into bed. *Tomorrow, more trouble.*

It was well after midnight before Sloan got back to the flat. He had collected a bottle of pretty good champagne, a plate of roast pork and potatoes, and a bag of nice pastries. He had a copy of the afternoon paper. He was tired and hungry and more than a little aroused. He had thought of nothing but Anita, of nothing but returning to Anita, for all the hours he had been away from her. Coming up the stairs, taking them three at a time, he was excited and breathless and felt a little foolish.

No matter. He got out his key and went through the door and found the apartment empty.

He knew it was empty as soon as he got inside. The air was stale. The windows had been closed for hours. And there was no sound in the room. Sloan put his packages on the counter in the tiny kitchen and went back to the front room.

On the table was the note he had left for her. Scrawled at the bottom of it were the words *Me too. I love you. A.*

She had never said "I love you" to him. It made his heart quake. He went to the sideboard and inspected the bottles there. Some scotch remained in one of them, some rum in the other. He poured the scotch into a glass, and went to the window and opened it. The air blew in hot and salty from the port, bringing with it the clatter of a car going over the cobblestones below. He took his whiskey and sat and waited.

He was still waiting, and drinking, when the sun came up. As the room lightened, Sloan's mind darkened. She was gone. She had written, *Me too.* For hours, he had wondered, What did that mean? I have gone out, too? I have gone out to meet a friend, too? I will be back at midnight, too? What friend, then? And what had happened with the friend that had kept her past midnight?

It didn't matter. Sloan's heart ached and then hardened. She was gone. Again. She had left him, again. It was just like Las Vegas. She was there, and then she was not. And if she was not with him, she was with someone else.

Had she gone back to Calloway? Or to someone else? Was she that kind of woman? Did she not love him, then?

It didn't matter. If she was not here, it was because she was somewhere else. She was with someone else.

He had fooled himself once, in Las Vegas, because he knew she was young and couldn't have known any better. Now he had fooled himself again, in Havana. She wasn't a child. She was making a choice, and she knew what the choice meant. And he, having fallen for it again, was the weasel of the Western world. What a chump. He'd done it again.

Some time after dawn Sloan shut the window and pulled the shutters closed. The room went dark. His mind went dark. The whiskey was gone. Sloan lay on the bed with his clothes still on. Soon he was asleep.

5

They were stuck behind an oxcart when the truck full of soldiers opened fire on them. The oxcart saved their lives.

Delgado and a man who called himself Paco had been driving for three hours. They had come to a tiny village set in an enclosed valley surrounded by fields of boniato and malanga. Just past the village the road rose steeply out of the valley. Ahead of them was an oxcart pulled by two of the enormous humpbacked beasts and filled with produce. A sun-blackened man in a straw hat switched at his animals and waved to Delgado and his companion to show them that he was driving the oxen as fast as they would go. The road was too narrow to pass. Paco slowed the car to a crawl and lit a cigarette.

"Tell me something," Paco said. "In Havana, do they sell ice cream in the park in front of the Hotel Inglaterra?"

"I imagine so," Delgado said. "Why?"

"It is the thing I miss most about the city," Paco said. "I was a student there for one year. I had very little money, only what my family could save and send to me. Sometimes I would go to the park and eat an ice cream. It meant no dinner that night. But I was young and foolish, and I didn't care."

"We are all foolish when we are young," Delgado said. "Your foolishness seems very sensible to me, anyway."

"I can taste the ice cream still," Paco said. "I was particularly fond of coconut. ¡Coñó! Soldiers!"

The oxcart was winding its way around a corner. More than half the road was blocked. A truckload of soldiers was coming down the hill toward them. They were forced to stop. The driver shouted something unkind at the black man in the straw hat. Then he saw the dark sedan behind the oxcart. He shouted, "You! Pull to the side."

Paco panicked. He yanked the wheel and stamped on the gas, and the car spun sharply. But the road was narrow. He could not complete the turn. He jammed it into reverse and backed across the road until his rear bumper hit the oxcart.

Then the soldiers opened fire. Delgado leapt from the sedan and crouched behind the oxcart. The air was full of bullets. He could hear them ricocheting off the top of the sedan. He could hear another sound, too—a *thunk-thunk* sound of bullets hitting something soft. Just then one of the oxen bellowed, and its front legs collapsed: the soldiers were killing the animals. Then a punctured tire fizzed, and Delgado heard Paco cry out in pain.

Delgado bolted for the trees. The hill rose sharply before him. He scrambled, clutching at the ground, his feet slipping on the steep slope. Bullets flew. He could hear the soldiers firing for a full minute or more after he left the road. Then it was quiet. Delgado ran on until he could run no more. Twenty minutes later he collapsed into a thicket near the crest of the hill and lay gasping for air, his face in the dirt.

No one followed. Delgado lay a long time, catching his breath. He had left his knapsack in the car. It held his water bottle and pistol and a little sack of sandwiches he had taken from the Remedios café in Santa Clara. Now, in the woods, he would have to stay off the road for a full day. And he was without food or water. When he had caught his breath, he got to his feet and began walking. After picking his way through the brush for fifteen minutes, he came upon a trail. Judging from the sun, he guessed the trail was leading away from the road. Where? Someplace the soldiers did not go, Delgado hoped. He took up the trail and began following it.

For four days Calloway sat and waited. Calloway drank and smoked and tried to read. No word came. For hours at a stretch Calloway sat and listened to the plumbing, to doors that swung shut in the hallways, to the mechanical burr of the elevator rising and falling. Sometimes he sat on the balcony, overlooking the plaza. Men working there had drained the water from the fountain and were repairing a gaping hole in the concrete. The time moved just as slowly there as when he lay on his bed, staring at the ceiling.

He left the apartment on Calle San Lázaro only twice, to help conclude negotiations for Mo Weiner with the Miramar and again with the Sunset. He was too distracted to be of much use. But the business went forward. The casinos would all be open by the end of August. Mo would open three casinos on the same night. It would be a sensation, like nothing Havana had ever seen. He would put searchlights on the streets in front of all three. The Havana night sky would crisscross with blue-white beams.

As long as Batista didn't scare all the money out of the country by August, Mo said, the casinos would be a big hit—as long as the rebels didn't take over the city by August, either.

As summer approached there was increasing violence in the streets. One night, while Calloway sat and drank and waited, a series of explosions seemed to encircle the city. Calloway could see flashes of light against the imposing exterior of the Presidential Palace. The squeal of sirens followed. Calloway would learn the following morning that the rebels had bombed the offices of some of the leading Cuban and American business interests around Havana—IT&T, Royal Sugar, Ford, Coca-Cola, and Bacardi among them. The only casualties were two cleaning ladies who were sweeping the Royal Sugar offices and two rebels who were injured by their own firebombs

at the Coca-Cola corporate offices. The cleaning ladies were treated at
a hospital and released. The rebels died—whether of their wounds or
at the hands of the police was not known.

On the fifth day, at midday, there was a telephone call. Calloway
was in the sitting room with a whiskey and a cigar, looking out over
the sea. Guillermo took the call. He was spending most of his time,
when he wasn't behind the wheel, posted in the apartment. There
was another man sitting on a wooden chair just outside the apartment door, facing the elevator. There were two other men standing in
the lobby. There was a plainclothes policeman, too, posted somewhere on the block in front of the building.

Calloway was gradually becoming convinced that the kidnappers,
if kidnappers they were, could not get to him. They would not be
able to cut through this cordon of security that the Security officers
had made. They would not be able to contact him for the shakedown.
He sat with his cigar and whiskey, imagining frustrated criminals
locked in a room with a gun and a phone, dialing and cursing. He
imagined them circling the apartment, unable to approach. He
imagined all sorts of bad endings.

But then Guillermo came into the sitting room, his face drained
of color, and said, "The telephone, señor. It is *her*."

Calloway stumbled up and spilled his whiskey going for the
receiver in the front room. He grabbed at it and shoved it to his ear.

He said, "Anita, darling—"

Her voice said, "Nick? I—"

And then she was gone. The line went dead. Calloway stood with
the telephone pressed to his ear, listening to a buzzing silence.
Guillermo stared, expectant, hopeful, breathless. Calloway put the
phone down.

He said, "Well, she's alive."

Then the phone rang again. Calloway put the piece to his ear and
said, "This is Calloway."

"Señor Calloway, you know the sound of your woman." The voice
was rich, deep, Cuban. It said, "We have taken her. We are holding
her. If you want her to come back to you . . . you will pay money."

Calloway said, "I will pay anything."

"Good, señor," the voice said. "Very good."

And then the line went dead again. Calloway stood with the telephone in his hand and waited. Guillermo stared. The phone did not ring again. Calloway sat and lit a cigarette, and watched his hands shake. He said to Guillermo, "Make a drink, will you? For both of us."

When he had finished his drink and the phone had not rung again, Calloway called the Security offices. He got Cardoso and told him what had happened.

Cardoso said, "This is a good development, señor. She is alive, and the men who have taken her want money. They will not hurt her, if they want your money. This is excellent."

"I am glad it pleases you," Calloway said, and regretted it.

"Of course it does not," Cardoso said gently. "It has been several days since your woman is missing. If there is no telephone call, she is probably dead. If there is a telephone call and no discussion of money, it is probably a political problem, or a personal problem. Then, perhaps she will be dead, too. But if it is a kidnapping . . . I am sorry, señor, but that is much better."

"I understand," Calloway said. "And I apologize."

"You are feeling a great deal of pressure," Cardoso said. "With your woman gone away, and your business with the Miramar and the Sunset and the Presidente. This is a difficult time."

Calloway said, "Why do you know about these things?"

"Please, señor," Cardoso said softly. "We know about many things. Most of them, they do not interest me. But still I must discover them."

"That's just business," Calloway said. "It has nothing to do with Anita."

"Of course, señor," Cardoso said. "A woman has disappeared from your apartment. A man has been murdered in your apartment. Imagine, señor, if the girl is also murdered. What if you are the killer? I must discover these things, too."

Calloway said, "I understand," and he did. "What should I do?"

"Wait, señor."

Guillermo had specific instructions. Someone was to stand over the telephone, all hours of the day and night. If Calloway was not there, someone who knew how to find him was to dispatch a messenger immediately and keep the line open until he returned.

This limited Calloway's movements, but he had no appetite for anything, anyway. Food and drink came in. He had a book or two. Guillermo went for a box of cigars. On the fifth night Calloway suddenly felt he could not bear the apartment any longer. He told Guillermo, "I am going to the Floridita for a daiquiri. If the telephone rings, do *not* alert the police. Send a runner to the Floridita. Continue speaking to the man on the telephone. I can be here in ten minutes."

Guillermo understood. He looked terribly pained. It was as if his woman, too, had been taken from him. Or as if it were his fault Anita had disappeared.

But the Floridita did nothing for Calloway's spirits. It was early, for one thing. The Floridita was always quiet until after eleven or twelve o'clock. It was ten now. The only drinkers were the tourists and the real drunks. The tourists looked up and around every time someone moved in or out of the room. They were praying for a glimpse of Hemingway or some other celebrity. The drunks didn't look up at all.

Faustino the bartender greeted him with great ceremony. He had, of course, read the newspaper accounts of the murder in Calle San Lázaro and the disappearance of the American woman. And he had heard the gossip. Cubans are great gossipers, so naturally the stories that reached Faustino's ears were preposterous. The American woman had run off with the rebels. She had been taken by Batista's men and turned into a prostitute. She was already a prostitute, but now she had become the lover of Fidel. She was a spy. She was a lesbian spy. She was a Hollywood movie star who was the lover of Batista and was living now in an apartment in the Presidential Palace.

Faustino knew this was all rubbish—the hysterical imaginings of small-minded, provincial Cubans. He himself was more sophisticated. He privately suspected that the woman was torn between her love for the rich American playboy Calloway and the powerful Jewish gangster Meyer Lansky. Perhaps she faked her own kidnapping—or faked her own suicide—in order to escape them both and run off to the Sierra Maestra with a masculine young Cuban revolutionary.

Faustino brought Calloway a pitcher of daiquiris and poured out a glass. He said, "Good ni', Señor Calloway."

"Faustino. Good evening to you."

"I am well, thank you. And I am sorry you have some trouble in your life."

"Thank you, Faustino. All life is trouble."

Havana Brown, the 'shine from the park in front of the Hotel Inglaterra, drifted in with his shoeshine case. Calloway nodded to him and said, "Good evening, Mr. Brown."

"Evening, suh," the Negro said. "How about I get you a shine?"

"How about I get you a drink?"

"Yes, suh," Havana Brown said. "A drink indeed."

They stood at the bar together. They talked of baseball. Brown had followed the Dodgers all his adult life.

"I was *born* in Brooklyn," he said. "Now they gone to Los Angeles, I don't care what happens to 'em."

"You don't like them in Los Angeles?"

"You cain't play no ball in *Los Angeles*," Brown said with disgust. "It's too damn hot. Like tryin' to play ball in Havana."

"I thought they made some pretty good ballplayers down here," Calloway said. "In fact, wasn't that rebel leader Castro a ballplayer?"

Brown said, "That's right. Scouted by the Washington Senators. He was a pitcher. They didn't pick him up."

"Too bad," Calloway said. "Might've saved everybody a lot of headache."

Calloway felt oddly warmed by his presence. In the United States, a poor Negro and a rich white man could not stand side by side at a bar and have a drink and a talk. Even if they wanted to, which Calloway imagined most Americans of either color did not. But it was strangely comforting. The tourists were laughing and yelping behind him. The real drunks were snoozing into their beakers. Calloway looked down at Havana Brown.

Havana Brown said to him, "I'm sorry about yo' troubles."

Calloway was surprised. "You've heard, then?"

"Oh, yes, suh. But I hear a lot of things."

"Do you hear where she is?"

"No, suh."

"Or when she's coming back?"

"No, suh."

"Me neither. Let's have another cocktail."

No one came for him. No breathless Cuban rushed in to say, "Señor! The telephone!" Calloway bought another pitcher of daiquiris.

Calloway said, "Who do you like for the Series?"

"It's got to be them Yankees," Brown said. "Mantle gonna break that home run record, maybe."

"A toast to Mickey Mantle, then."

Havana Brown and he toasted the Mick. Then the Yankees. Then the Los Angeles Dodgers. Havana Brown spat on the floor. They toasted each other. Calloway, who had not eaten a proper meal in several days, became intoxicated. This, too, like the presence of Havana Brown, was soothing to him.

But then he was drunk. Havana Brown was gone. Calloway was slumped over the bar, his arm curled around his empty glass. Suddenly, it seemed, it was very late. The bar was very crowded. Calloway had forgotten himself. He said, "Faustino! A taxi!"

But Guillermo was at the door. Had they come together? Calloway did not remember. Guillermo had him. They were in the big black car. They were home. Calloway was smoking a cigarette he did not remember lighting. Guillermo took it from his fingers and pulled him to his feet. They were inside the apartment.

The phone was ringing when they came through the door. Calloway reached for it.

"Señor Calloway?" It was the same rich, deep Cuban voice.

"Yes, yes. ¡Sí!" Calloway said. "Talk to me."

"Señor Calloway, listen to me closely. You will have one hundred thousand dollars. You will go alone to the Cementerio de Colón. Do you know this place?"

"Yes, I know it."

"You will go there with your money. You will go there at midnight tomorrow. There is a statue of *La Milagrosa*—Amelia Goyri de la Hoz. Do you know it?"

"No."

"You will find it. The woman with her baby. Very famous. You will put *there* a sweetcake with the money inside."

Calloway said, "A sweetcake? What the hell is a sweetcake?"

"A sweetcake, señor. A bag. *Una maleta, señor.* A sweetcake for traveling."

"A suitcase?"

"*Sí, señor.* A sweetcase."

"I understand. What about Anita?"

"What about her, señor?"

"When will I see her?"

"She will be there, beside La Milagrosa."

"What is *milagrosa?*"

"Oh, señor." The voice became weary and old. "The *Milagrosa* is the name of the statue of the lady and her baby who is dead. Your woman will wait for you there."

"I understand. Let me talk to her now."

There was silence, replaced by buzzing. The voice was gone. Calloway slunk into an armchair. Sweetcakes, and a lady with a baby who is dead. And only one hundred thousand dollars! What fools! Calloway felt the night air close around him. He had almost twenty-four hours to get the money, to get to the cemetery, to wait, to see Anita once more. What a long time it seemed. He would tell Guillermo to fetch him up a drink. He would tell Guillermo to fetch him up a pot of coffee and a sandwich of some kind. He would telephone Cardoso. But then he was asleep.

Guillermo went into the bedroom and pulled a blanket from the bed. He draped it over his employer and then knelt to remove the man's shoes. He switched off the light and dropped into an armchair across the room. He slept, too.

* * *

"He is drunk," Vicente Chibás said to his comrades. "Americans should not drink."

"But he understands?" Alemán asked him.

"He understands. Perhaps tomorrow he will forget, but he understands. How is the girl?"

"She is fine. I saw her an hour ago."

"Go see her again."

They had been in the farmhouse for almost a week. It was not pleasant. The night air smelled of animals and dirt. Chibás had grown up on such a farm, his father a poor field hand, his brothers and sisters and himself raised on a dirt floor in a thatched *bohío*. Chibás never saw the inside of the big house. Now he was staying in the big house, just like that one, the main residence of a farm he and his men had liberated from the *imperialistas* who claimed to own it. Chibás and Alemán and two others had come here in the early spring. They had watched the house for a day. Then they had crept into the house that night and murdered the owner and his wife in their beds. They had buried the bodies in the dirt behind the house before dawn. The next morning they had run the workers out of their huts and off the land altogether.

Their comrades on Calle 15, from whom Chibás and the others were meant to take orders, never knew how they'd secured the house. It was Chibás's plan, and his alone.

As was the kidnapping. Alemán believed there were orders from Fidel directly. Chibás had told him so. This was nonsense. But he was not a smart man, and he was new to the revolution.

Chibás had driven here, the first night, with Alemán. The girl was bound and gagged in the trunk. She thrashed a little when they took her out. So Chibás hit her on the head with the butt of his pistol. She went down like a sack of grain. Alemán slung her over his shoulder and locked her in a room they had already prepared for her. The windows had been boarded shut and all the furniture removed, with a lock on the outside of the door. Alemán poured the girl onto the mattress they had put on the floor. He pulled the sack from her head and removed the gag and the rope that tied her hands. He saw that she was very beautiful. Alemán had, for one dreadful moment, one dreadful thought. Then he rose to his feet, shuddering, and hurried from the room. Chibás said, "Lock the door."

The next day their comrades Fermín and Losada came from Havana. Fermín was just a boy. He had been arrested and beaten badly during an interrogation in the Security offices. His left arm hung at a funny angle. Losada was a veteran of the movement who had lost an eye in a battle following the attack on the Moncada barracks. Like Alemán, Fermín and Losada thought the kidnapping plan came from the Sierra Maestra.

Both men wanted to see the girl. Chibás said they could not.

"Alemán watches her," he growled. "You will be watching the Cementerio de Colón."

During the next several days, Alemán never heard her speak. He took her water and food. He waited while she went to the bathroom, then marched her back to the bedroom. She did not look at his face. She showed no expression—no fear, no anger, no sadness—except when she heard the voice of her man on the telephone and then had the telephone taken out of her hands. She looked lost and afraid then, but only for a moment. Then once, rising from the bed, she seemed to stumble. She reached up and touched the back of her head—where Chibás had struck her with his pistol, Alemán thought—and winced. Alemán felt shame. Who would hit such a woman? The revolution was hard work sometimes.

He was eager for this part to be finished. He said, "Soon we will give back the girl and take the money to the mountains—to the Sierra Maestra."

"Perhaps," Chibás said. "If this drunken fool pays for the return of his woman."

"Who would not pay?" Alemán said. "If I were rich, I would pay."

"Then you are also a fool," Chibás said. "Check the lock on her door, and go to bed."

Alemán checked the lock. It was secure. He listened for the sound of the girl inside. He could imagine her, soft and brown and warm, lying asleep in her bed. He had those dreadful thoughts again, and again he felt shame.

Soon this will be over, he knew. He would get a woman in Havana perhaps, and his dreadful thoughts would be over, too.

In the front room Chibás was telling Losada and Fermín again how the exchange would take place. "You must go now and begin watching the cemetery," he told them. "The night watchman is my cousin. He will let you drive in. Watch for three nights. See that it is secure. Then we will finish the plan and invite the American to come with his money."

The first day María Fuentes had been taken as far as Colón. The bus was old, there were holes in the floorboards, and the air inside stank of exhaust fumes. The road rose up and away from the sea, moving farther from Havana than María had ever traveled, and the view was marvelous. But María could hardly keep her eyes open. She was uncomfortably hot, sticking to the seat in her thin cotton dress. A man who got on the bus in Havana kept trying to engage her in conversation. But the talk and the view did nothing for her. She was through with talking, and scenery. She closed her eyes and slept, dreamlessly, as the bus rolled eastward. She awoke after dark, her head clanging, and got down from the bus in the center of town.

María had taken with her all the money she could scrape together. It was enough to get her to Ciego de Ávila or Camagüey, or Bayamo even, if that's how far she had to go to meet the rebels. But it was not enough for her to enjoy any luxury getting there. The few things she had brought with her could not be sold for anything, either, should she run short of money. Her small suitcase held only a few pieces of clothing, a Bible, photographs of her mother and father, a certificate showing that she had graduated from high school, and a straight razor she had taken from Juan Obregón's apartment. She wasn't sure why she might need a straight razor, but it made her think of Juan, and his strength, and made her feel protected.

María bought a *medianoche* sandwich and ate it slowly, sitting in the town square for an hour watching the small-town night come to life.

There was a round policeman, middle-aged and slow in his stained uniform, strolling the square. When it was time, María approached him.

"I am traveling," she said. "I need to find an inexpensive hotel near the center of the town."

"Why would you need a hotel?" the policeman said. "You are a beautiful woman! There are a hundred men who would gladly take you in for the night. I myself, were I not a policeman . . ."

"Good-bye," María said, and moved away.

There was an old man selling fruit from a stall across the square. She went there. The man appeared to be dozing behind his wares. But he spoke without opening his eyes. He said, "Yes, *mi niña?* What do you want?"

"I need to find a place to sleep for the night," María said. "A hotel. I haven't much money."

"El Batey," the old man said. "It is only two blocks from here. Behind the *Teatro Municipal*. It is owned by my son, Juan Pedro Guzmán. He is a good man. You may tell him his father sent you."

"You are kind, señor," María said.

"I am old and blind and tired," the man said. "I have no time for unkindness anymore. Go with God, granddaughter."

Juan Pedro Guzmán did not have his father's gentility. He said, "We are full," when María came into the lobby of his hotel. It was wooden and old. It smelled of cooking and soiled laundry. Ordinarily, María would sooner have slept in the open. But nothing was ordinary now.

She said, "Please. You must have something. I will stay only one night. I have money. I am not asking for any charity. Just a bed."

"Perhaps," Guzmán said. "Wait."

When he returned, he said, "I have one bed. It is in a room I keep for myself. You can have it for tonight only."

"Thank you," María said. "I have come by bus from Havana. I am tired."

"Follow me," Guzmán said. "Bring your bag."

The room was on the ground floor, behind a storeroom. It was a windowless room with a concrete floor, lit by a bare bulb hanging from a long black wire, and contained a toilet, sink, and a cot with a thin mattress. The air was close and stank of urine.

María said, "Thank you. May I pay you in the morning?"

"Of course," Guzmán said. "If not sooner. Good night."

When he was gone, María pulled down the thin sheet covering the mattress. Neither looked clean. She put her suitcase next to the bed and lay back without removing her dress. She was asleep within minutes.

But Guzmán returned and woke her. He came into the room, a slash of light behind him stabbing through the doorway, and then closed the door and stood, panting. María could not see him in the dark, but she heard him fumbling with the buttons on his clothes. She reached down and slid open the top of her suitcase, and slipped out of the bed.

Guzmán said, "Here. I have come for you. Your man has come for you."

"And I am waiting," María said in a low voice. "I have a razor in my hand. If you touch me, I will cut you open with it."

"A razor, eh? I am not afraid of a woman with a razor."

Guzmán lunged. María stepped aside. The man bumped his leg on the cot and cursed. María got her hand on the doorknob and yanked it open. Light poured in. Guzmán stood with his hands on his undershorts. María stepped toward him with the razor glinting in her hand.

"Get out," she said. "I am tired. I need to sleep. You are a pig, and I will cut your throat like a pig if you come near me again. Understand?"

Guzmán, eyes red with rage, nodded.

"Then get out," María said.

María put the straight razor in her bag and sat on the cot. She knew the man would not return. But she knew she would not sleep anymore now, either. She pulled the sheet from the bed, folded it and put it in her bag, and left the vile room. She went back to the town square. There were park benches under the shade of some low trees. María spread the hotel sheet over a bench and stretched out on it. Perhaps she would be safe here, unmolested by the police, if only for an hour's sleep. With that, she felt, she could go on. Just an hour's sleep. The slightest breeze was blowing as she closed her eyes and pulled the thin sheet close around her shoulders.

Mo Weiner had not seen Deacon, or rather Sloan, for two days. He wasn't on the bandstand. The boys in the band didn't know where he was—or they wouldn't say. Mo went to the manager and made it sound like a personal thing. The manager came back and said, "Perhaps he is not well, señor. He has not been here for several days. I spoke to Baby Ruth personally."

"Baby Ruth?"

"He is the bandleader, señor. He says Señor Sloan was not here."

It wasn't like Vegas. There, Mo would only have to ask one person one question, and sometimes back the question up with, say, a fifty-dollar bill. Information was provided. Here, not speaking the language, not surrounded by the machinery of business, Mo was at a loss. You asked. No one answered. Then what? Call for Philo Vance? Call for Charlie Chan?

Mo said, "Does Baby Ruth know where Sloan lives?"

"No, señor. I ask him that, too. He does not know."

Mo went to the big bar off the lobby, the bar where he'd first met Calloway. A bright-eyed Cuban bartender, a guy who looked like he heard things and knew what they meant, mixed Mo a Manhattan. Mo sat at the bar and sipped the cocktail, folding and unfolding a fifty-dollar bill on the bar. The bartender was cool. He paid Mo no more attention than he would have any Florida floozy. Mo had another cocktail. The bar was full of tourists, plus a couple of local sharps who looked like they were hunting tourists.

During a lull, Mo said, "I'm looking for a friend."

The bartender said, "Señor, we are all looking for a friend."

"Yeah, yeah," Mo said. "This one's got a name. He's called Sloan. He plays cornet in the band here. I'm looking for him."

"I don't know any Sloan, señor."

"Yeah, yeah," Mo said. "Nobody knows anybody. Some mornings I don't even know who *I* am. But this is important."

The bartender excused himself to mix up a pitcher of daiquiris for a group of three wild-looking young American women. They had hair piled high on their heads. One of them wore a pair of pointy-ended eyeglasses with jewels in the frame. They all had on cocktail dresses and high heels. They'd had plenty to drink already. They squeaked when they talked.

The bartender came a little too casually back down the bar. Mo thought, *Okay, I got him. He sees the fifty now—General Ulysses S. Grant going into his pocket.*

Mo said, "You saw something in the papers about an American girl, a tourist, in Havana. Some guy was shot in her apartment. She disappeared. She was with this rich American named Calloway. Ring a bell?"

"I heard something about that," the bartender said.

"The girl is missing. She's in trouble—either with the law if she killed the guy in the apartment, or with the guys who *did* kill the guy in the apartment. Sloan doesn't know about this. He needs to know. Pick up that fifty and tell me you can help me."

The bartender looked down the bar at the three American girls. He looked back at the fifty. His hand went to it, slippery and sly, and the bill was gone.

He said, "Sloan sleeps in an apartment in Old Havana. In Plaza Vieja. He drinks sometime in La Coronita, on the street called Lamparilla."

"Does he have a phone?"

"No, señor. No one in Old Havana has a phone."

"What time do you finish?"

"Me, señor? I finish at two o'clock."

"I'm coming back here at two o'clock. I've got more pictures of General Grant in my wallet. You can have some of them. We're going to Plaza Vieja, and La Lampa, or whatever it is. Got me?"

"Okay, señor. Two o'clock."

Hours later, in the taxi, Mo said, "What's your name, anyway?"

"Phil."

"Your name is Phil?"

"Yes and no, señor. It is Filomeno. But this is difficult to say. So I am Phil."

Phil was a snappy dresser. He had changed out of his Tropicana black-and-whites into a pair of soft brown slacks and white and brown two-tone shoes. He was ready for a night on the town.

They stopped first in Old Havana, near Plaza Vieja. Phil said, "La Coronita is here." He led Mo down one dark street, onto an even darker street, which had no name, into an extremely dark doorway. Over the doorway was a small neon crown. Phil pointed to it and said, "Little crown. *Coronita.*"

Inside, the music was thick as mud, oozing out of a trumpet, sax, piano, and bass at the back of the room. The air was heavy with blue cigarette smoke and the smell of bodies. There were black bodies and white bodies, jammed in tight, jammed together on the dance floor, jammed into small tables beside the dance floor, jammed in at the bar.

Mo turned to Phil to say, "This is not the place," but Phil had gone. Mo stood alone on the threshold. He focused on the white faces in the room, trying to pick which of them might belong to Deacon or Sloan. There weren't that many. It didn't take long to see that Deacon wasn't around.

Phil returned with cocktails. He had two glasses of some pale, cloudy beverage.

Mo said, "What's this?"

Phil said, "Delicious," and threw his down in one gulp.

Mo looked at the clouds swirling in the glass, which smelled of rum, then handed it to Phil. Phil smiled and said, "Delicious," and threw that one down, too. He raised his eyebrows and said, "I get more?"

"No," Mo said. "He's not here. Let's scramble."

"Scramble?"

"Out."

In the street there was silence and oxygen. Mo shook the cigarette smoke out of his jacket. He said, "What's next?"

Phil said, "There is another club."

"Is it as nice as this one?"

"More nicer," Phil said. "Is good. Come."

"Wait," Mo said. "First, let's try to find his apartment. You go back in that bar and ask if anyone knows where he lives. Okay? Then we'll see another bar."

Phil looked doubtful. Or hurt. Mo hit his pocket and came up with a twenty. He said, "Go get another delicious. Find out about the apartment. I'll wait."

Phil shot back into the Coronita, opening a vent of smoke and mambo. Mo stood on the uneven cobblestones and looked around him. Depressing to think of Deacon in any of these holes. The apartment buildings were dark and dank. The gutters were damp with sewage. Rats ran through the shadows. Babies cried. Somewhere a radio was playing American music. It sounded like some of that hillbilly stuff. The Anderson Brothers. The Emerson Brothers? No. Something like that. The song was "Wake Up, Little Susie." They were a kind of Elvis act. The Elvis Brothers. The *Everly* Brothers. Mo didn't get it. He was a Harry James man himself. He liked music with some meat on it. He could listen to Ella Fitzgerald or Sarah Vaughan all day long. And Sinatra. And Satchmo. But the new stuff was lost on him. The Everly Brothers and Elvis and Pat Boone, and this Bill Haley "Rock Around the Clock" and Buddy Holly "Peggy Sue" monkey business. Kids had been going nuts over this thing called "At the Hop" when Mo left Las Vegas. He didn't understand any of it.

Deacon had said to him, "I think this rock-roll stuff is here to stay."

"Why not?" Mo answered. "Everything else is turning to crap."

The door of La Coronita swung open, disgorging smoke and noise and Phil, who stumbled once over the curb. He had another of those cloudy drinks in his hand. He said, "For you, señor."

Mo said, "No. Thank you."

Phil swallowed the drink whole. He said, "Delicious. No one knows the apartment of your friend. We will go to another club."

*   *   *

It was late. Or it was early. It didn't matter. It was dark and Sloan was drunk, and that was good. He was in some ratbag joint in Old Havana. He had been there for hours, blowing and drinking and jamming. It was hot as hell. He'd lost his jacket. He had no money. This didn't matter. There were drinks and more drinks. And hot mambo and dark, jivey jazz, and then more drinks.

He had not been out at all in several days. Anita was gone. No. Anita had *left*. He felt like the guy in some dumb joke. Guy goes out for a pack of cigarettes. He had left her for half a day. He had come back to find her gone. And she stayed gone. Well, chump, what should a guy like you expect? Rummy old ex-hype jazzbo. A guy who couldn't even stay afloat in *Las Vegas*. A guy who couldn't show his face in Chicago or Los Angeles, and who was barely holding his own in Havana. Why *wouldn't* a girl like Anita run off?

So Sloan sat and drank. The second night he sat and drank and pulled his trumpet from its case and blew softly at the balcony. The third night he drank a lot and blew not so softly. He blew until it was so late that someone came and pounded on the door and told him in Spanish to shut up. Or that's what it sounded like. Sloan didn't know how to say "shut up" in Spanish. He didn't know how to tell someone in Spanish that he wasn't going to shut up. So he kept playing. An hour later there was someone shouting at him from the street. Sloan swayed on the balcony and looked down. A guy he sort of knew said, "Hello, my freng! Good music!"

Then Sloan was in a nightclub. The guy he saw from the balcony was Carlos. Then there were some other guys. They were going to some joint in Miramar. Sloan told them he wouldn't go to Miramar. Then they weren't going to Miramar. They were going to a club *called* Miramar. Or Mirador. Or Mirror Door? The guys were snapping their fingers and laughing and grinning like Cheshire cats. One of them was carrying a pair of drumsticks stuck in one back pocket and pair of wire brushes in the other. He was leading. The sticks and brushes switched like tail feathers. Sloan was lost before they got halfway there, staggering along with his horn in his hand. Someone said the word *taxi* and then they had a taxi. Then they were inside some dark place and Carlos said, "*¡Mojitos!*" and they were all drinking.

It was hot jazz after that. Carlos was a piano player, and they had a piano, and the other men were playing bass and sax. The man with the drumsticks in his pocket was behind a trap set and he was going rat-a-tat on it. And they were playing. The room filled up. There were women. The air got heavy with cigarettes and the smell of women's perfume and hot bodies. It smelled like jazz and sex.

There was a wonderful-looking dark-skinned Cuban woman sitting next to him. Her eyes were shiny, and she smelled like roses. Sloan was watching Carlos hit the keyboard. The girl was watching Sloan.

Sloan said, "He can really navigate them eighty-eights."

The girl said, "*¿Cómo?*"

Sloan laughed and said, "Nobody talks English down here. I'm saying that the man can really navigate them eighty-eights. Them piano keys. He can *play* the black-and-whites. He can navigate. He can applicate. Dominate. He can *radiate* the eighty-eights."

The girl grinned and said, "*Payaso.*"

Sloan said, "*Payaso* to you, too, baby. *¡Vamos mojitos!*"

When he woke up, he was back in his flat. He didn't remember coming home. He didn't remember leaving the club. His head was thick and his clothes reeked of cigarettes and rum and the crowd. Someone else's cologne was everywhere. Sloan gagged slightly at the smell of it on his shirt collar. He would need to get his suit shook out if he was going to wear it anymore, and he was going to need some laundry on the shirt. He took his head into the bathroom and ran it under cold water until the ringing in his ears stopped. Then he had a smoke and opened the shutters. It was getting dark. That was a very good sign. He had gotten through the day. Soon night would come. At night you could drink and smoke and blow your horn. It was easier to make the nighttime go.

Midnight came and went. His clothes had been cleaned. He had showered and had a shave. He was beginning to think that he ought to eat something. He was beginning to wish he had a drink, too. He was trying to figure out a place where he could do all that. He could get a bite on Obispo. Maybe La Zaragozana? Someplace like that. Maybe a snack at Bar Monserrate. Maybe something down by the

water? No. Make him think of Anita. Sloan was making up his mind
when there were voices shouting up from the street again. He went
to the balcony. Carlos was standing downstairs with some guys and
the dark-skinned Cuban girl from the night before. Carlos was waving something shiny.

He said, "Jew whore, mang."

Sloan said, "What?"

"I hob jew *whore,* my freng. Con dow-side!"

Sloan said, "Wait." He went to the closet where he kept his trumpet. No trumpet. He understood: *I have your horn, my friend. Come
downstairs.*

He went back to the balcony and said, "I'm coming downside, my
freng."

It was like long-lost brothers in the street. There was much shaking of hands, much slapping of backs. Carlos said, "We go to a new
club, my freng. Tonight, El Cruz Azul."

Sloan took his horn from Carlos and said, *"Vamos mojitos."*

They went off Plaza Vieja, across Mercaderes, to Lamparilla. The
night thickened around them like smoke.

Cardoso had been thinking for several days that he ought to contact
the Spaniard who had first introduced him to the Calloway. There
might be something there.

Or not. That was police work. Very little was where you expected
it to be or where you looked for it. And everything you found came
from someplace unexpected. Like Calloway knowing about the Calle
15 arrests. That was entirely unexpected. Cardoso did not know what
it meant, yet.

Each day he expected to receive word from Calloway that he had
been contacted by the kidnappers. He had plainclothes officers
posted around Calloway's apartment, in case there was violence
directed at the American. But he expected nothing of the sort. He
expected a phone call, or a note, or a runner with a message. For days,
though, there had been only silence.

Each day he expected also to learn something new about Calloway's connection to the Calle 15 group. There were new bits of information arriving all the time, from suspects being interrogated, from detainees volunteering testimony, from new facts being uncovered. Cardoso had pieced together most of the pertinent details of the Calle 15 operation, including the cell's connection to Carlos Delgado. He learned from papers he had seized from the residence that Delgado's passage had been arranged in Mexico City, that he had sailed from Veracruz, that the boat was owned by an American, and that there would be a shipment of cash on board when he sailed. There was nothing to indicate the source of the cash, nor was there any information regarding the ownership of the boat.

Both of those things, though, could point to Calloway. Which brought Cardoso back to the irony of the kidnapping: If Calloway was connected to the Calle 15 group, he could be connected only as a financial supporter; and if he was a financial supporter, why would the rebels kidnap his woman? And if it was not the rebels who had kidnapped his woman, where was she?

Maybe it was no kidnapping at all. Maybe it was all much simpler—a jilted lover, a jealous man, the old story. Perhaps Calloway himself had triggered the dead man in his apartment.

Cardoso clicked off the bright desk lamp and left his office.

Matos and Bustillo were sitting in the front area, drinking from short glasses. The air smelled of alcohol and urine and the acrid smoke of Matos's cigarillo. There was a ragged lump of a man, a creature from the street, black as soot, sitting between them. He looked dazed—drunk or starving or beaten senseless, or all three.

Matos said, "Hey, Commandante, drink with us."

"Perhaps it is not safe," Cardoso said. "It doesn't seem to agree with your friend."

The two policemen turned to stare at the man sitting between them. His face was filthy. His clothes were torn. His hair was matted to the density of old carpet. But his eyes were bright. He grinned black teeth at Cardoso.

He said, "Money for me, señores. No rum."

"He wants to sell us information," Bustillo explained. "He thinks we are interested in information."

"Eso es más negro que el betún," Matos said. "He's as black as shoe polish!"

Cardoso pulled a chair close to the man. Matos gave him a short glass filled with rum. Cardoso lifted it to his nose. The sharp smell of alcohol burned. He took a sip and said, "We are always interested in information. What does it concern?"

"Ghosts," Bustillo said.

"Ghosts and grave robbers," Matos said.

"A new miracle at the tomb of La Milagrosa," Bustillo said.

Cardoso reached into his pocket and found a ten-peso note, and drank off the rest of his rum. He handed the money to the bum and said, "Tell me about the ghosts."

"They are not ghosts, señor," the man said, shoving the money into his pants. "They are men who move at midnight, like ghosts. For three nights they have come at midnight to the Cementerio de Colón, señor. They gather at the tomb of La Milagrosa—may God rest her soul."

Cardoso said, "And what do they do, these men?"

"They wait, and watch," the man said. "Then they leave. They take nothing. They do nothing."

"And you? What do you do?"

"I watch and wait also, señor," the man said. "But I do not leave. I sleep, and I dream, and nightmares come to me in my dreams. These are evil men—and foul!"

Matos said, *"¡Coñó!* It is you who are foul. You wait and you watch. No time for bathing, eh? You stink!"

Cardoso said, "Stop that." Then he turned back to the man. "Do they always come at midnight?"

"Every night, señor. At midnight."

Cardoso checked his wristwatch. It was just before eleven o'clock. He said, "We will go together, you and I. We will watch the ghosts come and go."

"Thank you, señor," the man said. "La Milagrosa cannot rest with these men watching her and waiting every night. She must rest."

"We all must rest," Cardoso said. "Will you have a drink now?"

"No, señor," the man said. "I have not eaten today. I must not drink."

"Come, then. You also, Bustillo. We will have a sandwich and go to the cemetery. Bring your rum, if you like."

The man rose. Waves of stink rose with him. Matos said, "My God! The smell of him! Like rotting flesh."

"We are all rotting," Cardoso said. "*Venga conmigo, mi viejo.* Let us go and see the cemetery."

Phil led Mo to three more joints before Mo called an end to the hunt. He said, "Phil, I'm finished. *Finito. No más.* I'm going back to the Tropicana."

"No, señor!" Phil said. "One more club! One more cocktails!"

They were standing in a crowded barroom where music played from a bandstand in the corner. The room was full. All the rooms had been full, and smoky, and loud and rank with heat and sweat. Mo had lost track of the names and locations. Phil was drunk. Mo was tired. Mo was done.

Then Phil said, "We go to the Blue Cross."

"I need the Red Cross," Mo said. "What's the Blue Cross?"

"El Cruz Azul!" Phil said. "Very famous. Nightclub for Cubans. The most hot of all Havana."

"Then why didn't we go there first?"

"El Cruz Azul is later club," Phil said. "Two o'clock, three o'clock, four o'clock . . ."

"Yeah, yeah," Mo said. "I get it. Where is it?"

"Miramar, señor. Near to Tropicana."

"Let's go."

"Okay, señor. *¡Pa' El Cruz Azul!*"

This joint was bigger and fancier than the others, but inside it was just as hot and dark and close. The foyer was lined with sweeping palms and men in some sort of royal uniforms. Each wore a medallion on his chest bearing a cross of blue.

The club itself was downstairs. Mo descended, feeling the air get hotter and tighter and the music more insistent. Phil was already at the bar, shouting friendly words at the bartender and several of the patrons. The noise was overpowering. It came like a blast from a stage at the far end of the room. Over swaying heads, through a field of blue smoke, Mo could see a dozen musicians wrestling with their instruments. Phil handed him a glass of something that smelled like gasoline, with a lime in it.

Phil raised his glass at the stage and said, "There is your freng, my freng."

At that moment the sound of the trumpet cut through the smoke. It was Deacon. Mo knew the horn before he could make the face. And then he saw. Deacon was onstage with the six other men, clutching his horn and blowing heat through it. A cry went up from the floor. There was something like electricity in the room. Mo had not heard that kind of music, nor seen that kind of electricity, since the night the Ivory Coast opened. When Deacon blew out the last of his solo, voices shouted at him. He dropped his head, as if this embarrassed him, and stepped back on the stage.

At the break Mo pushed his way through the crowd. He caught Deacon on the sleeve.

He said, "I've been looking for you all night. We need to talk."

"Talk?"

"Yeah," Mo said. "Come down from there."

Deacon slid his horn under his arm and stepped off the stage. Mo could see that he was drunk. He wobbled badly on his feet, and his eyes swam in his head. Mo said, "You all right?"

"Swell, Mo," he said. "Jus' swell. Wussup?"

"It's about Anita."

"Nevermind 'bout Anita," he said. "Don't care about Anita, no mo'."

"I understand," Mo said. "But this, believe me, you want to know."

"No. Don't want to know no mo'," Deacon said. "Know no mo', Mo!"

"Very funny. She's been kidnapped, Deacon."

That got his attention. His eyes swam. He was still wobbly. But he was paying attention now. He said, "Who is this?"

Mo turned. Phil had come up from behind and was breathing over his shoulder. Mo said, "Meet Phil. It's short for Philodendron."

Deacon looked at Phil and said, "Does Phil know?"

Mo said, "No."

Deacon said, "Does Phil *habla* English?"

"A little."

"Tell me about Anita."

"She's been grabbed."

"By who?"

"We don't know."

A dark, slinky girl slid out of the crowd and applied herself to Deacon, who turned to investigate. He peeled the girl off him and said, "Not now."

The girl said, "Dance me."

Deacon said, "Later," and then to Mo, "What are we going to do?"

"We wait. Anita was taken from Calloway's apartment. I guess someone will contact him."

"Calloway."

"Calloway. The man she was with."

"Yes. The rich man. Another rich man. He would pay the ransom."

"Yes. He will pay the ransom."

The dark and slinky girl said to Phil, *"Oyeme tú. ¿Qué haces con él?"*

"Trabajando, niña. ¿Igual que tú con ese flaco, no?"

"Qué va," the girl said, sadly. *"Ese está borracho completo."*

"¡Coñó! Qué lástima."

The band struck up again. Deacon flinched. His eyes clouded over, then focused again. He patted the slinky, dark girl on the arm and said, "I gotta get out of here."

"Come with me," Mo said. "Let's all get out of here."

The streets were empty. A cab saw the two men come to the curb, and rushed there to catch them. They got inside.

Mo said, "You can drop me at the Tropicana and then take the cab home, Deacon."

"Home. *Ha.* And you said *Deacon.*"

"No one calls you that now, do they?"

"No. No one calls me that now," he said. "I'm Sloan. I'm the dead guy."

"Dead drunk," Mo said gently. "Go home and sober up. Call me in the morning. We'll figure an angle on this thing."

"An angle," Deacon said. "It's all about the angles. It's all about Los Angeles. I should never have left Los Angeles."

Mo said to the driver, "Go to Old Havana first. Then the Tropicana."

Once they got near, Deacon was able to identify his street. The cabdriver pulled slowly down a dark, dark block and emerged in Plaza Vieja. Deacon said, "Here is where I live."

Mo said, "Show me." Then he handed the driver a five-dollar bill and said, "Wait."

He helped Deacon navigate the cobblestones and steps to his apartment building. It was one flight up and very dark. Mo smelled the smells of poor people. He remembered the smells from his childhood in Chicago, when he would accompany his father on his rounds. They would visit apartment blocks where white people did not live. Those buildings smelled like this—of onions and head lice and cockroaches.

Deacon found a light switch on the second-floor landing. Then he got a key out of his pocket. He leaned heavily on the door and almost fell into the room as the door swung open.

Mo said, "I'm leaving. Sweet dreams. Good night."

Deacon said over his shoulder, heading for the bathroom, "Stay and have one *más mojitos* with me."

"Good night," Mo said. "I'm leaving. I'm gone."

He swung the apartment door shut and went back down the stairs. The cabbie was waiting. He crossed the cobblestones into the plaza, got into the backseat, and stuck a ten-dollar bill on the front seat. He said, "Tropicana. Please."

It was a short ride. Cardoso drove the black Security car up La Rampa, across the wealthy section of Vedado, and into the poorer part of town. At the huge Cementerio de Colón, he awoke the night watchman with a flash of his policeman's badge and forced him to unlock the main gate. He said, "Tell no one we are here, eh?" The night watchman nodded sleepily and waved them into the cemetery.

"It is there," Cardoso's tattered companion said. "I have seen the men there."

Cardoso drove the car down a long lane lined with enormous crypts. He killed the headlights and pulled the car close to a stone tomb modeled on Havana's own Capitolio. In the dark, with the car lights off, it was difficult to make out anything but vague, gray shapes.

"Here!" the old bum said, pointing a shaky hand past Cardoso. "Here is La Milagrosa."

"Lies!" Bustillo sneered. "Only a fool believes in such things."

"Please, señor," the old man said. "This is a holy place. This is a place of sanctity."

"Lies!" Bustillo said. He pulled the bottle of rum close to him. "All lies, coñó. This is a place of dead people. You will join them soon, and you will see if it is holy or not."

"Stop, Bustillo," Cardoso said gently. "Drink your rum and be quiet."

"You will see, señor," the old man said. "They will come soon."

Cardoso swung his door open and stood beside the car. He said, "Let them come, then, mi viejo. You eat your sandwich. We will wait."

Guillermo had the car ready. Calloway had the money, wrapped in towels, stowed in a black gladstone bag. Half the money was in fifty-dollar bills. The other half was in hundreds. Calloway didn't know how you passed hundred-dollar bills in Cuba, except at the casinos. But that wasn't his problem. The money probably wouldn't be spent in Cuba, anyway. It would be spent buying someone a new life in a new country.

They left the building just after eleven o'clock. The streets were quiet and wet. It had rained briefly just after sundown, and everything looked shiny and new and the air was sweet. The car slid through Havana, along Reina, along Carlos III. Calloway saw the university go by, and thought of the Calle 15 house and the students there. They would be locked in cells now. The lucky ones, anyway. Calloway did not like to think where the others would be now. In Paradise.

Guillermo didn't look good. His eyes were wild, and his skin was gray in the dim light. Calloway said, "Guillermo, tell me, how are you doing?"

Guillermo's eyes widened in the rearview mirror.

"Okay, señor. Fine."

"No, Guillermo. Not fine. Are you frightened?"

"Yes, señor."

Calloway laughed, and ran his hands through his silvery hair.

"Good! I am frightened, too."

"Señor, we must not go," Guillermo said. He pulled the black sedan to the curb and idled it there.

La Rampa lay to their right, a long slope down to the water. The lights of the Hotel Nacional twinkled at them. The hulking edifice that would be the Havana Hilton stood before them. Even now, near midnight, workmen were hurrying along, trying to ready the building for its late-summer opening. On the opposite corner, in the park, the benches were empty.

"Please, señor," Guillermo said. "We must not go."

"But we must go," Calloway said. "Or *I* must go, anyway. Why don't you step down here? I'll take the car. You go to the apartment and wait for me."

Guillermo said, "But why, señor? This is a problem for the police."

"No," Calloway said. "This is a problem for me. If I bring in the police and Anita is hurt . . . That would be unbearable."

"But what if *you* are hurt, señor?"

"Oh, I don't care so much about that," Calloway said. "But midnight will be here soon. Get out and let me drive on."

"No, señor," Guillermo said. "We will go together."

"You are a good man," Calloway said. "Drive, then."

Five minutes on, Guillermo pulled close to the huge wrought-iron gates in front of the Cementerio de Colón. A gatekeeper appeared, rubbing sleep from his eyes, shaking his head no. Guillermo held a bill out to him. The gatekeeper took the bill and stuck it in his pocket, then resumed shaking his head no. He said something about the time. Calloway heard the word *mañana,* which he knew meant "tomorrow." Guillermo held out another bill. The gatekeeper took that one, too, and turned and looked at the gate, then turned his head higher and appeared to study the sky. Calloway heard him say, *"Medianoche,"* which he thought meant "midnight." Guillermo reached for one more bill. The gatekeeper took it and drew a huge iron key from his pocket and began to unlock the gate.

Calloway said to Guillermo, "Do you know this place?"

"Yes, señor. It is famous, La Milagrosa."

"What is it?"

"A famous lady, she died when her baby was born. Then her baby died also. Very sad. In the *cementerio,* they put the lady and the baby in the same place. In one . . . *cómo se dice* . . . one box?"

"Coffin."

"Yes. One coffin. Together. The baby is by her feet. But then, the next year, they open the box. The coffin. And the baby is in the arms of the lady. Like Jesus and María. It is miracle. *Milagro.* And the lady is La Milagrosa."

"The miracle. The miracle worker."

"Exactly, señor. And now people come to see La Milagrosa, to ask for help with love, with money, with problems. And very many girl come to ask for help with a baby. They want to have a baby. La Milagrosa will help."

Calloway said, "How incredibly macabre."

"It is here, señor."

Guillermo stopped the car and cut the headlights. They were in a long, dim avenue. Ornate grave markers and crypts rose on all sides of them, some as large as houses. Rows of graves extended as far as Calloway could see, thousands of rock and marble statues standing gray and silent like a city sleeping in the dead of night. Guillermo pointed. He said, "That one, señor."

La Milagrosa was a statue of a woman, cradling a child, her free hand outstretched. There was a low, flat grave marker of marble surrounded by a low iron fence. The grave itself was almost entirely covered in flowers. Calloway's eyes adjusted to the darkness. He opened the car door and sat listening to the night. Trees waved slightly in the breeze, the fluttering leaves the only sound. Nothing moved in the shadows. Calloway got out of the car.

It wasn't quite midnight, Calloway guessed. He couldn't read his watch in the dim light. He picked up the gladstone bag, and stepped across the avenue to the monument to La Milagrosa. He stepped over the little fence, cleared a spot for himself on the low marble grave marker, and sat down. He lit a cigarette. Guillermo, standing uncomfortably by the car, said, "Señor, I think it is bad luck to sit on La Milagrosa."

Calloway said, "Sorry, old boy. But I think I've got the bad luck already."

He finished his cigarette, then had another. Guillermo shifted on his feet, sat back in the car, got out again and stood leaning against the fender. He was about to sit down in the car again when a voice called out, from somewhere in the darkness.

"Meester Calloway."

Calloway stood with the gladstone bag in his hand. He said, "I'm Calloway."

"And the money?"

Calloway held up the bag. He said, "I have the money."

"Put the money on La Milagrosa."

Calloway placed the bag on top of the marble slab. He swung his eyes back and forth. He could see nothing but shadow and blackness among the headstones and statues.

He said, "Where is the girl?"

"The girl is here."

Calloway said, "Where?"

"Move away from the money, señor."

Calloway stepped over the low wrought-iron barrier, took a few steps toward the voice, then stopped. He said, "Show me the girl."

"I'm here, Nick."

It was Anita, suddenly there beside him. He pulled her into his arms. The voice said again, "Move away from the money, señor."

Calloway pulled Anita toward the car. He said to Guillermo, "Start the car."

Guillermo got behind the wheel. Calloway opened the back door for Anita.

The night was suddenly full of noise and light. Car headlights flooded the street before them. La Milagrosa rose like an ascending angel.

A new voice shouted, "Police! Stop at once! Drop your guns and drop the money! *¡Suelten las pistolas!*"

Calloway heard a scrambling of feet and saw the flash of gunfire before he heard the shot. The blast came from behind a gravestone to his left. To his right there was a groan and the sound of a body falling. Then more gunfire—lots of gunfire. There were muzzle blasts from both sides. Calloway grabbed Anita and pulled her to the ground and held her close beneath him. One of the headlights was shattered and went black.

"Do not run!" the police voice shouted now. "If you run, you will die!"

Feet were moving in the darkness, followed by more gunfire. Calloway felt the ping of bullets hitting the big black car parked behind him. He pulled Anita tighter beneath him. There was a fresh blast of gunfire, then a moan, nearer now. Calloway knew without looking that it was Guillermo. No one else was there, so close to him.

"Last chance!" the police voice called. "Surrender or die!"

The answer came in gun blasts. Feet pounded, close to Calloway. He looked up to see the Security officer Cardoso come bounding over a wide gravestone, gun barrel aflame. Across from him there were more gunshots, the cry of someone struck by bullets, and the sound of several men running. A voice said, "*¡Por una Cuba libre!*" Cardoso's gun blared. Other guns answered. A bullet blew the other headlight to darkness. La Milagrosa disappeared and then was illuminated again by muzzle flashes.

Calloway knew they were going to be killed. They were caught in the cross fire between the police and the kidnappers. Bullets whizzed and whirred. The air was full of lead. He pulled Anita close to him and said, "We have to move. I will count to three, and we will run toward the gate where we came in. Are you ready?"

Anita nodded.

"Okay. One. Two. Three!"

Cardoso saw them and shouted, "Stop!" But they were up, and moving. Calloway and the girl got six feet from the car before a new blast of gunfire took them down. Cardoso cursed and began blasting at the place where the gunfire was coming from. He heard the sound of a bottle breaking. The air filled with the smell of rum. Someone moaned.

Anita felt Calloway crumble in the darkness. She fell with him and lay as close as possible to the ground. Then there were feet running around her. Hands grabbed her and lifted her. *The policeman will help me now,* she thought. But the hands went to her throat and covered her mouth, and she knew it was the kidnappers. She was yanked to her feet and dragged away from *La Milagrosa.* Someone—some man, or some two men—shoved her into a car. There were more blasts of gunfire. The car started and squealed away.

Then there was silence. Stillness. A car horn came from somewhere on the street. Then there was the sound of a radio playing an insistent mambo, from an apartment nearby. Car doors slammed far behind La Milagrosa, and tires crunched on asphalt.

Cardoso rose from behind a gravestone, pistol in hand, eyes mad. He said, "You fool! Why did you shoot?"

Ponce's high, shrill laugh answered him. "It was so dark, *mi socio.* And so noisy with guns."

"You have killed them all," Cardoso said. He stood over the bodies of two men who had been crouching behind the statue of La Milagrosa.

"Qué pena," Ponce said. "Who are they?"

Cardoso said, "One is Vicente Chibás. He was a student leader. He was connected to the safe house on Calle 15. The other is an old man with only one eye."

"Excellent," Ponce said. "They are no loss to anyone but their poor mothers."

Moving down the drive in the dark, Cardoso saw the rest of the wreckage.

"You have also shot the American, Calloway," he said. "He is dead. His driver is dead as well. And the money is gone. And the girl."

Ponce laughed. "That is too bad, *coñó*. About the money, I mean. And also I know you were interested in the girl."

"You know nothing. What are you doing here?"

"I was following the American."

"On whose orders?"

"Escalante's orders," Ponce said. "What else? Do you think you are the only policeman in Havana? You fool. I have been following Calloway for several days."

"You knew about the kidnapping, then?"

"No," Ponce said. "Only that the girl was gone. I was concentrating on the other gringo, the man she was sleeping with. We have nice pictures of them together."

"Excellent police work," Cardoso said. "You have ruined everything."

Ponce laughed at him. "And who is the other man there?" he said, pointing toward the black Security car. "Did I score another rebel victory for you?"

Cardoso turned to look. Bustillo lay beside the car, clutching the neck of the broken bottle of rum, bleeding heavily from bullet wounds to the chest and neck. He was dead.

"*¡Coñó!*" Cardoso said. "You have killed Officer Bustillo."

"*I* have killed him?" Ponce said. "Not I, amigo. From the look of his wounds, I can only guess a rebel bullet killed him. Or one from your weapon, perhaps. He appears to have been shot in the chest. I was behind him."

The cemetery bum had climbed up from the ground to inspect the statue and the grave. He looked up now, and said, "Señores! La Milagrosa is not harmed."

"*¡No jodas!*" Ponce said. "Can you be serious? It's another miracle!"

"Shut up, Ponce," Cardoso said. "If I have to look at you another minute . . ."

"What, *coñó?*" Ponce said, and laughed. "What will you do? What *could* you do? Nothing, my friend. But I will call an ambulance, to help you clean up your mess."

Driving out of Vedado, Alemán said over and over to himself, *"Ay, Dios mío. Ay, Dios mío."* He was not an especially religious man. But he could think of nothing else to say. He was in deep trouble. He had a kidnapped American woman in the backseat. Alemán had never been in on the plan, but he knew that the plan—whatever it was— was now ruined beyond recognition. Chibás was dead. Losada was dead. Only he and the boy Fermín remained, and neither of them had ever been told what was supposed to happen with the girl. Go to the Sierra? Return her to Havana? Alemán had never even been told what they were going to do with the money they were supposed to get in exchange for the girl.

He had no idea what to do now. Had any policemen been killed at the cemetery? Dead policemen were the worst thing. No: dead Security men would be worse than that.

He said again, *"¡Ay, Dios!"* A glance in the rearview mirror told him that the girl, at least, was not going to be any trouble. She sat like a block of stone, looking neither right nor left, not the slightest trace of emotion on her perfect brown face.

"Did you see?" Fermín asked him again. "We were shooting like *banditos!* Like the cowboys and Indians in the movies!"

"Ay, Dios mío," Alemán said.

"I remember one of the men from the torture chamber on La Rampa," Fermín said. "I hope he died like a dog, from the bullets from my gun."

They were nearly out of Vedado when Alemán noticed the bag on the floor.

Alemán said, "The money is here?"

Fermín lifted up a dark leather overnight bag. Inside were stacks of American dollars. Fermín said, "Of course! I took it during the shooting."

Alemán decided their only hope was the Sierra Maestra. If they could drive an hour, then steal a car, and continue into the mountains, they had a chance. It might take as much as an hour for the Security men to work out what had happened and mobilize. But it would take longer than that to get to the farmhouse. After that, Alemán and Fermín would have to be off the road in less than an hour.

Alemán said, "We will drive to Viñales."

Fermín looked up from the money. He said, "That's the wrong way."

"Yes," Alemán said. "That's why we will go there. The road from Havana to Cojímar, and from Cojímar to Matanzas, there will be roadblocks. We will never make it to the Sierra. We have killed a policeman. And a rich American. We are dead men ourselves. But perhaps if we try for Viñales, we can hide in the hills there. I know a farmer."

"You are a fool," Fermín said. "And a coward."

"It is true," Alemán said. "But I do not know what else to do."

"I will stay in Havana and fight," Fermín said.

"Of course," Alemán said. "You are young."

"I will take the money and buy weapons."

"No," Alemán said as quietly as possible. "For that you are *too* young. The money and the girl do not belong to us now. They will stay together, and I will watch over them."

"I say you are a fool," Fermín said.

"And you are right," Alemán replied. "Where do you want me to leave you?"

Delgado walked for hours through the deepening woods. The sun left the sky overhead, and the light grew dim. The trail continued but seemed to go nowhere. Delgado came upon no sign of habitation—and no water and no fruit.

Once the Ciboney and Taíno had walked these woods. Then the Europeans came. The indigenous people were enslaved or slaughtered. As a boy, Delgado had read of Hatuey, a Taíno chief who led a rebellion against the Spaniards during the time of Diego Velásquez and his conquest of Cuba. Hatuey and his men killed many Spaniards before they were subdued. Hatuey was burned at the stake after refusing to convert to Christianity, on the grounds that the salvation his captors promised him ensured only a future in their heaven full of Spaniards.

Now his country was dominated by a different sort of *conquistador*. Now the conquest was done with dollars. One American company, Delgado knew, owned 90 percent of Cuba's iron industry. The Americans owned one of the country's two railroads. The other was British-owned. The telephone service was run by IT&T. In Havana, Batista and his supporters were mostly white men of Spanish heritage. In the countryside, or working on the docks or in the mines or in the fields, were the brown and black men of Caribbean or African heritage. The terms of enslavement had changed. Nothing else had changed.

Delgado tramped on, hungry and thirsty. He had come upon a stream at midday and stopped to drink his fill. But that was hours ago, and he had no canteen to carry water in. Soon night would come. Were there animals in these woods? Perhaps. Nothing so dangerous as the soldiers he had left behind.

Later, when it was almost dark, Delgado caught the smell of a wood fire. He followed the trail a while longer. The smell of smoke grew stronger. A voice came to him through the trees. He slowed his pace and walked on. Soon he could smell meat cooking, too. And something else. Tobacco smoke? Someone was smoking. Delgado was cheered. Food and tobacco! And water, no doubt. And perhaps a bed?

"Stop there, señor," a voice behind him said.

Delgado stopped, and let his hands fall to his sides. He turned his head to look. Two teenage boys, both with cigarettes dangling from their lips, stood holding machetes in their hands.

Delgado said, "Good evening, señores. I am lost in these woods. I am without food or water. Take pity on me."

"Come," said one of the boys. "Our village is nearby. You can have water."

The boys took him down the trail to a collection of *bohío* huts with thatched roofs. The wood fire Delgado had smelled had a spit of goat on it. Delgado met the village elders. There were fifteen families collected here. One old man told Delgado the village had once been prosperous. The village families had worked a mill at a river in the next valley. But soldiers had come and mistaken the village for a rebel stronghold. They had destroyed the mill. Later, the rebels had come and given the village two cows and some sacks of rice and beans. But they had long ago eaten the rice and beans and had been forced to slaughter one of the cows.

"We thought perhaps, when you came, you were bringing more food from the rebels," the old man said. "We are sorry to see you carry nothing."

"I am sorry, too, to come and share the food of people who cannot feed themselves," Delgado said.

The old man gestured at the meat on the fire. "You are lucky to come today, señor," he said. "Two of the young men stole a goat earlier today. We will have meat tonight."

"You should have meat always," Delgado said. "Perhaps I can help you. I will be seeing the rebels soon. I will ask them to send you supplies, if you write down for me the name of your village."

The old man stared at the ground. "I am sorry, señor," he said. "There is no one in the village who can write."

"Then tell it to me," Delgado said gently. "I will never forget it."

It was almost dawn before Anita understood what had happened. She still did not feel it. Was this shock? She had heard about people being in shock. She had seen the victims of a car accident once, when she was waiting tables for her "uncle" in Shipton Wells. There was a woman with blood on her face. It was not her blood. Her man had been killed in the accident. The woman looked like a department store mannequin—smiling almost, but somehow expressionless and inhuman.

The little round Cuban driving the car had stopped for a few minutes, sometime in the darkness, and left Anita locked in and alone. Then he had returned, driving a different car. He had very gently escorted her from the old car to the new one, sat her in the backseat, and locked the doors again. Then he had driven the old car off the street, into some shadows, and returned to the new car. They had continued driving for some time, in the dark.

The sky was beginning to brighten now. Anita felt like that department store mannequin, or the woman wearing her husband's blood. She kept thinking, over and over, *Poor Nick.* He had been so determined to bring money to the rebels. And he had done so. Just not the way he planned. Nothing was what anyone planned. She had planned to run to Deacon, if she could be free of Calloway. Now she was free of Calloway. And Deacon, who might not even know she had been kidnapped, probably would not have her even if she could return to him. She was soiled now. Things were different now. Everything was wrong now. Would Calloway have found it ironic, and funny? He found odd things funny.

Then her sobs came suddenly and powerfully. Her shoulders shook. Her chest heaved and ached.

Alemán, driving west alone, didn't even glance back at her. Best to leave it. Best to forget it. Best to drive on. He had gotten past the turnings for Las Terrazas and Soroa. If he could continue unseen past San Cristóbal, he could turn into the mountains. It was not far now. The sun would be up soon. He would be in the hills. He and the girl would be safe. Let her cry. She would be safe now. He would take care of her.

For the newspapers, it was a sensation. They had a rich dead American—a handsome Yankee millionaire, shot dead at midnight in Havana's most famous cemetery, at the feet of the most famous dead woman in Cuban history. Calloway, dead at the feet of La Milagrosa. Beside him lay his loyal Cuban chauffeur. Behind them was their bullet-riddled automobile, as long and black as a hearse.

The story improved with every detail. Headlines in *El Tiempo, La Prensa,* and even *Bohemia* screamed scandal. Calloway, the millionaire industrialist and international playboy, had come to the Cementerio de Colón at midnight to pay a million-dollar ransom for his girlfriend, an exotic mulatto from Las Vegas. The kidnappers had tricked Calloway and his chauffeur. They had escaped, after a fierce gun battle with police, with the girl and the money. Calloway and his chauffeur and two of the kidnappers had died on the cemetery streets. Police had no leads on the whereabouts of the mulatto beauty or the missing million dollars. The famous statue of La Milagrosa was, miraculously, unharmed.

Reporters for United Press International, the Associated Press, and *The New York Times* peppered Escalante's office, demanding details and explanations. Escalante had them all turned away. One reporter insinuated himself into the office of William Dickens, the assistant U.S. ambassador to Cuba. He returned with some boilerplate comment about the safety of U.S. citizens abroad and American confidence that the perpetrators of this heinous act would be brought to justice by the Cuban authorities. The reporter had to look up the word *heinous* and then changed it to *cowardly* because it read better. A Cuban stringer for the AP managed to get a lead on the dead chauffeur. He interviewed the chauffeur's widow, one Alicia Sánchez, at length. Unfortunately, she knew even less than the police. But she did provide some background on the kidnapped mulatto girl—Las Vegas, big money, Hollywood, the movies, and now death in Havana. It was dime-store-novel stuff, but the AP desk made good use of it.

Cardoso, sitting in his office the following afternoon, drinking *café con leche* and wishing it were rum, felt chilled by the heat around the story. The facts were all wrong, of course, and they kept getting more so. Calloway got richer and more handsome with every retelling, and the girl younger and more beautiful. The ransom money started at one million and rose to two. The death toll started at four and rose to ten.

Most of the papers mentioned the death of Bustillo. One of them noted that he was a nephew of the president.

That would mean trouble. Escalante had been a good cop, and he had been a cop almost longer than Batista had been his president. But he was ambitious as well. Nothing good could come from a nephew of the president being killed on his command. Someone would have to swing for that. And since Ponce had been conducting surveillance on Calloway, on Escalante's orders . . .

Coñó, Cardoso thought. *This is very bad for me.*

The *café con leche* brought beads of sweat to Cardoso's forehead. It was stinking hot, this afternoon. The air hung in sheets of humidity. There was the promise of rain. Until it came, the air was almost too thick to breathe. Cardoso put his feet on the floor and his hands on his knees, got up, and walked stiffly down the hall. He found one of the station house boys and flipped him a coin. He said, "Get me a pack of cigarettes and hurry back here." The boy ran off, shoeless, immune to the sodden afternoon air.

Cardoso would go see Scarfioti tonight. He would attempt to get him to provide an introduction to his friend the mobster, the one Cardoso had heard was in town legging for Lansky. There were rumors of a new syndicate of casinos. Ownership or control of the Presidente, Miramar, and Sunset was shifting. That meant money coming in and changing hands. Calloway was connected in some way. It was probably not any way that tied his girlfriend to the kidnappers, but Cardoso would not know that until he had snooped around a bit. And he probably wouldn't know much then, either. He would be snooping far above his station, in places that probably didn't welcome much snooping from anyone—especially a mid-level lieutenant with Cuban Security. Could he count on Escalante's backing? No. He could not count on anyone for anything, except trouble.

Cardoso tipped the boy again when he returned, and sat in his office, smoking, until the sky outside darkened. The temperature did not fall. It seemed to rise as the night descended. Cardoso snapped off the light on his desk and sat in the shadows. *Home,* he thought, *and a shower and a shave, and a clean suit and tie, and maybe a shoeshine.* Then he would make the rounds until he found Scarfioti or Lansky's legman. What would he ask them? He would have to decide that between now and then.

On the way out of the station, Cardoso stopped beside a policeman he did not know, who was dozing over the afternoon papers. There was a photograph of Calloway and a headline full of scandal. The policeman looked up and said, "*Coñó.* What a story."

"Almost unbelievable," Cardoso said. "I wish I had been there. Who is watching the chauffeur's girlfriend?"

"The newspaper says 'wife,' " the policeman said.

"Girlfriend, I think. Who's on it?"

"Colón."

"At the Calle San Lázaro apartment?"

"She lives in the basement. With the chauffeur."

"See that Colón stays on top of that," Cardoso said. "It may be the only place we will see any movement."

"*El capitán* says we should forget it."

"He's the boss," Cardoso said. "But we're not going to."

An hour later, scraping shaving soap from his chin, Cardoso realized that *el capitán* Escalante was probably right. There was nothing useful to learn in this investigation. And there would be no one to arrest or prosecute, anyway. The main perpetrator, Vicente Chibás, was dead. Whoever had paid him to kidnap the girl was gone. There was no point in attempting to show that Cardoso's own colleague, Lieutenant Ponce, had probably fired the bullets that killed Calloway and his chauffeur.

But there was still the question of the missing money. And there was still the question of the girl. Toweling off, laying out his clothes, feeling worn and tired but strangely aroused, Cardoso wondered: *If she were ugly or old, would I care? Would I continue?*

He got no answer. Instead, he got dressed, slung a pistol into a shoulder holster hidden under his arm, and went out. He would go to Old Havana, to El Floridita and the Monserrate and La Bodeguita and Café de Paris and Hotel Inglaterra. He would find the right person and ask the right question and get the right answer. And hope that the girl was still beautiful, and alive, when he found her.

María Fuentes had gotten as far as Camagüey. It had taken two and a half days of travel. The bus had been stopped frequently by roadblocks and breakdowns. A flat tire, in the hills outside Jatinbonico, had taken eight hours to repair. She had husbanded her money, buying food only when she was faint with hunger, sleeping one night on the bus rather than waste money on a hotel room. She needed a bath and a bed, but she was determined to be frugal.

Coming into Camagüey, she remembered reading about the town heroine. She was Ana Betancourt, who had led military assaults against the Spanish in the 1870s, in the first war of independence. She had been instrumental in bringing emancipation of her country-women. Would there be a statue of her? María imagined not.

When the bus stopped, heaving with exhaustion under the trees that lined Parque Ignacio Agramonte, María took her suitcase and began to walk across the plaza. There would be cheap hotels, she knew, near the rail station. A woman selling lemonade from a stall directed her that way.

"Go toward *Nuestra Señora de la Candelaría* and continue past *Nuestra Señora de la Soledad*," she said. "The station is down that road."

It was twenty minutes' walking. María was light-headed before she was halfway there. She stopped at *Nuestra Señora de la Soledad*, an enormous church built long before the war for independence. María crossed herself and sat in a rear pew, breathing in the dusty, cool air. When she felt well again, she returned to the street and walked to the station.

The hotel was called El Agramonte, after another hero of the town. María paid for her room in advance. There was a day-old newspaper on the counter. María took it to her room and lay on the bed, reading the headlines.

Security forces and government troops had been routed at Las Tunas, Bayamo, and points in between. The far end of the island, from Baracoa to Santiago de Cuba and as far west as some parts of Camagüey Province, was in rebel hands. This told María that she was close—close enough, perhaps, to stop riding the bus.

The following morning María went to a workingman's café near the station. She sat and ordered a *café* and *pan con mantequilla*. Unmolested, she drank her coffee and watched the men come and go. Many of them were carrying metal lunch pails. They would be factory workers. Others had blackened hands and faces. *Dockworkers, unloading coal,* María thought. *Or blacksmiths, maybe.* Still others wore cheap suits and shiny suits. They might be salesmen. *So many jobs for men,* María thought. *So few jobs for women.* The only other females in the room, María saw, were domestics, grabbing a quick bite before going off to clean the house of someone wealthier.

When she was restored, María went to the center of town, walking back the way she had come the night before. The morning air was fresh. The hills were green. She could understand why the Spanish, led by Velásquez, had established a city here. Back at Parque Ignacio Agramonte, María sat on a bench and began to scan the passing men and women.

It wasn't long before she saw what she wanted. A group of students had come from their university and gathered in a grassy area. There were five men and four women. None of them was younger than María, probably, but they all looked like children. They were the children of wealth and privilege. As were their leaders: Fidel Castro himself was the son of a rich sugar plantation owner in Santiago, and he had married a woman whose family's money and political connections earned them cabinet posts in the Batista government. Revolutions were not begun by poor people, María knew. Poor people are too hungry to demand justice.

María Fuentes approached the group cautiously. "Excuse me," she said to one of the women, and knelt beside her in the grass. She was suddenly aware of her cheap cotton dress, and how her hair must look, and what a long time it had been since she put on proper makeup.

The girl looked at her, not alarmed but wary.

"I have come from Havana," María said. "My man was murdered by the police. He was suspected of helping the rebels. I have come to Camagüey to find the men he was helping. I need you to help me, please."

"But, help you . . . how?" the girl asked.

"The rebels are near," María said. "I need to know where they are."

"No one knows where they are," one of the girl's companions said stiffly. He was well groomed and well dressed, and carried himself with arrogance. He looked like a medical student or a young officer out of uniform. "We know nothing of rebels. You should go away now."

When she hesitated, the stiff young man said, "*Vámonos*. This woman is trouble." The young people rose and left. María, alone again, looked around the park. There were no other young people, no other people at all who looked likely to help a city woman searching for revolutionaries.

What a fool I have been, María thought. *So naive! Perhaps I should just get a taxi. "Take me to the revolution, señor, and keep the change!" What a fool.*

María calculated. She probably had enough money for the bus back to Havana. She would return to her job. She would listen for the voices of revolution. Someday, perhaps, she would be able to be of some help. For now, she was useless. Worse than useless. Worse than the children of privilege who laughed at her in the park. At least they would make good targets for revolutionaries when the shooting started.

Leaving the park, María heard amplified voices—urgent, over-heated, metallic voices coming from a street off the plaza. María followed the sound. Soon the voices had words.

"After seventy-six days of unceasing fighting, the rebel army has repulsed and virtually destroyed the cream of the forces of tyranny, bringing about one of the greatest disasters ever suffered by a modern army," the voice called. It was a rich, angry voice, filled with venom and pride. María recognized it at once. It was the voice of Fidel Castro. "I am speaking to the people today, and to the forces of tyranny. These are the conditions for peace. First, the dictator must be arrested and brought to justice. So must those responsible for having upheld the tyranny. . . ."

María walked toward the thundering voice. As she walked, the voice grew fainter, then stronger, then fainter again. María followed a side street into another plaza, close to where the night before she had passed the church called *Nuestra Señora de la Candelaría*. In the center of the plaza now, María saw a small black sedan with a broadcasting megaphone attached to its roof. The car sat empty. Men and women in the plaza stared at it, as if it were about to perform a feat of magic.

"The rebel columns are prepared to advance," the voice said, gaining strength and volume now. "The civilian population must be prepared to aid the combatants. They must be ready to endure the privations of war. May the fortitude demonstrated by the people of the Sierra Maestra—where even the children help our troops—arouse the emulation of the people of all Cuba. There is revolution because there is tyranny! There is revolution because there is injustice. There is and there will be revolution while a single shadow menaces our rights and our liberty!"

The air crackled with energy. But the voice was gone. The people standing in the plaza remained immobile, staring at the little black car. Then a truck of soldiers shrieked into the plaza. The uniformed men stumbled out, rifles ready, trained on the black sedan. María moved slowly off the plaza, sinking into the shade of the great cathedral.

Stepping onto a side street, María was met by the arrogant medical student from the park. He smiled now. He said, "Hello again, comrade. Fidel has spoken! I know you wish to see the guerrillas. We will go together. I leave for the Sierra Maestra tonight."

Morning came, dragging Sloan with it. It was noon before he opened his eyes, and another hour at least before he slid out of the bed. His head felt cracked, pierced by knitting needles, and he was dizzy. His first cigarette didn't help. His first beer did. He would have chased that with a whiskey, but there was none in the house. He chased it instead with a second beer, and a second smoke. The pain began to subside.

He remembered a lot of what had happened the night before, but not enough: his horn was missing, he saw, and he didn't know where he had left it. He imagined it might have been several places. He remembered being in several places. He remembered playing in several places. If he could remember the last place he'd played in, he had a good shot at finding the horn. But he had no shot, it seemed, at remembering what the last place was. He didn't remember getting home. So he didn't remember how he got home. So he didn't remember where he'd been right before he left for home.

Mo. He had been with Mo. Mo had told him about Anita. There

had been a dark-skinned Cuban girl with Mo. They were in a place with a low bandstand and walls of blue—El Cruz Azul.

Now he remembered. The crowd below his window. A guy named Carlos. There was always a guy named Carlos. Like in the States— there was always a guy named Steve in any crowd, at least one guy named Steve. Sloan lit another cigarette. The beer had settled his stomach and was going boozy in his head. The relief was enormous. So enormous that he temporarily forgot all about how bad he had felt upon waking, and all about that brief idea he'd had about not drinking anymore. There was a guy named Carlos. And a dark-skinned girl. Who did not remind him all that much of Anita. Who, according to Mo, had been kidnapped.

Sloan went for another beer and found there was none. The sun was beginning to stab shafts of light into the room, through the shutters overlooking the plaza. Sloan thought that with a shower and a shave and a pair of sunglasses, he might make it to the street. From there he could get to the corner café, hurl down a cup of mud, and begin to get his lid screwed back on. Then maybe he could get his horn back.

The street was busy and burning hot. Sloan had found a pair of thick, dark shades and had stuck a hat on his head as well. Still the light was awful. He lit a cigarette with shaking hands and wobbled down the block on his long, uncertain legs.

The coffee worked. He had another, and a coffin nail with it. The ground stopped pulsing. He'd have to watch the *mojitos*. Something about the sugar, he imagined. Or something about the lime juice and the sugar. Or something about the fact that he'd drunk about twenty of them. Either way, worth watching. He did not want to feel the way he felt this morning more than was entirely necessary.

His legs secure under him again, his head fixed on El Cruz Azul, Sloan was just out the door. The afternoon papers were up. Newspaper boys, some of them not even in their teens, spilled down the street, screaming headlines. A boy half Sloan's size said, *"Un Americano muerto en el cementerio de Colón!"* Sloan didn't know what that meant, exactly, but he gave the kid a coin and took the paper.

It was Calloway. The subhead and the caption said so. The picture itself said so. Sloan, now that he saw it, knew the man's face from the magazines. He was square-jawed and silver-haired and dead, lying facedown in a dark pool of blood. Near him was another man, Sloan guessed a Cuban, in front of a bullet-riddled automobile. Behind them rose a statue of a woman cradling a child and reaching in supplication to heaven.

The body of the story told Sloan the rest. Even with his spotty Spanish, he could string the big bits together. Shoot-out. Calloway and chauffeur dead. Rebels, two or more of them, also dead. Also two policemen. A word that Sloan did not know—*secuestrada*—referred to an American woman, a young woman. It looked like "sequestered." Under arrest, then? No. Because she was *secuestrada por los rebeldes,* which seemed to say "sequestered by the rebels."

Sloan sat down hard on the curb. Kidnapped, then. By the rebels. That explained the words *dólares* and *millones* that cropped up in the story. The ransom. Paid by Calloway, who was then gunned down, for Anita, who then was taken into the Sierra Maestra.

Sloan folded the newspaper lengthwise and stuck it inside his jacket. He lit a cigarette. He got to his feet unsteadily and began walking . . . where? He'd best find his horn first. Then he'd find Mo. He'd get Mo to lend him a few bucks. He'd find out where the Sierra Maestra was. And he would go there and bring back his woman. She was his woman now. She had to be. Calloway was gone. Who else's woman could she be?

6

Carlos Delgado had been in the Sierra Maestra for
two days before he was summoned to see Fidel. He had been given
his own tent. He had been given meals. He had embraced long-lost
comrades. Many he had not seen in years, since the training camps he
and the others had used years before, in the mountains to the east,
and in Mexico when they were all exiled. In those days they had beds
of hard ground, and for food only what could be begged or stolen
from the campesinos.

But he had not been summoned to see Fidel. He knew that Che
was busy conducting raids in Las Villas. He knew that Raúl was in
Oriente somewhere, training troops. Camilo Cienfuegoes was com-
manding battalions in the west. Delgado thought Fidel was here, in
the Sierra Maestra compound. On the second day there, he had asked
a young soldier whether he had seen the bearded, black-spectacled
leader.

"No, señor," the soldier said. "But I believe he exists."

Delgado tried to enjoy the relative luxury of the camp. It was like staying at the Hotel Nacional, after the rough time in exile. There were canvas-sided cabins with wooden floors for almost all the soldiers. There were proper latrines. There was a medical tent, as well as a communications tent and a place where food was served. There was running water. Wires strung between structures carried electricity.

The men were more civilized, too. They were trained soldiers now—guerrillas, to be sure, but trained. It showed in their bearing and carriage. In the beginning only the very dedicated joined the cause. Now it was a true people's army.

Nilsa Fernandez was unrecognizable to him at first. She had come to his tent shortly after his arrival. She shook his hand and said, "Welcome home, comrade. It is good to have you with us again."

Delgado remembered a moonfaced student, the Nilsa who had gotten involved with the revolution and become part of the University of Havana movement and later became a key member of the Calle 15 cell. She was as round as she was tall then, doughy, self-effacing, bright-eyed, and bubbly.

This was not the same young woman. This woman was lean and muscular, abbreviated in her movements, cautious about the eyes, and scarred badly on her face. There were nicks and cuts across one cheekbone. A gouge of flesh had been torn, or burned, from her jawline to her ear. The scar tissue made it appear that she was sneering.

But she was not. She was smiling. She said, "I know it is not easy to recognize me. I have changed. I have been changed. My own mother wouldn't know me."

Delgado took her in his arms and said, "I know your bright eyes, Nilsa. But now they are the eyes of a woman. Before, you were only a girl. Now you are a hero of the revolution."

"Come now and see Fidel," Nilsa said. "He is returning to Santiago tonight and is very distracted, but he wants to see you."

They went. Fidel was distracted. He served coffee and welcomed Delgado like a brother—a respected elder brother. He thanked him, in oratorical tones, for the sacrifice he had made, the risks he had taken bringing the arms and money in from Mexico. But then he was off, haranguing against Batista's close ties to the Americans, with the Mafia, with big business.

"The Americans have promised to sell no more weapons to the dictator Batista," he said. "Instead, they sell the weapons to Trujillo of the Dominican Republic and Somoza of Nicaragua, and *they* sell them to Batista. But why shouldn't the *people* give one another a hand? A few days ago we received weapons purchased by our friends in Costa Rica. In Cuba we are fighting a battle for the democratic ideal of the entire continent."

Delgado laughed at his old friend and said, "Nothing has changed, then. We are still winning the losing battle. We have no arms, no men, no supplies, and no chance of victory—and still we are victorious. What a campaign you have led!"

"Against the odds. And I need a dentist," Fidel said. "I cannot think in peace. Before, when there was no food, my teeth were good. Now we have food, and I cannot eat. Later, there will be no food again. Perhaps my teeth will be better then."

"I don't believe you," Delgado said. "You're the picture of health. You look like a boy—a boy with a cigar and a beard, but a boy just the same."

"I turned thirty-one, you know. When I was twenty-nine, I never expected to see thirty. Now, I don't know what to expect."

"You have become your people's leader. You must live long. And the fatigues suit you."

"Today I put on this new uniform that was sent to me," Fidel said. "I am going to begin the final campaign in it. We are getting ready for the long struggle. The dictatorship will use its greatest strength to beat us back. And we are oiling our weapons."

"I am happy to join you," Delgado said.

"I am happy you are here," Fidel answered. "And I must leave you."

Carlos Delgado had not seen Fidel since then. Reports came, daily, of the campaigns waged by Che, Cienfuegos, and Raúl. Fidel appeared and disappeared, in bits of gossip and pieces of real news, everywhere in Oriente Province. Santiago was secure. Bayamo was secure. There were new victories north of Guantánamo. The news from Havana was all good. After the devastating arrests on Calle

15, cells had reorganized. The year had already seen raids on police barracks, sabotage of factories and electric and gas works, the seizure of arms, and successful attacks on government offices. A night of anti-Batista rioting, organized by the student factions, had left nearly a hundred dead or seriously injured. Many of them were policemen, but most were students. This was a terrible blow to the future of Cuba, but it was also a public relations coup for the revolution: Batista's men were now murdering the nation's young people.

As the weeks passed, Delgado found himself in the unaccustomed position of senior officer. Héctor Bolinas, who was nominally in charge of the rebel village, often came to him with questions. There were issues of protocol, of justice, of military logic. Delgado was ill equipped to answer most of them. Instead of offering advice, he would ask the mulelike, lumbering Bolinas what he thought. Bolinas would approach the problem anew, and out loud, and usually work himself forward to the most sensible conclusion. In each case, he thought Delgado had given him brilliant guidance. Delgado was only letting him think for himself.

He came one afternoon with a puzzle. Nilsa Fernández had been put in charge of two young women. One of them had been the girlfriend of a man the police had detained in Cojímar. The young man had been devastated by the interrogation. He'd been beaten and tortured and threatened. He had left the movement entirely and abandoned his woman. Now she had caught his revolutionary fervor.

"And the other?" Delgado asked.

"She is the woman of the American millionaire who was murdered at La Milagrosa's gravesite," Bolinas said. "The men who kidnapped her brought her here—with the ransom money."

"These are two different situations," Delgado said cautiously. "What do you suppose Fidel would do?"

Bolinas chewed at a hangnail for a few minutes. He said, "The girlfriend of the man interrogated at Cojímar is a true convert. Her heart was broken by the brutality of the police. She was forced by the government into becoming a revolutionary. I think she should be allowed to train with the others and take up arms as soon as she is ready."

"Excellent," Delgado said, quite sure this was the correct answer. "And the other?"

"She is more difficult," Bolinas said. "She is very beautiful, and she is an American, and she did not come to us willingly. But we do not know how to take her back to Havana without endangering ourselves."

"Has she demanded to be returned?"

"No," Bolinas said. "She has hardly spoken."

"Is there any urgency? Must she be returned at once?"

"None," Bolinas said. "So, perhaps it is best to wait. Perhaps she will tell us what she wants, and we will be able to help her."

"These are excellent solutions," Delgado told him.

"You are wise," Bolinas said. "I wish I had your wisdom."

"You are wiser than you think," Delgado said. "A wise man seeks counsel. Only a fool thinks he can decide such things on his own."

But even with the promise of counsel, Bolinas entirely abandoned responsibility for some matters. There was today's exercise, for example. A journalist and photographer for *Life* magazine were being escorted into the mountains by a squad of Fidel's men. They would be brought into the camp for a series of pictures and interviews. Fidel and his information officers believed that the journalist was on the right side of the cause and that sympathetic photos and interviews would be useful in future fund-raising efforts in the United States. Delgado had been asked to host.

It was an easy assignment. The journalist was Ernest Claymore, a florid, gin-soaked veteran of the field. He understood war, having covered the bloody battles for independence in Algeria and Indochina. He understood revolution. He and his photographer rolled into camp—Fidel's men carrying most of their gear—looking as if the walk into the mountains had worn them down badly. But Claymore greeted Carlos Delgado with deference.

He said, "Señor Delgado, you are kind to welcome us to your camp. But what is your rank? I do not know how to address you."

"You must call me Carlos, as everyone else does. I have no rank."

"No rank! A leader in the field with no rank?"

"I was away when the current military architecture was designed," Delgado said. "They ran out of ranks before my return."

"Fantastic!" Claymore said. "Then join me in a drink, Carlos."

The American had done difficult reporting in difficult circumstances, making contacts in Havana without any assistance from the rebels. He had written most of his story, in his mind at least, before he even arrived in the mountains. For the next two days, Claymore drank and ate and joked with the men, asking them questions about their hometowns, their ambitions and post-revolution plans, and their daily life. To Delgado's relief, the journalist stayed entirely off politics. If there were communists here, he didn't seem interested— unusual in an American reporter, for most of them seemed obsessed with the question of political affiliation. Delgado had explained to several writers that the revolution was the people's war against tyranny, not a political movement. Few had understood. Few had printed it. But Claymore understood. He told Delgado he was in the mountains for "color" and "background."

Slurping a gin and tonic—one of Claymore's many suitcases seemed to contain nothing but bottles of one or the other—the journalist said, "This is going to be like what Ernie Pyle did for the dog-faces in World War Two. Show 'em the common man, the average Joe, making the sacrifice for something bigger. I talked to a boy today, couldn't have been more than eighteen, who's lost six of his brothers in this thing. And his old man!"

"That's Abelardo Sánchez," Delgado said. "He's a good boy."

"He's a hero. He told me that he was afraid to fight, that he felt like a coward when the battles begin."

"He is an interesting case," Delgado said. "During his first fight, he became frightened. He dropped his rifle and ran. His commander in the field that day was Che."

"And he wasn't shot for desertion?"

"Some men would have been," Delgado said. "Perhaps Che was saving bullets. Or he saw a better man behind the coward. But here is what happened. Abelardo came to him in tears. Che told him he was finished as a soldier. The boy begged. Che made him a deal. He would allow him to rejoin his brothers in arms only if he was willing to fight unarmed until he could seize a rifle from the enemy. And so he did. There was a skirmish that day, and Abelardo went into a camp carrying only a knife. He returned with a Garand rifle and several boxes of bullets."

Claymore said, "He's a hero. I've known hundreds of soldiers. I was in Italy in 'forty-three and 'forty-four. Only the idiots and the psychopaths are not afraid. Tomorrow we'll take our pictures. Then we'll get out of here."

"You honor us with such a long stay," Delgado said.

"Nonsense," the red-faced reporter said. "I love it here. Clean air, lots of sun, good chow. It's safe, too. I thought I was gonna get my nuts shot off in Havana."

"You were there for the insurrection."

"Insurrection, my eye! It was mayhem. No one in charge."

"It was the voice of the people. An anguished people."

"The voice of the people is always the voice of insanity. That is where the strong men come from. Hitler. Stalin. Mussolini. Franco. They hear the insane voice of the people and speak back to it in its own language. Beware the strong man, Carlos. Don't let your Fidel turn into Stalin."

"Fidel is not a strong man. He is just a man."

"Sure," Claymore said. "And how long will his people accept that?"

The following day was given over to photographs. Claymore's partner was a thin, mousy fellow with thick eyeglasses. He shot pictures here and there in the camp, staging shots of the men in casual poses—with their rifles, with their books, with their plates of dinner. Delgado was bullied into sitting in.

"That's the cover," Claymore said. Delgado was standing with a circle of men and women around him, his pin-weave Panama low over his eyes. Nilsa was nearby, standing with two other rebel women.

Claymore said, "Fantastic! Look at that beauty."

"The mulatto," the photographer said. "Some dish."

"Make sure she's in the shot."

Delgado saw them off the following morning. Claymore shook his hand vigorously and said, "What is it you people say? About the inevitability of victory?"

"¡Venceremos! We will win."

"The people united can never be defeated?"

"That's correct," Delgado told him.

"I hope you're right," Claymore said. "I'm writing this as if you were. Don't make me look like a fool."

Later, Delgado said to Bolinas, "I want to meet the American girl, the woman of the dead American. Bring her to me in an hour."

Bolinas, his eyes hardening slightly, said, "Of course."

She remembered him from that day on the road. It was the hat. Or it was the hat and the beard and mustache and the dark, flashing eyes. She was in the car with Guillermo and Alicia, going to . . . Varadero? Yes. The day she was refused service in that restaurant. He had been standing beside the road. He had raised his hat and smiled.

Now he was here, and she was here as a captive, or a sort of captive, of the rebel army he commanded. How strange, she thought. How unlikely. A man beside the road and a passing automobile, and now this.

She was escorted to his tent by a pair of young women. One had terrible scars on her face. The other was pretty, but cold and reserved. Her name was María—or so the woman with the scars called her. The woman with the scars said to Anita, "You will come with us now."

Anita rose from the place she had been sitting. Outside her tent sat Alemán, the man who had brought her to the mountains. The look on his face made her shudder. He had been staring at her with that face for weeks.

The rebel leader was waiting for her at a camp table behind his tent. She knew him at once. He rose and introduced himself, formally and in English, as Carlos Delgado. He introduced the two women as his "comrades," Nilsa and María Fuentes. Then the two women left. Delgado called out, "¡Felipe! Dos cafés, por favor, con azucar."

Then he said to Anita, "How do you take your coffee?"

"With cream," she said, surprised at the steadiness of her own voice. She had not spoken, to anyone, in more than two weeks.

"*Uno con leche, Felipe.*" Delgado smiled and removed his hat. He said, "I hope you are not too uncomfortable here?"

"No. I am comfortable," Anita said slowly.

"Is there anything you need that I can bring to you?"

"Other than my freedom?"

"Yes," Delgado said. "Other than that."

"No," Anita said. "There is nothing."

"Ah," Delgado said. "Here is the coffee."

Over his cup, Delgado said, "I am sorry that you are here, under these circumstances. You must know that the men who took you from your apartment were not part of the revolution. They were renegades, acting out of greed. The leader was killed at the cemetery. The others are dead also, or will be punished."

Anita said, "And the others? Did the American and his driver die?"

"Yes," Delgado said. "They died at once, at the cemetery, before you were even taken away. Did you not know?"

"I knew. But I hoped . . ."

When Anita did not continue, Delgado said, "Soon we will be able to return you to Havana, along with the money your man tried to pay for your release. For now, that is not possible. The roads are dangerous. Anyone trying to escort you to Havana would be ambushed and killed. It is very possible that you would be killed also. For now, you must stay here with us."

Anita still did not answer. There was nothing to say. She had lost the habit of conversation over the weeks, with no one to talk to. Now there was someone to talk to, but nothing to say.

Delgado said, "As you see, we have many women here living with us. Women like Nilsa, and María Fuentes. Nilsa was very active in the movement in Havana, before she was injured. María Fuentes's man was murdered by the police. She was brought here by a medical student from Camagüey, after setting out from Havana alone, traveling by bus, in search of the movement here in the Sierra Maestra. They are both very much part of this revolution. Perhaps there is a place for you here also."

Anita looked at him but did not answer.

He said, "You must do something, anyway, to pass the time. Do you cook or sew?"

"No."

"Do you have medical training?"

"No."

"Can you handle a rifle?"

"No."

Delgado smiled. "Then you would not be very useful as a revolutionary. All the women here, just like all the men, have some sort of a job," he said. "Without that . . . Some of the men might imagine another use for you, I'm afraid."

"The man who has been watching me, Alemán, he is one of those."

"I will see that he stays away from you, then," Delgado said. "The men are only human, after all. Many of them have been in the mountains for months. And you are very beautiful. But there is no call for you to be in jeopardy. We have put you in jeopardy already, when we should not have done so. For that, I am very sorry."

It was the first kindness Anita had experienced in weeks. She fought back tears and failed, and began to sob. Her shoulders shook and her chest heaved. Delgado began to reach for her, as he would reach for a suffering child or any other suffering woman. Then he stopped, rose to his feet, and walked to the front of his tent. Nilsa and María Fuentes were there. He said, "She is crying. Comfort her. And find her some sort of job, in the kitchen."

Delgado walked down the hill to the tent where Alemán had been waiting. Delgado was distressed by the American woman's complaints, but this was not a bad man. A bad man would have raped the girl, abandoned her, and taken the $100,000 in ransom money and run. Perhaps this Alemán thought of these things—but Delgado would not condemn a man for what he thought. Delgado removed his hat and said, "Get to your feet, señor. You are relieved of duty."

"¡Mi capitán! Who will watch the American girl?"

"Not you. Report at once to Bolinas. Tell him I sent you. Tell him you are to be assigned to a forward position. Can you operate a grenade launcher?"

Alemán shuddered visibly. He said, "No, señor! I am not a soldier."

"You are a soldier now," Delgado said. "You must learn to fight. Go!"

It was a long struggle ahead, Delgado thought as he walked slowly back up to his tent. First, liberate the men from the tyrants. Then, liberate the women from the men, lest the men become tyrants themselves. One farmhouse at a time. One family at a time. One tyrant at a time. A free Cuba for free Cubans. And then what? Overthrowing a government was not the same thing as operating a government. Perhaps he would not survive long enough to find out whether the rebels were up to that challenge. Perhaps that would be best. Delgado was tired. He put his straw hat back on his head and forced a smile onto his face. Enough of grim leaders.

A messenger arrived about noon and knocked at the door until Mo answered it. The boy bore a small white envelope on a small silver tray. Mo took the envelope and gave the kid a buck, then sat down to read the bad news.

It wasn't so bad. But it was from Lansky. It read, "Call me at once," and was signed, "Eleanor." One of Meyer's little jokes. Mo didn't get it. He didn't get half of what Meyer said. Mo picked up the phone and told room service to bring him a pot of coffee. He took a hot shower and got dressed. An hour later he was on the horn again, asking for a number in Miami.

"Talk to me about the American," Meyer's voice croaked.

"Which one?"

"You know which one."

"Okay," Mo said. "There isn't much to tell. Someone snatched his girl. He tried to get her back. Something went wrong. He got shot. Is that what you mean?"

"No," Meyer said. "Who cares about that crap? I want to know about his business interests and how they are affected, and how that affects you."

"It doesn't," Mo said. "He was helping. We hadn't made any deals."

"Is everything in place, for your new . . . nightclubs?"

Mo smiled. So cautious, even this late in the game. Mo said, "Everything is fixed. We open in a couple of weeks. Three joints."

"You'll need a partner. Someone strong. I'd like to help."

Mo smiled again. So greedy, too, even this late in the game. He said, "I welcome your help and your partnership. Why didn't you offer it earlier?"

"I have a history with the American. Not a good history. We had some trouble in the desert. There was bad blood. Now, though . . . Do we understand each other?"

"Perfectly," Mo said. "I will be in Miami soon. May I stop and see you then?"

"I'll send a car to the airport."

Then he was gone. Mo sat like a fool with the telephone in his hand, saying, "Thank you. I think we are going to do quite a good business—" before he realized he was talking to himself. Just to be safe, he said, "Good-bye for now, then," and hung up.

What a life! Men died and were buried, hearts were broken, families were ruined, history was altered . . . and business went on as usual. The machinery ran on its own. The hotels and the nightclubs, the hookers and the dope racket, the numbers runners and the bookies and the ponies and the unions, all of it rushed forward into its future, crushing under itself all those who fell and those who tried to stop it and even those who tried to run away from it.

Mo had been lucky. He hadn't exactly planned it this way, but he had been left more or less alone. He had the good fortune of never having had tremendous good fortune. The hotels were successful, but not ruinously so. He shot the swaggo from the Starburst and the Thunderbird to the men in Chicago and Cleveland. He took the hit on the Ivory Coast on his own. He never asked anyone to clean up his mess or make good on his losses. He left the desert, came to Havana, and made his deals—with Meyer's blessing but without his help. Now, with Calloway gone and Meyer nosing back in, Mo could only hope he had the same kind of success with the three new clubs.

Money, but not big money. Money was good. Big money was deadly.

After lunch Mo had the hotel get him a car and driver—if he was now going to be Meyer's guy, he decided he might as well take advantage of Meyer's privileges—and went into Havana. He had meetings at two of the three new locations. He also wanted to speak with Deacon again. With Calloway gone, Mo felt strangely exposed. Calloway had set him up, and Mo had been promised the benefit of Calloway's connections. Now he had three businesses opening, and no connections. And no friends. Except Meyer's, which was the same as having none at all. With Meyer, you inherited as many enemies as friends—and the enemies were much deadlier than the friends were helpful. He could depend on Meyer only to rake a percentage from whatever he earned. He could not expect to use Meyer for anything heavy.

For that, he needed someone whose loyalties were certain. He needed to get Deacon on board. Or Sloan. Or whatever he was called. It was time to call in that favor.

The only thing that saved Cardoso from a visit to *Paraíso* was Escalante's cop instinct that Cardoso was telling the truth. The shoot-out at the cemetery and the death of the president's nephew were a terrible embarrassment to his department. Escalante was furious. But he was not suspicious. That saved Cardoso's life.

Leaving the station house in his street clothes, one cardboard box of personal belongings under his arm, Cardoso was relieved. If Escalante had suspected for a moment that the fiasco at the cemetery could be explained by Cardoso's involvement with the rebels, the Security officer's former colleagues would have had his eyeballs hanging from their sockets by dawn.

Instead, Escalante had dressed him down, railing at him for incompetence and idiocy, and fired him.

"You are finished, you shit," Escalante spat. "Not for treachery, not for corruption, but for stupidity. For allowing the nephew of the *presidente* to be killed. *¡El coño de tu madre!* This could end my career as a policeman."

"You have been a policeman a long time," Cardoso offered.

"Longer than *el Presidente* has been *presidente*," Escalante said. "I intend to outlast him, too. But not with assistance from you, *maricón*. You are finished. I should have expected nothing better from you. *'Tiene el negro,'* they told me. I didn't listen. You might as well be black as night."

Cardoso blanched. These were words that led to violence, and death. Cardoso would never have stood for them from a man in the street. He stood for them now.

He said nothing of Ponce—of his having shot Bustillo and murdered Calloway and the chauffeur. He said nothing of Ponce's earlier murder, and robbery, of the dead American movie star. It was not from any loyalty to Ponce, who was a wretched man and a crooked cop. Nor was it from any sense that cops don't rat on cops. Cardoso simply didn't see the point to it. When a man as angry as Escalante gets as angry as he was now, he must strike out and hurt someone. Cardoso was the only one there.

When he was finished railing, Escalante slumped in his seat, exhausted by his own rage, and said, "Out."

"I'm leaving," Cardoso said. "But one thing. If we meet again and you speak to me as you have spoken today, I will kill you. Good-bye."

Cardoso left him, thinking only of drink. Beer and whiskey. Now.

The night was hot and wet. Cardoso came out of the station house on La Rampa, cigarette dangling from his mouth, and began thinking of rainstorms. Too much to hope for now, he imagined. In his hometown, in the countryside, this kind of hot, heavy air sometimes foretold a summer downpour. The clay dirt earth of the fields would run rust-red with water, and the trees would flap in the wind like hysterical women. If it was severe, the children would be sent running home from the open-sided schoolhouse to help their mothers and fathers prepare for the storm. What a fine memory it was—dashing from the school, splashing through the rust-colored puddles, scattering chickens in the wind, running headlong home, a hero, needed and wanted.

Cardoso spat his cigarette into the gutter and went up La Rampa to the top of the hill. Young men and women were lined up for a movie.

Lovers walked hand in hand in the park. Vendors sold paper bags filled with popcorn or peanuts. The smell of the salt and the oil broke over him like a wave, reminding him—but enough of memories.

There was a workingman's drinking place just off Calle M. Cardoso went there, his cardboard box bundled under his arm, down half a flight of stairs to below street level.

Inside it was all cigarette smoke and men calling out. Cardoso welcomed it. The noise was almost deafening, almost loud enough to quiet his brain. He shouted, "¡Cerveza!" to the bartender, and got a mug with a head on it. He drank half of it away, wiped his lip on the back of his sleeve, lit a cigarette, and said, "One more." When the bartender ignored him, Cardoso began to think of the various ways he might show the man exactly who he was and exactly why he shouldn't treat him with disrespect. Then he remembered: *I'm not even a cop anymore. He can treat me any way he likes.*

Cardoso said, "¡Óyeme! Another beer, and soon. I'd like to be drunk sometime before tomorrow." The bartender heard this and laughed, and came down the bar with another mug of suds.

He said, "Here you are, my friend. I didn't realize you were drinking to get drunk."

"Isn't everyone?" Cardoso asked.

He knew he could get work. With the increasing violence in the streets and the continuing corruptibility of the police, businesses were hiring private security men. He'd have to make the rounds and see whether the Nacional or the Presidente or one of the other big hotels was looking for a security boss. It was galling. But working for the Security police had become like working private security, anyway—for a big rich company called Batista. He would exchange weeks of surveillance in the cities, stalking Cuban rebels intent on blowing up American-owned factories, for hours of surveillance in the lobbies, stalking Cuban rapists intent on violating American-owned women.

An hour later he was drunk, having slid from beer to whiskey after the third beer began to make him feel bloated and gassy. He drank, called for more drink, splashed money on the bar, and drank some more. No one spoke to him. No one bought him a round. No one expected him to buy anyone else a round. He was obviously busy drinking, getting drunk, and he didn't need any help or want any company.

Then it was midnight or later. The sky had fallen. The air was as thick as gauze. Cardoso was staggering onto the sidewalk, the half flight of stairs a Matterhorn of concrete steps and iron railing. When he was upright again he panicked, having lost his cardboard box, until he realized it was still tucked under his arm. He got to the curb and waved for a taxicab that wasn't there.

"Ponce was a crook," he said to his companion. "He was a bad cop and a thief, and no gentleman."

His companion, who was not there, silently agreed.

"No," Cardoso said. "He was. A thief. I am sorry if he was a friend of yours. He was a bad man. A bad cop."

The bartender, who had finished sweeping and mopping his barroom floor and was heading home for the night, said, "Commandante! You're drunk! Let me help you."

Cardoso said, "You are a fine fellow. Bighearted and brave. You will receive a citation from the Security forces. But for now, I must go home."

"We will find a taxi, then, Señor Cardoso," the bartender said. When Cardoso snapped back in reaction, he explained: "I remember you well from the student riots of 1956, señor. My two brothers were imprisoned. One of them went to *Paraiso*. They were innocent—too stupid to spell the word *revolution,* much less become rebels themselves. You had them released."

"Ah," Cardoso said. "I am no Ponce."

"No, señor. Let us find a taxi."

Mo had Lansky's car and driver make the rounds of the casinos he would manage. It was time to show himself. In one afternoon he saw the people at the Presidente, the Miramar, and the Sunset.

The problems he saw were the usual ones. Get rid of that flocked red wallpaper. Get new carpet. Bring in a few waiters who didn't look so much like morticians.

At the Presidente, the staff had a list of demands, which the translator supplied by the hotel presented to him while the workingmen stood with their arms folded across their chests.

When they were all done, Mo smiled and said, "Here is the answer to your questions. The Hotel Presidente is losing fifty thousand dollars a month from its non-hotel activities. If I don't take over, the hotel will be out of business within two months. You'll be out of a job. If you cooperate with me, you will keep your jobs. If you don't, you'll be fired now."

Mo turned to the translator and said, "Tell them that in Spanish, and don't make it sound nice. Tell them I'll be back in the morning to see who wants to work here."

Leaving the hotel, Mo said to his driver, "Take me over to that Plaza Vieja."

The air outside Sloan's apartment was overcooked and sweaty. The plaza was busy with people—fruit seller, newspaper boy, black shoeshine, a man with a wheel for sharpening knives—but not with anyone who looked like his horn player. Mo sat in the back of Meyer's big black car, waiting, thinking, waiting some more. By now Sloan would know everything Mo knew about Calloway and Anita and the rebels and the money. What must he feel? Misery. Again.

Mo said, "Say, Pepe? How's about getting me something to read? Is that a newsstand on the corner?"

"Yes, señor."

"See if they have a newspaper in English, will you? Or a magazine?"

Mo handed the driver a handful of Cuban bills and sent him to the corner. He waited, watching the shoeshine sit and wait patiently, and modeled himself on the old black man. He looked serene, at ease, waiting but not waiting. Just . . . sitting. Mo did that for about two minutes. The driver returned to the car with some printed material in his hand.

He said, "Only this, señor," and handed Mo a copy of *Life* magazine.

The cover story was about Roy Campanella, the legendary Dodger catcher who'd been paralyzed in an automobile accident. But inside was also a story called "Inside Rebel Cuba." Words and pictures told the story of Fidel and his men. The word REVOLUTIONARIES was splashed across the top of a black-and-white photograph of the rebels in the mountains. At the center of the image was a strikingly handsome Cuban man, bright-eyed and bearded, wearing military fatigues and smiling broadly from underneath a Panama hat. Around him were soldiers, some of them boys barely out of shorts, some of them women. One had terrible scars across her face and neck. The other, staring straight at the camera, was Anita.

Mo jerked his head up as if he had been slapped. There was no mistaking the image. That was Anita.

And here was Sloan. At that moment he came into view, moving a little uncertainly down the sidewalk, a paper bag under his arm. Mo guessed that the bag contained a bottle. He guessed, from the way he was walking, that Sloan contained *at least* a bottle, too. He said to the driver, "Wait for me."

He slid across the backseat of the car and got onto the sidewalk and walked up the street to greet Sloan. He took him by the elbow and led him to a bench on the plaza.

When he had Sloan parked on the bench, Mo said, "There's something you need to see," and pulled the magazine from his back pocket.

Sloan, who was pretty drunk already, said, "Aw, who cares about those rebels?"

"Not me," Mo said. "But look who's with 'em."

Sloan looked at the photograph, and saw. He swore under his breath, stared at the sky for a minute, and then got the paper bag open and the bottle of rum out of it. He cracked the seal and took a long gulp. He pointed the nose of it across the plaza and said, "There's Havana Brown."

Mo glanced over and said, "Who's that?"

"Havana Brown. He's an American. From Mobile, or someplace like that. Used to be one of the great Chicago piano players."

"And now he shines shoes?"

"Yeah. He came down here chasing a woman, story is." Sloan had another long pull on the bottle. "God *damn,* Mo. What am I gonna do?"

Mo said, "We'll fix it. I think I have a plan."

Mo would contact Lansky. Mo would find out who inside the revolution was Lansky's man. He would find him, and find out how much money the rebels wanted to release the girl. He would let them know it was Lansky's money. That would probably shake them up a bit. They would either set a price or return the girl. Either way, she would be freed.

And either way, it would be good for business. Mo would have Sloan on his team. He would have the loyal lieutenant his Havana operation was going to require. He could finesse it so Sloan would never know that was the deal he was making.

Mo would have to step more nimbly with Meyer. The old man could refuse. He could cut Mo off. He could have the girl eliminated, even.

But he wouldn't. It would be bad for business.

Cardoso found Scarfioti two nights later. It was midnight at El Floridita. It was the first time he had been out of his apartment since his booze-up at the joint on Calle 23. He'd slept all the following day. That night, he'd risen and clumped around his apartment for an hour, taken a bath, and then fallen back defeated into a state of hungover stupor. Today he had eaten, bathed again and shaved, and tried to formulate some kind of scheme. Over coffee and a cigarette in the late afternoon, he'd finally seen a way forward. It wasn't by the book, or legal, but that was not his concern anymore.

Cardoso spotted Scarfioti across the room as he entered El Floridita. The Spaniard had his head back and was laughing so hard that Cardoso thought his teeth would fall out. He was perspiring heavily, mopping his forehead with a handkerchief, and saying in a language that Cardoso didn't understand, *"Mi amas vin.* However, *mia hundo amas vian katon!"*

Scarfioti saw Cardoso come through the door and waved a hand at him, beckoning him over to his corner. Cardoso nodded and moved across the room, checking faces, like a cop, as he went. He recognized two men—they fenced stolen goods—standing by the end of the bar

eyeing the tourists. Behind them, at a table in the back, Cardoso recognized the American actor Gary Cooper. He looked old and lined and hard—more like the characters he played in the pictures, Cardoso thought, than an actor playing those parts should look. He was showing some sort of card trick to one of his companions, a petite Cuban woman with huge earrings. Near the Cooper party was another group of Yankees. Cardoso knew they were athletes from their sunburned faces and their chunky builds. Baseball players, probably. But he couldn't have said what sport or team they represented. The Dodgers and the Yankees trained in Varadero. The Cuban Sugar Kings, an American-managed team that played the International League, was housed there permanently. Half of the players were Americans.

When he was a boy, Cardoso had seen some of the legendary Americans walking the streets of Old Havana. He remembered Whitey Ford and Duke Snider and Dolph Camilli. Cardoso had seen Babe Ruth once, too, at a Christmas party at the Hotel Nacional. He had been just a boy, but the effect was profound: here was a great American sports legend, and he was fat and vulgar and he was smoking a cigar and drinking rum and he was repellent.

This group of Americans had cigars and rum, too. The man who appeared to be explaining Cuba to them was a high-level pimp Cardoso knew from the Vedado area. Cardoso hoped he'd get them into a cathouse, and soon, before the heat under those sunburns turned violent.

Then he remembered, *I'm not a cop anymore. Let them all boil over.*

Scarfioti embraced him energetically and said, "My friend the policeman! They have given you a night off! Meet Monsieur Lemoin. He cannot speak Spanish, and his English is execrable, but he has a very serviceable Esperanto. We've been exchanging pleasantries. Tell Faustino what you will have to drink."

"*Mi amas vin,*" Limoin said. "*Mais, se vi gajnus la loterion, mi amus vin.*"

Scarfioti said, "Yes! *If you win the lottery, I will love you.* As opposed to, simply, *I love you.* Wait, Señor Cardoso. *Se vi gajnus la loterion, mia hundo amus vian katon!* Yes! If you win the lottery, my dog will love your cat! Excellent!"

Cardoso drew Scarfioti aside, excusing himself from the Esperanto expert, and said, "I need your assistance on a personal matter. May we speak for a moment outside?"

The Spaniard, who was perhaps not as drunk as it first appeared, said, "Meet me outside in two minutes. We cannot speak seriously in El Floridita."

Cardoso stood at the bar and had a rum and Coca-Cola, and waited until Scarfioti stopped gesturing and cackling to the Frenchman.

They walked uphill from the bar, into Parque Central. The wedding-cake exterior of the Hotel Inglaterra rose before them. Higher and nobler was the dome of the Capitolio, where the Cuban flag fluttered in the light breeze. The air had cooled a little. Cardoso, with a rum and cola gurgling inside him, had begun to feel human again.

He said, "I hope I can trust your discretion in this matter. Can I speak to you confidentially?"

The Spaniard looked almost offended. He said, "Señor! You wound me. Of course!"

"This is not a police matter. It is beyond the reach of our Security force. There is a rebel, newly returned to Cuba from exile, named Carlos Delgado. Do you know of him?"

Cardoso thought he saw a light of recognition in Scarfioti's eyes. But Scarfioti said, "No. I do not."

"It is not important. He is a revolutionary, very highly placed, very highly regarded. Close to Fidel Castro. He appears to be the man behind a kidnapping, of an American girl who was the girl-friend of the American millionaire Calloway."

"Of *this* I have heard," Scarfioti said.

"Calloway is dead. The girl is alive. I want to get the girl."

"Of course," Scarfioti said. "And why not? She is beautiful!"

"No, no. You misunderstand me," Cardoso said. "My interest is not in her beauty."

"Then what *is* your interest, señor?"

"Ah, that," Cardoso said. "That, I'm afraid, must remain confidential. And it is a secondary concern. You were friendly with the dead American, Calloway. Did you know the girl?"

"No. I never met her."

"Then it will need to be an associate of Calloway's. Who else did he know?"

"He was not here for very long," Scarfioti said. "It is not so easy."

Cardoso could often smell a lie. He could always smell discomfort. Scarfioti was becoming uncomfortable. He removed the straw hat from his hairless head and mopped himself with a handkerchief. Cardoso let him sweat. He waited a full minute, rocking on his heels and looking around at the night sky, while Scarfioti composed himself.

"It is always so serene at this time," Cardoso said. "Look at the Capitolio. Such a brave, handsome building. And the sky is clear tonight. And there are no gunshots in Havana. So peaceful—until about three o'clock. There is always trouble at three o'clock."

"I am always in bed before then," Scarfioti said. "I cannot bear gunshots."

"What about Calloway's friends?"

Scarfioti said, "I can tell you only this. There is a man named Morris Weiner. Everyone calls him Mo. He is a gangster, connected in some way to Meyer Lansky. He is in Havana now, making arrangements to do something with some casino. I don't know what. But he was making his business with Calloway, before Calloway was killed."

"This is excellent," Cardoso said. "Thank you. Can you make the introduction?"

"No," Scarfioti said. "I cannot. I do not know Mo Weiner. And for a man in my position, it is not wise to be associated with American gangsters."

"I imagine it is not," Cardoso said. "What is your position?"

"Ah!" Scarfioti caught himself. "What indeed! Now, if you will excuse me, I must return to my Esperanto-speaking friend. We are planning to take in a cockfight tonight, in Cojímar. Can a policeman enjoy such a spectacle?"

"Not this policeman," Cardoso said. "Tell me where I can find this Weiner."

"At the Tropicana, I believe. And with that, I will say good night, señor."

Scarfioti saluted ridiculously, turned on his heel, and left Parque Central. Cardoso could feel his urgency. But he didn't understand it. Did it matter? Maybe not. Scarfioti was afraid of the American. He was afraid of the gangsters. Who was not? Cardoso himself was afraid of them. They were rich and strong and powerful, and they killed their enemies without pretext or warning. What was not to be afraid of?

Across Parque Central sat the old American black man they called Havana Brown. He had fallen asleep, apparently, over his shoeshine kit. His head was on his chest. He looked peaceful. Perhaps he was dead? Cardoso had a fleeting, almost nostalgic thought: *When I die, I want it to be exactly like that. A park bench, my head on my chest, resting.* Then reality returned. *When I die,* he thought, *it will be nothing at all like that.*

At the corner of the park, where Neptuno and the Prado come into the plaza, Cardoso hailed a taxi. A busload of American women had gathered in front of the Inglaterra. Going out? At this hour? That could mean only trouble. Perhaps they were headed for Scarfioti's cockfight. Cardoso slid into the back of the taxi, feeling like a tourist. Or like a civilian, anyway. He said, "To the Tropicana, please."

"Yes, Lieutenant."

Cardoso shot his eyes at the rearview mirror. Havana was too small. The *taxista* was a man he'd interrogated several times over the years, a petty thief who at one time had tried to move into the arms-trafficking business as a supplier to the rebels.

Cardoso said, "No, Morales. I am just a citizen tonight, not a lieutenant. You are a taxi driver now?"

"It is easier than being a thief," the taxi driver said. "These days, no one has anything to steal. But the tourists always want a taxi."

"Crime doesn't pay, like I always told you," Cardoso said. "This is especially true in a bad economy. Now, drive."

For the first week that Anita was among them, the rebels in the hills seemed more like a motion picture company than a revolutionary army. Or they seemed like comic book rebels. They were very energetic. They were very cheerful. They sang songs at night, and sang snatches of songs to one another all day long. There was always an enormous amount of activity. Men gathered wood and built fires and cleaned rifles and boxed ammunition and hunted for food, or collected food from the local peasantry. They held meetings almost around the clock—big ones, involving a hundred men or more, and small ones, sometimes involving only Carlos Delgado and one or two other men.

The women, meanwhile, cooked or sewed or mended camouflage netting or gathered water from the river or made bandages or tended the sick in the field hospital.

The food preparation was amazing, and unceasing. Anita had worked in a café at Shipton Wells. She knew about food. But she had worked only around food that was packaged for commercial use. She had never seen food gathered and prepared in the wild. The quantities seemed vast. There were slaughtered cattle, big enough to last a lifetime, and mountains of bananas and sacks and sacks of rice and dried beans. In the evening, when the men came in from the field and gathered for their meal, it was as if the women were an army to themselves. The younger girls carried great steaming platters to the table—of fried chicken, roast pork, boiled beef, boiled potatoes, fried bananas—while their mothers and aunts and elder sisters stayed in the kitchen, serving bowls of rice and black beans from their huge, smoking cauldrons.

The talk of battle was unceasing, too. Every day Anita heard bits of conversation about the rebel army's triumphs and tragedies on the battlefield. There had been hard-won victories in places with exotic-sounding names—Las Minas de Ocujal, El Dajao, Limonar, Zanja de Mayarí, Cupeyal and Baltoney. There had been terrible defeats, too, at Imias and Yateritas, at San Rámon de las Yaguas and Sagua de Tánamo, where hundreds of civilians had been killed when Batista's airplanes dropped bombs and napalm on farms and fields where the rebels were believed to be hiding.

The names of the soldiers, too, were exotic and strange. Fighting with Fidel in the eastern Sierra, or with his brother Raúl in Oriente

Province, were Ciro Frías and Efigenio Amejeiras and Manuel Fajardo. Anita repeatedly heard mention of Toto and Anibal and Lusson and Tomasevich, and men with nicknames whose real names she never learned, men called Cheche, El Guajiro, and Chucho, or El Abogado, El Profesor, El Moro, or El Gordo.

She heard about women as well—Vilma Espín, who ran operations in the city of Santiago, and Celia Sánchez, who was responsible for provisions in the Sierra and who was as close to Fidel as Che or Raúl. She heard about Haydée Santamaría, who was known as Yeyé. Haydée had been with Fidel and her brother and her fiancé in the attack on the Moncada police barracks. During the interrogation following the rebels' defeat, the soldiers had brought Haydée her brother's eyes, ripped from his head, and her fiancé's testicles, ripped from his scrotum. She had told the soldiers nothing, and now ran the rebels' finances out of a safe house in Havana.

To Anita, these were impossible acts of heroism. They were mythic and unreal. It was three weeks before reality interrupted the storytelling.

In the late spring, Fidel's brother Raúl had fought to victory in the towns of La Lima, La Guanabana, San Antonio, and Santa Ana, collecting arms and prisoners on the way. Batista's military, in May and June, had begun an aerial campaign against the rebels. Despite the "arms embargo" declared by the U.S. government in March, which decreed that the American military would remain apart from the fighting in Cuba, the aerial campaign was waged from the American base at Guantánamo. The bombs that fell on rebels and peasants were American bombs. Raúl began a pointedly anti-American counterattack. As the summer wore on, his forces captured U.S. Marines stationed at Guantánamo, managers of metals companies around the mountain city of Moa, and United Fruit Company employees at Nicaro and Caimanera. Raúl had taken almost fifty Americans hostage—thirty of them soldiers from Guántanamo, the rest civilians. He had held them at a mountain camp in the east, in Oriente.

Batista's army, in response, had intensified its assaults against the rebel bases in the mountains. Camilo Cienfuegos had suffered terrible attacks in the Santa Clara region. Che Guevara and his men were being pummeled around Baragua. Then the fight came to Carlos Delgado in the mountains.

It was the dawn of a quiet, still morning. The sky was clear. The heat, rising from the ground like steam, was already intense, and the air was heavy with damp and the smell of the woods. Anita had been to the river, had washed and brushed her hair, and was dressing in preparation to join the women in the kitchen tents. She had just folded a blouse and put it on her bed when a man ran past her tent and said, "To the center of the camp, at once!"

Outside her tent men and women were running. They looked afraid. Overhead was a high, whining sound Anita had not heard before—a swarm of bees in the distance. A woman Anita knew as Gloria caught her by the elbow and said, fear everywhere on her face, "We are being attacked. There is no time."

For what? Rebel soldiers sprinted past, carrying rifles and machine guns. They were running away from the camp, uphill, farther into the mountains. The buzzing overhead increased. Anita saw Nilsa and the girl called María Fuentes moving determinedly across the camp, carrying a heavy bag of freshly made bandages toward the field hospital. Anita said, "Can I help you?"

Nilsa, the scars on her face white with rage, said, "*Regresa a mi campamento*—" and then stopped and said, in English, "In my tent. More bandages."

Anita nodded and turned and ran back down the hill. The horrible man Alemán, who had taken her from the cemetery and kept her with the pigs on the farm in Viñales, saw her running and said, "*¡No, mi vida!* Not that way!" Anita ran past him without answering. Then she was at Nilsa's tent. There were bags and bags of bandages, many too heavy for her to carry. She found a bag she could lift, hoisted it onto her shoulder, and began moving back uphill.

The buzzing of the bees was now an overbearing drone. Then it went quiet, or seemed somehow to get quiet. Voices around her shouted, "*¡Al suelo!*" Everyone dove to the ground. Anita fell near a camp table. A rebel soldier rolled to the ground beside her, and grabbed and held her close.

The ground exploded. Anita was lifted from the dirt and dropped. The noise was impossible. Then the ground exploded again. Soil filled the air, as did the screams of men and women around her, and then came another explosion. Metal whistled. Sharp bits of wind blew. The soldier pushed Anita deeper into the dirt. She felt choked by dust and the sound of the earth shaking.

Then the soldier went slack and grew heavy on her. Anita rolled her shoulders until he fell away from her, and then turned around on the ground. His eyes were open and his face was close to hers. He was dead. Anita flinched, and just then the ground heaved again and the air filled with screams.

Something was burning. The woods around them were burning. Voices called out, "¡Fuego! ¡Fuego, állà!" Anita began to be afraid in a new way. She got to her feet, dizzy, almost hysterical. Men and women were dashing past her, through clouds of smoke that hung close to the ground like fog. No one seemed to see her. They were running, crying, bleeding. Anita turned and began to run with them.

The whistling came again, along with a strange wooden *chunk-chunka* sound, which came from the trees. The air smelled of fresh pine, as if woodcutters were working. Anita looked back over her shoulder. There were men chasing them now, men in uniforms, which were not the uniforms of the rebels. They had guns, which they were firing uphill at the fleeing rebels. There came again a whistling quite near her. Anita felt a whoosh past her ear. Then the *chunk-chunka* of the bullets hitting the pine trees.

A hundred yards ahead was a clearing. Anita, running headlong uphill, broke out of the trees and dashed for the cover of the woods beyond. Two men fell in beside her. Anita could hear one of them breathing heavily and cursing from beneath his bushy mustache. She did not know the words, but the sounds were vicious.

Then, just ahead, something confused her. A woman was walking downhill with a cow—walking behind the cow, firing her rifle over the cow's back. It was the woman Nilsa. She was moving slowly, patiently, a look of calm determination on her face, firing her rifle methodically at targets down the hill behind Anita.

The whistling came again, and that *chunk-chunka* sound. The cow raised its head and groaned horribly, and its forelegs collapsed. Nilsa sat down on the ground and continued firing.

Then there was more whisling, close again to Anita's ears. The *chunk-chunka* came from two men running beside her. They fell straight forward, arms outstretched, soundless. The cursing stopped.

Anita gasped—and knew then, right then, that she was about to die. Instead, she tripped over the outstretched arm of the man who had just fallen in front of her. She herself fell straight forward, struck her head on the root of a pine tree, and went black.

Delgado had been given advance warning, but just barely. A runner came in about four o'clock. Delgado was awakened at five. A battalion of Batista's men had overrun Cienfuegos's troops near the coast. They had armored cars and two trucks and were coming into the mountains. Lookouts had seen their approach. It was evident that they knew where they were going. This was no search party.

Then a field telephone call reported that planes loaded with bombs and napalm had left the temporary Batista airfield at San Jose, near Santa Clara. This was routine. But the planes had executed left-hand turns upon takeoff and had set off for the west.

Delgado ordered his men to heightened readiness. He ordered a cache of arms and ammunition to be moved out of the camp at once, on board a camouflaged truck kept in readiness for this specific emergency. He sent advance troops down the hill in three directions. His own men could hold the summit, and the camp, if necessary.

But the air strike was devastating. An informer, a very well-placed informer, had reported the rebel camp's location with great accuracy. Someone had fed the coordinates to Batista's pilots. The camp was too well hidden to be that well assaulted without assistance. Delgado was thinking these things as the first wave came. He left his tent and looked at the sky. There were seven or eight airplanes. The first wave loosed at least twelve bombs. The planes shot past and began broad turns to the north. They were making a return run. Delgado said to Bolinas and his captains, "Evacuate the camp immediately. Uphill, to the summit. Tell everyone to take cover in the brush. Leave the wounded."

He returned briefly to his tent. There were maps and memos that must be carried off, and not by Batista's men. Delgado collected several maps, rolled them up, and stuck them together in a metal tube. He folded a sheaf of papers together, too, and stuck them into a knapsack. Enough. He went quickly from the tent and, with another glance at the sky, headed uphill.

The attack was surprisingly well executed. Delgado had gotten near the summit, where a clearing afforded a view of the camp area. There had been three sweeps by the airplanes. The pilots had dropped bombs on the first two runs, and napalm on the third. Now the woods were on fire. Half the camp was destroyed. And soldiers with rifles and grenade launchers were firing on his fleeing men. He saw two rebels go down hard, shot in the back, onto their faces in the dirt. Then the American girl, the beautiful Anita, fell between them. *¡Ay, Dios!* This was turning very sour. But the vantage point, right there, was marvelous. Delgado called out to a soldier running past, "Place a machine gun exactly here. Begin firing as soon as the soldiers are within range." The soldier stopped, terror in his eyes, and set his machine gun and ammunition belt on the ground. Then he turned and ran.

Delgado cursed under his breath. He ran to the machine gun and got it onto its tripod. Two other machine gunners were running nearby. He called to them, "Men! We will post a line here. Stop and mount your guns. We have only a minute."

The two men stopped and began preparing their guns. In less than a minute, Batista's men were through the woods and moving toward them into a little clearing. Delgado said, "*¡Todavía no!* Wait thirty more seconds, *compañeros.*"

They began firing. Batista's men were not prepared for it. They fell in waves. Delgado, who had never experienced the invigorating terror of battle, felt exhilarated and nauseated in equal measure. He took deep breaths, as he had been schooled to do, and exhaled slowly, keeping his eyes upon the approaching men. He saw thirty or more fall before the retreat began.

As the smoke cleared, Delgado saw a rebel soldier firing upon Batista's men from behind a cow. Or behind the carcass of a cow. The soldier had taken cover behind the cow's fallen body and, well hidden from view, was sharpshooting government soldiers as they crested the hill and came out of the woods below. Delgado laughed out loud. What creativity!

If the bombing had continued, there would have been no survivors. But the planes did not come back after the third sortie. Hours later, when the rebels were able to retake their camp, it was clear to Delgado that the last bombs had fallen on the lines of Batista's men as they ran between the tents. That and the field hospital. There were no survivors among those previously wounded. Delgado said to Bolinas, "Let us bury the men and women who died fighting first, then those who died in the field hospital." He excused himself and walked downhill fifty feet. When he was alone, he vomited behind a pine tree and then wept silently for a minute or more.

Unlike some of his comrades, Delgado felt no joy when he fired upon Batista's men. He was a Cuban. He was not a killer. He was especially not a killer of Cubans.

Several hours later the young man who had dropped his machine gun and run from the battle was brought to Delgado. He was escorted by two older men. One of them, Delgado thought, was his uncle. He said to this older man, "What is it?"

The man said, "My nephew was a coward today in battle. He is sorry. He feels shame. He wants your forgiveness."

The boy was not yet twenty. He was ashen and shaking. There was dried blood on his chin. Had he bitten his lip? Had his nose bled? Delgado could not tell. His heart ached for the boy. What a thing, to be a coward in the field.

He said to the older man, "Of course I will forgive him. It is a terrible thing to run when those around you are fighting and dying. What is your name?"

The boy tried to speak but could not. His uncle, his throat tight with emotion, said, "He is called Diego Santana Quevedo."

Delgado said, "There is no penalty for cowardice. But the penalty for desertion is death."

The uncle said, "But señor . . ."

Delgado hesitated. He said, "Too many Cubans have died today already. Leave the camp at once. If you are seen here again, you will be shot on sight. Shame on you. Now go."

Hours later, alone in his tent, Delgado thought, *What is my penalty, then? To have let the boy go, without punishment, is dereliction of duty, at least.* Delgado imagined the boy finding his heart, finding his courage, and leading an assault against the rebels. He would shoot his own uncle. He would make Delgado pay for shaming him. After killing him, he would dismember Delgado's body, tearing the fingers from their joints.

Delgado rose from his cot. He would go down to the field hospital. The men he had visited yesterday were all dead. There were new men to see.

And the camp would have to be relocated. Everything that had not been damaged must now be moved to a new location, and hidden there. Soon. The government planes would not be back today, but they might return tomorrow. Bolinas had mentioned an alternative camp, under better cover of trees, that he and some of his men were proposing as a new location. Now they would get their wish. But first the dead.

Mo Weiner was not at the Tropicana the first three times Cardoso asked for him there. The ex-policeman didn't leave a note. He didn't walk the halls, calling out Mo's name. He only asked for him at the front desk. Still, after the second night, Mo was made aware of his presence.

The first night, Cardoso called the front desk from a telephone in the lobby. He watched the man working Reception pick up the receiver and glance over his shoulder at the wall of mail slots behind him when Cardoso said, "Is Mr. Weiner available, please?" The desk clerk said, "I'm sorry. May I take a message for him?"

Cardoso sat in the lobby bar for an hour, drinking, watching. He'd been a cop there too many times to start asking questions. Even out of uniform, he was too obvious. So he watched, and didn't start asking anything.

The following night Cardoso returned to the Tropicana, but earlier in the evening. This time he bribed a doorman, feeding him an American twenty-dollar bill and saying, "I have to deliver this envelope personally to Morris Weiner's room. Can you show me where it is?"

The doorman led him around the back of the Tropicana to where the gangster Meyer Lansky kept his apartment. Cardoso took pictures, in his mind, the whole way. Here was the high window, probably for a bathroom, behind the building. There was a service door that might lead to the hall in front of the apartment. There were two wide windows, covered now in heavy drapes, that must be the front room of the apartment. By the time the doorman had shown him the front door and he slipped his envelope under it, Cardoso had a complete image of the place. The envelope contained nothing but a blank sheet of paper, but now he knew where Weiner cooped when the day was done.

Between times, Cardoso did his work quietly. He had to. He wasn't a cop anymore. He didn't have the cop resources he'd used before. He couldn't throw his weight and his badge around on the street. He didn't like the idea of bracing some creep and having the creep laugh and say, "You're not even a cop anymore!"

So he was discreet. He knew people who worked at the Presidente and the Miramar. He spent a few hours in each, wandering, admiring the gift shop, riding up and down the elevator, having a cocktail in the bar, taking a coffee in the lounge, picking up what he could. It wasn't much more than the street had already given him: This guy Mo was bringing new money into the casinos at the Sunset, Miramar, and Presidente. He was going to open new gaming venues in all three. From the size of the army of workers Cardoso saw on the job, it was serious and it was happening soon. There were lots of men, and they were working fast.

A bookie Cardoso knew from long ago said, conversationally, over a drink at the Miramar, "All of it belongs to the American gangster Lansky."

The bartender, whom Cardoso had interrogated once about a ring of jewel thieves working the hotels, said, "That's not what I hear. Mo Weiner *is* Lansky now."

Cardoso leaned on a newspaper reporter he knew from the old days, and spent an hour combing through news files. He'd come up with a photograph of Morris Weiner, or Mo Weiner, attached to a story about the building boom in Las Vegas. The clip was ten years old. Mo Weiner was a slight, handsome man with silvery gray hair, standing with his hands clasped behind his back, twinkling at the camera. Cardoso was surprised: this was a likable-looking guy. He'd been prepared for the opposite.

Sitting with a beer at the workingman's bar on Calle 23, next to a man he'd followed from the staff entrance at the Sunset, Cardoso said, "Big money going into the Sunset, eh?"

"Big money is right," the man said. "Good jobs, too."

"Yankee money?"

"Completely," the man said. "Everyone else is leaving Havana. This new group is coming in."

"It's that millionaire Calloway, isn't it?"

"No, señor," the workingman said. "That man was murdered. This group is led by an American hotel owner from Las Vegas."

"Ah, *claro*," Cardoso said. "I remember now. There was a woman, who was kidnapped."

"Exactly." The man raised his head at the bartender, who began drawing him another beer. Cardoso nodded to indicate he'd have another, too.

He said, "These are on me, señor. What happened to the girl?"

"The *rebeldes* took her to the mountains. The ransom money is many millions now. She is a great beauty."

"She must be something," Cardoso said. "Will anyone pay the ransom?"

"Perhaps the first gambler to break the bank at the new Club Paraiso, señor."

"Paraiso? What is it?"

"That is the name of the new casinos, señor. In the Sunset and the Miramar and the Presidente. The Paraiso Sunset, the Paraiso Miramar . . ."

It was too grotesque. To name the casinos after the prison . . . Horrible.

Cardoso paid for the drinks, raised his glass to the workingman, and drank off the top inch of his beer. Havana now boasted four nightspots known as *Paraiso*. Three casinos, one torture chamber.

Cuba! A country with everything for the tourist!

It was several days later that Cardoso returned to the Tropicana for a third visit. He looked for the doorman from the preceding time but found he was not on duty. He checked the desk and phoned from the lobby, and was told that Mr. Weiner was in the hotel but not available at the moment. He looked into the lobby bar and was just sitting down to order a drink when he recognized Mo Weiner, the man from the newspaper files, coming toward him. He was flanked by a couple of men Cardoso knew were professional muscle. Cardoso was just figuring out what he might say to such a pair of men when the trio turned and came across the lobby directly toward him.

One of the musclemen said, "Señor Weiner wants to talk with you. Now."

Cardoso said, "Good. I want to talk with him, too."

The muscle said, "Okay. Better give me the *pistola*."

The big man moved close to Cardoso, as if he were going to begin a rumba. Cardoso slid his left hand into his jacket and drew out his sidearm, holding the grip between his thumb and forefinger. The bodyguard buried the pistol in his pocket and said, "Good. Come."

Weiner and the other goon had turned away and were moving toward the main ballroom. Cardoso and the bodyguard followed. The four of them sat at a back table.

There were no dancers onstage. But the orchestra was in place, the musicians urging a soothing wave of rumba and *son* from their instruments.

Mo Weiner said, "You're bird-dogging me. Why?"

But then a waiter was with them. Mo ordered champagne for himself, and two coffees for the bookends. He raised his eyes at Cardoso, who said, "Brandy."

When the waiter left, Mo said, "Well? Why?"

"I am looking for the girl," Cardoso said. "The American girl."

"Why?"

"It is personal, señor."

"That's not good enough for me," Mo said with a smile. "I know a couple of things, but not things I'd tell to a man with secrets."

"We all have secrets, señor."

"Of course! But an officer with the Security forces who has just been fired—and has secrets? That's too much trouble for me."

"Then let me tell you the truth," Cardoso said, lowering his voice. "I have made a terrible mistake. The American, Calloway, was killed as a result. And the American girl is being held by the rebels as a result. I would like to obtain her release."

"Anyone can obtain her release," Mo said. "She is for sale. Here is your drink, Mr. Cardoso."

Mo let the waiter pour him a glass of champagne, then raised it to his lips and winked at Cardoso. The policeman raised his brandy similarly, and said, "To your health." One of the bodyguards, his nose buried in a cup of coffee, grunted his assent.

"What else have you got?" Mo said. "So far, I don't hear anything that interests me."

"I can get to the girl, and I can get the man who kidnapped her," Cardoso said. "Both those things are important to me."

"But they are not important to me. Why are you bothering me with this?"

Cardoso decided to overlook the *bothering*. He said, "The girl was your partner's *papaya*. She is very beautiful, and young. I understand you want to get her back."

"Really?" Mo was surprised. Just a good guess? Or had he heard something? He said, "That's good detective work, Mr. Cardoso. Your logic is faulty, but your timing is pretty good. I am not interested in the girl. But someone else is—and he has asked me to help him. Perhaps you and I can do business after all."

"I am sure of it, señor," Cardoso said. "But I am only what the Yankees call a 'flatfoot,' eh? Explain to me how it will work."

Mo smiled. One slick Cuban playing dumb. He said, "First thing, we need a little privacy. Gentlemen? Will you leave us?"

The two goons looked at Mo, then at each other, then back at Mo. He said, "I'm serious. Scramble." The goons got up and shuffled off toward the bar.

When they were out of earshot, Mo said, "It's not real difficult. We offer the money. They accept. You go get the girl. What happens to the man you're after is not important to me. You bring back the girl. You get paid. The end."

"The end?"

"That's right. After that, I don't know you. We don't do any more business together. If you were to come around again looking for me, it wouldn't turn out good for you. You understand?"

"Perfectly, señor," Cardoso said. "When will you make the offer?"

"Tomorrow. How can I contact you?"

Cardoso drew a slip of paper from his pocket and wrote a telephone number on it. He said, "Ask for me at this number. Any hour. They will bring me to the phone."

Mo penciled a telephone number on a blank business card. He slid it across the table to Carsoso.

"This is the number you can call for me. Don't call unless it's an emergency. If you do call, explain exactly what the problem is. It will be solved. Got me?"

"I got you," Cardoso said. "I will take your money and buy back your woman. There won't be an emergency."

"Excellent!" Mo said. "Now, finish that drink. I'll whistle up those gorillas, and we can get out of here."

Carlos Delgado visited the field hospital in the new encampment every day for the next week. It was part of his job. The men needed to see him there. There was also the American girl. She didn't need to see him. But he went to her, anyway.

The first day had been a shock—a happy shock. She was lying on a cot at one end of the tent. She was the only woman injured in the firefight. Two other women, Cuban women, had been killed by Batista's bombs. But all the other injured were men. Someone had bandaged the American girl's head. She had taken a fall—the fall that Delgado had seen, when he thought she had been shot in the back like her fallen comrades—and bruised her head. She was unconcsious, or sleeping, the first time he visited. She was, in repose, impossibly beautiful. Something wrenched in his chest. He turned away. Later he was sitting with two farm boys from Oriente, brothers who had been knocked unconscious by a bomb blast and had bomb fragments in their legs and backs. He said to the elder of them, "You have taken a blow for the revolution. That is heroic in itself. And you will live to fight another day."

The younger brother smiled and said, "Here is La Vaca!"

Delgado turned. It was Nilsa. Delgado said, "*¿La Vaca? ¿Por qué se llama así?*"

"Haven't you heard? She is the warrior who fights with the cows!"

Delgado asked Nilsa to sit with them. They listened as the younger brother retold the story of Nilsa's defense of the camp. She had stood behind a milk cow, exchanging rifle fire with enemy troops, until the cow had dropped, gut-shot, to its haunches. Then Nilsa had squatted behind the cow's corpse and continued her assault. She had killed several government soldiers. When it was over, the cow was a slaughtered mess. The women from the kitchens refused to butcher it for meat.

"But she is La Vaca forever!" the boy said.

"Viva La Vaca!" his brother shouted.

"As I said, heroism takes many forms," Delgado said. "Come with me, Nilsa. I want to talk to you about the American girl."

Nilsa told him the girl's injuries were minor. She would recover quickly. What, she asked, was his interest?

"We must get rid of her," Delgado said. "She is a danger to us. She represents the interests, the *worst* interests, of the imperialists. If we wait long enough, someone will come for her. And they may not come nicely. Besides, she is not good for the morale of the men."

Nilsa smiled. The skin around the scar on her cheek went pink.

She said, "The morale of the men? Or the morale of El Gato?"

Delgado laughed, but the words stung. He said, "No, Nilsa. The only threat to my morale is the threat of La Vaca. What a heroine you are to these men!"

"A heroine without beauty. I would have died for the revolution, happily. I didn't count on the rest of it."

"None of us gets the bargain he makes," Delgado said. "Maybe that is as it should be, though. I did not set out to be El Gato. You did not ask to be La Vaca. But think of those who have died. They are no longer able to serve, as we are."

Nilsa put a hand to the scar on her cheek and covered it. Delgado reached and pulled the hand away, then kissed her on that side of her face.

"Come," he said. "I understand we are expecting a truckload of new kitchen supplies. Perhaps the food will improve now."

The natives were restless. Mo could sense it. There was too much movement in the streets. There was too much noise. It felt wrong. Furtive movement, anxious noise. Setting forth in Lansky's car but without Lansky's muscle, using Phil as his driver again, Mo was looking for Sloan. The streets made him nervous.

A clot of men standing on the corner in Vedado melted into the shadows as Mo's car approached. A block on, another collection of men swarmed under a streetlight and then dispersed. Mo said, "Hey, Phil. What's going on tonight?"

"Tonight? Is usual, señor."

"No, it's not. Something's happening. There are too many men in the street. And no women."

Phil brightened. "You want woman?"

"No," Mo said. "I'm just saying. There are no women on the street. There are almost no single men on the street. Just little groups, and they look dangerous. What's going on?"

"Tonight is estrike."

"Estrike?"

"Sí, senor. Estrike. The *rebeldes* say no more nightclub, no more casino, no more restaurant, no more bar."

"For what?"

Phil accelerated to catch a green light turning to yellow, scattering a pair of men onto the sidewalk. He said, "The *rebeldes* want to stop Havana nightlife. Bad money for bad men. For Batista and the Yankees. So they say, all the Havana stay home. No more casino, no more nightclub, no more get drunk and spend money."

"Great," Mo said. "Keep driving."

There was no answer at Sloan's door. There was no doorman to question. No helpful street monkey to quiz. Mo said, "Let's go to the place we went before. What was the one where we found him?"

"El Cruz Azul. But no one go to El Cruz Azul until two o'clock."

Mo sighed. "Where, then?"

Phil watched Mo in the rearview mirror and said, "Maybe . . . Floridita. Monserrate. Bodeguita del Medio. El Gato Tuerto. Café de Paris."

"Those are popular places?"

"The *most* popular, señor."

"Which one would *you* go to?"

"I, señor? *I* will only go La Coronita."

Mo sighed. "I remember it. Let's go there, then."

Sloan was slumped over a corner table, alone, his horn tucked under his arm, almost unconcious. A half-empty glass of something that looked like scotch sat in front of him. Mo, taking this in, amid the general decrepitude of the joint, saw trouble. He had never seen Sloan leave a glass of anything sitting half empty before him. He'd have to be pretty drunk to leave a cocktail unfinished.

But he smiled when Mo sat down across from him, and said, "Hey, old man. What's a nice guy like you doing in a place like this?"

"I could ask you the same question."

"Not really," Sloan said. "I'm not a nice guy."

"It's still a crappy joint."

"Yep. Have a drink. It gets better when you have a drink. *Everything* gets better when you have a drink."

The bar was dark and stank of spilled booze and stale cigar smoke. Music rushed from a radio on the bar. A man and woman in the back of the room were all tangled up in each other. Through the darkness Mo could not see their faces, nor those of the two or three men slumped over on barstools.

Phil came out of the blackness behind them and said, "*Mojitos,* my friends," and put a tray of cocktail glasses in front of them. The smell of rum and lime rose from the table.

Mo said, "You go ahead, Phil. You drink 'em all. You're driving."

It took Phil twenty minutes to drink all the *mojitos.* Sloan seemed to come and go. Mo made small talk. He wanted Sloan outside and sober. He didn't want to have the conversation twice. When Phil drank off the last of the cocktails, Mo said, "Come outside. Walk with me."

The mood in the street had darkened. Now even Havana Vieja was silent. Nothing moved on the sidewalks. Mo motioned up the hill to his right and said, "Can't we walk that way up to that park?"

Sloan glanced up the rise before them. He said, "This street is O'Reilly. It goes to the park."

Mo said to Phil, "Get the car. Meet us in the park, in front of that big hotel."

"The Inglaterra, señor."

A block later, Mo said, "I've got this thing all cooked, for Anita. There's this ex-cop. Cardoso. He's going to broker the deal with the rebels. He's from the mountains. He knows these guys. He's going to go in and get her, and bring her back safe and sound."

Sloan listened and thought.

Mo said, "I'll take care of the money."

Sloan listened.

Mo said, "It could take a little time, is all. The roads between the Sierra and here are not safe. That's what Cardoso says. The rebels and the government are fighting for control of the highways. So it could take a couple of weeks to get there and back."

Sloan nodded.

Mo said, "So? What do you think?"

"I think it sounds dangerous."

Mo said, "Yeah? It probably is."

"I think it sounds dangerous for this guy, and dangerous for Anita."

"Not more dangerous than living with the rebels. There's real fighting going on up there. It's a real war."

"I know. I read the papers. And I don't like this plan. Who's this Cardoso? Why isn't he going to screw it up the same way it got screwed up the last time? When Calloway got killed?"

"Cardoso was the cop on the job that night."

"Great," Sloan said. "This guy has had a shot at making the rescue, and that winds up getting Calloway killed and Anita kidnapped. He sounds perfect for the job."

They had come up O'Reilly into the central square. The Hotel Inglaterra shimmered before them, rising out of the general darkness like an ice castle. The park itself seemed empty. Mo was struck, again, with a sense of eeriness. Sloan did not seem concerned. On the other hand, he was half crocked.

"Maybe he's not the perfect guy," Mo said. "But he's the only guy I got. Unless you've got some other idea."

"I do," Sloan said. "Let's say he's the guy. He knows the mountains. He knows the rebels. Maybe he's straight."

"So?"

"So, I'm going with him."

Mo was surprised. He said, "But why? This guy's a pro. This is what he does for a living. You're a musician."

"Let me ask you this," Sloan said. "Is Cardoso in love with her?"

"No!" Mo said. "It's not like that at all."

"Then that's why I have to go. It matters more to me than it does to anybody else."

Mo said, "I understand that, but you gotta—"

"Shit!" Sloan said. "This looks bad."

Four men came rushing out from the shadows, moving quickly and silently past Sloan and Mo. At the same time, two cars came into the central square, from opposite directions, into the boulevard fronting the Hotel Inglaterra.

Sloan said, "Get down!"

He grabbed Mo's elbow, and the two of them dove into a bank of shrubbery.

The two cars screeched to a halt. A voice shouted, *"¡Pa' una Cuba libre!"* The night shook with explosions. Sloan and Mo could feel the heat on the tops of their heads and the backs of their hands. The night sky went orange. Sloan jerked his head up to look. A line of twenty cars, parked in front of the Inglaterra, had burst into flames. A dozen men were dashing away from them, disappearing into the shadows around the central plaza. Glass shattered. A car tire popped and then hissed empty with a sigh.

Sloan sat up, scanning the shadows for men, watching the sky. From the distance came the cry of an ambulance or fire truck, followed by the clanging of its bell. Shutters on apartments overlooking the plaza began to clatter open. Voices fell on them. Mo brushed dirt from his forehead and raised his eyes to the burning line of automobiles in front of the hotel.

"Otherwise," Sloan said, "if I don't go with him, this is what's going to happen to Anita."

"Okay," Mo said. "You got it. Do you think we can get up now?"

"It's over," Sloan said. "But I'm afraid your man Phil and your car were part of the barbecue."

Sloan was only half right. The black Lansky car was indeed among those melted to the ground in front of the Inglaterra. But Phil was alive, standing on the sidewalk, his arms crossed over his chest, hopping anxiously from foot to foot. When he saw Mo and Sloan approach, coming across the park garden that faced the hotel, he began wringing his hands.

"I sorry, I sorry, I sorry, señor. There is *nothing* for me to do, señor. The car—*boom!*"

Mo said, "Are you all right?"

"Yes, señor. I was inside."

"Inside the hotel?"

"Sorry, señor. I have only one *mojito,* in the kitchen, with my friend. He is a cook."

"I'm glad you're not hurt," Mo said. "Don't worry about the car."

"But, Señor Lansky! He will be very, very angry."

"Forget about Lansky. How about getting us a taxi?"

"Señor! At once."

Phil dashed across the plaza. Sloan and Mo watched the last of the cars burn itself out.

Sloan said, "When can I meet this guy?"

"Cardoso? I'll set it up for tomorrow."

Much later that night, a well-dressed man with a Spanish accent approached Phil as he sat nursing a brass monkey at a Vedado bar popular with the off-duty Tropicana workers. The man with the accent admired the cocktail, asked what it was, and said to the bartender, "Two more, please," then sat down next to Filomeno. When the cocktails arrived, he said in a low voice, "Listen to me, my friend: you are in terrible danger. I have come with a warning. Stay away from the American gangster. This deal he is making for the kidnapped girl is very dangerous for you."

"For me? Why for me?"

"Because you are a Cuban. To the rebels, it is a betrayal."

"But I am only his driver. I'm helping the American find his friend."

"You are part of the deal."

"But I am not! The young American wants his woman back. The gangster is going to pay the money. They are using a policeman to deliver the ransom. I have no part in it."

"It is not up to me. I am sorry."

"But you can speak to them for me. Tell them you warned me, and I explained everything."

"You have explained nothing," Scarfioti said. "Perhaps you know nothing. If you could tell them when the ransom would be delivered, perhaps . . ."

"I will find out," Filomeno said. "This is easy. I will find out, and I will tell you, and you will tell them. I am not a traitor. I am only a driver!"

"I will try to help," Scarfioti said. "Find out what you can about the delivery of the money. And I will order two more brass monkeys."

The following night, when they met again at the dim Vedado bar, Phil told Scarfioti, "The policeman is going to the Sierra Maestra, and the American musician is going with him. They leave tomorrow."

"Have the rebels been informed?"

"I don't know."

"And the money?"

"It is the gangster's money. The policeman is picking it up tomorrow."

The Spaniard considered this information. He said, "How are they going to the mountains?"

"By car, señor."

"Ah," Scarfioti said. "I think I see the solution. You must drive them."

"Ay, no, señor. How?"

"I will make an arrangement," Scarfioti said. "You will go. You will report to me what happens. I will protect you. Also, you will be paid a large sum of money. The gangster will pay you. I will pay you also."

That night the Spaniard sent a carefully worded telegram to his contact in Washington, D.C. That man placed the telegram in a file and picked up the telephone on his desk and dialed. When a voice answered at the other end, the man said, "Get this. I've had a brief from Havana. Meyer Lansky is buying a girl from Fidel Castro for a hundred thousand bucks."

The man paused, then said, "Must be some broad. I'll file it under 'P' for 'poontang.'"

In the mountains Delgado said to Bolinas, "We have had a most interesting offer. There is an American gangster who is willing to pay us one hundred thousand dollars for the American girl. *Another* one hundred thousand dollars. Imagine what we could do with two hundred thousand dollars."

"Wonderful," Bolinas said. "We will buy cannons, and a tank. A helicopter, even!"

"No, *compañero,* we will not," Delgado said. "We cannot take the money. We cannot keep the money. We are not kidnappers. We cannot afford to be."

"But she is the girlfriend of an American gangster," Bolinas said. "This is the money of an American gangster! This money represents everything we are fighting against!"

"Yes, *compañero*. You are right, of course. But we must not become the thing we are fighting against, even to win, if we are to have true victory. We are not criminals. We are the hand of justice. We cannot be kidnappers, too. Not even for two hundred thousand dollars. What a pity!"

Bolinas said, "Even so, what would you buy?"

"One helicopter!" Delgado said. "And one nickelodeon."

"One what?"

"A nickelodeon. A jukebox. You put a coin and choose a song, and music plays. It is the only thing I miss about life in the city—music! I would pay one hundred thousand dollars right now to hire Bola de Nieve and his orchestra to play a night of mambo and *son* for us."

"Imagine it! Snowball here!"

"With Louis Armstrong."

"¡*Coño!* What a night!"

"Let us decide how to answer the gangster's offer. I suppose we will have to return the girl to him, for no ransom at all."

7

The newspapers were filled with conflicting reports about the explosions at Parque Central. Each front-page account insisted that the bomb blasts were the work of the rebels, but the extent of the damage and the death toll varied. At the high end, in *El Tiempo,* two dozen cars had exploded, destroying six storefronts and killing five citizens. At the low end, in *El País,* nine cars had exploded, causing no property damage and resulting in no deaths at all.

The details did not interest Escalante. His interest was nailed to a report from an informer who chanced to be in Parque Central at the time of the blast, with his hand up his girlfriend's skirt. He told Escalante that two gringo foreigners and a Cuban were part of the assault. He saw the foreigners approach the park, while their Cuban driver left their car in front of the Hotel Inglaterra, and wait in the park until the blasts occurred. Then they made a rendezvous with the driver and escaped on foot.

Escalante cursed. Gringos! It was bad enough that Yankee communists were fueling the insurrection with money and arms. But foreigners taking part in bombings! That was a new development.

Escalante said, "This is good police work, but incomplete. Without their identities, we have nothing."

The informer, a nervous man made more nervous by Escalante, said, "I can try, *Jefe,* to discover their identities."

"Let me show you some pictures." Escalante pulled a file from his desk and removed a black-and-white photograph, which he slid across the desk.

"Was this one of the men?"

The informer said, "Yes, *Jefe!* This man was in the park."

Escalante grunted. He called out, "Redondo! Bring brandy!"

A rabbitlike sergeant stuck his head in the door and said, "Yes, *Capitán*. At once," and dashed away.

Escalante grunted again. He said, "Here is one more photograph." The captain pulled another picture from his file and slid it across the desk. The informer's face lit up with astonishment.

"It is incredible, *Jefe.* This is the other man. You are a magician."

"Not a magician. But not stupid, either. We will have a brandy, to celebrate your good work."

When he was alone again, Escalante shut his office door, poured a fresh snifter, and sat with his feet on the desk. It was beyond logic that the American gangster Mo Weiner and his friend the musician could be involved in the blasts at Parque Central. It must be coincidence, just as it was really nothing but coincidence that Escalante had their pictures in his desk. One matter could have nothing to do with the other. The kidnapping of the American girl and the murder in Cementerio del Colón of her lover, and now the rebel bombing of Parque Central—these must be unrelated.

And yet there were common elements. And common elements made for opportunities. Escalante could have the two Americans brought in for questioning. He could have Cardoso begin investigating the connection between the two Americans, and their connection to the death of the man Calloway. He could—except that he could not. Cardoso was gone. Escalante slid his heavy feet off the desk and went to his office door.

He said, "Matos! Come here at once!"

Matos was an idiot. But Matos would have to do.

They were coming for her. Men were coming for her. The girl Nilsa had stopped by Anita's tent one morning to tell her that a ransom arrangement had been made. She would be returning to Havana.

Who, Anita asked? Who was coming for her?

Nilsa did not know. She said, "Is it important? You will be free."

Anita said, "Am I free now, here in the mountains, where I don't know anyone and can't go anywhere, and people are dying all around me? Are *you* free here? If that is free, then I will be just as free when I leave here. No more. Unless . . ."

"Unless what?"

Anita turned away. "Forget it," she said. "I had a thought. It was a stupid thought."

She had imagined, for a second, that it was Deacon coming for her. But that was foolish. Deacon had no money. Deacon didn't know the revolutionaries. It would be Calloway's people. Or someone else's people.

If you are for sale, she thought, *you do not get to choose the customer.* A wave of self-disgust and self-pity broke over her.

"When are they coming?"

"Soon," Nilsa said. "Tomorrow."

"Excuse me, will you?" Anita said stiffly. "I need to pack my things."

There weren't any things to pack. The rebel women had gathered together a few necessaries for her—a toothbrush, a hairbrush, a nightgown, some underclothes—when she was first brought to the mountains. Someone had given her a book to read, too. It was a dog-eared copy of *The Good Earth,* a story about peasant women in China that had not interested her. She would leave it for the next captive. She rolled the brushes and a change of underclothes into the nightgown, tied its sleeves into a package, and sat on her cot with the package on her lap.

I have been here before, she thought. *I have always been here—waiting for some man to come get me, for some person to come and take me away.* When she was a child and her grandmother died, she went to the bus station and waited, imagining that a family would take pity on her and take her in. It was the cops, though, who mistook her for a prostitute and ran her off. Later, she waited for her "uncle" to take her to Las Vegas. He took her only to the wretched café in Shipton Wells, where he worked her like a mule and tried to force her to make love with him. Later still, she waited for Deacon.

And he *did* come for her. He *did* take her away. Until he was shot, he lived for her. But that ended. Then she waited for Albert Sherman, who took her to Hollywood, and for Nick Calloway, who took her away from Sherman and in the end brought her here. Then it was the rebels, and the police, and the ransom money . . .

She watched Nilsa walk away from her, across the muddy center of the camp. Anita didn't know where she had gotten the scars on her face, but they didn't get there nicely. Anita didn't know what made Nilsa a revolutionary, but she knew that she hadn't signed up for it at summer camp. All these rebels, maybe the women *especially,* had a hardness to them. Anita saw it even when they were kind to her.

Anita longed for a little of that hardness, or whatever it was. To be hard, to be tough, to be protected against the world. Against the men who were coming for her.

She longed, too, to have the purpose these women had. Watching Nilsa or María Fuentes, she saw women with powerful reasons to live. They had a place in their revolution, in their country, in their lives. Anita had no place. What was she for, really? Not for anything.

Anita left her tent. No point in moping. Tomorrow would come, whether she waited for it or not, whether she was afraid of it or not. Perhaps she could busy herself with the women in the kitchen. She followed Nilsa's footsteps, trying to miss the biggest of the mud puddles, going across the camp. When she got to the kitchen tent, she said to the group of Cuban women there, who were chopping vegetables and boiling water and plucking a chicken and singing a country song, *"¿Puedo ayúdate?"*

A fat Cuban woman with a kerchief on her head stopped her singing and said, "O-kay! You espeak Espanish? O-kay!" She handed Anita a towel, put a hand on her shoulder, and pointed to a stack of dishes. She said, *"Óyeme, tú. Ayúdame con los platos.* O-kay?"

Anita smiled and said, "Okay," and picked up a dish and began mopping at it with the towel. The Cuban women resumed their singing.

Sloan's head was bad. He woke an hour before he had been told to. The light from the street was killing. He had left the shutters open when he went to bed, knowing the early sun would wake him. Now he wished he hadn't. He cursed the light, and rolled from his bed thinking of beer and aspirin and Alka-Seltzer.

He had none of those. There was a couple of fingers of rum left in a bottle in the kitchen. Sloan poured that into a glass and swirled it around for a second. Then he threw the rum into the sink. The fumes rose and gagged him. Enough. He went back into the front room and lit a cigarette. He found his wristwatch. It was seven-thirty. He had half an hour.

He used it to get water splashed on his face, and a clean shirt and underwear on his body. He dusted off his shoes and shook the wrinkles out of his dark suit, and shook his draggy, baggy self down to the street. He went across the plaza to the café, where he had two cups of *café con leche* in quick succession. They made his head swim. Regretting the rum he had thrown into the sink, he said to the waiter, *"Traime un ron, mi socio."* When the waiter brought the rum, he drank it down in one swallow. A moment later the smoke in his brain began to clear. He was fixed now. His wristwatch said it was almost eight o'clock. He could see the front of his building from here. He told the waiter to bring him another rum, paid the bill, and settled in to watch for Cardoso.

He wasn't long in coming. Prompt, people like him. Sloan hadn't been introduced to the man, but there was no mistaking him, even from across the plaza. He had the long black cadillac, with the official driver behind the wheel. He had the square black suit. He had the square black shoes and the dark hat to match. Sloan got up from his seat at the café and stepped onto the curb. Cardoso was already watching him, his cop eyes sweeping across the plaza and picking out Sloan before he had hit the curb.

Cardoso had seen him in the café. There was no missing him. Why were Americans so obvious? There was something too loud about them, too obvious, too open. Even a cool customer like this guy—jazzman, ladies' man, nighttime bar-crawling man—stood out on the plaza like a shiny penny.

Cardoso said, "Stop the car here." The driver, who like the car had been supplied by the American gangster Mo Weiner, drew the car to the curb.

He was a jumpy young Cuban named Filomeno, and he said, "In the café, señor. That's him."

"I know," Cardoso said. "Keep the car running."

Cardoso got out of the car and opened the rear passenger door, watching as the American came across the street. They would spend the next two days together, at least. He took the opportunity to measure what he could now.

He saw a lean, wiry guy with dark, hollow eyes. Something about him looked beat. Was he a drug addict? He had that look, Cardoso thought. He had a demon. Maybe the demon was the girl? She was beautiful enough to be someone's devil.

Sloan gave Cardoso a weak handshake. He said, "Thank you, for helping out on this. I wouldn't like to go into the mountains on my own. Especially not carrying the big money."

"You are welcome," Cardoso said. "It is my pleasure. *Our* pleasure. This is Filomeno. I understand some Americans call him Phil."

"Phil and I have met," Sloan said. "We did a little honky-tonking one night. I think it was La Coronita, or El Cruz Azul."

Phil's face brightened. He said, "*Sí, señor.* La Coronita! Much drinking!" Then he looked at Cardoso and got quiet.

Sloan said, "What's the plan?"

Cardoso gave him about half of the available information, or a quarter. They would drive from Havana to Colón, then to Santa Clara, and on to Camagüey. There they would rendezvous with an operative from the rebel base in the hills. They would be taken to the rebel camp where Anita was being held. They would exchange the money for the girl and be escorted back down to Camagüey, and promised safe passage on the return to Havana.

This wasn't entirely true, but Cardoso felt it was true enough.

Sloan said, "How much money is it? And whose money is it?"

Cardoso said, "Señor, I do not know. I am only delivering a package—two packages. One package of money, to trade for one package of woman. Beyond that . . ."

Sloan recited, "Theirs not to reason why / Theirs but to do or die."

"Aha," Cardoso said, and laughed. "You know the poem. 'The Charge of the Light Brigade.' A great tale of heroic death, no?"

Sloan said, "It's Tennyson, I think. I studied it in school."

"I also," Cardoso said. "But the line says 'Theirs but to do *and* die,' señor—not do *or* die. Perhaps our situation is different."

"I hope so. Let's get going."

"*Vámonos, Filo,*" Cardoso said.

It took them three hours' hard driving to make Colón, and another three to make Santa Clara. The countryside was like nothing Sloan had ever seen. The red dirt reminded him of Georgia, but the trees were all wrong and too mixed up, and so was the livestock. Driving out, they rose through fields bordered with palm trees into hills blanketed with piney woods. There were great beasts that looked like water buffalo in the rice fields and braces of yoked oxen with upturned horns and humps on their backs pulling carts on the streets of the little towns. Down the main avenue of a hamlet east of Colón, one of these beasts was pulling what looked like the back half of a flatbed Ford, filled with laughing schoolchildren. They gave the black car a stern going-over as they passed. Then one of the boys said, "*¡Mira mira! ¡Un yanqui!*" and all the children began to wave.

For Cardoso, it was like going home. He felt it as soon as they passed out of Matanzas. It had to do with the smells—of the fields, the loamy soil, and of things burning. Everywhere were little fires—

rubbish fires, fires burning corn husks, cooking fires in the small towns—and their brown, ashen odors made Cardoso feel like a child again. The salty air of the coast gave way to the green, yeasty smell of the crops. The breeze carried hints of hay and cattle and things alive and dying. They passed tobacco barns and open dirt fields where rice was being dried, and acres and acres of sugarcane. The road, once they passed Colón, was clogged with farm trucks carrying workers, carrying bananas or pineapples, carrying bales of hay and barrels of dried rice. What a rich land! Cardoso had forgotten why he left the country, forgotten how he hated the backbreaking work in the fields, the dirt and the heat, the lean times. He remembered now only the honesty of the workingmen and -women and the good cheer of the poor farm families, the purity of their labor and their lives.

Cardoso glanced into the backseat. Sloan was asleep with his face pressed against the window. Like an innocent. All Americans are innocents. Even the criminals.

The highway was slower after Santa Clara. The roads had been disputed and fought over there for two years. There were craters where Batista's bombs had fallen, and craters where the rebels' grenades had exploded. A huge truck carrying cattle had broken its axle in one pothole, near the village of Jatibonico. Traffic in both directions came to a halt while men from ten vehicles postured and argued on the pavement. There was no ramp to lower the cattle. The truck, with the cattle inside it, was too heavy for the men to move. Without a rear axle, the truck would not roll. Cardoso got out of the black sedan to attempt to bring order to the chaos. His voice was not heard.

One man was saying, "*Señores,* we will cut a tree and build an axle for the truck, and together we will lift the truck from the road."

Another said, "No! We will butcher the cattle in the truck and distribute the meat. We will eat like men! Then we will be strong, and the truck will be light, and we can move it wherever we like."

Sloan woke up and said, "Uh-oh. Men at work."

Cardoso ordered the other cars and trucks off the road, and drove through the collection of vehicles. They had lost an hour in the confusion.

Ten miles on, the air became thick with a new smell of something burning, and soon the road was covered with smoke.

Cardoso said, "The rebels have been busy."

"What is it?" Sloan asked him.

"They are burning the sugarcane fields."

"Why?"

"Ask them when we get there," Cardoso said.

When it became dark, somewhere near Ciego de Ávila, he said, "This road is not safe at night. We will stop here to eat and sleep, and continue again in the morning."

Mo Weiner spent the day inspecting the final stages of construction on his three casinos. It was just over a week until their planned opening nights. Everything was on schedule.

By nightfall, having stopped at the Miramar and the Presidente and the Sunset, Mo needed a drink and a meal. He told Meyer's driver to take him to the Nacional. It was closest to the Sunset, of the joints he knew. He could sit in the big lounge, with its picture-window view of the sea, and have a sandwich and a glass of champagne.

The driveway was deserted, and the lobby was quiet. The Nacional, like the other places, didn't move until midnight. At six P.M. it was like the graveyard shift. A few tourists sat in the lobby lounge chairs, writing postcards, reading paperbacks, or scanning newspaper headlines.

The lounge was empty but for a couple of slicks at the bar. One of them was George Raft. Mo knew him from the pictures, and from Vegas. Raft had come up hard, a tough kid from Hell's Kitchen. All his best pals were street hoods who wound up in the mob. Raft went to Hollywood and started playing hard guys in the movies. But he stayed connected. He made deals for his friends in Hollywood and New York. He helped them invest in movie studios and in gambling halls and restaurants. Mo had heard that Raft was part owner of the Capri, where he sometimes worked the main room like a maître d'. What a life! First you're the star of *Scarface* and *Johnny Angel*. Now you're an overdressed headwaiter at a casino in Havana.

When the waiter came, Mo took his eyes off George Raft and said, "I want a chicken salad sandwich and a bottle of decent champagne."

"*Sí, señor*. At once."

Raft and his companions at the bar glanced up as the waiter sped by. Raft left the other drinkers and went over to Mo's table.

"Hello, my friend. Long time."

Mo said, "Hello, George. It *has* been a long time."

"You're doing well."

"I can't complain. Will you join me?"

Like a lot of actors, Raft had a large head and a big, expressive face. He was more lined, and older-looking, than Mo remembered.

Raft said, "You're coming on strong with the Sunset. Opening soon?"

"Next week. Along with the Presidente and the Miramar."

"Meyer's pleased."

Mo blanched.

"Relax," Raft said. "Down here, everybody knows everybody's business."

"I don't like 'em knowing *my* business."

"You'll get used to it. Is it true you're calling all three joints Paraiso?"

"That's right. Paraiso Miramar. Paraiso Sunset . . ."

"You know about the prison, right? The torture chamber?"

"Coincidence," Mo said smoothly. "I didn't mean it as a joke."

"It's some joke," Raft said.

When the champagne arrived, Mo said, "Have a glass, George."

Raft said, "No can do. I got to get back. That's Meyer's brother, Jake. You know him, right?"

"I've never met him."

"You should keep it that way," Raft said. "He's upset that Meyer's giving you so much action. He thinks *he* shoulda got the Miramar and the Sunset. And the Presidente."

"He couldn't deliver them," Mo said. "I delivered them."

"Easy," Raft said, and stood away from the table. "You get no argument from me. I'm just saying."

"I appreciate the warning," Mo said. "How's business at the Capri?"

"Couldn't be better," Raft said. "We're losing a few customers because of the bombings, you know. But the real gamblers, you can't scare them away. I'll be seeing you around."

"I'll be around."

Raft moved back to the bar like a man on greased wheels. One of his companions turned to look at him, then sent a look at Mo. He was heavy-faced and dark-browed over his black eyeglasses and looked as if he'd escaped from the ape house. *That's Jake Lansky,* Mo thought. Two of the other men at the bar also turned and glanced at Mo. Jake said something to them, under his breath. Mo, knowing it was the wrong thing to do, raised his glass in a silent toast and winked at Lansky—mud in your eye, big shot—and then took a long, cool slug.

Scarfioti, the Spaniard, came in just as Mo was picking up his chicken salad sandwich. Mo saw the shiny bald dome and then made the face. Scarfioti glanced once around the room, casually, and seemed not to notice Mo. Instead, he went to the bar and shook hands with George Raft and Jake Lansky and the other gorillas drinking there. Mo watched Scarfioti's back. He had expressive hands, and he gestured the way a conductor leads an orchestra. His hands rose, fingers in the air, to say, "Listen," then went flat, fingers out, to say, "Shhhh," and then turned palms up to say, "And what do you think happened next?" You could almost hear the story without hearing the words. At the conclusion, Scarfioti's hands came slowly together, like the curtain drawing shut at the movie theater. The End.

Then he turned and looked directly at Mo. His face broke into a smile. He said, "My friend from Las Vegas!" and went across the room to him.

He lost his smile on the ten-foot walk from the bar to the table. By the time he arrived, hands out, shaking Mo's one in his two, he had no smile at all.

He said, "We must talk. There is some trouble."

"Tell me."

Scarfioti glanced over his shoulder, at the crowd at the bar. He turned back to Mo. He said, "There is going to be a problem with the delivery of the ransom money. The *rebeldes* in the Sierra, they have been told to expect a trick. They believe the men delivering the ransom money are officers with the Security force. They believe they are going to be arrested. Or worse."

Mo took a bite of his chicken salad sandwich, and a sip of champagne, without taking his eyes off Scarfioti and without any expression on his face. When it was clear that Scarfioti was finished, Mo patted his lips with a napkin and said, "This is an interesting story. But I have no idea what you're talking about."

Scarfioti smiled. It was a cracked, difficult smile. "But, señor . . . The ransom money! And the girl."

"I have heard something about this," Mo said. "But it doesn't involve me in any way. May I pour you a glass of champagne?"

The Spaniard's smile soured. He stood up straight, so formally that Mo thought he might click his heels and say, "Heil Hitler." Mo grinned at him, high wattage, to show there were no hard feelings. And to show that he could not be intimidated.

Scarfioti said, "Well, I have told you, señor. I hope the information will be useful. I will return now to other concerns."

"Thanks, pal. I'll be seeing you around. Say hi to Jake for me, will you?"

Scarfioti got that sick smile back on his face and said, "Of course, my friend. Good day."

Mo watched Scarfioti go back to his friends at the bar. Mo thought, as if the idea hadn't occurred to him before, *I can't do that. I can't go stand with my friends at the bar. I have no friends.* It was an interesting thought. He had another glass of champagne, finished his sandwich, and looked out the big picture window at the bright blue sea below.

Jaime Matos was no fool. Irrespective of what Escalante thought of him or what Escalante actually shouted at him, Jaime Matos was not an idiot. He had been given an impossible assignment, and he knew it.

All that day he did in a hurry what he was accustomed to doing slowly. He went around, asking questions, listening to gossip, entertaining rumors, paying attention to the details, and doling out small sums of money for the details that interested him most. He spoke with two bartenders, four barbers, four taxi drivers, one cousin who owned a butcher shop, another cousin who was a pilot for hire, a third cousin who was a waiter at the Nacional, and two friends who were professional drinkers. He didn't say what he was looking for.

Each of them told him a lot, in return. The Cuban is a talking man, Matos reflected, coming out of a barber shop for a haircut he didn't need, on Vedado's Calle 23. The average Cuban is gossipy and social by nature—to a fault, just as he is musical and comical and romantic. Everyone told him something useful.

Matos flagged down a taxi after the haircut and told the driver to take him to Old Havana, across the port, to the restaurant at the fort guarding the harbor. Here was Matos's true Cuba. The driver circled the monument of Máximo Gómez, a leader of the war of independence against Spain. They passed the ruins of the notorious prison of Tacón, where José Martí, the father of Cuban independence, had been held. Across the water, work was under way on an enormous statue of Christ. He was made of marble and would stand with his hands outstretched, in peace, facing the water, when he was finished. Behind the Christ, the ruins of the grand Fortaleza de San Carlos de la Cabana. From those ramparts the Cubans defended Havana against the British in 1762. What a brave history!

Matos told the *taxista* to wait for him and gave him a ten-peso note to buy some lunch. He then told the headwaiter at the café that he was on police business and wanted a meal, but did not want to be disturbed. The headwaiter led him solemnly to a table overlooking the harbor. Matos ate his meal in silence.

The silence didn't help. He spread his cards before him. What he knew did not make sense. The rebels had kidnapped an American girl and were holding her for ransom. Her boyfriend agreed to pay the ransom but was murdered while trying to do so. The rebels had reclaimed the girl and taken her to the mountains. Now another man, an American gangster, had agreed to pay another ransom. Matos's disgraced colleague Cardoso had been hired to deliver the ransom money and had gone to the Sierra Maestra with a driver and a hit man supplied by the American gangster.

Those facts, if they were facts, made sense. It was a good day's work. Matos ate his meal—black beans and rice, and a pork *chuleta,* cooked with plenty of garlic and *sofrito,* and fried plantains—and considered which of these facts, when he reported them to Escalante, might hurt him. He did not think any of them would. They might hurt Cardoso, but Cardoso was no longer his concern.

Two hours later, sitting in Escalante's office, his heart fluttering slightly as it did in the presence of this difficult man, Matos laid out the facts as best he could. Escalante listened, puffing at a huge double corona, nodding, making notes with a pencil.

"It is as I thought," he said when Matos paused. "Cardoso is a turncoat and a traitor. He was probably working for the American gangster Lansky the entire time. That is why he shot Señor Calloway—to get the ransom money—before he was outsmarted by the rebels. Now he will try again. It is a double cross."

"Yes, *Jefe,*" Matos said. "It must be so."

"The roads will be quiet," Escalante said. "The rebels are burning sugarcane fields from Matanzas to Ciego de Ávila. Cardoso's car will not be hard to find. We will track them. They will lead us to the rebels. You have done good work. You are not to speak of this to anyone."

"No, *Jefe,*" Matos said. "Not to anyone."

"Go away, then," Escalante said.

Matos was halfway to the door when Escalante said into a telephone, "Put me through to the airport." Matos pulled the door closed behind him.

Scarfioti, who was a gambling man, figured he had one shot. It was a long shot. He had played the outside points one way, and it hadn't played out for him. He had one more play. There wasn't a lot at stake. But he liked to win. Even more, like every inveterate gambler, he liked to *play*. And in playing, the thing that mattered most was the thing that was about to happen. The whole thrill of gambling was the thrill of the wheel as it spun and the ball as it bounced—not the winning, not the losing, not the getting of the money or the paying out of the money, but the great, agonizing, impossibly sweet moment of not knowing where the ball would fall. The higher the stakes, the longer the shot, the more agonizingly sweet that moment was.

He'd been disappointed by Mo Weiner's behavior at the Nacional. Scarfioti was certain that his information was correct, that the American gangster was bankrolling the ransom and rescue of the girlfriend of the dead Calloway. He was certain because he had sent Cardoso that way, and he knew Cardoso had no other way to go. His little spies, the men and women around Havana who saw things and then said things—for a little pocket money—had convinced him that Cardoso had set out, using the American gangster's car and driver, for the mountains. His spies told him that they had a third man with them and that he was another American. Scarfioti was sure this was one of Lansky's people, or else some muscle Mo Weiner had brought in to cover the money on the journey to the Sierra.

The question now became this: how to unsettle the deal, once the deal was in play? The Spaniard could find no value, for himself, in Weiner's paying $100,000 in ransom money to the rebels for the freedom of some American slut whose millionaire boyfriend was dead. Scarfioti could not get a piece of that money, and he did not benefit in any other way. If the deal broke down, though, the ensuing crisis might produce an opportunity. Scarfioti profited from crisis. He made loans to businessmen in crisis. He earned his keep with the men in Washington by reporting details of crisis. His ability to deliver information to Batista's operatives convinced the men in Havana that he was valuable to them—which meant they kept their hands off him.

There wasn't any way to profit from this—unless he could trade on the information or somehow foul it up.

It took several hours of patient waiting and intuitive wandering.

Scarfioti was like a hunter, quietly moving through the woods, secure in the knowledge that his prey would present itself when the time was right, that he must only be calm and remain ready. Scarfioti hit the tables at the Capri and the San Souci. He lost a little at the Capri, but he won a little at the San Souci, where he also had a genial moment with two of Trafficante's boys, two red-eyed triggermen who looked hungry for trouble.

Scarfioti found the man he needed to see at El Floridita. It was three or four o'clock in the morning. The crowd was still thick at the bar. The air was heavy with cigar smoke and drunken gossip, chopped into inaudible chunks by the whirling ceiling fans. Scarfioti came through the door and waved at Faustino, who winked at him suggestively and nodded his head to the back of the bar. Scarfioti went there. Faustino said, "Your friend was looking for you, señor."

"Ay, Faustino! I have too many friends. What friend?"

"The American ambassador. No. The *assistant* to the ambassador. I cannot remember his name. Like the famous writer."

"Dickens? Dickens was here?"

"He is here now, señor. In the back."

The Spaniard thanked Faustino and palmed him an American ten-dollar bill. Going across the crowded room, which filled now with the sound of a blaring Cuban rumba, he realized he still didn't know exactly how to make his play. He was like a man gone drunk on dice. He would suddenly know, just *know,* what the next tumble would show. He'd lay his money down, looking like a chump, and say, "Hundred dollar six the hard way." Heads would turn. Then he'd hit the six.

"Señor Dickens!" he said. "I am pleased to see you!"

The wretched-looking Yankee diplomat was paler and more wrinkled than usual. It surprised Scarfioti, every time he saw him, that the Americans would employ a man so badly groomed. His hairpiece looked like something shot by the pioneers. His skin was yellow-white, unhealthy. His suit didn't fit and looked slept in. He had two women with him, middle-aged American frumps who'd obviously been away from their makeup mirrors for many hours. The Spaniard bowed formally and greeted them.

Dickens rose from his seat and said, "Señor. Good evening. Nice to see you. Let me introduce Mrs. Gorman and Mrs. Hall. They are from Seattle."

"Really?" Scarfioti made himself look astonished. "Welcome to Havana, señoras. We are lucky to have you with us. Do you find Havana romantic?"

The two women blushed and giggled.

"So do I!" Scarfioti said. "When an American visits Havana, it is like one country making love to another."

Leaving them to consider that, Scarfioti leaned close to Dickens and said, "How have you been? Are you cockfighting recently?"

"No, no," Dickens said, pulling Scarfioti away from the table. "And I don't like people to know about that, actually. Not becoming for a member of the diplomatic service. Cockfighting. Jai alai. Gambling. Not good. I do hear *this*, though. . . ."

Dickens beckoned Scarfioti farther forward. The Spaniard winced. Dickens's halitosis was infamous. He smelled tonight of old rubber. Of old *rubbers*, even. Scarfioti inhaled sharply and tried to breathe through his mouth, smiling sideways at the two gaping American women.

"I hear that Favela is going to run in front tomorrow at La Paloma. It's fixed."

"Ah," Scarfioti said. "What a tip! Is it good?"

"The best," Dickens breathed.

The Spaniard laughed out loud. He said, "Faustino! Daiquiris, please!" Dickens looked like a man who'd just proposed marriage. What an idiot! The fix at La Paloma was one of the oldest gimmicks in Havana. Someone puts the word on the street that this horse or that is going to run first, that the race is fixed. Usually the news is accompanied by the inside dope that the race is being fixed for someone special. Meyer Lansky has a senator in from Washington. Batista's mistress is going to be at the track. The word gets out, the odds start to shift, and pretty soon there is a favorite. The odds on the true favorite drop accordingly. The natural winner comes in with long-shot odds. Sometimes the gimmick goes the other way, too. Someone puts the word out that the fifth at La Paloma is fixed, that

such-and-such a favored horse is supposed to run *out* of the money—
it's a double cross. The odds start to shift. Someone places a bundle
on the favored pony anyway.

In several years of playing around the tracks of Havana, Scarfioti
had never been given a tip that was legit. He was surprised at Dickens's gullibility. But then Dickens was an American. The Americans
fell for everything.

When the daiquiris came, Scarfioti returned to the table and
poured. He said, "For the tip!" and toasted Dickens. He said to one
of the two women, "He is the future of American diplomacy in the
Caribbean. Believe it!"

Half an hour later the Spaniard said, "Well, señoras, it is past my
bedtime. Señor Dickens, may I have a word with you privately? A
matter of some diplomatic urgency."

Dickens looked alarmed but rose from his seat just the same. He
accompanied Scarfioti to the door.

"I have received some troubling information," Scarfioti said. "It is
not my business, but perhaps it will be useful for you."

Dickens looked over his shoulder at the two women from Seattle. They had their noses in the daiquiri and were paying no attention to him. Nevertheless, he said to Scarfioti, "Yes, please. But let's
go outside."

In the street Dickens huddled close. In the open air his halitosis
was not so noticeable. Scarfioti breathed more easily. He took Dickens's elbow.

"You have heard, of course, that the rebels are still holding the
girlfriend of the dead American, Calloway."

"Of course. My people are monitoring the situation."

"Good," Scarfioti said. "Here is what you need to know. The ransom money is being paid by Meyer Lansky. It is being paid through
one of his operatives, the American gangster Morris Weiner. Weiner
has hired two men, one Cuban and one American, to take the money
to the rebels. They are carrying one million dollars."

"A million!"

"*Sí, señor*. One million. But it is a trick. The two men do not
intend to pay the ransom money. One of the men is a Security officer.

He intends to trick the rebels. He will capture or assassinate the rebel leader, Carlos Delgado, and return with the money."

"What will happen to the girl?"

"The girl?" The Spaniard was surprised at the question. "The girl is of no importance. She will be sacrificed."

Dickens grew even more pale and yellow. He said, "This is alarming news. Here is the thing that worries me. Does Lansky know it is a trick?"

Aha! Scarfioti almost burst into tears. Of course! That was it! The duck had risen from the blind, directly in front of him. He had been patient. His patience had paid off. The shot was his to take.

He said, "No. Lansky does not know."

"Crikey," Dickens said. "This could be catastrophic!"

"I thought you would need to know," Scarfioti said. "I have told no one else. Please, be careful with this information. It is explosive."

"Crikey," Dickens said again. "I have to go. Thank you. I can't tell you how grateful I am."

"It is nothing, my friend. You will return the favor someday."

Dickens swallowed hard, nodded, and turned and ran back into El Floridita. Scarfioti walked half a block, into the central plaza. He saw the old shoeshine man, Havana Brown, slumped and sleeping on a bench. *I would like to end up like that myself, one day,* Scarfioti thought. Such peace! Not tonight, though.

He had set the wheels in motion. He had placed his bet. He must wait now, to see where the ball would fall.

The morning broke calm and still. Ciego de Ávila, a simple, square town of whitewashed houses surrounding a central *parque* and plaza, awoke slowly. Cardoso had come down at dawn to look for *café con leche.* He'd been given a mug in the lobby of the Hotel Ávila. He sat watching the heavy horse-drawn carriages lining the plaza, waiting for fares.

He had not slept well. Doubt consumed him. He was not certain that his plan was the right one or that he had planned it the right way. Because he had not seen the rebel camp, though, and because he was working with too many unknowns, it was the best plan he could muster. The American might foul it up. The American girl might foul it up. The rebels themselves—for who knew, really, their game?—might foul it up. There was nothing in the police manual for this kind of situation.

So, working with what he had, Cardoso ran scenarios in his head, like a chess player anticipating an attack and planning a counter-attack. If this . . . then that. If *that* . . . then *this*.

He had a second *café con leche* and plate of *pan tostado*. Filomeno the driver came downstairs an hour after Cardoso. He, too, ordered his *café con leche*. He said, pointing at the horse-drawn carriages parked in the town square, "That was my father's job."

"The driver, or the horse?" Cardoso said.

"You may joke, if you like," Filomeno said. "He kept his family fed."

"And the horse as well, perhaps. I am going upstairs to see about the Yankee."

Cardoso knocked on Sloan's door twice without getting an answer. He was about to go downstairs to beat the desk clerk out of a passkey when he heard feet fall on the floor and move toward him. The door opened. A rumpled Sloan squinted at him from behind a lock of hair.

Cardoso said, "I am sorry to wake you. But we must go."

Sloan said, "I get it. I got it. Give me five minutes."

"We are waiting in the lobby. Do you take *café?*"

"Yes."

"It will be waiting, too."

Sloan swung the door closed on Cardoso's stern features. This waking at dawn was like rising for an execution. Sloan half expected to see a sad-faced old *padre* waiting for him in the hall with a Bible for the long walk to the gallows. The sun wasn't even up. Or was it? Sloan went to the shutters on his windows and pushed them open. The sun was bright and clear, shining down on an empty cobble-stone street lined with shops painted pink and green and blue and ochre.

He was five minutes throwing his wrinkled suit back onto his lanky frame and throwing cold water onto his tired, pale face. He reflected, at his reflection, that there was a time when he might have been mistaken for a handsome man. From about twenty feet. In dim lighting. If you'd had a few cocktails. Which was the way that most people saw him, after all—at night, across the orchestra pit, onstage, after a highball or two. Then he remembered, *That was not how Anita first saw me, and I was good enough—better than good enough—for her.* The thought gave Sloan strength. He got downstairs and got the *café con leche* down his throat, and asked for another.

Cardoso said, "We'll bring the car around. Meet us in the plaza." He threw coins on the table and left Sloan waiting for his coffee.

The rebels had issued only one set of instructions. Cardoso was to drive east, past Camagüey, leave the main highway at the turnoff for Coronella, and proceed from there at not more than twenty-five miles per hour. He would be met by an escort vehicle, which would lead them into the rebel camp. He was not to leave his automobile, or engage the escort vehicle, until he arrived in the camp and was told to stop.

Filomeno drove in silence. Cardoso could feel his anxiety. He didn't look like a coward. But you never knew. Men who were afraid could be capable of immense courage under fire. And brave men could turn and run, too. Filomeno did not know what Cardoso had planned for this day. Neither did the American. His anxiety, then, must be confined to simpler things. They were going to a place of violence, occupied by men of violence. Of course they were afraid.

The American looked calm, though. He sat in the center of the backseat, his arms spread onto the cushions, his head lolling back, watching the sky through the back window.

It was two hours on the road before they came to the turnoff for Coronella. Cardoso saw it first. He said, "Here is the road to the mountains."

Filomeno said, "Yes, señor."

"It is not much longer. Watch for the rebels' car. They may appear at any moment."

"What do you think about the airplane?" Sloan asked him.

Cardoso said, "What airplane?"

"Haven't you seen it?" Sloan tilted his head toward the back window. "The same airplane has flown over us three or four times. Since about an hour ago."

"*¡Coñó! Qué jodienda,*" Cardoso said. "The rebels have airplanes now. They are watching, perhaps to make certain we are coming alone, without the army following us."

"That's okay for them," Sloan said. "But what about us? How do we know these rebels don't have their own army following us? After we give up the ransom money, why would they let us go? Why wouldn't they just kill us?"

Cardoso turned to him and smiled. He said, "Why, indeed? That is a possibility."

Sloan winced. He said, "Then you'd better give me a weapon."

"You have no weapon?" It had not occurred to Cardoso that Sloan would be unarmed.

"Of course I have no weapon. I'm a cornet player."

Cardoso opened the glove box. There were matching black Luger pistols, German-made, along with two boxes of ammunition. He drew out one of the Lugers, checked that it was loaded, and handed it to Sloan.

"You know how to use this weapon?" he asked.

Sloan said, "Let's see. I point it and pull the trigger, right?"

Cardoso smiled. He said, "That's correct. Make sure you point it at the person you want to kill. For now, please stop pointing it at me."

Sloan stuck the pistol in his waistband.

Cardoso said, "And please do not shoot anyone at all, no matter what happens, until I give the order to fire. Is that understood?"

"Yep."

"Have you a weapon, Filomeno?"

"No, señor," the driver said. "I am a bartender. I do not want a weapon."

Cardoso paused, reflected, and said, "You are a bartender?"

"*Sí, señor*. I am a bartender in the main bar of the Tropicana lounge."

"You are not Morris Weiner's driver—or Meyer Lansky's driver?"

"No, señor. Only I drive three or four times for Señor Mo, for extra money."

Cardoso turned to Sloan. He said, "Did you know this?"

"Not me, boss," Sloan said. "I wasn't on the planning committee for this caper. I thought Phil was with you."

Cardoso scanned the road in front of them, cursing his own short-sightedness. Why hadn't he checked up on Filomeno? What a stupid mistake. If he was just a bartender, as he said, why was he asked to take part in this dangerous work? If he was not one of Lansky's professionals, why had he been sent along? *¡Coñó!*

The woods were getting thicker. Low farm huts were scattered here and there behind the trees. Donkeys and oxen huddled in pairs around them. There were no people. The car rolled past a roadside store with a bright red Coca-Cola sign in front. There should, Cardoso thought, be knots of children playing in front of a store like that and pairs of women carrying bags and baskets. But the road was empty. The rebels must have put out the word that there would be activity in the region, to help the locals protect themselves from danger. That meant the rebels expected trouble. Did they expect to be firing on their visitors, or to be fired upon? The road ahead, rising into the mountains, was clear.

Cardoso stuck the other Luger back into the glove box. He said, "It won't be long now."

Escalante had never before received any communication from Guantánamo. He had never been to Guantánamo. But he understood the communication clearly. A voice at the other end of the line said, in foreign-accented Spanish, "I am phoning on behalf of the American commander of the United States military base at Guantánamo. I have been asked to translate for the commander. Is this a secure line?"

"Yes," Escalante told him, and then wondered if that were true.

"One moment."

Escalante heard English being spoken. He heard *rebels* and *kidnapped* and then other words he did not understand.

The translator spoke again in his stiff, American-school Spanish. "It has come to the attention of the commmander that Cuban rebels have kidnapped an American citizen and are holding her against her will in the Sierra."

"Yes."

"It has also come to the attention of the commander that you have a surveillance aircraft in the vicinity."

"Yes."

There was another pause. Then the translator said, "What do you intend to do?"

Escalante was frightened. What if this were a trick? What if it were not a trick? How to know? He said, "Once we have a location for the rebel base, we will begin an assault."

The commander listened to the translation, then barked something back. The translator said, "With what?"

"We have support aircraft standing by, and we have troops within one hour of the suspected rebel site."

The translator said these words in English, then said, "Please wait."

Escalante waited. Shapes passed by the smoked glass of his office windows. He smelled coffee brewing. Someone was smoking an expensive cigar. Who? No one in the building except Escalante could afford decent cigars. Unless there'd been a shakedown, or a bribe. Which meant it could be anyone. Except Cardoso, who was taking the ultimate bribe, or Matos, the idiot who was chasing Cardoso. Escalante wondered what amount of money Cardoso had been promised.

"The commander would like to offer you a suggestion," the translator said at last. "Our intelligence operatives inform us that a large ransom is being paid in exchange for the freedom of this hostage. The money belongs to an American citizen of some importance. The commander will offer you his assistance in the form of air support. But the hostage and the money must be retrieved."

Escalante said, "But why? Who does the money belong to?"

The translator repeated this question in English. Escalante heard the American commander say to the translator, "None of his goddamn business."

The translator said, "We are not able to share that information at this time."

Escalante imagined the rebel base. He imagined the dirt roads leading to it, the thick woods surrounding it, the spotter plane, the rebel troops dug in, the government soldiers making the assault. It was impossible.

He said, "It is impossible. I do not know how to attack the rebels and guarantee the safety of the hostage and the ransom money."

There was another long pause. The translator had placed his hand over the telephone this time, and Escalante could not hear any words being spoken.

Then the translator said, "It is not impossible. You will wait until the surveillance aircraft has located the rebel base. Then you will report its location to us, as well as the information regarding the location of the car carrying the ransom money. We will make the assault. You will be responsible only for retrieving the car with the ransom money."

Escalante considered this. Something was wrong. He said, "But what about the girl?"

The translator asked this question in English. Then he said, "The ransom money, the primary concern. We assume the girl will not be among the combatants. She will probably survive the assault."

"I understand," Escalante said. "How will I communicate with you?"

"We will have a man in your office in fifteen minutes," the translator said after a pause. "He will communicate with us when your information becomes available."

"I understand."

When the line clicked dead, Escalante slumped in his seat. He was limp, damp, and intimidated. He knew he owed his job to the Americans. Without the support of the big businesses—Coca-Cola,

United Fruit, Pan Am, Meyer Lansky, Santo Trafficante, and others—
the government that employed him would have collapsed long ago.
For this, if for nothing else, he hated the Americans. The rebels were
wrong. Their solution was the wrong solution. But the Yankees . . .

Fifteen minutes later, almost to the minute, there was a rap at his
door. Escalante stood up and said, "Enter."

Through the door came the trembling Redondo, leading an
impeccably dressed man carrying a Panama hat and walking stick.
He was entirely bald and had a brilliant white smile. He said, in an
accent that came straight from Madrid, "Capitán Escalante! What a
pleasure to meet you! I am here today on behalf of the American military commander at Guantánamo. May I sit down?"

"Of course," Escalante said. "Redondo, bring us brandy and soda."

The visitor sat. Escalante sat facing him. He said, "I was expecting
an American. But you are from Spain?"

"I am an American citizen," the visitor exclaimed. "Of course!
How else would I come to call on you? But you have a fine ear. By
birth, I am a Spaniard! But my name is Scarfioti—an Italian name!"

"Ah," Escalante said. "And you are employed by the American
military?"

"Employed? No! I am never employed. But I make myself available, here and there, now and then, where I can be helpful. In return,
others are helpful to me. After today, perhaps, you and I can become
helpful to each other."

"Perhaps," Escalante said. "Here. A drink."

The shaky Redondo clattered in with a tray carrying a bottle,
glasses, and a syphon and deposited it on the desk. Escalante rose and
began mixing drinks. He handed a highball glass to his guest.

"To Cuba, señor," Escalante said.

"And to the revolution!" Scarfioti answered with a grin. "Without
it, what would we do?"

Nilsa, who was now known only as La Vaca, came away from Carlos
Delgado's tent at midmorning. They had met for an hour. Delgado was
very concerned about reports coming from Havana. The government

forces were again moving aircraft from the capital to the U.S. military base at Guantánamo. This action was in direct contravention to the official American policy and broke the American promise to no longer supply the government forces with arms or assist in arming or refueling government aircraft at their military base. But there could be no other explanation for the transfer of Cuban military aircraft.

The rebels had occupied the hills surrounding the U.S. base for over a year. Lookouts there would know at once if any Cuban aircraft took off and began flying inland. There would be at least thirty minutes' warning, then, if an assault were launched. Delgado wanted Nilsa's opinion on the readiness of the camp. Could they evacuate to a safe location in thirty minutes or less?

Nilsa thought so. Losses would depend on how much time was available and on how much equipment was to be salvaged. If all the weapons and ammunition had to be moved, thirty minutes was of course not enough time.

Delgado had surprised her. He said, "We can always get more weapons and ammunition. We cannot always get more true Cuban patriots. We will concentrate on saving them, and hope for the best as far as *matériel* is concerned. You know that today is the day for this ransom money."

"I know," Nilsa said.

"We had reports from Ciego de Ávila. They left shortly after eight o'clock."

"Then it will not be long. Shall I tell the *gringa* to get ready?"

"I am sure she is ready," Delgado said. "She has been ready for some time. But let us be on the alert, just the same. I am uneasy with this ransom business. Trading with gangsters."

"They are not worse than the government stooges you have negotiated with in the past," Nilsa said.

"Perhaps not, but they are Americans. I understand Cubans—even the evil ones. The Americans . . . I do not feel them the same way."

"They are only human," Nilsa said.

"The Yankees are human?" Delgado pretended to be shocked. "La Vaca, you are transformed. What next? Batista is not so bad also? You have been in the hills too long, my child."

Nilsa smiled. She was, at that moment, entirely in love with El Gato. "I have been in the hills too long. I would like to be on the beach, in the sun, playing in the water, as I did when I *was* someone's child."

"Soon, then," Delgado said. "I promise you this. Soon, we will all swim in Havana Bay."

"I will go tell the *gringa* that it is nearly time."

"Thank you," he said. "And also please send María Fuentes to me, eh? I have to speak with her today."

Nilsa found Anita working with the laundry women. She looked at home there. She seemed not so aloof as she had, not so foreign and not so feminine. She had hardened, as all the women in the mountains hardened. Her hair, her makeup, and her nails and skin looked as though they had been a long time away from the beauty salon. In that, Nilsa thought, she had become more beautiful. She was less feminine, but more of a woman. Did that make sense? Would a man like Carlos Delgado feel the same way—about Nilsa, perhaps? Nilsa could hope so.

She said, "Commandante Delgado tells me that your friends are coming soon."

Anita nodded without expression. She said, "I am ready."

Nilsa said, "The women will be sorry to see you leave."

Anita nodded, still without expression. Then her face clouded over. She put her head in her hands and began to weep.

Nilsa moved to her and put her arms around Anita's shoulders. Several of the women put down their work and stared. Nilsa said, in the English that the rebel women did not understand, "What is the matter? What is wrong?"

Anita said, "I'm sorry. That's never happened to me before."

"What has not happened?"

Anita said, "No one has ever been sorry to see me leave. There was never anyone there, to be sorry, when I left. I am sorry to be so emotional."

"It is nothing," Nilsa said. "We are all emotional. But we don't cry so much anymore. We have all cried too much already. We have lost the habit. Come with me. Tell the women good-bye."

Catching sight of María Fuentes, she said, "*Óyeme, compañera.* El Gato wants you in his tent."

Some of the women hooted and whistled at that. María, blushing, left them with her head down.

At the other end of the camp, Delgado left his tent and stared at the sky. He could hear, high overhead, the thrum of an airplane. It was moving slowly, high and out of sight. Surveillance? Probably. He knew the camp was not visible, though, from that height. If he could not see the aircraft, the aircraft could not possibly see him—or anything but the woods that surrounded him.

He went across the clearing in the middle of the camp, looking for Bolinas. Time to prepare for these American gangsters.

When Delgado found him, Bolinas was drinking coffee and smoking a cigarette, gossiping with two men who were replacing the axle on a truck. The truck was covered in leaves and branches, and the men were covered in grease. Delgado said, "Bolinas! I need you."

When he had him away from the mechanics, Delgado said, "We will need four or five sharpshooters, with good rifles, posted outside the camp today."

"For the Americans?"

"Exactly," Delgado said. "I am concerned for the safety of our people. I have guaranteed the safety of the American woman as well. She must be allowed to leave here, undisturbed, with the Americans—and with the money. We cannot allow her to be hurt."

"And the sharpshooters? Who are they to shoot?"

"I don't know. It is only a precaution."

"It will be done, *Commandante.*"

"Don't call me that," Delgado said. "You know my name. Let me know when you have picked your men. I will tell you where they are to be posted."

"Yes, *compañero.*"

Going back across the camp, he saw María Fuentes waiting for him in front of his tent. How powerful she looked. How beautiful. The women in the Sierra Maestra were all beautiful to him now. Strange to think he had once dreamed of Rita Hayworth and Ava Gardner and Veronica Lake. Now they seemed as unreal and undesirable as department-store mannequins. A woman like María Fuentes was a real woman.

When he was close, he took her elbow and said, "Come sit with me a minute. I have an important request to make of you."

"Anything," María said.

"Don't be hasty," Delgado said. "You won't like this. I want you to leave the mountains today and return to Havana."

María wilted. She said, "I understand."

"No," Delgado said. "You don't understand. But thank you for saying so. You know the Calle 15 cell was destroyed. We lost much of our leadership in the city in the raid—the one that disfigured Nilsa."

"How can I not know of that?" María said, turning away from him. "It was the arrest of my man, Juan Obregón, that led to the raid on Calle 15. It was my fault."

"It was not," Delgado said. "But if you feel that way, this is your chance to right the wrong. You will return to Havana. I have specific instructions for what you will do when you arrive. We must rebuild the Havana cell. You know the city better than anyone else here. You must go and prepare for our eventual invasion."

"Will I go alone?"

"As you came, *mi niña*." Delgado took her hand. "I am sorry, for me personally, that you are leaving. But I am proud for you also, that you have this work to do."

María Fuentes put her face down. She thought, *If I look at him, I will begin to cry. I mustn't cry*. She got to her feet and said, "Thank you. I will prepare to leave at once."

"After the Americans have come and gone," Delgado said. "You will be given an escort as far as Camagüey. It will not be so hard from there."

María left the tent without looking back. Delgado allowed himself one moment, and one thought: *When I see you again, it will be Havana, after the revolution is victorious.*

*   *   *

Mo found a cable waiting for him when he woke up that day. It was coded, but it was from Meyer and it meant that Mo was to make a telephone call at noon to a certain number. Mo had coffee and toast sent up to the room, then showered and shaved and dressed. Lansky wouldn't see it, down the telephone line from Miami, but Mo felt he needed the grooming. Look sharp, act sharp. He was on the phone on schedule.

Lansky said, "There is a rumor going around up here. I'm paying a million bucks to buy a piece of tail. What the hell is going on?"

"I'm sorry, Meyer," Mo said. "The girlfriend of a friend of mine got kidnapped by the rebels. I'm helping him out. And it's only a hundred thousand dollars."

"That's not the point, Morris. And it's embarrassing. To have my name involved with such a thing! It's not professional."

"I'm sorry," Mo said again. "It's not professional. And it's unfortunate that your name got involved."

"It is unfortunate that my *money* got involved, Morris."

Mo squirmed. "This is a business expense, just like the other business expenses."

"This is a high rate for a high-end hooker, is what it looks like to me," Lansky said. "And you're doing business with the wrong people, too. The rebels constitute a terrible threat to our way of life in Havana, Morris. If they are successful . . ."

"I understand," Mo said. "I'm sorry. I will put out the word that you are not involved in any way. I am sorry for the inconvenience it has caused you already."

"Never mind the inconvenience," Lansky said. "Worry about the cost. And my reputation. At my age, I can't afford for people to think I will spend a million dollars for a piece of tail. I'm paying too much as it is. Good-bye."

Leaving the Tropicana later that afternoon, Mo had a different piece of tail—the tail that picked him up as he and his driver left the Tropicana driveway, and then followed them across Vedado. The tail would be Meyer's, no doubt. Which was funny. Meyer's tail was tailing Meyer's car and driver, keeping an eye on Meyer's man in

Havana. Unless, perhaps, it was Meyer's bad-tempered brother, Jake. Mo knew Jake was jealous of the spread Meyer had given Mo. Natural enough, then, that Meyer might have Jake keep an eye on Mo. Someone would be watching Jake, too, of course.

"To the Presidente, first," Mo told the driver. "But stop at that park by La Rampa."

"The park, señor?"

"I might take a little walk," Mo said.

The driver drew up La Rampa and slowed near the corner of Calle M and Calle 23. Mo pointed at the curb and said, "Pull in there, and wait for me."

The driver slid to a stop, and Mo got out. Over his shoulder, he saw a dark blue Cadillac pull to the curb a block behind them. Mo grinned.

He went through the park, under the shade of the plane trees, until the Cadillac was out of sight. No one seemed to be following him. He walked straight across a wide green lawn. When he came out of the shadows and into the sun again, he was alone. He left the park on the side opposite the block where he'd left his driver, and went through an alley that connected Calle L to M, and from there went quickly down M to Calle 21. There was no one following him. He followed Calle 21 directly into the driveway of the Hotel Nacional.

The Spaniard was waiting for him in the bar, as planned. He rose, florid and courtly, head polished to a high sheen, and said, "Good morning, my friend! Have a daiquiri with me!"

"Too early for me, señor. I'll start with a coffee."

"Hey, *camarero! ¡Un café!*" Scarfioti sat and smiled.

Mo thought, not for the first time, *This guy gives me the creeps.* He said, "Do you hear anything about our friends in the mountains?"

The Spaniard returned a conspiratorial smile. He said, "Our friends, the ones that you know nothing about, in the mountains?"

"Yeah. Those ones."

"I hear nothing, except what I have already told you. The rebels are laying a trap. They will not welcome their visitors. They believe the Security forces will try to take the girl and the money *and* capture the rebel *commandante.*"

"Have you any way to communicate with them?"

"*I*, señor?" Scarfioti looked horrified. "Communicate with the rebels?"

"Or with the Security forces?"

"No, señor. I have no connection to such people. If I had, of course, you would be welcome to them. But . . . why?"

"I don't know," Mo said. "A personal guarantee?"

"Of what?"

"That Security is not involved. I could guarantee that the men with the ransom money are there only for the girl."

"Could you really, señor?" Scarfioti smiled. "I am impressed. But it is too late for such gentlemanly behavior, my friend. The situation here in Cuba no longer allows for such things."

"Then forget about it," Mo said, and smiled. "It's not a big deal. And it's only money, anyway."

"But it is *your* money, señor!" Scarfioti said indignantly. "And here is your *cafecito*."

Mo said, "Cheers," and after the waiter had poured a cup, lifted it to toast his companion. "Better days ahead."

"I hope so," Scarfioti said. "But not in Havana, I am afraid. Dark days are ahead here."

"How come? And how soon?"

"Señor, this is what you would call the $60,000 question."

"It's the $64,000 question, actually."

"Indeed," Scarfioti said. "Or even more. But it is the question without an answer. The rebels are pressing from the mountains. The government is in a state of panic. Many of the richest men in the country have already placed their millions in foreign banks. Batista himself has made inquiries—of Costa Rica, of the Dominican Republic, of Brazil—about where he will find a home if the rebels march on Havana."

"It's a bad time to be starting a business here, isn't it?" Mo gave the Spaniard a wry smile.

"Terrible!" Scarfioti said, and laughed. "But that is why you have the opportunity. Mr. Lansky and the others would not be making a place for you if their future was secure, no?"

"No, of course not," Mo said. "That is the gamble."

"It is all a gamble, señor," Scarfioti said. "And soon Havana will have nothing left but gamblers. We are all taking a risk, one way or another, even staying here."

"But not you, eh?"

Scarfioti waved at the waiter and pointed to his glass. He said, "Not I, what?"

"You are a little more protected than the rest of us, I guess."

"Why do you say this, señor? I have no special protection."

Mo laughed now. He said, "Aw, don't be so bashful. I happen to know you carry a U.S. diplomatic service passport, and your salary is paid by the American State Department. So don't push that 'we're all taking a risk' bunk with me."

"But señor. You misjudge me."

"Sure, sure," Mo said. "My mistake. Forget I said it. But remember that I *know* it. And if it isn't too late, pass the word along the line that the ransom money really is supposed to buy back the girl. There's no other plan."

"Of course, my friend. I will 'pass the word,' as you say."

"Thank you. Here's your daiquiri. Cheers, again. Better days ahead."

Mo left the Spaniard in the Nacional bar. He went out the side door, just to play it safe, and checked the driveway. There was no dark blue Caddy waiting for him there. Mo grabbed a taxi and said, "Take me over to the Miramar."

"There is the escort," Cardoso said. "Slow down the car."

Filomeno saw the dark green sedan nose out of the trees ahead of them and ease onto the road. He glanced in the rearview mirror. Another vehicle, a dark green military truck, had pulled onto the road behind them. For an instant, Filomeno's blood went cold. Ambush! He saw rebel soldiers and guns and bullets flying.

But none of that happened. The dark green sedan in front of them, and the military truck behind, remained stationary for a full minute. Nothing moved.

Sloan said, "Do we get out?"

Cardoso said, "No. We wait."

"For what?"

"For that," Cardoso said. The dark green sedan began to move forward slowly. The military truck behind them did the same.

Cardoso said, "Okay. We'll follow."

For thirty minutes the three vehicles convoyed through dense, deep, green woods. At times the track was no broader than the width of the truck. Other times it opened up to reveal an abandoned farmhouse or *bohío*. A pen of horses and donkeys stood untended around one corner. A small cooking fire burned untended around another.

The heat had risen with the sun, which was now directly overhead, and with the sun had come the humidity and the whine of insects. Filomeno drove slowly up the potholed red dirt road, all four windows down, the air limp around him.

Cardoso said to Sloan, "Make sure the safety is off, on that Luger. But don't let the soldiers behind us see you."

Sloan said, "I checked that already. And I checked their weapons. We are outgunned by a factor of about a hundred."

"It is true," Cardoso said. "If they turn on us, we haven't a chance."

"Thanks," Sloan said. "I feel better now."

Cardoso turned to look at him. He said, "Are you frightened?"

"Of course I am," Sloan said.

"Good," Cardoso said. "I am frightened, too. It would be foolish not to be."

"Excellent. I'd hate to die a fool."

Cardoso laughed. He said, "When this is over, we will have a long talk, over a bottle, about fear and the meaning of fear, and the meaning of bravery."

"And the meaning of stupidity," Sloan said. "Are they stopping?"

Up ahead, the green sedan had slowed almost to a halt. There was a crossroads. The heavy truck behind them ground its gears and drew to a stop as well. The forest was silent but for the hum of the three vehicles. The driver of the green sedan, Cardoso saw, was speaking into a field telephone.

"They are communicating with the base camp," Cardoso said. "Now we will see what they truly mean to do with us."

It wasn't until the third time the spotter plane passed overhead that Delgado put two and two together and got four. How obvious! The spotter plane was not looking for the rebel camp. The spotter plane was looking for the car, carrying the ransom money, that was being escorted to the rebel camp.

Delgado left his tent and jogged over to where Bolinas was squatting with three of his sharpshooters. They had drawn a map of the camp in the dirt. Bolinas was making plans with a pointed stick.

Delgado said, "No time for that now. We must change plans. Can you get the escort vehicle on the radio?"

"Of course, *Jefe*," Bolinas said.

"Get them now. Tell them to stop and report their position, and wait for orders."

Bolinas ran to the communications tent. Delgado went across the open center of the camp to the kitchen. He had seen Nilsa and the American girl go in there earlier. Now he saw only Nilsa.

He said, "La Vaca! I need you."

When she went to him, Delgado said, "Get the *gringa* and bring her to me. And bring also the green knapsack from my tent."

"I understand."

Delgado met Bolinas back at his tent. He was followed by a young man, hardly more than a boy, carrying a field telephone transmitter. He was cranking and talking into it at the same time. As Delgado arrived, he began nodding to Bolinas, and handed him the transmitter. Bolinas indicated Delgado, who stepped forward and took the equipment in his hands.

"This is El Gato. Where are you?"

A crackling voice replied, "Near the turning, down the hill."

"Stop there," Delgado said. "How many in the car?"

"There is a driver and two men."

"Americans?"

"One only."

The line crackled while Delgado considered his options. One American. One Security man. One driver, probably also a Security man. Three guns. And certainly more hidden in the car.

And other cars, receiving reports from the spotter plane, coming up the mountain behind them.

Delgado said, "Send the truck back down the mountain to the rendezvous point. Place your men around the truck for an ambush. You men must leave your car and return on foot to the camp. At once."

There was a long crackling pause. Then the voice said, "I understand, *Jefe.*"

"Tell the visitors to wait right where they are."

The voice said, "I understand, *Jefe.*"

Delgado handed the transmitter back to the young man and said, "Pack up that transmitter. I will take it with me."

Bolinas was staring at him. He said, "What do you intend to do?"

"I will go down the hill myself, with the *gringa,*" Delgado said.

"It is not safe for you, *Capitán.*"

"It is not safe for anyone," Delgado said. "But it is the only way. We cannot allow the visitors to come here. They are being watched by the plane that has been going overhead all morning. We must move fast. Here is the woman now."

Nilsa was coming across the camp with Anita. They stopped in front of Delgado. Anita swept a lock of hair from her forehead and put the straw hat low over her eyes, and smiled at Delgado.

She said, "*Listo. Listo?* Is that right?"

Delgado smiled back. He said, "*Listo* is correct." He handed her the green knapsack and said, "You will carry this. *Vámonos.*"

Delgado turned to Bolinas and said, "Take your sharpshooters down the road, after we have gone. Remain on high alert. I do not know what is going to happen."

Delgado slung the field telephone onto his back. Then he said to Anita, "Come. We will go to meet your friends."

"My friends?" Anita said. "Maybe. Maybe not."

"If they are not, they will become your friends. As we have, here in the mountains."

"Was this the plan?" Sloan asked. The military truck had turned and began moving back down the road. The men in the green sedan had gotten out and began moving into the brush. One of them was walking slowly toward the black Cadillac.

"No," Cardoso said. "Or, maybe yes. Maybe part of *their* plan. Be still."

The rebel wore green fatigues, stained filthy with dirt, and a battered bush hat. He had a droopy mustache and tired eyes, and a limp cigarillo dangling from his lip. In his right hand he carried an M-1 carbine. With his left, he drew the cigarillo from his lip and eyed it sadly before throwing it into the dirt. When he got close to the car, he smiled and slowed his pace. He stopped ten or twelve feet away, and faced Cardoso.

"We stop here," he said in Spanish. "You will wait."

"For what?" Cardoso asked him.

"For . . . ten minutes," the rebel said, smiling at his own joke.

Cardoso smiled back in spite of himself. What nerve! The rebel's finger was not covering his trigger. He was calm. There was no trouble here. Cardoso said, "Good. We wait, for ten minutes. And then?"

"Then another man will come. He will have something for you. So remain calm, enjoy the beautiful mountains of our Sierra Maestra. I will leave you now."

With that, the rebel turned and moved to join his men. Soon the woods were silent, and Cardoso and Filomeno and Sloan were alone. Cardoso said, "Turn off the car. I want to listen." He got out of the car and sat on the hood, turning his face toward the road before him. Sloan got out of the car, too, and went to stand beside Cardoso.

He said, "What do you think?"

"I think we wait ten minutes and see."

Nothing moved. The whirring of the insects returned. Soon it was all that Sloan could hear. He closed his eyes and turned his face up to the sun.

*   *   *

Delgado put the Panama hat on his head and slung an M-1 carbine over his shoulder—his own M-1 carbine. Che had given it to him a month earlier, just after he and his men had overtaken the barracks at San Jose. It was a great victory because it had been bloodless. The government soldiers had simply put down their weapons and left the building, on the promise that they would not be hurt. Che said it was the turning point, the moment at which the entire nation declared that the rebels were the side of justice—even though several of his men were furious that they had not gunned down the soldiers when they marched, guilelessly, out of the barracks. Che had difficulty getting the men to understand that not killing them was, in fact, the point of the victory.

Delgado was glad to have the weapon. He had been carrying an ancient Springfield. It was inaccurate and heavy. The M-1 was its opposite. Delgado felt protected.

Anita fell in beside him. At the turning, a quarter mile down the road, she looked back. But her comrades, no sentimentalists, had returned to their duties. There was no one waving to her when she turned. A hundred feet on, the woods had consumed the camp. There was nothing around them but green and the heavy damp heat and the nattering of the insects.

Delgado said, "You will be happy to return."

Anita did not answer. It wasn't a question.

Delgado said, "Are your people in Los Angeles?"

"My people?" Anita said.

"Your family," Delgado said. "Someone told me your home is Los Angeles. Is your family there also?"

"I don't have any family," Anita said. "Especially not in Los Angeles."

"But your mother and father?"

"They are gone. Dead. Long dead."

"And your brothers and sisters? Your aunts and uncles? And cousins?"

"I don't have any. There's just me."

Delgado sighed. The Americans, he knew, were not all Catholics. They did not come from large families. He had read that in *Life* magazine. But still. No one? It was impossibly sad. He said, "To be among one's own people, even so, this is good. To be in the land of your birth."

"Yes," Anita said. "It's hard not speaking the language. Everyone here has been awfully nice to me, but it's hard when you don't understand what people are saying. On the other hand, where I come from, you can understand *everything* people are saying, and that's hard, too. People don't always say the nicest things."

"Come with me here, quickly."

Delgado grabbed Anita by the hand and pulled her off the road, into the woods. Overhead, but much lower now, the spotter plane rattled across the tops of the trees.

Delgado said, "I'm sorry. That airplane has been passing overhead this morning, looking for the camp. I don't think they saw us."

"Your hat's crooked."

Delgado adjusted the Panama. Ahead, something glittered in the sun. Delgado put a finger to his lips and made an exaggerated gesture of silence to Anita. She smiled, like a child, and nodded. Delgado indicated a path leading into the woods, and with his forefinger showed Anita that they would walk there. She nodded. Delgado moved forward at half pace now and unslung his carbine.

Through the trees came glimpses of an automobile sitting in the road up ahead. It was a black Cadillac, shiny and new, but with mud caked around its wheels and fenders. Across the road in front of it was the rebel car, the camouflaged sedan. The bumpers and other chrome parts had been removed. It hung flat and low, like part of the landscape. The black Cadillac, by contrast, looked like something off the showroom floor. Delgado winced. The spotter plane could not possibly have missed it.

Fifty steps ahead. Delgado was moving slowly. The ground was wet. Nothing crackled beneath him. As he drew closer, he began to make out shapes. Someone was lying on the hood of the Cadillac. Someone else was sitting in the driver's seat. A third man was sitting on the back bumper, smoking a cigarette and watching the road behind the car. Delgado glanced over his shoulder. Anita was directly behind him. She had not seen the men ahead of them yet. Delgado turned to her and pulled her close to him. It was strangely intimate, as close to a woman as he had been in a long time.

He said, "They are just ahead. Very near. I will go on. You wait. Do not move until I call you. If there is shooting, lie down and wait until everything is quiet. Then return to the camp. Yes?"

"Yes."

It felt like good-bye. Delgado wanted to embrace her. He didn't. Instead, he cradled the rifle a little higher in his hands and moved forward.

The men were not watching. They were listening. Delgado stepped out from the woods and said, in his most cheerful voice, "Good afternoon, gentlemen. I am Carlos Delgado. Welcome to the mountains."

The American sitting on the back bumper stood up abruptly and began to reach inside his trousers, but stopped. The man lying on the hood of the car, a man Delgado took to be Cuban, had his hands full of a gun already. He had it up and trained on Delgado, and he did not lower it. He held it like a professional, though. Delgado was unconcerned for the moment. The man sitting behind the wheel of the car smiled unsteadily and nodded.

The man with the gun slid off the hood. He said, "This is not the rendezvous."

"No," Delgado said. "There has been a change of plan. You have seen the airplane overhead? It is a government spotter plane. It followed you here—by design or not, I do not know. We cannot escort you to our camp, with the plane overhead. You understand."

"It is not our plane," Cardoso said. "You have my word on that."

"It is not important," Delgado said. "I sent the other men to a different rendezvous. They are watching the roads. The airplane may have seen us, and they may send soldiers. We will be ready for them. It has nothing to do with you now, anyway."

"No," Cardoso said. "We have come only for the girl."

"And what will you do with her?"

Cardoso was surprised by the question. He said, "What do you mean?"

"What is your plan from here?"

"We will take her back to Havana. After that, it is not my concern."

"Who is your companion?"

"That is her lover," Cardoso said. "He is an American. A musician."

"Ah," Delgado said. The man standing behind the car did not look like much of a man. He was tall and thin and had long dark hair that fell over his forehead. He looked like that American singer Elvis Presley. He looked . . . soft. Would a woman like a man like that? A woman like Anita? There was no explaining women.

Cardoso said, "Can you guarantee safe passage on the road?"

"No," Delgado said. "Have you brought the money?"

"Of course," Cardoso said. He turned to Sloan and said in English, "He wants to see the money."

Sloan opened the trunk of the car. Instinctively, Delgado raised his rifle and turned it toward the American.

Cardoso said, "Be careful, señor."

Delgado nodded but held his rifle steady.

Sloan pulled up a small suitcase, closed the trunk, and stepped forward and put the suitcase on the road. He opened the top of it and spread the handles so Delgado could see the money inside.

Delgado said, "Good. Put it in the other car."

Cardoso said in English, "He says put the money into the other car."

Sloan walked over to the camouflaged green rebel car, opened the passenger side door, and put the bag on the seat.

Delgado nodded to him. Then he said in English, over his shoulder, "It is all right, now, Anita. You can come out from the trees."

In Havana, at the station house on La Rampa, Escalante and Scarfioti had been given various murky reports. The spotter plane had followed a car, determined that it was the wrong car, and then determined that it was the right car. They had no useful details, but it was a black Cadillac, new, that had left Ciego de Ávila. By the time the car made the turn for Coronella, there was no doubt that it was the vehicle in question. The car left the paved road sometime later. It was met by two other vehicles, both camouflaged in greens and browns. One was a military truck of some kind.

"That is it, then," Escalante said. "This is a rebel convoy. They will take the ransom money to the camp."

He was excited. He was too excited. He rose from his seat and went to a large map tacked to the wall. He tapped the center of the map, over the town of Coronella, and said, "They will make the exchange in the mountains near this town."

Scarfioti sat calmly across from him, listening to half the conversation as the telephone calls came in, smiling politely at Escalante's reports. He did not share his excitement. He was curious to know the outcome, but he had nothing riding on the result. He did not stand to profit either way.

Thirty minutes later there was bad news. Two pieces of bad news, in fact. The rebel convoy had *not* escorted the kidnappers to the rebel camp. The convoy had stopped the Cadillac deep in the woods. The soldiers had left their vehicles and dispersed. And the spotter plane had been forced to land for refueling.

"Bad luck," the Spaniard said.

"Horrible," said Escalante, and shouted at his assistant, Redondo, for more brandy. "It is very bad timing. Still, it is not over. I have men positioned less than thirty miles away. One report, with one location, and they will attack."

"I haven't ever visited that part of your beautiful country," Scarfioti said. "I imagine the vegetation is quite lush."

"Like a jungle," Escalante said, waving his hand over the map in front of him. "You can't see your hand before your face."

"Difficult to find the rebels there, then."

"Almost impossible," Escalante said. "That is why the airplane is so important."

Escalante sat again, and the two men shared a brandy. Scarfioti drew a brace of Partagas cigars from his breast pocket and offered one to his companion. The two men groomed their cigars and lit them in silence. Five minutes ticked by. The telephone rang again. Escalante grabbed at it and listened with eyes full of desperation.

"Yes," he said. "Continue reporting."

He put the phone down and said to Scarfioti, "The Cadillac is leaving the area, escorted by one of the rebel cars. They have made the exchange, don't you think?"

The Spaniard considered this. He said, "No. Not yet. If they had made the exchange, the rebel car would not escort them. No? They are going somewhere else to make the exchange."

"To the rebel camp!"

"Perhaps," Scarfioti said. "Isn't this a fine cigar?"

Escalante did not seem to hear him. He rose from his seat and began staring again at the map on the wall, tapping the town of Coronella with his forefinger.

"I am calling in the strike now," he said, and went back to the telephone. "Surely we can hit something, even in that jungle of woods where the cowards are hiding."

Sloan went dizzy when he saw her. Anita stepped out of the woods like a vision and moved toward him slowly. His head went soft. He had just put the bag of money in the rebel's car. The Cuban had just told Anita it was safe to come out. Sloan turned toward the woods, and there she was. Her hair was loose and wild under a straw hat, her skin was darkened by the sun, and she wore no makeup. She looked more like a woman than Sloan had ever seen her look. He moved toward her, without regard for the others, without any thought in his head.

He said, "You're all right."

She smiled and said, "I'm fine."

Then he was with her, and hugging her, and holding her, and she was fine. He heard Cardoso and Delgado speaking Spanish behind him. They weren't talking about him, or for him. He crushed Anita close to him and shut out the world. Then she drew away from him and pulled him toward the others.

Delgado introduced himself to Sloan and Filomeno. He told them his plan. The road was not safe. He had guaranteed the safety of the American woman. He would not tell Cardoso and Sloan and their driver what to do, but he was responsible for the safety of the American woman.

They would take two cars out of the woods. Filomeno, Sloan, and the girl would ride in the rebel car. Cardoso would drive Delgado in the Cadillac. They would drive north, down from the mountain, away from the rebel camp, to an airstrip near Coronella.

Cardoso said, "Why an airstrip?"

"We have a plane fueled and waiting," Delgado said. "It will take the girl back to Havana."

Anita recognized, suddenly, the man that Delgado was addressing. He was the man she had seen, that first night in Havana, in the plaza below the room on San Lázaro. His partner had shot the driver of the car that had crashed. He had been putting his hat back on his head and had looked up to where she stood on the balcony. She saw him again now, and she was afraid.

Sloan said, "What's wrong?"

"Nothing," Anita said. "I'm just . . . happy. I'm happy you're here."

"Well, I'm not. I'll be happy when we're *away* from here. These people make me nervous."

"Who is the man with you?" she asked him.

"The driver is named Phil. The other guy is Cardoso."

"He's a policeman. A Secret Service policeman."

"No," Sloan said. "He's just a tough guy. He's okay."

Overhead came again the thrum of the spotter plane. Delgado said, "*Vámonos*. We have wasted too much time. Anita, you will go in the car with your boyfriend and this driver. You will follow us. Yes?"

Anita said, "Yes. Of course."

She took Sloan's sleeve and tugged him toward the rebel car. Filomeno, moving away from Cardoso with eyes full of fear, said, "*¿Está bien, Jefe?*"

Cardoso said, "*Está bien. No te preocupes. Yo te voy a proteger.*"

Don't worry, Delgado thought. *I will protect you?* And who will protect him? Who will protect any of us? He said, *"Ya, vámonos."*

Inside the Cadillac, as Cardoso sat behind the wheel and started the engine, Delgado unslung the field telephone and ground up a signal. He said into the mouthpiece, "We are going to the airstrip now."

A crackly voice replied to him, *"Hay tres aviones."*

"I understand," Delgado said, and put the phone down. "We have the spotter plane and two others now."

Cardoso, gunning the car into the woods, said, "I'm sorry. It's not my people."

"You are a former policeman with Security," Delgado said. "Have you any people?"

"No," Cardoso said. "And the airplanes are not part of my plan. I am here to exchange the money for the girl."

"So you have said," Delgado replied. "Turn left at this next clearing."

Following in the rebel car, Sloan told Filomeno, "You follow the Cadillac. They'll get us out of these woods."

"But where do we go, señor?"

"To safety," Sloan said. He had no idea, even as he said it, what he thought he meant.

The Cadillac ran down a quarter mile of the red dirt road, then came to a clearing and turned left, and began picking its way downhill. The road improved as they dropped out of the mountains.

Inside the Cadillac, Delgado said to Cardoso, "Tell me: You are being paid by Meyer Lansky?"

"No," Cardoso said. "By a man named Morris Weiner. He is connected to Lansky."

"The money belongs to Lansky, I am told. Why does the American want this woman?"

"I do not know. For himself, I think."

"And the boyfriend?"

"This is not my concern," Cardoso said. "I was not given any instructions about him, except that he was to accompany me."

"And what about you? Are you a gun for hire now? A mercenary?"

"For the moment, I am only doing this job. I was fired from the

Security forces, you know. In large part because I failed to bring you to justice."

"Justice!" Delgado said, and laughed. "You failed to bring me to a kangaroo court and a band of torturing tyrants. And so we both escaped. You will earn more money today rescuing the American girl than you would have earned in a year as a Security agent."

"If we survive it."

Behind them in the rebel car, cruising slowly down the narrow track, Filomeno mopped sweat from his forehead and breathed unevenly. Sloan said to Anita, "It won't be much longer now. We are coming out of the mountains fast."

Anita said, "Do you know where we're going?"

"No," he said. "But this cat Cardoso is nobody's fool."

Filomeno said, "He is a *keeler*. Very danger!"

Sloan said, "Thanks, Phil."

Anita said, "He's on our side, right?"

"I think so," Sloan said. "For now, anyway."

Delgado, watching Cardoso maneuver the Cadillac, said, "Slowly now. Here is the main road. We'll turn east. We must cover about six miles fast. Just before the village of Coronella, there is a sugar refinery. We turn there, to the right. Half a mile in there is an airstrip. Our airplane is waiting there."

Cardoso said, "I understand."

Several miles on, Delgado said, "*Está pinta mal*. There is the spotter plane."

It was low on the horizon, tracking the highway and coming straight toward them. Cardoso nodded and said, "At that height, they may not know who we are."

Delgado said, "Trust me. A new Cadillac, on this road, is all they need to see. They will not mistake us. Turn away now, to the right. There!"

Cardoso yanked the wheel to the right. There was a dirt track leading up a hillside into the woods. The Cadillac hit the soft soil and spun slightly before catching traction again and shooting up into the trees. Cardoso checked the rearview, but there was too much dust for him to see what the green rebel car had done. Delgado turned and looked out the passenger window.

He said, "Do not slow down. They are with us still."

The track through the woods was rough. The car shook violently. Cardoso kept an eye on his passenger when he was not fixed on the road. The field telephone was on the seat between them. The rebel leader's M-1 was slung between his legs. His hand had not left it since he joined them at the rendezvous. Sooner or later, Cardoso thought, he will set the rifle down. At the airstrip, perhaps, if we make it to the airstrip. He will use the telephone. Or he will shake the American's hand. Or he will use two hands to lift the bag of money. Or he will embrace the girl. Of course he will embrace the girl. Cardoso thought, *Who would not take the opportunity to embrace the girl?*

Delgado said, "Here. Take that road on the left."

The woods were very thick now. There was no possibility the spotter plane could track them. The only question was whether it had seen them on the highway.

The airstrip was a crude stretch of asphalt running between two sets of low hills. The Cadillac crested the first set of hills, the green rebel car following. At one end of the airstrip was a limp wind sock and a stand of royal palms gathered around a pair of Quonset hut hangars. Two small planes, both Cessnas, stood next to the hangars. At the other end of the strip, on the runway, was a C-103 Grumman transport plane.

Delgado pointed to the pair of Cessnas and said, "There."

"There?" Cardoso asked. "Not the Grumman?"

"No. Go over there," Delgado said.

Cardoso, nodding and turning the Caddy toward the Quonset huts, thought he could see a man in the cockpit of the Grumman. Something was rotten here. He said to Delgado, "No tricks, please, my friend. Remember, we are three and you are one."

Delgado smiled. "You are a hundred, and I am one. That is the story of revolution, my friend. Pull the car close to the two planes."

Cardoso parked. The green rebel car was close behind. Delgado got out of the Caddy, carbine in hand, and beckoned Filomeno and

Sloan out as well. Then he glanced at the sky. He said, "We have been followed. Listen."

The noise of the spotter plane grew louder, and then the spotter plane itself burst over the horizon, coming low over the airstrip from behind the wind sock. Behind it were two Douglas C-1s, military gray, fitted with .50-caliber machine guns.

Delgado said, "And they have brought guns."

The three planes buzzed low over the airstrip and began to bank heavily to the right for a return pass.

Delgado said, "We have one chance. We will stay here, right here, and let them have a run at us. If we are lucky, they will destroy one of these Cessnas. We will let them strike until they do. Then they will think they are finished. Then we can move."

"Move where?" Cardoso said.

"To the other plane," Delgado said. "Listen now, and wait."

Delgado cocked his head to the sky and glanced at his wristwatch. Anita stood close to Sloan, her hand in his, slightly behind Filomeno. The doors to the green rebel car stood open. Filomeno desperately wanted to jump in and drive away. This was not a safe place. He watched Cardoso—calm, dark-eyed, still—and even more desperately wished he could feel the way Cardoso looked. He hated being afraid. He was often afraid.

Delgado lifted his finger to the air. Cardoso could hear nothing. Ten seconds passed, then he picked up the low whine of the approaching planes. Delgado turned to Anita and Sloan, and then to Filomeno, and said, "Get behind the building."

The three of them ran to the side of the nearest Quonset hut. Delgado and Cardoso stood next to the Cessnas. Delgado looked at his wristwatch again and said, "We will have about three minutes between one pass and the next. That is how long it takes them to turn and approach again."

"It is not long."

"It is long enough. Get ready. On my signal, we will turn and dive."

The three planes came over the horizon more slowly and deliberately this time, cresting the wind sock, correcting slightly to the left, and bearing down. The spotter plane dropped almost to the level of the airstrip. The C-1s dropped behind it. There were soldiers in uniform manning the .50 calibers now.

Delgado said, "Ready . . ."

The C-1s began blasting when they were not yet level with the Quonsets. The first bullets struck the metal side of the buildings. The second burst kicked up a line of soil next to the runway, between the buildings and the two Cessnas.

Delgado said, "Now!"

He and Cardoso turned and dove, rolling on the grass away from the two planes. Behind them, the machine-gun fire pinged holes in one Cessna and blew the windows out of the black Cadillac. A shower of windshield glass rained down on Delgado and Cardoso. Delgado lifted his rifle, and began firing at the closer of the two C-1s. He scored half a dozen hits into the side of the plane, then buried his head in the dirt again. Machine-gun fire continued cutting strips of soil as the gunships passed out of range.

Delgado said, "That was very good. We will have to sustain one more, I think. They are missing the point entirely."

"What is the point?" Cardoso said. "They will destroy our planes."

"Not at all," Delgado said. "Our plane is the Grumman at the other end of the strip. They are ignoring it altogether. Three minutes now."

Delgado ran to the green car and pulled out the bag containing the ransom money. He gave the money a quick look and then closed the bag and carried it over to Cardoso.

He said, "You will return this money when you return the girl?"

Cardoso was surprised. "You trust me with it?"

"No. But I don't want it here. Too many people have died fighting over it already."

Cardoso laughed. "You would prefer them to die for your revolution."

"Surely it is better to die for what you believe in."

"Is it?" Cardoso asked. "I would not want to die fighting for a girl. Or for money. But, really, does it matter what you die for?"

"Of course!" Delgado said. "As much as it matters what you live for. Not to you, perhaps, after you are gone. But to the ones you leave behind, it matters immensely. What legacy will you leave, señor, for the people who will remember you?"

"No legacy," Cardoso said. "No one will remember me."

"We have one minute," Delgado said. "Bring the others."

The five of them waited out the last thirty seconds in silence. Delgado raised his finger. They all moved close to the Cessnas. Delgado had the bag of money in his hand. The whine of the spotter plane became audible. Sloan gripped Anita's hand and smiled at her, feigning excitement. Filomeno looked sick. Delgado said, "Ready now."

The three planes blew over the airstrip again, much closer this time to the Quonset huts and much lower to the ground. Delgado said, "Go!" Sloan dragged Anita across twenty feet of grass, then pulled her to the ground. Bullets struck the Quonset behind them. Phil froze in his tracks. At the sound of the first bullets, he fainted and dropped. Delgado set the bag of money next to the airplanes, dropped to his knees, and began firing the M-1 at the Douglas gunships. Bullets raked across the two automobiles and then the two airplanes. The tires blew out on one Cessna, the windshield shattered, and the plane listed badly to one side. The other Cessna, its gas tank punctured by machine-gun fire, burst into flames. Delgado continued shooting, piercing the side of the C-1. He saw the soldier manning the .50 caliber go over sideways. Then the C-1 veered away. As the spotter plane and the other Douglas pulled up at the end of the runway, the second C-1 skidded the opposite way in the sky. Then it slammed into the hillside and exploded.

Delgado leapt to his feet and said, "That's it. Let's go."

Cardoso helped Anita to her feet. Sloan went to Filomeno. Delgado said, in English, "Give me the money. Leave the driver. We do not have time for him."

Sloan picked up the suitcase and handed it to Delgado. Cardoso got behind the wheel of the Cadillac again and started the car. Anita and Sloan slid into the backseat. Delgado jumped into the front seat, carrying his M-1 and the money. Down the runway, the propellers of the Grumman started to turn. Cardoso wheeled the Cadillac onto the airstrip and drove straight toward the waiting plane. The big C-103 engines roared to life. Delgado, the carbine resting on his lap, said, "The Grumman is not damaged, then. We have a chance."

It took less than thirty seconds to get to the end of the airstrip. Delgado checked his watch. Two minutes remained. The Cadillac screeched to a halt fifteen feet from the Grumman. Cardoso could see the pilot clearly now. He waved from the cockpit.

Delgado jumped out of the car and said, "Hurry, now. We have no time to waste. Anita, get on the plane."

Cardoso whipped his revolver from inside his jacket and shook it at Sloan and said in English, "You also." Then he turned the weapon on Delgado and said in Spanish, "Give him the money."

Delgado smiled sadly and said, "Of course. I would never have accepted it from you, anyway. We are not kidnappers."

Cardoso said to Sloan, "Get the money. Get on the plane."

Sloan picked up the bag of money and said, "What about—"

"Go!" Cardoso shouted.

Sloan said, "Sorry. I'm not leaving Phil." He dropped the bag of money at Cardoso's feet. Anita was halfway up the steps of the Grumman. Sloan said, "I'll be back."

Sloan sprinted back to where Filomeno had fallen. He found him facedown in the grass. He expected the worst—blood, open wounds, guts. But there was nothing. He put his hands on Filomeno's shoulders and said, "Phil! Talk to me!"

The Cuban jumped to his feet, terror in his eyes. He said, "¡Coño! They shot me!"

"No, man," Sloan said. "You're okay. But we have to go now. Look."

At the end of the runway, two truckloads of soldiers were approaching fast. The men in the back of the truck carried guns that bristled like hairs as the truck came toward them.

"Come on," Sloan said. "Run."

Seeing Sloan on his feet again, with Filomeno running beside him, Cardoso said, "Good. It is finished." He shouted out to Sloan as he neared, "Get on the plane!" When Filomeno was closer, he said, "Not you. You wait."

Then he trained his pistol on Delgado again. He said, "Now you. On the plane. But first drop your weapon."

Delgado lay the M-1 on the ground in front of him.

"What else?" Cardoso asked.

"I had only the carbine."

"Show me."

Delgado slowly pulled open his jacket. Cardoso nodded and said, "Get on the plane."

Delgado looked at the ground and shook his head wearily. He checked his watch. He said, "No. You can shoot me now, but I am not getting on the plane."

"You will return to Havana. You will stand trial."

"I would never survive to stand trial, señor. You know that."

"Get on the plane."

"No, señor. I will not."

"¡Escúchame lo que te digo! I have chased you across Cuba. I have lost my job because you escaped. This ridiculous kidnapping has made me a fool. You will return with me to Havana, or die here."

Delgado smiled. He said, "Then I will die here, señor. Today, or another day. But I am not going to Havana. And you are going to be shot in the back if you do not lower your weapon now."

Cardoso glanced over his shoulder. A young woman with a badly scarred face stood in the doorway of the plane, training a pistol on him.

Delgado said, "Please, compañero. No more killing today. Get on the plane and leave me here, and live."

The Grumman was now gunning its engines. Cardoso lowered his weapon and glanced at the pilot. He was spinning one finger in the air, calling out something inaudible, and pointing to the far end of the airstrip. Cardoso looked. Two transport trucks, full of government soldiers, were pulling onto the asphalt runway.

Cardoso said, "Government soldiers. Now you will have to join us on the plane."

"No," Delgado said. "I will stand and fight. But you had best get on board now, unless you want to fight with me."

The young woman with the scarred face came down from the Grumman, her pistol aimed at Cardoso's belly. He couldn't place her, but he had seen her before. In Havana. In a nightclub? On the street? What had her face been before she was scarred? He could almost see her.

Delgado said, *"¡Ven, Nilsa!"* The woman came to him. Delgado bent down and picked up the M-1 carbine lying at his feet. Cardoso could hear the government aircraft coming now, too. He reckoned they would come over the side of the airstrip, as they had before, ready to strike again at the twin Cessnas. The wreckage of their own C-1 was still smoking and burning on the hill behind the Grumman. The spotter pilot would not be looking for them on the airstrip.

Delgado turned now to the other Cuban, the driver they called Phil. He said, "And you? *¿Qué haces, compañero?*"

Filomeno said, "I cannot go on the airplane, señor. I am afraid to fly."

Delgado said, "You may stay with us if you like, but you must decide now."

Delgado checked the end of the runway. The trucks were coming fast. Cardoso stood still before him.

Delgado called up to the pilot, "Go! Now!" and then turned to Cardoso. "Last chance. Take the money and the girl and her friend, and leave Cuba. The pilot has been instructed to fly to Havana, or to Mérida, if he is asked. Go."

Cardoso hesitated. Mérida? In Mexico? A whole world opened and beckoned. The government trucks of government soldiers were on the airstrip now.

Delgado said, "Go."

Delgado turned and ran, carbine in hand. The young woman ran with him. Cardoso turned and ran the opposite way, to the Grumman, as it began to taxi. Sloan was inside, ready to pull him aboard. Cardoso took the first step at a run. Sloan got him by the arm and pulled him up. The pilot dropped the levers. The Grumman roared forward.

Anita, seated by a window, watched Delgado below, running from the airstrip. She suddenly realized she was still carrying his green knapsack. She pulled it from her back and looked inside, and gasped: *Money.*

Below, Delgado fell to the ground and faced the approaching soldiers. Behind him rose a tower of orange and black smoke and fire where the government C-1 burned. Delgado lay flat in the dirt, training his rifle on the airstrip. Nilsa lay beside him.

Cardoso and Sloan watched, too. The pilot shouted back at them, "¡Siéntense, señores!"

Cardoso said, "Sit down."

As they did, the Grumman left the ground and banked violently to the left, then almost immediately again to the right. Out the side window, as the ground screamed up at them, Cardoso saw the spotter plane and the remaining C-1 blow by. The C-1 appeared to be firing upon the two Cessnas on the ground. Near them, Cardoso saw, Phil was creeping into the woods at the edge of the airstrip.

Cardoso thought he could hear rifle fire now, too. He hoped Delgado had the sense to empty his rifle at the airplanes and then leave the field. He would be no match, no matter what kind of marksman he was, no matter how much help his companion was, for the two trucks full of soldiers.

The plane rose fast, struggling. Cardoso did not know enough about airplanes to guess, but he hoped the C-1 they'd left behind would not give chase. Could a Grumman outrun a C-1? Cardoso had no idea. He had never been in a plane before. He had never seen his country from the air. Out the window, he saw the strip of red dirt road they'd driven to the airfield. Far off to the left he could see something that must be the village of Coronella. Then the airplane banked steeply again to the left. Suddenly there was nothing below but blue. They were over the Caribbean.

Cardoso rose to his feet and struggled up the gangway to the cabin. Inside were two men in civilian clothes wearing headphones. Cardoso tapped one of them on the shoulder. He turned, pulling the earphones halfway from his head.

"What is it?"

"Where are we going?" Cardoso asked.

"That is up to the passengers," the copilot said. "Havana or Mérida. We have fuel enough to fly about three hours."

"Miami, then."

"Miami?"

"Yes. Can you communicate with anyone on the ground?"

"We have radio contact."

"Have someone in Havana call this number. Tell them we are flying to Miami. Have them notify the authorities in Miami."

"This is an American embassy phone number?"

"No," Cardoso said. "It is a Meyer Lansky phone number."

Back in his seat, Cardoso calculated his chances. He did not think
Escalante would chase him to the United States. He did not think
the gangster's people would want him killed, if he delivered the girl
and the money to Miami. He did not know what kind of life he could
make for himself in America. But he knew what kind of life he had to
face in Havana. If the girl and the money were not safe, he would
have to run from Meyer Lansky. If he delivered the girl and the
money but not Carlos Delgado, he would have to run from Escalante
and his Security men. That kind of running was forever. One day,
someday, they would find him and kill him. One day in America,
maybe, he would not have to run at all.

He made up his mind. He said to Sloan, "Do you have people in
Miami?"

"People?"

"Friends? Or family?"

"No," Sloan said. "I have no one. Why?"

"Because that is where we are flying."

"Do you have people there?"

"No one at all," Cardoso said.

Sloan thought for a moment. Anita. The money. The rebels. Mo,
and Meyer. He said, "What about the money?"

"What about it?"

"What will you do with it?"

"It is not my money," Cardoso said. "You decide what happens
to it."

Sloan settled back in his seat and nodded.

At just that moment, Cardoso remembered the woman with the
scars on her face. She was called Nilsa. She was one of the rebels
arrested in the safe house on Calle 15. She had been tortured by
Ponce and the other Security men. And here, today, on the ground in

Coronella, she had not killed him. Why? Nothing that had happened today, nothing he had seen, made any sense to him. But if he was leaving Cuba forever, it didn't matter anymore.

Escalante, in Havana, got the news first. The nervous police officer named Redondo entered Escalante's office. The captain and his friend from Spain were far into the bottom of the bottle of Fundador. Redondo said, his voice cracking, "Your telephone call from Coronella, *mi capitán*." Then he left the room.

Escalante grinned at Scarfioti and said, "At last!" and picked up the telephone. He said, "*¡Dígame!*" Then his face colored deep red. He said, "*¿Qué pasó?*" and listened, and said, "*¿Y qué pasó con los otros?*" Escalante stood up and ripped the phone from the desk and hurled it at the wall, then lifted his desk chair from the floor and, swinging it like a club, began to demolish everything on top of his desk. His lamp and cigar humidor exploded into splinters.

The Spaniard smiled and stood up and placed his hat on his head. He turned and walked from the captain's office without a word.

Across Havana, a wide American man with a face made for violence stepped out of a taxicab in front of the Hotel Miramar. He went down a sidewalk lined with palms, through a gaily painted lobby, past an indoor pond stocked with bamboo-legged flamingos. He had been told he'd find this guy Mo in the main ballroom, which the messenger thought was a pretty weird place to be in the middle of the afternoon. But these guys were all fruity anyway.

He found a group of men huddled around a single table, in a sea of tables, in the darkened ballroom. From the distant stage came the harmonic wonders of the Orquesta Cubana. A singer in a red tuxedo jacket was whining something about *amor* while fifty or more musicians strummed and stroked and blared and blasted their instruments around him.

The man he wanted, the guy Mo, was staring at the line of conga players. There were four of them. In front of the four were the drums, tall and short, narrow and broad, made of wood the color of bamboo and wood the color of mahogany. The four men were pounding the skins, transfixed, in four syncopated, synchronized trances.

The American didn't think he could be heard over the beaner racket coming from the stage, so he waited. When it ended, sounding like a trash truck colliding with a load of accordions, he touched Mo on the shoulder and said, "I got a message for you."

Mo took the brute's arm and led him toward the back of the ballroom. When they were out of earshot of the others, he said, "Bad news, huh? Gimme."

The big man said, "Alls I know is this. The ransom gimmick didn't work. Somebody broke up the party. But the musician and the girl got away, along with the detective. They're in Miami."

Mo looked up as if he'd been slapped. He said, "Miami? What the hell are they doing in Miami?"

"Beats me, boss. Alls I know is they're in Miami."

"And the money?"

"Beats me, boss."

"You said that already." Mo looked at his watch. It wasn't three yet. They were in Miami. The ransom swap went sour. They got a plane and went to Miami. What about the money? What about Deacon helping him with the casinos? What about that cop?

Mo said, "I got it. Thanks for the news. Who tipped you by the way?"

"One of Meyer's guys. They got the call about an hour ago."

"From Miami? Or from Cuba?"

"Beats—"

"Don't say it. Tell the guy that tipped you I said thanks."

"Sure, boss."

Mo went back to the table, took a deep breath, and said, "Look, fellas. We want the folks to get hot in here, but not so hot that they gotta run home and hop in the sack. So gimme an hour's worth of material, just like that last number, and we'll have it licked. For now, I gotta go to the Sunset."

Going past the flamingos, Mo tried to imagine Deacon and Anita on their own in Miami. He tried to see them normal, like folks. He put Anita in an apron. He put Deacon in a gray flannel suit. He put a couple of brats in the front yard, on tricycles, behind a white picket fence.

It didn't work. He couldn't see any of it. All he got was Anita on Deacon's arm, crossing a hotel lobby sort of like this one, some night, somewhere in America. That was more like it. That was good.

That, Mo thought, *and me all alone—in Paraiso. My paradise.*

Carlos Delgado had stayed on the little hill at the end of the runway just long enough to do some damage. He and Nilsa crouched with their weapons, then took up positions. The driver named Filomeno had said, "Señor, I am no soldier," and had run back across the runway toward the Quonset hut.

Delgado had watched the Grumman carrying the Americans go down the runway, get speed, and get off the ground, lying with his carbine ready, his back to the burning C-1. The spotter plane and the remaining C-1 blew over the horizon just as the Grumman was getting airborne. The C-1 saw it first and jerked upright, beginning its turn. It was banked almost sideways by the time it got to the end of the runway. Delgado had a clear shot at its belly. He squeezed off a dozen rounds before the plane was out of range. He was sure that several rounds had found their mark. Then he had half a dozen more clear shots at the spotter plane. The C-1 began to sputter and smoke before it got back to the other end of the airfield. Delgado could almost see the pilot make the decision: the C-1 turned away from the airfield, made a sweeping left hand turn, and began its approach. It was going to land where the Grumman had been.

The two trucks of soldiers had stopped next to the crumpled Cessna. Half a dozen soldiers dashed toward the Quonset hut and other airport buildings. Delgado guessed they had seen Filomeno running there. The rest of the soldiers began to run, in formation, to the end of the airstrip. Delgado reckoned he could stay on the hilltop another four or five minutes. He could certainly knock down six men or more with the carbine before the return fire became serious.

But why? These were new recruits, a mountain unit that had probably not yet seen any action. Six more dead Cubans? Six more dead young men who would never learn what they had been fighting, and never live to see their new Cuba, once the revolution was over? Why?

He turned to Nilsa, lying beside him in the dirt, and said, "I think it is time."

Nilsa said, "I am ready. Do we attack?"

Delgado smiled. "No. We retreat. Now!"

He retrieved his Panama hat, stuck it on his head, took up his rifle, and made for the trees. Nilsa ran beside him. The C-1 was just landing. The spotter plane circled up, turning toward Havana. That told Delgado that it would not, in any case, pursue the Grumman.

It was a shame about Filomeno, if they caught him. It was a shame about the camouflaged car, too. There would be no reclaiming that. And it was a shame about the money. It would have been difficult to accept it, but that kind of cash would buy a lot of bullets.

Slipping into the trees, Nilsa running beside him, Delgado thought, *One day soon we won't need bullets at all.* He took a last look at the sky, then ducked into the shadows and was gone.

It was a small airfield outside of Miami. Cardoso stared out the window as the Grumman rolled down the runway. From the air, the city was impossibly beautiful. Rich. Shiny. Surrounded by blue water, like his Havana, but otherwise as different as night from day.

Behind him sat the American, beside his girl. He was still holding the bag full of money. Cardoso wondered which kind of police or Secret Service or customs officials were going to come for them, and what they were going to say.

The Grumman rolled to a stop. The engines died. The two pilots pulled themselves up from their seats and walked toward their passengers. Both wore black aviator's sunglasses. Cardoso could not have said whether they were Cuban or American.

Then one of them spoke. He was Cuban, but to judge from his accent he had been away from the country for a long time. He said, "Welcome to Miami. Welcome to the United States. This is where you get off the plane. If you walk toward the control tower, you will be met by a car and driver. He will take you wherever you want to go."

Cardoso rose from his seat. Sloan and the girl were already moving to the door.

The pilot held a hand up to stop them.

He said, "Leave the bag, please."

Sloan said, "Leave the bag? Leave the money?"

"That's right," the pilot said. "Leave the money."

"This is Meyer Lansky's money, pal," Sloan said. "You don't want to be stealing from Meyer Lansky."

"We can argue about it, if you like," the pilot said. Then he pulled a pistol from his waistband. "Or you can put the bag down."

Sloan said, "Are you working for the Cubans? Or the Americans?"

"Never mind that," the pilot said. "Put the bag down and get off the plane. I don't have any more time to waste."

Sloan put the bag down. He took Anita's hand. They walked to the door and left the plane. Cardoso went down the steps behind them. The door swung shut. The Grumman engines started up again at once.

On the tarmac, Cardoso put on a pair of sunglasses against the sunlight and looked at the control tower and the small terminal below it. Nothing was moving. No soldiers. No policemen. No one in any kind of uniform was coming for them.

He said to the American, "Now what?"

Sloan said, "Hell if I know. I guess we're on our own."

Cardoso nodded. Behind them, the Grumman was gaining momentum as it ran down the runway. Cardoso heard it leave the ground. He didn't turn to look.

In front of the terminal building were two men in dark suits and mirrored sunglasses, standing with their arms folded beside the fender of a long black car.

Sloan saw them first, and his mouth went dry. He said, "Hold up a minute," but it was too late. The men with the sunglasses saw him, too. They moved forward like machinery. Sloan said, "Steady now. And keep your gun down, right?"

The bulkier of the two men said, "Welcome to Miami. Meyer
Lansky extends his greetings to you."

Sloan nodded.

The man said, "If you'll get in the car, we will take you into
Miami."

Sloan looked at Cardoso, and at Anita. He had no idea what he
was expected to do next. It didn't seem that they had much of a
choice. They had no money. They had no contacts. They had no plan.

Sloan said, "And then what?"

"And then nothing," the man said. "You wanna go to the Fountainbleu or the Eden Roc, or whatever, we'll take you there."

Sloan said, "Give us a second, will you?" and turned to Cardoso
and Anita. "What do you think? I've got a hundred Cuban pesos and
about ten American bucks."

Anita pulled him close and said, in a whisper, "It's okay. I have
money. A *lot* of money. In the knapsack. I think it's the ransom
money."

Sloan said, "But the pilots just got that."

"The money from before," Anita said. "From the cemetery."

"La Milagrosa!" Cardoso said, and began to laugh. "Que milagro! A
new miracle."

Sloan turned Anita around by the shoulders and peeked into the
knapsack. Bound packets of money. Big money. But whose? Calloway's? Did it matter anymore?

He turned back to Lansky's man and said, "To the Fountainbleu,
then."

The sedan left the airport at a gallop. Cardoso got a pair of sunglasses from his pocket and put them on. He glanced over his shoulder to confirm what he already knew: the Grumman had left them.
He saw it arcing up into the sky. Headed back to Havana? He
couldn't have guessed.

And he was going where? He couldn't have guessed that, either.
When they got to this Fountainebleu, he thought, he would slip
away. It wouldn't do for him to be seen with these two Americans.
Not even in Miami. He would be safer alone from now on.

Twenty minutes later the sedan pulled into the driveway of the grand hotel. Two bellmen came down the steps and opened the car doors. Anita and Sloan slid out. Sloan pulled a bill from his pocket and handed it to one of the bellmen. Cardoso slid out of the car behind him.

Sloan said, "What about you?"

"What about me?"

"Are you coming?"

"No," Cardoso said. "I think I will go somewhere else."

"Where?"

"I don't know," Cardoso said. "But not here. It isn't safe, for you, to have me around."

"Depending on where that money went, it may not be safe for any of us," Sloan said.

"What will you do?"

Sloan said, "Stop here. Get cleaned up. Get a meal. Stay the night. Then run."

"Run where?"

"Away from Meyer Lansky. This is his town."

Cardoso nodded. "I will run also. I have always wanted to see New York."

"You won't go back to Havana?"

"No," Cardoso said. "I am a dead man in Havana. I think I will stay here."

"Take this, then," Sloan said. He reached into the knapsack and palmed out a pack of bills. "It's enough to get you started."

Cardoso took the money and nodded. He turned to where the bellmen were posted. He said, "Taxi, please." One of the bellmen whistled shrilly. A cab sprang to the curb.

Cardoso said, "Good-bye, then. And good luck."

Sloan shook the Cuban's hand. Then he took Anita by the elbow and escorted her toward the front of the hotel.

Cardoso got into the taxi. He said to the driver, "Can you take me to the center? To a bus station?"

The driver said, "Biscayne Boulevard," and pulled away from the curb.

Cardoso turned and looked out the back window of the cab. The

American man and his woman were going through the front doors of the hotel. He watched them disappear. They were no longer his concern.

Now he had only the rest of his life to figure out. When the cab reached the downtown strip, Cardoso said, "Here. I will stop here."

He thanked the taxi driver, gave him a twenty-dollar bill, and watched as the driver made change. Then he slid across the seat and got out.

The sun was strong, strong like in Havana, and the air smelled of the sea. The buildings were sleek and shiny and ugly. There was too much metal glinting in the sun. Cardoso was glad he had sunglasses. He put them on, and Miami softened. Cardoso stepped onto the sidewalk, hesitated one moment, then turned left and walked into the city.

ACKNOWLEDGMENTS

The author would like to thank Julie Singer for her enduring love, A. J. Langguth for his constant friendship, Joshua Kendall for his delicate editing, David Vigliano for his aggressive agenting, Vincent Castellanos for his assistance with Cuban Spanish, and the people of Havana for their kindness.